"Do I appear in the guise of a grieving widow to you?" Lisette challenged. "Have you not noticed that I am quite able to control my tears?"

"You can't expect me to believe that you rejoice," Caid argued. "I murdered your husband in something akin to cold blood. His death at my hands caused you to lose your status as a respected member of a noted family—"

"You allowed my freedom, for which I owe you unending gratitude," she interrupted.

Stringent thoughts scoured his mind like acid, leaving behind a single conclusion. "So you feel I deserve a permanent place in your household because of it?"

She lifted a brow. "Only if you desire it."

Oh, he desired it. He desired to snatch her up and take her somewhere private where he could strip her naked and shatter the cool composure she wore like a cloak. "To rescue you was never my intention, Madame Moisant. I owe you restitution, or so you once said, and on that head agreed to your demand for my protection. The debt is reasonable and will be discharged. More than that is beyond my ability to perform."

She watched him, her gaze fathomless. Then her lips curved into a smile. "Not quite. You offered a demonstration of…of passion, I believe? Unless, of course, that is withdrawn, as well?"

It was a challenge of the most flagrant kind, something he had been conditioned never to refuse. "By no means, madame," he said in soft promise as he paced forward. "For that, as in anything short of the most holy of unions, I am yours to command."

Also by JENNIFER BLAKE

CHALLENGE TO HONOR
GARDEN OF SCANDAL

The Louisiana Gentlemen Series

WADE
CLAY
ROAN
LUKE
KANE

JENNIFER BLAKE

Dawn Encounter

MIRA

ISBN 0-7783-2213-0

DAWN ENCOUNTER

Copyright © 2006 by Patricia Maxwell.

All rights reserved. Except for use in any review, the reproduction or
utilization of this work in whole or in part in any form by any electronic,
mechanical or other means, now known or hereafter invented, including
xerography, photocopying and recording, or in any information storage or
retrieval system, is forbidden without the written permission of the publisher,
MIRA Books, 225 Duncan Mill Road, Don Mills, Ontario, Canada M3B 3K9.

All characters in this book have no existence outside the imagination of the
author and have no relation whatsoever to anyone bearing the same name
or names. They are not even distantly inspired by any individual known or
unknown to the author, and all incidents are pure invention.

MIRA and the Star Colophon are trademarks used under license and registered
in Australia, New Zealand, Philippines, United States Patent and Trademark
Office and in other countries.

www.MIRABooks.com

Printed in U.S.A.

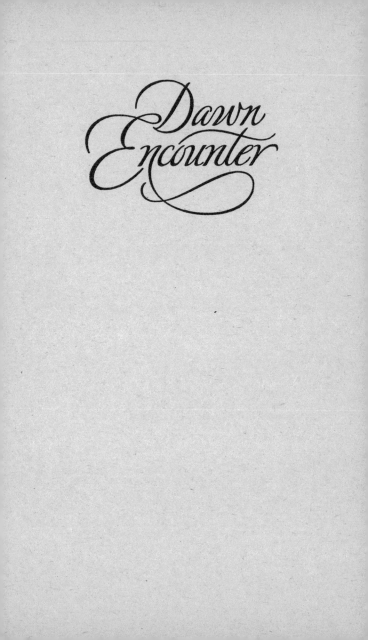

Dawn Encounter

1

New Orleans, Louisiana
March, 1840

To walk homeward through the cemetery after midnight was Caid Roe O'Neill's personal penance. He did it not as a reminder of his own mortality but rather to prevent himself from becoming too fond of death.

For a man who wielded a sword for his living, the possibility of a fatal blow, given or taken, was a constant specter. The errant flick of a wrist, a second's hesitation in parrying a clever feint, and it was over. Then would come the broken sword, the black armbands worn by his friends, the grim parade to the burying ground. Sometimes, when darkness lay like a thick miasma over New Orleans and the only sounds were the distant rattle of carriage wheels and the occasional bark of a dog, it was far too easy to think of that end as natural, or even one to be accepted with gratitude.

Such introspection was not a sign of a melancholy mind. Rather, it was the natural bent of Caid's Black Irish heritage allied to a strict upbringing at the hands of priests and nuns who thought a bog Irish kid needed a close acquaintance with the more somber aspects of life. They had been right in their fashion.

On an early morning just a month ago, Caid had felt his sword pierce the heart of Eugene Moisant, and the sensation had caused neither guilt, shame nor even triumph, but rather the most unholy satisfaction. It was not something Caid wanted to feel again.

He strode with his head up and his sword cane gripped loosely in his hand as he glanced around at the white marble tombs like small houses with their gables and cupolas reflecting the star shine. He wasn't looking for trouble, but neither would he shy away from it. It was always dangerous on the streets at night but even more so here in this so-called City of the Dead. The tombs that were constructed above ground because of the low water table, the tall monuments and marble mausoleums, provided excellent cover for sneak thieves and cutthroats.

The oyster-shell path crunched under his booted feet, while the billowing edges of his cloak brushed dust from the dried weeds along its edges. He could smell that arid mustiness, and also a whiff of the lime used to whitewash the enclosing brick walls. The night was cool for early March in these latitudes. The chill had seeped down from the north earlier in the day, ousting the usual mildness. Now his breath fogged a little as he kept his steady pace.

Turning a corner in this silent city whose narrow, meandering pathways had been laid out at need instead of with logic, he saw ahead of him the Moisant tomb. It was of gray marble shaped like a large fainting couch and surrounded by an iron fence wrought with the time-honored mortuary design of a weeping willow. There was something white lying on the tomb, something with a tender shape, pale skin and flowing raiment....

Caid halted. For long seconds, he stood perfectly still. Then he drew a swift breath and moved forward again. The grating of his footsteps on the shells seemed profane, as if it might disturb the rest of the many carved angels that surrounded him, including the one which lay supine and white as alabaster upon the Moisant tomb. Drawing closer, he saw the soft auburn-gold tresses that spilled around her head and over the tomb's edge, the symmetry of her features, her arching brows and finely molded cheekbones. Memory clicked abruptly, producing an image seen just once before. Regret twisted sharply inside Caid's chest.

The woman was—had been—Lisette Moisant, young widow of Eugene Moisant, the man he had killed less than a month ago. If the death of the husband was on his head, then so would be that of his lady.

Caid leaped the low iron fence then went to one knee beside the tomb. With care, he reached to close his fingers on Lisette Moisant's slender wrist and take her hand in his own warm grasp. Cool, she was so cool to the touch. Her lashes lay upon her cheeks, resting on their own fanlike shadows. A soft breeze stirred the waves of her hair so that a fine, auburn strand, fragile as a spiderweb, lifted and caught on the wool of his cloak. He knelt motionless, as if tethered, held fast by its strength.

When last he'd seen Lisette Moisant, she had appeared pale and unhappy in her mourning clothes of deepest black. She had met his gaze for a single instant before recognition flared in her face along with a wash of color. Her gaze had passed over him then, and her lips had tightened. She had refused to acknowledge him, and who could blame her? Regardless, Caid had seen nothing, heard nothing since, to indicate that she might come to this, lying still and cold in her nightgown of fine virginal white, as if she had taken too much of some sleeping potion. The choice had been laudanum, he thought, for he could catch the faint scent of it about her.

A suicide, and for the sake of a man like the late Eugene Moisant. It was not a suitable fate for any creature, and certainly not for such a lovely young woman.

Caid replaced her hand beside her and sat back, staring for long seconds at the delicately curved lips and the decided point of her chin that just prevented her face from being a perfect oval. Such a tragic waste of life, so much tender promise gone unclaimed, undeveloped. The pain of it shifted inside him. Lisette Moisant had doubtless been as wronged in her way by her lout of a husband as had Caid's sister Brona. That fact deserved some acknowledgment, some salute, however futile.

Caid leaned over the bedlike tomb and bent his head to brush his lips gently across the soft, cool mouth of the lady. As he drew back a little, his chest rose and fell in a deep breath as he sought to relieve the ache in his throat. And in return, he felt the faintest intimation of a sigh brush over his cheek.

His eyebrows snapped together in a frown. Without ceremony, he set his hand palm down flat between Lisette Moisant's breasts, splaying his fingers over and around the gently resilient mounds beneath their covering of white batiste.

A heartbeat. It was there, that gentle throbbing, faint and not quite even. He cursed his mooning stupidity and waste of time even as he stripped off his cloak and laid it over her, wrapping her in its voluminous folds. Then he thrust one arm under her knees, the other behind her back, and lifted her high against his chest. Swinging with his burden, he kicked open the gate of the iron fence and started off toward his lodging.

After three long steps, he paused. He could not carry a respectable woman to his rooms, not even if she was dying. Should she survive, she would be compromised beyond repair, her life hardly worth living. To show up on the doorstep of the Moisant household, the man who had killed the son of the house, would hardly be wise, might even be enough to get him hanged if Lisette Moisant failed to live. The house of Dr. Labatut, the young physician called upon to attend the injuries of the fencing salons, was many blocks away, too far under the circumstances. What was he to do?

A soft sound, like a cross between a gasp and a moan, came from just beneath his collarbone. Caid looked down and was snared by the wide gaze of the woman in his arms. Her eyes appeared silvery-gray in the pale light of the moon, with centers so dark and fathomless that they threatened to engulf him. Angel's eyes, wide spaced, clear behind their thick fringe of lashes, their expression was infinitely beguiling. There was no fear in them, but only bewilderment overlaid by wonder. Abruptly, she shivered, a movement that seemed to catch her unaware. She reached with her free hand to clutch the lapel of his coat under his cloak as her lashes closed again, then turned her face into his shoulder.

Caid felt his heart alter its rhythm. Heat flashed over him in a surging wave. He stood with his legs braced while he wrestled with a morass of impulses that were as amazing as they were impossible to deny. He wanted to take the woman in his arms away somewhere and hide her where she would be forever safe from harm. He felt a strong need to lie down with her on the nearest marble surface and sleep for an eternity with her in his arms. He yearned to have her lift her lashes and smile at him, to acknowledge him and say his name. He was desperate for her forgiveness, her absolution, her acceptance of him into the pantheon of those she loved. He longed to be pure and noble in her eyes. He wanted to turn back the clock so she might see him as untainted by past mistakes or bloody deeds done in anger. He ached to warm her cool lips until they opened to him, until she turned to him in sweet passion, asking that he possess her, make her safe and happy and whole by the healing power of his touch, his…

He was an idiot.

Think. He had to think. He needed a refuge for the lady he carried, some place where she could be cared for and kept safe from harm. Safe from him and all he had done to her sheltered world, all that he could well do to it.

The answer came to him as in response to a prayer.

Maurelle Herriot.

The Herriot town house was not far away, on the rue Dauphine. Maurelle was likely to be up still, being like a cat in her habits, keeping late hours and sleeping well into the afternoon. She would not be entertaining this evening, Caid knew, as he had received no invitation, nor was she likely to be keeping an assignation. Maurelle might affect a Bohemian lifestyle, but relied on her impeccable lineage among the aristocratic French Creole families, which allowed her that eccentricity; she was much too circumspect to do anything that might seriously jeopardize her place in society. Being at the center of interesting events was meat and drink to her, however, and she would not mind being disturbed for such a titillating adventure. Even if she did mind, she would forgive him. She had been Caid's friend since their first meeting in Paris a few years ago. She always forgave him.

Caid began walking again.

Maurelle was dressed for an evening at home. Scorning the simple Gabrielle wrapper preferred by most women on such occasions, she had donned flowing Oriental robes of rust-red silk brocade and a matching turban draped with pearls. The exotic fashion suited her, lending mystery to her fine dark eyes while subtly enhancing an opulent figure kept comfortably rounded by a love for multicourse dinners and chocolate bonbons. She swept forward in a flutter of draperies as her butler showed Caid and his burden into her second-floor salon.

"*Mon Dieu, cher!* What have you done? Put the poor thing down there, on the settee near the fire." Turning to her butler of many years, who hovered in the doorway, she clapped her hands. "Hartshorn and water, Solon. At once."

"The lady requires a doctor," Caid said as he deposited Lisette where he had been instructed, then knelt beside her and began to chafe her icy hands. "Also a warm coverlet."

Maurelle nodded at the butler. "You heard."

When the door had closed behind the man, Caid went on. "I didn't harm the lady, in any case. She was in this state when I found her." In a few brief phrases, he described how that had come about.

"And you suspect this poor girl of drinking laudanum because of Eugene Moisant's demise? Nonsense! Champagne, possibly, but nothing more deadly."

"I'll admit to seeing no cause for her to destroy herself, but it's entirely possible she may feel otherwise."

"The man had the sensibility of a clod," Maurelle said with precision. "I would be surprised to learn that he knew how to treat a wife. She should be profoundly grateful for the release which elevated her to the fortunate status of a young widow of independent means."

Maurelle believed in plain speaking, one of many things Caid liked about her. Married at sixteen to an old satyr nearly thirty years her senior, she had been widowed a scant four years and many prayers for deliverance later. As a consequence, she was no advocate of love and marriage, another thing he found attractive since he need not fear rousing expectations he could not fulfill. "Just because you hummed the jubilant death song from *Don Giovanni* while your husband was laid to rest doesn't mean all women are so inclined," Caid said over his shoulder. "But is the lady wellplaced?"

"You were not here two years ago when Lisette Saine and Eugene Moisant were wed, were you? Her late husband's father, Monsieur Henri Moisant, was thought to have achieved the coup of the season when he arranged the marriage of his son to the Saine heiress. The properties alone would have been enough to attract a baron for the girl, if not someone more exalted, had Madame Saine cared to travel to Europe. Too bad she didn't look higher for an eligible *parti*."

"What are you saying?"

"Madame Saine drove a hard bargain, so they claim, insisting that the bulk of her daughter's enormous dowry remain in Lisette's control—this in return for paying Eugene's gambling debts and making a sizable contribution to the Moisant family coffers. Madame had little trust in the Moisants, father or son, and thought to ensure that Lisette would be well treated. It seems she knew she had not long to live."

"Her efforts were not successful?" Caid's voice was distracted as he studied the lady on the settee. Her lashes fluttered a little, but she did not open her eyes again. Alarm tightened his chest until he could hardly breathe.

"Just so. One hears that Monsieur Henri Moisant was dissatisfied from the moment the vows were spoken. He thought it unseemly that his young daughter-in-law should have so much wealth at her disposal, felt also that her unwillingness to place her affairs in his hands showed a disinclination to submerge her personality and become a true Moisant. He had been sure he could persuade her to sign a power of attorney giving him control of the monies once he had her under his roof. Lisette proved less malleable than expected. In fact, she was amazingly obstinate about it."

Caid, distracted, merely shook his head.

"I mean, only look at her, so young and with hardly a spare ounce on her body. Who would suppose she could stand up to a man of Monsieur Moisant's age and stature?" Maurelle gave a short laugh. "He was used to commanding the females of his household, from his ghost of a wife, before she died of some mysterious, ravaging disease, to the lowliest maid in the kitchen. It was demeaning to him that his son's bride should be impervious to his demands."

"Her contributions to the household must have been adequate. Eugene seemed to spend freely enough when I first saw him."

"One must keep up appearances, yes? Still, it was done mainly on account. He and his father always outstripped their monthly stipend."

"Had they nothing of their own?"

"Debts," Maurelle said succinctly. "Henri Moisant invested unwisely just before the bank failures three seasons ago. The Saine fortune effectively rescued him from the moneylenders. But if you think he was grateful for it, you would be mistaken. He was merely annoyed that he could not buy and sell Lisette's holdings at will."

"Poor lady," Caid said as he smoothed his thumb over the fine, blue-veined skin of her hand. "I doubt Eugene's death mended matters."

"As you say. Eugene's methods of extracting funds from his wife involved payments to keep him from her bedchamber, or so it was whispered. Perhaps it's true as he left no heir. The elder Moisant lacked that leverage so has found himself in strained circumstances. He has been heard complaining of the ungrateful behavior of his daughter-in-law and generally speaking unkindly of her."

"She must have relatives who could intervene?" In Caid's experience, nearly everyone in New Orleans was connected by blood, at least in the French section.

"None that matter. Madame Saine came as a young girl from Saint Domingue with an uncle after her parents and older sister were killed in the slave uprising there some forty years ago. When she was married and off his hands, the uncle sailed for France where he bought an estate that had belonged to one of Napoleon's ministers. He has never laid eyes on Lisette, and can hardly be expected to concern himself now."

"Her father and his people?"

"He was lost in the cholera and yellow fever epidemic of eight years ago."

There was no need for her to say more. Caid had heard over

and over again of the lives lost at that time, when whole families had been decimated, the dead piled up in the cemeteries like cordwood as the population of the city was cut nearly in half.

The butler returned with the hartshorn and water then. Lisette Moisant did not respond to the remedy, however. Nor did she rouse when the doctor arrived.

A dapper man with center-parted hair, luxuriant side-whiskers, and his coat and waistcoat thrown on hastily over his nightgown so its neck band served in place of a cravat, he seemed competent enough in his initial examination. He directed that young Madame Moisant be installed in a bedchamber, and then called for a basin and pitcher of water while he set out an array of corked brown glass bottles that made Caid shudder to look at them. Accepting a cup of strong coffee laced with cognac to fortify him for the ordeal ahead, the physician sent everyone from the room and shut the door firmly behind them.

To simply walk away from that bedchamber seemed like desertion to Caid, still he could find no excuse to remain. When Maurelle took his arm, turning with him to move along the rear gallery back toward the central salon, he walked beside her. They didn't speak for long moments, but breathed the crisp night air as they moved from one to the other of the squares of golden lamplight that fell from the windows onto the gallery floor.

To their right lay the courtyard, a small, pleasant space flanked on one side by outbuildings that included the kitchen, laundry, storage shed and a rather elegant brick privy and on the other by a tall brick wall softened by a green curtain of night-blooming jasmine. The house had no *porte cochère* as Maurelle disliked keeping a carriage with its attendant horses and their inevitable dung, hay litter and flies. Otherwise, it was a typical town dwelling of two stories with the living area on the second floor and its interior life centered on the rear courtyard. A *pharmacie* shop occupied the *rez-de-chaussée,* or ground floor facing the street, ignored by Maurelle who was the proprietor's landlady.

"You need not stay, you know," Maurelle said after a moment. "I can look after Lisette."

Caid sent a frowning glance toward the woman who glided along beside him. "Am I in your way?"

"Not at all. There is simply no reason for you to remain."

"I feel myself responsible."

"*Mon cher,* how can you suggest such a thing?"

"If I had not challenged Eugene, had not left him lying on the field…"

"You would have been less than a man, certainly less than a loving brother to your sister. If anyone is to blame, it is Eugene Moisant for his own conduct. Please don't speak to me of responsibility when you had no hand whatever in this wretched girl's misfortune."

"It still seems coldhearted to deliver her to your doorstep then abandon her."

"I will send word to the Moisant town house so they may come and take her away in the morning. That is, if she survives the night. If she does not, it will do your reputation no good for it to become known that you were nearby."

"My reputation." The words were flat as he scowled down into the dark courtyard below them where a wrought iron bench of the kind normally placed in cemeteries sat beneath the dark green branches of a sweet olive. The small white blossoms that starred the tree sent their sweet fragrance pouring into the night air. There had been a similar fragrance about Lisette Moisant as he carried her in his arms, Caid thought. She had been so fragile, so helpless in her drugged state. Her death was unthinkable, but then so was the possibility of seeing her return to her father-in-law's house.

"I was referring to the repute of your fencing salon,"

Maurelle said, reclaiming his attention again. "Attendance declined after the duel with Eugene, or so you've said, because the elder Moisant told all who would listen that you tricked his son, killing him by a stratagem beneath the dignity of a gentleman. This turn in the affair can hardly mend matters."

Caid understood that well enough. Only the allowances for a father's grief had prevented him from calling out Moisant over the accusation. "Regardless, but I'd like to hear from the lady's lips just why she tried to do away with herself."

Maurelle lifted a plump shoulder. "Despondency over her circumstances, despair at being virtually alone in the world. Such things occur."

"You said yourself that Lisette Moisant had little reason to mourn her husband, and a woman who can stand up to Eugene's father doesn't sound the type to swallow laudanum merely because she's lonely. Besides…"

"Besides which," Maurelle mocked with a tilt of her turbaned head that sent iridescent light flowing along its pearl ropes, "the lady is attractive and mistreated, and you have just rescued her from dying of an inflammation of the lungs at the very least. So gallant, so romantic, yes? I wish I might have come upon that means of attaching your favor."

Caid recognized the reproof behind the wry humor. Maurelle might have scant notion of entering into a serious affair with him, but she still had her vanity. Spirited flirtations were her life blood and she was quick to resent any defection by the rakes and rogues like himself which she gathered around her. Reaching to take her hand, he brushed the backs of her fingers with his lips. "You have my complete devotion already, *chère,* as you well know. Why should you need more?"

"Flatterer," she scoffed, though in more gentle tones. "If you won't consider your own good name, then think of Lisette's. It will not enhance her social standing if it becomes known that you carried her here in your arms and remained by her side afterward."

Caid was forced to concede the point, still he hesitated. "Returning her to her home may have worse consequences. What if Moisant is the cause of what occurred tonight?"

"I doubt even he would stoop so low. He is a gentleman, after all. Besides, losing her good repute, being excluded from society, what could be worse? She might as well be dead."

Caid could not quite see it in that light, but then what did he know? As a *maître d'armes,* a fencing master with an atelier in the Passage de la Bourse, the short pedestrian way which led from Canal Street at the upper edge of the French Quarter to where the St. Louis Merchant's Exchange and Hotel had been before it burned last month, he held a strange place in the social hierarchy of French New Orleans. Without background, lineage or means to speak of, he still had prestige. It was his prowess with a sword that gained it for him, that and the fear instilled by his ability to look death in the face on a regular basis. Men gave way for him in doorways; young fops in their first seasons aped his manner of tying his cravat or the color of his waistcoat; elderly gentlemen vied for the honor of paying for his drinks or meals, and small boys followed him in the street. He was welcome at the male entertainments given by gentlemen of standing and also in the salons of the more adventurous ladies such as Maurelle. Women smiled at him behind their fans and sometimes extended veiled invitations to visit in the dark of night.

Regardless, he was not received in homes where young ladies resided, nor was he presented to them at the opera or during the winter subscription balls. It was not *comme il faut.* He was made ineligible because of his bloodlines, that all-important criteria in the city, but more importantly by his profession. A gentleman might become a lawyer, physician, banker or commission merchant, but he did nothing that might cause him to perspire. He certainly did not teach others the grueling art of swordplay for his living.

Caid had no quarrel with this position most of the time; it was not too dissimilar to what he had encountered in his native Ireland, after all. Yet there were times when it rankled.

"I still don't like it," he said finally.

"What would you, then? Where else is she to go?" Maurelle's voice held a defensive note.

"Why could she not stay with you for a few days, just until she is better?"

"You can't have considered, *cher*. Moisant will be searching for her. People will see her here and wish to know why she is with me rather than him. All manner of speculation will arise. Besides, the lady may not care to remain."

"Yet if she does?" How to explain his reluctance to lose touch with the woman he had rescued when he didn't understand it himself? It almost seemed he was being forced to part with something necessary to his peace of mind.

"We must see what Moisant has to say about it. Her place is in his house, after all."

Maurelle was right, he knew, still Caid felt a deep resistance inside him. It was ridiculous. He had no attachment to Lisette Moisant. She was lovely, but he certainly had not been felled by a *coup de foudre,* the lightning strike of love at first sight. He had no use for love, in fact. Lust, yes, but not love of the kind that turned intelligent men into mooning half-wits.

His disillusionment with such high emotion had begun as he watched his mother give birth to a new baby every year, most of which died before they learned to walk. It continued when he was seduced at fourteen by a barmaid who rollicked with him in the hay on two occasions for sport and mutual pleasure but demanded a shilling on the third. Then his last romantic notion was skewered once and for all by a

Parisian baroness who laughed his fervent infatuation to scorn while lying with him in a tangle of silk sheets.

Love was a cheat, an emotion that snared men and women in unions which ended in knife-sharp pain and disappointment. It was a convenient myth used by the church and the notaries to trap people in bonds that resulted in too many hungry, crying babes and not enough food, money or affection to go around. He wanted no part of it.

Nonetheless, he was forced to acknowledge some odd connection to Lisette Moisant that held him as surely as the shackles that had left scars embedded with iron rust on his wrists and ankles. He couldn't leave her, not until he knew that she was going to be alive to see the dawn. Not until he knew she was safe.

"Be reasonable, *cher,*" Maurelle said cajolingly. "You truly are not responsible, I promise."

"I'll wait a little while anyway, if you don't mind. I can make myself comfortable in the library if you are ready to retire for the night." The words were curt.

"By all means if you're determined to take the risk."

"Risk?"

"Moisant will not be pleased to discover how his daughter-in-law came to be here. The longer you stay, the more likely it is that the tale will reach his ears. He may feel compelled to call you out for having laid hands on her."

Caid felt heat burn the back of his neck as he remembered the brush of his mouth on Lisette's cool lips. His fingers curled slowly into fists in the dimness, still he spoke with conviction. "Unlikely."

Maurelle walked with him the few remaining steps to the library door. There, she turned to face him. "Why, *mon ami?* Why are you really involving yourself? Why did you bring Lisette Moisant here instead of merely reporting her whereabouts to those to whom she belongs?"

He gave her a crooked smile of deliberate charm. "Can you be asking my intentions?"

"Have you any?" She searched his face, her dark eyes serious.

"Of the kind you mean, no. How can I when I barely know the lady?"

"But of another kind, perhaps? If so, I suggest you reconsider. It would disturb me to know that my house was being used to capture a pawn in some devious game you may have a mind to play."

Temper rose inside Caid. It sounded as an Irish burr in his voice as he spoke. "You actually think I brought that poor girl here from spite, or that I would use her as a weapon for vendetta?"

"I have no idea. But I suspect many will wonder if it's not so, including Monsieur Moisant."

"I have no quarrel with the man. I exacted satisfaction from his son for what he did to my sister. It's enough."

"I am not sure Monsieur Moisant would agree. He hates you with a passion hotter than Hades itself and this will only fan the flames. Lisette Moisant doesn't deserve to become a part of your quarrel."

"I hope I have more consideration than to involve her."

"So do I, but Monsieur Moisant has few such qualms. He quarrels with everyone. And consider this. Eugene may have been a monster in your eyes, but he was Monsieur Moisant's beloved son and heir. He saw him as a man-about-town, no worse than many others in his habits and dealings with women. He was the last of the Moisant line, his father's one hope of immortality, and now he is gone. There is little Henri Moisant will not do to avenge Eugene's passing."

"His son destroyed Brona. If Moisant had been less proud of his lineage, if he'd been willing to accept into his family an Irish lass, there would have been no need for vengeance."

"Impossible and you know it. To him, she was a woman of no lineage, a mere…"

"A guttersnipe, a peasant's daughter born in a house beside a cow byre who by bad luck found her way here to the immigrant slums that people have named The Irish Channel?" he interrupted. "Or did you intend to indicate that she was a whore because she lived with a man who would not wed her?"

"Never would I say that, *cher.*"

"You think it." He looked away an instant. "Not that it matters."

Maurelle touched his arm lightly, her voice shaded with sadness. "But it does matter, *cher,* in this narrow little world in which we live. It matters to you, as well, much though you may deny it. If Moisant ever manages to hurt you, it will be that way, through this vast caring and your so-great pride."

"My pride," he said with emphasis, "doesn't depend on where I was born or how I live."

"No. It comes now from what you are, does it not? A *maître d'armes* capable of defending yourself against all comers, a dealer of death to your enemies and the enemies of those you love. But take away your sword, Caid, and what are you?"

He lifted one shoulder in a shrug. "A man like any other."

"Remember that, if the time ever comes when you are caught unarmed."

Maurelle turned with a silken swirl of her caftan and left him alone. Caid stood listening as her footsteps faded along the gallery. Then he stepped into the library with its glass-fronted cases of books.

Maurelle's dead husband had been something of a bibliophile, a spindle-shanked old fool who cared only for the ancient volumes he collected and the Havana cigars that gave him a constant cough, or so she said. His ghost lingered here in this small room with its embedded smells of leather bindings and tobacco, though it had been eradicated in the remainder of her house. Caid stepped to the window and lifted the velvet drapery that hung there to stare down into the street. The new gas lighting in use a few blocks over, on the rue Royale, had not yet been installed here. There was little to be seen in the dimness relieved only by a flickering whale-oil lantern on a street corner bracket. He dropped the drape and turned to seat himself in a chair. Reaching for a copy of the news sheet, *L'Abeille,* printed on one side in French and on the other in English as *The Bee,* that lay on a side table, he sat holding it, staring at nothing.

It was on a winter night like this that Brona had died of fever and loss of blood after a botched attempt to relieve her of the unwanted child she carried. She had been pregnant with Eugene Moisant's get, a baby conceived while she was his mistress kept in a small house on the rue de Rampart. Moisant had acknowledged the child readily enough, but insisted that she get rid of it. Afterward, when she remained sickly, he had pushed Brona out into the street and thrown her clothes after her. At least, so had said her neighbors, a pair of elegant quadroons with smiling lips and sad eyes who were themselves the *placées* of young French Creole gentlemen. Brona had been dead for months when Caid had traced her from Ireland to New Orleans then discovered where she had lived and with whom. He had never seen her as a young woman, had only memories of the sister who had been a freckle-faced kid with a missing front tooth when he was taken away by English soldiers.

God, but he could still smell the peat fires, still feel the chill Irish mist that had cooled his hot face as he jolted away in a prison cart. Mingled with the peat smoke scent had been the smell of burning thatch as they fired his home behind him. His mam and little sister had stood huddled into their shawls with their few pots and bundles at their feet, weeping in the rain. That was the last time he'd seen either of them.

They'd sent him to hulks, the bloody English. Treason, they called his fight against the oppression of his friends and neighbors and the stripping away of the ancient lands that were their birthright. Self-righteous and mighty, they had lectured him on proper gratitude and loyalty to the crown, as if he should be thankful for British rule that took away everything important to him. Because he'd been little more than a boy, they had relented finally and put him on a convict transport bound for Australia. It wasn't their fault that he'd never made it to the land of the Southern Cross, but had met with a storm off the horn of Africa, one that washed the ship clean of its prison stench before it sank her.

He should have died, Caid knew. He would have except for a friendship struck up weeks before with a grizzled fellow more beast than man. Called Troll, he had stood seven feet tall with one hunched shoulder, a battered face, three fingers gone from his right hand, and the strength of four men. He'd never had a friend before, Troll said, particularly one who could sing like Caid. Caid had sung him to sleep night after night, soothing the nightmares that so haunted the crippled giant that he was terrified to close his eyes. In return, Troll had taught him how to fight, both clean and dirty, and had protected him from the sordid fate of handsome but callow prisoners cooped up with the dregs of humanity. That was, until Caid could protect himself. The ugly giant with the soft heart had shared his rations and a few hard-earned inches of extra space. During the sea storm, he'd used his savage strength to rip free the chains that trapped them all below the hatches like skinny, ill-fed geese in a pen. But Troll hadn't been able to swim. He'd shoved Caid into the storm waves, but couldn't take the jump himself.

Caid could never recall the hours that followed, how he finally climbed onto the hatch cover that kept him afloat or even how long he'd remained in the water. By the time he'd been picked up by a French merchantman, he'd been tumbled and tossed until he was as naked as the day he was breached and sunburned to the shade of a boiled shrimp. He'd lain delirious and burning with fever for days. When he awoke, it was to discover that a fencing master on board the ship had paid for his medical care and passage to France. The only request the swordsman made in return was that Caid spar with him with *épées* to relieve the tedium of the long voyage. The merchantman's captain, a Breton with no love for the English and little inclination to return a prisoner to them, had found the arrangement more than satisfactory. So the lessons in swordplay had begun. While recovering his strength and gaining knowledge of the blade, Caid had also regained his self-respect, or at least a measure of it. By the time the ship docked at Le Havre and he journeyed on to Paris to become a master in the Frenchman's *salle d'assaut,* Caid had ceased to be a youth, callow or otherwise.

Behind him, there came the sound of someone clearing his throat. He turned to see Solon bearing a coffee tray with a decanter of cognac nestled among the silver service.

"I thought perhaps a touch of the same restorative the doctor prescribed for himself might meet with approval, Monsieur Caid," the butler said. His eyes were hooded, but his voice held a touch of sympathy.

"You are a man of rare understanding." Caid sat up straight as he watched the man put the tray before him.

"Madame has gone to bed. Shall I make up a spare chamber for you?"

The words were staid enough, though Caid thought he detected a note of reluctance behind them as Solon stood holding the salver. "I'm obliged, but no. I won't be staying so long."

"As you wish, *monsieur.*"

The butler bowed and went away. Caid watched him go, then shook his head.

The level of the brandy had fallen by a good inch and the silver coffeepot was empty when the doctor was finally shown into the room three hours later. "Ah, there you are, Monsieur O'Neill. They said I might find you here. Do I understand that you wish a report on the condition of the lady?"

"If you please," Caid answered politely, rising to his feet.

"The patient had a close call but is resting quite comfortably now. I was forced to exercise all my skill to…"

"She will be all right?"

"As to that, I cannot declare it with certainty. The effects of her exposure to the pernicious night air, her chilled condition, could easily lead to an inflammation of the lungs. However, she is quite strong for her size and, if I may say so, strong willed, so I can only surmise…"

"Yes, yes," he interrupted. "She is awake? She spoke to you?"

"Yes, assuredly. She is alert, more so than I expected when I first laid eyes on her. I endeavored to answer her questions but, alas, was unable to satisfy her. She wishes to speak to you since you found her. I do not advise it under the circumstances, but she is most insistent."

"Jesus, Joseph and Mary, man, why didn't you say so at once?"

Caid shouldered past the physician without ceremony and strode along the gallery to the bedchamber. He didn't hesitate since he knew his way, didn't wait for the medical man to take his leave with Solon who stood ready to show him from the house. Pushing into the guest bedchamber where the activity of the past few hours had been concentrated, he moved to the bed.

Lisette Moisant lay propped on satin pillows edged with Valenciennes lace and dressed in a nightgown borrowed from her hostess so considerably less demure than the one she had worn earlier. Her face was still pale except for twin spots of pink high on her cheekbones. These and the fiery highlights in the soft waves of her hair were the only color about her. Her lips were bloodless still, and the curve of her throat was as white and defenseless as a child's.

As he drew near, she pulled the coverlet up over her breasts in a nervous gesture, tucking it beneath her upper arms. "It really is you," she said, her voice a little husky as she studied his face. "I thought…that is, they said you brought me here."

"I'm sorry if it creates difficulties, but it seemed the only thing to be done." Her eyes were the gray of an Irish sky in winter, Caid thought, and as soft as Irish rain. He hadn't been entirely sure before.

Her lashes came down to conceal her expression, or perhaps because she was embarrassed by his close observation. "I can see that you had little choice. It was…very kind of Madame Herriott to take me in, particularly on such short notice. I am more grateful than I can say."

"She doesn't regard it, I'm sure."

"And you, Monsieur O'Neill, if you had not chanced to pass by…"

Caid shook his head. "Think no more of it."

"But I must. I shall be forever in your debt, *monsieur*."

"It is an honor to have been of service. If there is anything else I can do, anything else you need, you have only to command me."

She sent him a glance which held a trace of wariness, perhaps even fear, in spite of her valiance. Beneath it also was an odd, probing evaluation. "That is very kind. I wonder if you mean it."

"Every word, I promise. Can it be that you have a need?"

"As it happens."

"Yes?" Unease shifted through him. The hair on the back of his neck seemed to lift as at the intimation of danger. He watched with a drawing sensation in his lower belly as she moistened her lips with the flick of her pink tongue.

"I should not impose, really, I shouldn't. The matter is somewhat…delicate."

"Shall I send for Madame Herriot?" he asked as she paused. "Perhaps it's a subject you would be more comfortable discussing with a lady."

"No, no," she said hastily, looking back down at her arms clasped across her upper chest. "That wouldn't do at all. It's just that I'm not sure how things stand between the two of you and I would not wish to intervene in any way."

She thought they might be lovers, he and Maurelle. It was probably because of his presence at the town house so late at night. Caid almost smiled, but controlled the impulse as he surveyed the frown between Lisette Moisant's dark brows. "I assure you there is no complication. Please, just tell me."

"Very well." She took a deep breath that lifted her breasts under her heavy satin nightgown. Rich color rose to her hairline as she met his eyes, her own filled with clear and steady purpose. "You are a man who cannot be intimidated by my late husband's father—indeed, one who may create fear in him," she said, her voice only a little tremulous. "You are also, most unfortunately, one of the few who may understand the…the utter lack of concern for females shown by the men of his family, particularly those no longer of use to them. Because of these things I wish to ask, that is…I most earnestly request…"

"What, *madame?* Only say it."

"I require your protection."

2

"My protection."

Caid O'Neill's voice was without inflection. Lisette could hardly blame him. The idea of applying to the Irish sword master for aid had taken her breath when it first occurred to her. That had been some days ago, while listening to her father-in-law's bitter denunciation of the man's apparent invincibility. She had since become accustomed to it.

"If you please," she said politely, while her pulse throbbed so hard that she felt a little ill with it.

"What precisely do you mean?"

"Nothing too onerous. I simply thought, that is…I would first need you to arrange lodgings for me."

"You cannot be suggesting it should be under my roof!"

"Hardly, *monsieur!*" A flush warmed her cheeks. At the same time, she noted that the gentleman's French, even when freighted with irony, carried a musical lilt which gave away his origins.

"Just so," he agreed in grim tones. "Something eminently more respectable, I would imagine. A large order."

"You are more than capable of handling it, I believe." He looked capable of anything in fact, when seen at close range. He was taller and broader than expected, his presence more commanding. His skin lacked the olive hue of so many of her acquaintance, but was rather the healthy bronze of a man careless of the conventions which decreed that no gentleman should appear to have labored in the sun. His nose was classically straight, his jaw square and mouth well-defined with the curved lines of past amusement etched at its corners. Thick, straight brows and dark lashes framed eyes that appeared as sea-blue and fathomless as the Gulf of Mexico in the flickering light of the ornate candelabra on the bedside table. In their depths lay stringent intelligence that threatened to penetrate her desperate stratagem as easily as it shook her composure.

This man, this swordsman, had kissed her. He has pressed his firm lips to hers in a brief, romantic gesture that had awakened her in spite of everything. The mere memory of it made them tingle, a reaction that rippled through her in a strong a wave. It also led her to believe he was not as without feeling as he appeared, so gave her hope.

"And after you have been housed?"

"I should like to…to depend on you to see no harm comes to me."

"You require a guard then."

"In some sense," she agreed, while trying desperately to sound as if there was nothing unusual in the request.

"What of your good name?" he asked. "I have been reminded recently that it would be at risk in my company."

"No one need know of your partisanship unless there is some threat. Certainly, I would not expect you to dance attendance on me."

"In other words," he drawled, "you would not have it known that we are acquainted."

Her face felt even hotter than before. "I meant no insult, but was only thinking of your convenience. Well, and the proprieties, of course."

"Of course." His lips twisted briefly before he went on. "You have a quite proper home with your husband's family. What drives you to this measure?"

"Many things, none of them of concern to you, Monsieur O'Neill."

"You expect me to safeguard you without knowing the nature of your danger?"

"I am by no means certain this danger will continue once I am on my own," she declared, pushing a little higher in the bed as fear that he meant to refuse her brought the rise of annoyance. "I am no longer a *jeune fille* and have ample means to set up my own household. Why should I not emulate Madame Herriot and become independent?"

"Madame Herriot is older by ten years at least, and much more worldly-wise. She also had the company of an aging female cousin to lend respectability until the woman's death last winter."

"A companion is not the same as a duenna," she said with asperity. "As for the rest, I will age, and wisdom may be achieved."

"Not, perhaps, before you commit some *gaffe* that will put you beyond the pale."

"Of all the unkind things to say! I am not so heedless."

"You can hardly expect me to believe that when you go around asking men to take care of you."

"I've only asked one man, and he was chosen with extreme care." She sat forward a little so the sheet fell to her waist.

His features went blank. "And I am that man?"

"You are, or were before you showed yourself to be so disobliging."

He swung away from her so the thigh-length tail of his gray frock coat flared out then settled into place again over his fawn pantaloons. Lisette stared at his back, the width of his shoulders and the way they tapered to his waist, the sable black hair, cropped shorter than was fashionable, that curled just above his coat collar; the length of his legs emphasized by his pantaloons that were strapped beneath polished half boots. Purest female awareness unfurled deep inside her, and she was suddenly conscious of how alone they were in the sleeping house and how little she knew this man except by reputation. Her palms grew damp, and she smoothed them quickly over the sheet that pooled in her lap.

"It's impossible," Caid O'Neill said over his shoulder. "Surely you must see that."

"I don't see it at all. My situation can be laid at your door. You owe it to me to remedy it."

"Owe it?" he inquired with trenchant softness as he turned to face her again. "Now that you really must explain."

Power, masculine and not without danger, seemed to flow from him, touching her, surrounding her. Her heart redoubled its frantic beat. "I meant only that you removed my husband…."

"Removed. An odd way to put it."

"Would you have prefered that I had said you murdered him?" As the swordsman's eyes narrowed, she went on in haste. "No, please. I realize the duel between you was quite correct, that you could also have died. Yet I am left at the mercy of my father-in-law because of Eugene's death, and for that you are responsible."

"Very well, I will grant you that much. But what of it?"

She looked away again. "I hesitate to say. It will sound so…"

"So what? Petty?"

"Mad. It will sound mad. No one could credit it."

"Try me," he recommended.

Lisette bit the inside of her lower lip while she stared straight ahead of her. There was an ivory crucifix on the wall at eye level, one carved with lifelike realism. Her gaze slid away from it, passing over a skirted dressing table, a screen of woven bamboo, a large Mallard armoire with carved door panels. Nothing offered inspiration for further evasion. "I think…that is, I'm almost certain that my father-in-law is trying to drive me insane, even bring about my death. Or else he wishes people to think that I am in a decline so unable to tend to matters of a financial nature."

He made no reply. Greatly daring, she glanced at his face.

He watched her with a frown drawing his brows together over his nose.

"I told you it was unbelievable," she said, a slight catch in her voice.

"How is it that you make such an accusation?"

"He speaks to me as if to an invalid and insists that I drink concoctions I believe to be laced with spirits and sedative elixirs. On several occasions when he entertained guests, I was locked in my room to prevent my appearance in the salon. I was told later by the servants that he made my excuses, saying I was indisposed with a nervous complaint. I was not, I promise you! I am not, have never been, of a nervous disposition."

"The episode this evening—or last evening now, since it's almost dawn—this graveyard vigil of yours was not an attempt to join your departed husband."

"No." She shuddered at the mere thought of it.

"How did you come to be in the cemetery?"

"I have no idea, would not know I was found there except that I overheard Madame Herriot say so to Dr. Labatut."

"You didn't drink laudanum as a palliative."

"By no means."

"You're certain?"

She gave him an incredulous stare. "Of course I'm certain! I have no wish whatever to die."

"What did you have to drink with your evening meal? Wine? Coffee?"

"Of course. Doesn't everyone?"

"Did none of them have a strange taste?"

"Not that I noticed, but then everything tasted like the elixirs I have been plied with these past weeks."

"Yes," he mused, "I can see how they might."

"You believe me, then?" She hardly dared put the question.

He didn't answer but only stared at her with unnerving intensity, allowing his gaze to move from her face to her shoulders and then over the curves of her breasts. Glancing down, she saw that the satin of her borrowed nightgown lay against her of its own weight, outlining her feminine curves with extreme fidelity, even to the small protrusion of her nipples. For a brief instant, she wondered how he saw her. Most people tended to think of her as small of stature, perhaps because her bones were slender. She knew perfectly well that she was of average height and form, not so rounded of bosom as dictated by the current fashion, but adequate. Drawing the sheet higher, she covered herself again with its linen folds. When she looked up the sword master's gaze was on the wall above her bed.

"That doesn't explain how you came to be lying on your husband's tomb," he said in grim disapproval.

"It wasn't in a fit of melancholy. That is all I can tell you."

"You do realize that you could have died of an inflammation of the lungs, if not the overdose, had I not appeared?"

"So I am to be grateful for the rescue while any debt you might have owed has been canceled?" She scowled at him since it was a valid point, as little as she might want to admit it.

"I'm saying that there are worse things than to be driven mad."

"Yes," she said unhappily, looking away again toward the crucifix. "For instance, being carried to a cemetery to await whatever might come to me."

"Carried." His voice was tight.

"Since I had no reason to be there, I can only suppose it was managed in that fashion by Monsieur Moisant."

A long silence descended between them. Lisette hardly breathed as she waited for what the sword master might answer. From somewhere in the town house came the chiming of a clock announcing the hour of four in the morning.

Birds were beginning to twitter in the courtyard beyond the French door that gave access to the bedchamber, and somewhere a rooster crowed. How peaceful it sounded, though nothing of that quality existed between them there in the bedchamber.

Caid O'Neill turned from her, pushing a hand through his hair and clasping the back of his neck. "You must know how ineligible I am for the position you have suggested."

"You mean in a social way, I imagine. That is no great concern of mine at the moment since I require no escort. Mourning has closed off anything other than the most simple of entertainments."

"The period of grief will not last forever."

The urge to tell him that she felt little of that emotion was strong inside her. Yet how unnatural it would sound if she insisted that she did not mourn her husband except as one might a chance acquaintance. Her most niggling fear that he might sense it regardless. Caid O'Neill seemed more acute than her late husband or his father had ever been, as if he brought the intense concentration of the dueling field to their discussion. Troubling too was her awareness of him as a virile and commanding male presence. It was instinctive, she thought, quite apart from her recognition of his superior height and strength. Something primitive yet controlled reached out to her from inside him, letting her know that he saw her as a desirable woman. A small shiver ran down her spine, one she ignored with no small effort.

"The arrangement need not be for an extended period," she said, finally, "only until such time as I am seen to be in full possession of my faculties and beyond danger of morbid decline."

"That could take months."

"Weeks, rather," she corrected with conscious optimism.

"You will not care for living alone."

"On the contrary, I shall relish it beyond anything. You cannot know…"

"What? What is it that I don't know? What is it that you want?"

Did she dare to be truthful? Could this sword master possibly understand the near desperate longing inside her? She was quiet for an instant as doubt assailed her, then spoke in a rush. "To be free, I wish to be free."

"Free?" He turned to face her again, a frown between his brows.

"At liberty to do whatever I please without explaining my intentions, or go wherever I take a fancy without informing anyone of my whereabouts. I want to be alone, completely alone. I never have been, you know. I have always been accompanied by my governess, my mother and later by my maid or my husband. Even when I was locked away in my bedchamber I was not alone since a maid remained with me."

"What you are wishing for is impossible," he said quietly. "For good or ill, women require sheltering in this world in which we live."

She stared at him, meeting his unwavering blue gaze with all the courage that was in her. She thought a vagrant sympathy lay in its depths, something she had seen once before as they passed on the street. "To be sheltered is one thing, to be oppressed something quite different. That is why I am appealing to you."

"Your greatest safety, you know, could lie in finding a new husband. Nothing else could provide so permanent an end to Moisant's pretensions." He put his shoulders against the window frame behind him and crossed his arms over his chest as he waited for her answer.

"I require no replacement for Eugene. In fact, a husband is the last thing I want."

"Not at the moment, perhaps."

"Not ever."

"You are young and far too attractive to remain on the

shelf for long," he said with a dismissive movement of one shoulder.

He thought her attractive. That was oddly gratifying. "Any prospect of that nature is for the future, the very distant future."

"Of course, I understand."

She doubted it, but if thinking of her as devoted to Eugene's memory made him more likely to stand between her and her father-in-law, then she would willingly play that role. "About the lease of a house…"

"Later," he interrupted. "I've kept you talking long enough. You are well fixed here for the moment. Allow me to think what is best to be done, then we will discuss it at greater length."

It was a sensible suggestion; still she chafed at it. She wanted everything settled now, needed that to make her escape seem real. She could hardly believe that she was safely away from the Moisant town house and its master and might remain so. "Oh, but surely…"

"You need to rest," he said, pushing away from the window and moving to the door with muscular grace, as if his big, loose-jointed body was well-oiled by the hard exercise of countless hours on the fencing strips. "I will be close by, I promise you."

With that, she had to be content. The door closed behind him, settling into its frame with solid finality.

It was most peculiar, but Lisette suddenly felt exhausted, as if her strength and purpose had been fueled by the presence of the Irish *maître d'armes* and his departure had taken it away. She had cleared the first hurdle in her hastily concocted program, however. There were others, but they would have to wait on the sword master's decision.

Stifling a yawn with one hand, she gave her head a small shake. It had been some time since she had slept soundly, in all truth; she had hardly dared close her eyes since Eugene's death. Even when not locked inside, she had kept her door barricaded. Once or twice the knob had rattled, as if someone was trying to enter in the middle of the night. Who could it have been except Monsieur Moisant?

The memory sent a shudder over her. At least she would not be troubled by such visitations here. The doctor had also said the effects of the laudanum might linger awhile. She let her eyes drift shut, thinking she might doze just until daylight. She didn't care to impose on Madame Herriot's hospitality for much longer than that.

It was some time later that she roused from the numbing fog of near unconsciousness. Voices echoed, half in her dream, half within the house. One of them, masculine and layered with fury, sent a shaft of pain through her head, bringing her awake with a rush.

Henri Moisant burst into the room with hurricane force, breathing hard from his swift ascent from the courtyard entrance and still carrying his hat and silver-headed ebony cane as if he had not cared to surrender them to the butler. Attired in black from head to foot, his coat of fine wool had a velvet collar to match his waistcoat and the fobs that dangled from his watch chain featured a slack-jawed skull and a tiny funerary urn. His features were obscured by mustaches and a goatee, both with the same silver as his hair. Handsome in a suave fashion, he carried himself like a man who was aging well and knew it.

Lisette sat up in bed with alarm running like poison in her veins. Henri Moisant's thin lips formed a smile, but it was only on the surface, a pretense for the benefit of Madame Herriot who moved at his side. Rage gleamed in his eyes and darkened the skin of his neck; Lisette had seen the signs often enough to recognize them.

"What foolishness is this, *chère?*" he demanded as he strode toward her. "I could hardly credit the message sent by your hostess. You have been distraught of late, I know, but this behavior surpasses belief."

"It's a great mystery," she answered, her voice neutral. "Perhaps you might bring light to bear on the matter."

"I, when we've barely spoken in days? Your maid says you sent her to prepare a tisane for a headache after she had made you ready for bed last evening, then found your door barred when she returned. She seems to have been the last to see you."

His tone, so reasonable yet suggestive, set Lisette's teeth on edge. "Rather, she made the tisane at your order, as usual, and I drank it. Lying down for the night is the last thing I remember."

Henri Moisant, at her bedside, thrust his cane beneath his left arm and reached to clasp her hand. His grasp was hard enough to grind the bones together, though it might have appeared merely comforting to an observer.

"A nightmare's delusion, *chère*. It must be, for I refuse to believe you could so accuse one who has had only your best interests at heart since you became my son's wife. Perhaps you sleepwalked or your senses were disordered by pain. How affecting, that you so longed to be with our beloved Eugene. I am quite overcome by the sentiment."

Lisette glanced at her hostess, who had arrived at Moisant's elbow. "No, it wasn't like that…"

"Yes, of course," he said in the soothing tone used toward an unruly child. "We will say no more about it. Come, I have brought the carriage and coverlets to wrap you up snug and tight. We will take you home where we may cosset you and all will be forgotten."

"I don't wish to forget, *monsieur!* In fact, I find myself quite unable to do so. I almost died from your care and have no wish to repeat the experience."

"Repeat it? I should think not, but that is entirely up to you, *ma chère*. You are naturally the mistress of your fate as well as of your so sensitive emotions."

She caught the veiled reference to her supposed unbalanced state, also the glance he exchanged with Madame Herriot, but chose to disregard both. "Thank you for pointing it out so clearly, *monsieur*. If I am my own mistress, then I must tell you that I have decided to remain here until I am able to procure other lodgings." She turned to Maurelle Herriot. "That is, of course, if you will be so kind as to allow it, *madame*."

"Naturally, you are welcome," the lady answered with a troubled expression in her fine dark eyes.

"Nonsense," Monsieur Moisant interrupted while exerting pressure on Lisette's hand as if he meant to drag her from the bed. "Your place is in your own home where we may look after you."

Lisette tugged against his numbing hold, trying to free her hand. "I cannot be at ease there and much prefer the safety of my own household."

"What a thing to say! Your nerves are overset indeed by this ordeal. What will Madame Herriot think of such wild talk?"

He smiled at that lady with a sad shake of his head even as his fingers bit into Lisette's flesh. Seeing her hostess return the gesture, she felt the brush of despair. With her gaze fastened upon Maurelle's rich brown eyes, she said imploringly, "You must believe that I am not overwrought, *madame*. I have real need of shelter."

"It's very sad, is it not?" Her father-in-law gave an elaborate shrug. "That love for my son has led to this quite wrings the heart with pity. But I cannot permit that anyone else should assume the burden of caring for my son's wife. No, no, she is my responsibility for we are united in our grief."

"You must not believe him," Lisette said with a shade of desperation.

The lady of the house looked doubtful. "But *chère,* you do seem a trifle agitated, if I may say so."

"So would you be if someone meant to take you away against your will!"

"Enough," Moisant declared, reaching to drag her against his chest, beginning to lift her. "We will go before you become so hysterical that you actually claim I attempted to poison you."

Lisette flung away from him, breaking his hold. She grasped the post of the bed as he reached for her again. "But you did! I won't go with you."

"Indeed she will not. You must oblige me, *monsieur,* by releasing the lady."

The quiet rasp of drawn steel punctuated the request. Caid O'Neill stepped from the doorway into the bedchamber. There was no obvious threat in his manner, yet the very air that eddied around him, the brush of cloth against cloth as he moved, seemed to whisper of swift and easy death.

Lisette felt her heart leap inside her. Caid Roe O'Neill had come to her in her time of need. He meant to protect her, to stand between her and harm as no one had done since the death of her mother. This could mean that she had her champion and so her freedom. Nothing she had experienced had ever been so amazing or so gratifying.

"You!" Moisant's face mirrored stunned disbelief.

"As you say," Caid agreed, moving to the side of the bed.

Moisant released Lisette. Snatching his ebony cane from under his arm, he held it like a club as he swung toward the man who had killed his son. "What are you doing here? No, don't tell me. I might have known you would have a hand in this."

"Monsieur Moisant," their hostess said, drawing herself up in chill dudgeon. "Monsieur O'Neill is here only because it was he who discovered your daughter-in-law."

"How very convenient."

"An accident, rather," Caid said, "but not without its merits."

"You must think me a fool." Moisant shook his cane in Caid's face. "I have you to thank for this state of Lisette's,

I know it. Anything to be avenged against those of my name."

"You are wrong, as if happens, though I am glad to be of service to the lady."

"I'll wager you are, and I'll wager I know what form that service will take!"

Lisette sat up higher in the bed with her heart thudding against her ribs and heat burning its way to her hairline. Monsieur Moisant's suggestion was infamous without foundation, it must be. Even if it wasn't, not entirely, the rich satisfaction of the avowal made by the sword master remained. He was glad to be of service. It seemed promising.

"You forget yourself, *monsieur*," Caid said in sharp reprimand.

"What will you do? Call me out so you can butcher me, too?" Moisant gave a bark of mirthless laughter. "You'll catch *la grippe* at that. No one will believe it anything except a scurrilous vendetta."

"I have no quarrel with you, *monsieur*." Caid's reply was even.

"Well, I have one with you!" Hard on the words, Moisant lunged toward Caid, lifting the cane again as if he meant to strike him.

Caid sidestepped the blow, then flung out a hand and closed it around the shaft of the cane. Moisant gave a grunt and dragged his right arm back and down with a jerk. The cane parted with a grating of metal on wood, leaving Caid holding the empty shaft while the polished steel of a sword blade slid free to appear in Moisant's hand.

"Look out!"

Even as the desperate warning left Lisette's lips, she saw that it was unnecessary. Caid had flipped the cane shaft, gripping the larger end as he dropped into a swordsman's crouch. An odd thrill moved over her, though she could not have said whether it came from the excitement or dread.

"*Messieurs,*" Maurelle Herriot cried. "You cannot do this, not in my house."

Moisant's growling laugh was the only indication that he heard her. An instant later, he plunged to the attack.

Caid parried the short, flashing blade with a sharp clack and scrape, then recoiled like a banner unfurling in a stiff wind. Moisant followed after him, jabbing, lunging with vicious stabs. Maurelle skipped here and there as she tried to stay out of the way of the two men, finally whisking behind the bed where she screamed for her butler, Solon, for the gendarmes, for anyone who could stop the uneven match. Lisette sat forward with burning eyes and with her breath caught in her chest as she tried to follow the fight.

The small bedchamber gave Caid little room to maneuver, she saw, still he had the swift reflexes and smooth agility of one who avoided naked steel every day of his life. Moisant could not make contact in spite of slashing, whistling blows that sent blue fire gleaming along his sword's length as it caught the morning sunlight through the windows. His face turned a mottled purple, and his breathing sounded harsh and strained as he floundered around the bedchamber. His eyes glittered with hatred and bloodlust as he plunged after the Irishman who seemed to exert himself scarcely at all yet still could not be touched.

Abruptly, Caid halted his retreat. Splintering wood shrieked as he parried a particularly lethal thrust then swirled his jagged length of cane shaft in powerful movement too fast to follow. He forced Moisant's sword hand upward as he stepped into his guard, and the two men came together elbow to elbow, nose to nose. Instantly, the sword master exerted wrenching pressure. Moisant's hand opened, letting the sword cane clatter to the floor. Caid shifted, and suddenly the broken end of the cane shaft he held was pressed to the pulse that throbbed in Moisant's neck.

The blade Moisant had dropped rolled to the edge of the

high bed. Lisette threw back the sheet and slid off the mattress, dropping to a crouch to retrieve the weapon. With it clutched in her fist, she rose slowly to her feet. The vertigo of distress made her sway a little while her stomach clenched with a horrible sense of vulnerability, as if her father-in-law's sword thrusts had been directed at her as well as at the Irish *maître d'armes*.

Quiet descended. They all stood rigid, watching each other with wary mistrust. The seconds ticked past.

It was Madame Herriot who broke the impasse. "Thank God," she exclaimed. She glanced then toward the door where the butler had materialized. "Monsieur Moisant must leave us, Solon. Show him out, if you please."

"Yes, *madame*." The manservant moved back from the opening, standing stiffly to attention with one hand on the door handle.

Lisette's father-in-law shoved away from Caid then straightened his coat with a jerk. The only sign of his humiliation was the glitter in his dark eyes. "I go with pleasure since I am clearly too late to save my dead son's wife from her folly. I only hope she will not live to regret her decision made this day. And I trust she has thought well on the reasons why her husband's killer might come to her aid." He turned to Lisette then. "In the meantime, *madame,* you will not be surprised if I tell you that all connection between us is severed from this moment. I only wish that I might as easily take back my family name before it is dirtied beyond repair."

He nodded to Maurelle then strode from the bedchamber as if Caid did not exist. Solon followed after him with a measured tread. Their footsteps could be heard retreating, fading beyond earshot.

"*Mon cher,*" Madame Herriot said in low concern as she glided to Caid's side and took his arm. "You are all right? He didn't touch you?"

"Not even a scratch," he answered with a sardonic smile.

"What a devil, to attack you so. I was never more terrified in my life."

Lisette saw Caid glance in her direction though he still spoke to the older woman. "Perhaps you can see how important it is that your guest should stay well away from him then?" Freeing his arm, he walked to where Lisette stood. "What of you? Are you all right?"

"Perfectly," she said, though the word came out with less assurance than she had intended, and the sword cane she still held in her hand had an odd quiver to it.

Caid reached to take the weapon in his firm grasp. "I suggest that you get back into bed then have something to eat. It's past noon, you know, and you slept through breakfast."

She hadn't known, wasn't at all hungry, still she felt little inclination to argue. Turning, she mounted the bed step and settled back against the pillows.

"I will see that a little broth and bread are brought at once," Maurelle said over her shoulder as she moved from the room.

Lisette murmured her appreciation to the woman's retreating back. Then she lay staring at her hands a moment. Finally, she opened her mouth as if to speak.

"No," Caid said. "If you mean to thank me again, or even apologize, I beg you won't.

"You might have been killed." Her throat was so constricted that the words came out in a whisper.

"There was little likelihood of it, not with this toy." He flung the sword cane in his hand onto the bedside table.

"I never thought it would be like this. I see now that it was wrong to try to involve you. Believe me when I say that I had no intention of adding to the hatred between you and Eugene's father."

"What is a little more, given the degree he feels already? But you wouldn't be trying to abandon your request, now would you?"

"I think it may be necessary." She couldn't bring herself to look at him so she began to pleat the sheet between her fingers.

"Not for my sake. Unless, of course, you are afraid of me because of what you just saw."

She sent him a startled glance. "How could I be when it was to protect me?"

"Or afraid of Moisant's accusations?"

"That you might have some sinister motive for coming to my aid? Mere spite, I believe."

"No doubt, though it pleases me to hear you say so." He reached to lay his warm hand on her fingers, stilling their nervous activity. "Be easy now, if you can."

"Yes." The word was a mere whisper, all she could manage while her pulse leaped like a startled deer at his touch then throbbed along her veins so strongly that she felt a little ill with it.

"I will see about finding a suitable place for you today, and then return in the morning. We should have much to discuss then."

He pressed her fingers briefly, then released them and turned away. Seconds later, the door closed behind him.

Lisette lay still, barely breathing. He would return. They would talk. He had just agreed to her proposal, even if the exact words had not been spoken. He was really going to be her protector, someone she could depend upon to be nearby when needed, someone to prevent her from being coerced by Eugene's father. A few moments ago, the knowledge of that commitment would have made her happy, even ecstatic.

A few moments ago, she had not seen him face death and defeat it without turning a hair. She had not known the force of his personality, had not realized the armored hardness of the man he was inside or the deadliness of the power and skill he wielded. She had not dreamed of how he could smile while hiding secrets in the shimmering blue depths of his eyes with their elusive flashes of green like a sunset over deep water.

She had not known that she could tremble at his touch, or feel that she had been branded by it as the devil was said to brand his victims.

It was entirely possible she had made an error in her choice of protectors. She must pray to *le bon Dieu* that it did not prove fatal.

3

It was not Caid's day for fencing instruction. By common practice, the *maîtres d'armes* opened their salons on alternate days. This allowed clients to observe the techniques of the various sword masters and to receive instruction from more than one if they were so inclined. It also allowed recovery from the strenuous exercise of hours on the fencing strips. Caid almost regretted the arrangement just now. He could have used a few bouts to work off the anger that still burned inside him.

Emerging from under the arcade where the stairs mounted to his second-floor atelier, he paused. The Passage de la Bourse was quiet at this hour since the Vieux Carré kept the tradition of the siesta imported while Louisiana was ruled from Madrid and Havana. A clerk or two hurried along, carrying papers from some Canal Street establishment to the government offices at the Cabildo. Taking this pedestrian way devoted to male pursuits was speedier, even when they had to detour around where they were clearing away the ruins of the St. Louis Hotel, since it allowed them to forge ahead without stepping aside for the full skirts of the ladies or stopping to scrape and bow. Few females showed their faces here, where they might glimpse gentlemen in their shirtsleeves practicing in ateliers with doors thrown wide for air or be subjected to catcalls and frank comments from the young bucks lounging on the open balconies. Those who did were vendors of one thing or another, including more personal wares at night.

Caid paused on the pavement as he debated his choices

for a midday meal. He could take his pick of the half dozen coffeehouses in the area. He could also drop in at the new barroom opened by Alvarez since his place burned with the St. Louis Hotel. For the price of a tall glass of *bière* Creole, he could pick up a few slices of roast beef and a baguette from the cold collation served free on the bar there. Failing that, he could amble over to the City Exchange restaurant for fried oysters and redfish. Or if he wanted to venture farther afield or expend the funds, he could walk to the St. Charles Hotel and partake of their copious menu which included two dozen entrées and twice that many soups and salads served under gargantuan crystal chandeliers said to be the largest in America.

His problem was solved by the appearance of a gumbo vendor, a large woman with cinnamon skin, pristine white tignon tied with upstanding points like cats' ears and a comfortable bulk as advertisement for the quality of her wares. Her kettle of the winter concoction made popular by Alvarez's chef, usually prepared with sausage and chicken, smelled wonderful, and he stepped back inside his atelier for a bowl.

With his most immediate problem solved, Caid turned his thoughts toward the agreement made with Madame Lisette Moisant. What maggot of the brain had caused him to take it on, he could not say with exactitude, but thought it had something to do with soft gray eyes and desperate courage. Agree he had, however, and now must deliver.

The first requirement was to secure a house. He could handle that task easily enough for himself and his modest needs, but knew it would not be so simple for a wealthy young widow. Advice was what he required, and he knew where to find it. He turned in the direction of the atelier just down from his own.

He was hailed by the atelier's owner, Rio—or more correctly by Damian Francisco Adriano de Vega y Riordan, the recently elevated Conde de Lérida—the instant he stepped into the upstairs salon. With him was La Roche, though that was one of the *petit noms* beloved by the Creoles and conferred on the Italian because of his rocklike fighting stance. His name was actually Nicholas Pasquale, or perhaps something else entirely since many of the sword masters favored a nom de guerre and the code of the fencing salons did not encourage inquiry into such details. Both men appeared relaxed as they lounged in their chairs, but that was on the surface only. Little that took place in the salon or just outside its doors escaped them. It was a vigilance Caid understood very well since he shared it.

It was Rio's day to keep his *salle d'armes* open, but he was idle because of the three o'clock dinner hour. With a sweep of his hand, he indicated a chair at the table where he sat with Pasquale, then poured a drink for him from the bottle of Bordeaux which sat between them, next to what appeared to be a new sword case.

"So where have you been keeping yourself, *mon ami?*" La Roche asked as he leaned back at an angle with one booted foot propped on a rung of the chair next to him. "I came by your place last night and again this morning at dawn, but you were not at home."

"Accept my apologies," Caid answered, his gaze wry. "I trust it was nothing important? Just another outing to The Twin Oaks over one of your paramours or some such thing?"

"Some such," The Italian agreed with a shrug.

"That's all right then." Caid never failed to be amazed at La Roche's ability to stay out most of the night on clandestine rendezvous of which he seldom spoke a word, and then appear fresh and ready to take the strip at his atelier on the following morning. Dark haired, dark eyed, meltingly tender in his approach to females, his conquests had become legendary even in the short time he had been in the city.

"So where were you?"

"Occupied elsewhere."

"Ah," La Roche said wisely.

"You were with a lady?" Rio asked from where he lounged next to the Italian. "I thought you had no time for the petticoat contingent."

"It was unavoidable," Caid answered, even as he felt heat rise to the back of his neck. "And I never said I hadn't the time, only that I had better things to do than hang around some female's house like a stray cur. Just because you're about to be leg-shackled to the charming Celina doesn't mean the rest of us are inclined in that direction." Rio was betrothed to Celina Amalie Vallier, an obvious love match for all that the bride was an heiress of note.

"Who said anything about marriage?"

The amusement that lurked in Rio's eyes as he asked that question told Caid he had probably said too much. It was time to change the subject before he was truly indiscreet. "No one except you, who has it on the brain. How are the nuptials progressing?"

"Well enough, for all I can tell," Rio answered with careless bonhomie. "I sent off the *corbeille de noce* yesterday after two weeks of the most exhausting shopping. My responsibility is now at an end, and I have nothing to do except put in my appearance at the cathedral."

"Mademoiselle Vallier was pleased?"

Rio's grin slashed his face and shone silver in the dark gray of his eyes. "She seemed to appreciate the effort."

Caid had a fair idea of the form that appreciation might have taken, but manners and a healthy consideration for his own skin prevented him from confirming it. Doubtless, it had been an extravagant gift, given Rio's preoccupation lately with gathering it together. The *corbeille de noce* was the traditional wedding basket presented as the gift from the groom to his bride, so Caid had been told, a gilded extravaganza filled with the most beautiful and costly tokens to be found, cashmere shawls so finely woven that they could be pulled through a wedding ring, *parures* of jewels, delicately painted fans, carved hair combs, gem-encrusted gloves, and other such fripperies. To have it filled and presented was always an enormous weight off the mind of the groom.

"The big day will be here before long," he said. "You made your arrangements for the journey to Spain?"

Rio shook his head. "Celina prefers to remain in town until the *saison des visites* is over and the heat of summer is upon us."

"What of your preference? I'd think you'd be itching to see your old home."

"It's been so many years that a few weeks longer will make little difference," Rio answered with offhand ease.

The truth was, Caid thought, that Rio was besotted with his French Creole bride-to-be and would do anything to please her. That might have been a matter for sympathy except that his Celina was equally enamored. There were moments when Caid envied Rio his complete acceptance and unblemished future, but he was careful not to show it. "You will be here for the fencing tournament then?"

It was La Roche who answered before Rio could speak. "What use has he of crossing swords with other masters when he will no longer be a *maître d'armes* once he quits the city? Besides, he will hardly chance cutting short his days with the lovely Celina."

"True, on both counts," Rio agreed with lazy humor. "I leave it to one of you to take the prize."

"Meaning, of course, that he's certain we would have no chance otherwise," Caid pointed out to La Roche with a grin.

"For which consideration we thank him most sincerely." The Italian sword master raised his glass to him.

Caid had to admit that the odds were considerably improved with Rio out of the running. The Spaniard was a for-

midable opponent who had trained in Paris as he had, though
their paths, oddly enough, had never crossed. La Roche, an
expert in the Italian style, was just as formidable. The rivalry
between the three of them was friendly, however, which
could not be said about all the sword masters along the Passage. The upcoming tournament might well see a thinning
of the ranks. It had not yet begun and feelings were running
as high as the Mississippi in flood, particularly among the
masters who had been excluded from competition because
they did not hold a certificate from an approved academy.
Caid's had been gained in Paris of course. That training
meant he fought in the French style, rather than the Italian.
It should prove interesting to see which form was most successful.

Answering such a question was not the purpose of the
tournament, of course; it was purely for the glory. Well, that
and to increase interest in the art of fencing and present the
strengths and techniques of the different masters so new clients might chose among them.

"What is this?" Caid asked, indicating the sword case on
the table. "Don't tell me one of you has mortgaged your soul
for a champion's blade?"

"By no means." La Roche put down his glass then released the catch of the sword case. "The results of a fortunate wager. What do you think?"

Lying on the velvet of the case was a matched pair of
colichemarde, or rapiers, boasting the unmistakable
workmanship of Coulaux et Cie in Paris. Polished to a mirror shine, engraved with scrollwork, fitted with graceful
hilts and hand guards, they were miracles of the sword
maker's art. Caid took one out, sighting along the blade, hefting it for balance. It fit his hand as if made for him.

"Beautiful," he said simply, and had to fight to prevent
his envy from sounding in his voice. "You have the luck of
the devil."

La Roche lifted a shoulder. "On occasion. Let us hope that it extends to the lottery."

"You're still wasting money on tickets?"

"What would you? I'm a man of high expectations."

"At the very least." It was a harmless habit, Caid thought, but not something he was inclined to do with his hard-earned silver dollars. Or perhaps he just lacked that kind of optimism.

"I'm thinking of joining the Louisiana Legion while we wait for the tournament to begin," La Roche went on as he took the other rapier from the case, turning it in his hand.

"The militia? *Mon Dieu,* why would you do such a thing?" The amused inquiry came from Rio.

"Many reasons," the Italian answered. "First is my fatal sympathy for the underdog in any fight, since it appears enrollment in the Legion is being increased to make ready for intervention in this affair between Texas and Mexico."

"Not a bad thing," Caid commented.

La Roche inclined his head. "Then the drilling is being stepped up in anticipation of war, and I find I have a great deal of excess energy these days."

"And finally, as fever for the war grows, militiamen will be searching for expert instruction in swordplay in order to keep their skins unpricked, yes?" Caid asked.

"More regiments will be formed, more men enlisted as time goes on," La Roche said in agreement. "The gentlemen who are our potential clients will become officers of one sort or another with a sword as natural equipment to go with the uniform."

"If you are among their ranks, perhaps an officer yourself…"

"Then I will be able to demonstrate all the excellent reasons that they should frequent my *salle d'armes.*"

"You do have a point." Caid smoothed a careful thumb along the sword he held as he considered it.

"A uniform lends a man a certain cachet as well, not to mention the effect on the ladies."

Caid made a rude noise. "As if you need the help." Turning to Rio, he asked, "What say you, *mon ami?* Are you for the military?"

"Hardly." Rio leaned back in his chair. "I could be in Spain for months, even a year or more. This little contretemps with Mexico may be over before I return."

"You will not be reopening your atelier then, I imagine, so have no need to attract customers."

Though the suggestion came from La Roche, Caid was more than curious to hear the answer.

Rio gave them a lazy smile. "The two of you feel I should close? Oh, yes, and perhaps recommend your superior services to my clients?"

"Now why didn't we think of that," Caid asked, widening his eyes with spurious amazement. "After all, you'll hardly need the money once you and Celina are wed. I mean, her father is as rich as the legendary Valcour Aime. Then there is this vast Spanish estate of yours."

"Unfair, I agree." Rio sighed. "But I shall miss the clashing of blades, the exertion, and most particularly, the company of friends."

That hint of Latin sentimentality made Caid a bit uncomfortable though he knew what Rio meant. Beyond the obvious rivalry, sometimes friendly, sometimes cutthroat, there existed an odd sense of brotherhood among the sword masters. They were a class unto themselves, superior in strength and will, feared by many, lauded by most, imitated in all things and yet only quasi-respectable. Combination instructors, role models and gladiators whose exploits on the field of honor drew crowds of the curious, they formed a community of their own within the greater French Creole community of New Orleans, one whose center was the few blocks of the Passage de la Bourse. They made their own rules, supported and defended each other, even as they sought always to best both friend and foe on the strips. Each man was expected to fight his own battles, yet an insult to one was an insult to all, an injury that demanded instant amends. They were unique, a breed apart, and liked it that way, for the most part.

They spoke of other things, the three of them: the stabbing death of a prominent citizen and the lamentably frequent incidence of such things, a horrific explosion aboard a steamboat that had taken thirty-four lives, the presidential election shaping up between the Whigs and the Jackson Democrats, and the Whig slogan heard everywhere of "Tippecanoe and Tyler, Too." Finally, there came a lull into which Caid dropped the question that had not been far from his thoughts since he left Lisette Moisant.

"You surprise me, my friend," Rio said with a lifted brow. "I had not thought you had the time or inclination to set up a *chérie amie*."

"Nor do I," he answered shortly. "The lady is quite respectable. I require a house for her with a good, safe address."

"How did it come to be your responsibility? Has she no male relatives to take on the task?"

"None who will trouble to assist her."

"But you will? Come, who is this Fair One? And how do you mean to establish her without ruining her by the association?"

Caid set his lips in a firm line. He should have known he would have to tell the whole story. It went against the grain, though he had no fear that his friends would misconstrue his motives or spread the story. No, it was simply that there was something private about his acquaintance with the widow Moisant that he did not care to share.

There should not be any such aspect. It was because he knew this very well that he drew a deep breath and launched into the tale of their meeting.

"What a coil," La Roche said when he had finished. "Surely some other course is open to the lady?"

"She insists that there isn't."

"And you have pledged to help her. I wonder how she managed that."

"By asking," Caid returned, meeting the Italian's narrow gaze squarely. Not that he could blame La Roche for his suspicion. It would have been natural for Lisette to use feminine arts to acquire his aid. Why had she not? Was it because she was too naive to know the power of her beauty and feminine appeal, or only that she was too straightforward, too honorable to stoop to such a bribe?

Another possibility existed of course. She could consider him too far beneath her.

"You feel responsible, yes? Or is it that she appealed to your gentlemanly instincts and tender heart?"

"As if I had either," Caid answered with a cutting glance.

"But I think you do, my friend," La Roche said. "Perhaps more than any of us."

Ignoring that the Italian's too personal appraisal seemed better than answering it. "Set it down to duty, if you must have a reason. I am the cause of her troubles, so it appears, since I dispatched her husband. The least I can do is see she escapes Moisant's clutches—though responsibility for a headstrong female is the last thing I need."

"Ah. I begin to see."

"I doubt it." Caid frowned. "Moisant is…I just don't like the way he looks at her."

"My knowledge of the city is far from complete," Rio said, breaking into their minor clash. "Still, as with most towns built on the European model, the closer to the cathedral an address may be, the more respectable it seems."

"True," Caid replied, more than willing to change the subject.

La Roche gave a stubborn shake of his head. "If you arrange for a house, even if it is in the lady's name, someone is sure to hear of it. They will immediately wonder at your interest."

"Then how is it to be managed?"

"Madame Herriot might be enlisted for the task," Rio mused, rubbing a finger alongside his nose. "Involving her further could be unfortunate, of course. Moisant may be willing to overlook the fact that she took in his daughter-in-law for a night, but it's unlikely that he will forgive her for abetting the girl further."

"Maurelle is on shaky enough ground with her own artistic pretensions without deliberately making enemies," Caid said in agreement.

"A lawyer might be engaged," La Roche offered after a moment, "some discreet representative who can handle the transaction after you have chosen the location."

"But I still see difficulties," Rio said. "Moisant can't allow his former daughter-in-law to set up housekeeping on her own without giving up his source of income, and I don't see him doing that without a struggle. What is to keep him from invading her new home and dragging her away?"

"My protection," Caid said in soft reminder.

"But how will you manage it without being on the premises, especially at night?"

"A watch can be kept."

"You intend to sleep across her doorstep, I suppose? That may appeal to the knight-errant in you, my friend, but could cause comment—besides being damnably uncomfortable."

"Droll," Caid said without noticeable humor. What do you suggest then?"

"You could always offer to marry her."

He was even less amused. "It's unlikely she's that desperate."

"The only solution I see, then, is to place her in some

household with stout menservants, one where you may have easy *entrée* when necessary."

"Maurelle's, in other words."

"Just so."

"I doubt she will be so obliging as to take on a permanent houseguest."

"Unless you persuade her."

"Are you suggesting I have some particular influence?"

Rio shook his head. "Only charm and a facility with words. Madame Herriot might be led to recall her own past difficulties which could assure sympathy for her guest."

"I'm sure she feels that already."

"Well then?"

"I don't know," Caid said, testing the point of the rapier. "I'll have to give it more consideration."

Silence fell among them. It was Caid who broke it after some moments. "You know, my friends, I've been thinking."

"Take care," La Roche said with lazy humor. "It bids fair to become a habit."

Rio shook his head at the Italian in mock reproof. "To what purpose?"

"We three arrived in New Orleans with the same object in mind, as I understand it, a quest for vengeance. We achieved it, in our different ways, yet similar crimes to those we resented go unpunished all around us, mainly because of the odd division of the city into three municipalities a handful of years back. The gendarmes are spread thin, and there is scant cooperation between the police departments of the different jurisdictions. The streets aren't as safe after dark as they were before the Americans came, or so I'm told, and society is considerably less civilized. It seems something should be done about it." He stopped, embarrassed, suddenly, at putting his inclination into words.

"Allow me to guess," La Roche said in dry tones. "You

would use your trusty sword to rid the streets of thieves and cutthroats, frightening them into becoming good citizens."

Caid scowled at him. "My notion, insofar as I had one, was to put the fear of God into those who prey on women and children—the wife beaters, sadists and rapists who choose their victims from those who have no one to protect them and little recourse under the law. It's assumed that the frowns of society will prevent the worst inclinations of such men, but the truth is that it does not."

"And you would change that?"

"We could, if we wished it."

"We?" That soft query came from Rio.

"The sword masters, beginning with the three of us," Caid answered, turning to him. "It would take so little. A quiet suggestion with the weight of cold steel behind it might often be enough. If not, then a challenge would be forthcoming, followed by a salutary lesson in conduct. A few such meetings and the incidents of persecution should fall dramatically."

"These things happen already," La Roche mused. "Witness the impaling of Defossat upon the sword of his grown stepson just last week. The public tale is that it was over a matter of indebtedness, but the word among the servants is that Monsieur Murrett objected to the bruises worn by his mother who was widowed three years ago but married Defossat last spring. Such corrections of manners are a major benefit of the *code duello*."

"To make it a concentrated endeavor would be no great stretch."

"I don't know that I would say that," La Roche objected.

"Let it pass then. It was just a notion."

"Because of your sister," Rio said with trenchant understanding.

"Brona, yes, but also Maurelle Herriot, Lisette Moisant and others like them. Also because it seems that some good should come from the dread we generate."

"I like it," La Roche said. "By all the saints, I do like it." He reached with the blade he held to tap the one in Caid's hand. "In fact, I applaud it since it should go as far in giving me exercise as joining the militia. Shall we swear an oath to it on our crossed swords?"

He should have known they would be game for it, Caid thought. Regardless, he felt an odd tightness in his throat at that sign of partisanship. "By all means."

"What shall we swear?" La Roche mused. "Well, that's easy enough. For me, it shall be the obvious. To Vengeance."

"Yes, why not, since that's what we seek for those who have known cruelty?" Rio reached behind him to take an épée from the wall as he spoke. "I shall add, to Vigilance."

The crossed swords, held by his two friends who rested their corded wrists on the small table between them, formed the glittering shape of the letter V between their upright, polished silver blades. It seemed an inspiration. "To Valor in Arms then," Caid said, and placed his sword at the correct angle to repeat the design.

For a single instant, their eyes met and held above the blades. In that short space of time, Caid felt the stir of every chivalrous impulse he had ever known, a heart-swelling need to make the world a better place, to sweep it pure and clean in keeping with his most idealistic childhood image. Then it faded, replaced by discomfort that made him glance around quickly to see if anyone had noticed their extravagant gesture.

"Just so," Rio agreed as he took note of Caid's impulse even as he put the *épée* away. "Caution is required, I think. It will not do to advertise our aim."

"No. Results, not reputation, should be our purpose." Caid reseated the rapier he held in its case.

"Masks," La Roche said, snapping his fingers.

"Oh, I don't think…"

"But hidden identities are always so tantalizing in the books of the lady scribblers."

"Too melodramatic by half, except possibly during the weeks of Mardi Gras." Rio's mouth tilted in a wry smile. "In any case, the fact that there are three of us should be enough to make any chastisement appear random rather than planned. At least for a little while."

La Roche sighed as he replaced his own sword. "You two have no romance in your souls."

"True," Caid said in agreement. "It isn't a game, you know."

"I know. So deadly serious, both of you." La Roche shrugged. "So where shall we begin, then? I came across a situation these two days past that—"

He fell abruptly silent as a man appeared in the doorway. Tall, undeniably handsome, he had the café au lait skin which marked him as a mulatto. The newcomer wore a dove-gray frock coat with darker gray trousers, a waistcoat with satin stripes of palest gray and peach and a snowy cravat set with a large and finely carved cameo. Striding to where they sat, he swung out a chair and straddled it. "Well met, my friends," he exclaimed as he glanced from one to the other. "What are you plotting? You must tell me at once for I am dying of ennui, I promise you. Have no fear that I will betray you, for such a thing would surely end the amusement."

The newcomer was Bastile Croquère. Known throughout the city for his collection of cameos, sartorial perfection and dangerous skill with a sword, he kept an atelier close to the ruins of the St. Louis Hotel. His temper had once been legend, so Caid had heard, but he had learned to direct his anger into his swordplay. His salon was much frequented by the young bucks, though, like the famed Juan Pépé Llulla, he had been denied entrance to the sword master's tournament for lack of a proper certificate. It was a shame, since it meant that no contest could ever be definitive that barred either of the two from entering.

Caid exchanged a glance with Rio and La Roche. To add

the mulatto to their ranks was tempting since he would be a formidable asset. Still, it might be best to see how their arrangement turned out before involving others. He might be enlisted later, under special circumstances.

"We speak of brides and other ladies," Rio said easily. "Tell me, did you see Madame Julie Calvé in last night's performance at the opera house? I thought she was in rare voice, but Mademoiselle Vallier assures me I'm wrong and the diva was suffering from the effect of a spring cold. Do you support me or my lady?"

"Madame Julie Calvé at her worst is better than all the others at their best," Croquère said diplomatically. Then he turned the conversation to the races about to begin at the Métairie track outside the city and the moment passed.

It was late afternoon when Caid returned to the Herriot town house. He had thought to speak to Maurelle alone, but Solon showed him directly into the rear sitting room where the mistress of the house was consulting with a modiste. Caid found her directing the pinning up of the hem of Lisette's gown while her guest stood on a small, brocaded footstool with the seamstress at her feet.

"Forgive me," he said at once, turning to go. "I'll return another time."

"No, no!" Maurelle cried, gesturing him forward. "Give us your opinion, if you please. Do you not think this gown demure enough without a fichu? It's enough that poor Lisette is forced to wear black without her looking like a nun."

The gown was simple but well cut, as far as Caid could tell. It certainly hugged the slender waist of the young lady he had rescued while outlining the curves of her bosom with admirable fidelity. The contrast between the black silk and the fairness of her shoulders was marked, the softness of her skirts hinted at the softness beneath them, and the sablelike undertones of dark color brought out the auburn gleam in her hair. If by a fichu Maurelle meant the bit of lace Lisette was clutching between her breasts, then it was certainly redundant in his opinion. He said so without hesitation, while praying that the sudden, fevered heat he felt rising inside him did not sound in his voice.

"There, what did I tell you?" Maurelle twitched the fichu from her guest's clutches and tossed it aside. "Always ask a man if you wish the truth in these matters."

"Which isn't at all what she would have said if I had disagreed with her," Caid commented with a wry smile as he looked to Lisette on her stool. "But should you be up, Madame Moisant? I expected to find you still abed with a tray on your lap."

"I am quite recovered, thank you. Besides, I have no patience with the current fashion for wan ill health."

"No swooning or overwrought sensibilities for you? I will have to remember that."

She frowned a little as she stared down at him from her perch. "What do you mean? I assure you that I feel the shock and pain of loss as much as any."

"I never suggested otherwise," he answered, even as he wondered at the sharpness of her tone. "Permit me to say that it is a relief to see you feeling well enough for this." He waved at the modiste, a quadroon woman who had barely glanced at him since he came into the room.

"It's hardly taxing, since she is only having two or three garments fitted that I wore during my own mourning," Maurelle pointed out. "A few tucks here and there are all they require. The rest of her needs, new gowns for visiting and evening, walking and driving, may wait until she is in better form."

"One would think she had nothing to wear."

"Nor does she, *mon brave*. I sent a very polite request around to the Moisant household asking that the contents of her armoire be packed and sent here. It was refused."

It was just like Moisant to be as disobliging as possible

under the circumstances, Caid thought. "My apologies. I should have realized."

"The clothing left behind filled not even half an armoire and was not stylish in any degree," Lisette said with a lift of her chin. "I shall not miss it."

It was impossible to tell whether she was telling the truth or putting a good face on a difficult situation. Either way, Caid admired her for it. "I wish the problem of where you are to reside was as easily settled. The more I consider it, the less advisable it seems for you to remove to your own residence."

"Does it indeed?" Lisette's voice turned as chill as a wind from the north.

"I fear you may be too open to insult, or worse."

"I have considered the problem," she said regally. "I know just the lady to lend support and countenance to me, a veritable dragon of respectability."

"I'm sure she is, but something more is required. Madame Herriot has several strong menservants on the premises who serve to make this house secure. I'm sure she would give you house room for some time longer, at least until the end of the season."

"Caid, *mon cher*," Maurelle began.

"How can you not?" He turned to her with a hand out in appeal. "Have you no memory of how difficult it was to live with an older man of disagreeable temperament? I know you were happy to be free of that constraint. More than that, I am aware that you are all sympathy beneath your glaze of sophistication. Surely you can open your home and generous heart to this lady?"

"Naturally, when you ask in that manner," Maurelle said, two spots of color appearing on her cheeks. "However, I don't believe…"

"I much prefer to go my own way," Lisette said firmly.

"Even if it proves as dangerous as it is unwise?"

"Even so," Lisette answered with precision. "I cannot allow Madame Herriot to suffer for my sake, as she may if my father-in-law decides she is obstructing his wishes. Nor do I intend to allow that gentleman to dictate my behavior by default now that I have escaped his roof. I will not cower from him, fearing to go out in public, nor will I lie shivering in my bed while waiting to see if he will use force to compel obedience. I wish to be my own mistress, and I will."

"And then what?" Caid asked. "What will you do when you are ensconced in your house but no one calls, no one sends invitations or deigns to receive you?"

"No one? Or do you refer to the *haut ton?* I care little for society and its endless round of parties where one hears the same music and sees the same people. What I would wish is to entertain a few friends, those who share my interests and who can speak on topics which exercise the mind. And particularly those who are too intelligent to believe the lies that may be told about me."

"You don't mean that. You will not like being outside the pale, never going to the balls and soirées of the season."

"Really, *cher,*" Maurelle said in protest. "Must you paint such a bleak picture?"

"I am only pointing out the difficulties," he said shortly.

Lisette's eyes took on a militant gleam. "What he is doing, Madame Herriot, is trying to make me see that I am unlikely to find a husband unless I am out and about. He says that I should be married again, if you please, though I have told him I have no taste for it."

"Does he, really?" Maurelle murmured.

"It's clearly the best solution," Caid insisted. The prospect of freedom after living so restricted these past two years with her husband and father-in-law had clearly turned Lisette's head. She required curbing before it was too late.

"The best solution for whom?" Maurelle turned to

Lisette. "I am just now reminded of a town house on the rue Royale that might suit you, *ma chère*. It is owned by Monsieur Freret who took ship two or three weeks past to France, escorting his daughter there for the completion of her education. He and his wife are to remain in Paris with relatives for a year, and wish to lease their house for that period. By the time they return, you will surely have found a more permanent address."

"Excellent. I will be pleased to look at it," Lisette answered, meeting Caid's gaze with an air that in a man might have been called challenging.

"His agent will be most happy to meet with you, I'm sure. And should you be satisfied, the arrangements may be completed without further ado."

"You are very kind."

"Aren't you, though," Caid said, his gaze narrowed on Maurelle's features. "I trust it's a kindness you don't live to regret." She was siding with Lisette, he thought, out of annoyance at his attempt to foist an uninvited guest upon her.

"So do I," Maurelle said sweetly, "though I have no real fear. As the lady's protector, you must see to it that all is well."

So he must, Caid thought. God help him.

4

Lisette stared around at the salon with elation rising inside her like bubbles in fine champagne. Spacious and elegant, its twin fireplaces of gray marble faced each other on the end walls with tall mirrors rising above them, while stately draperies of dusty-rose silk framed two sets of transomed French doors. A pier mirror between the doors reflected an Aubusson carpet in muted woodland tones on which sat a settee, chaise and several chairs covered with tapestry and flanked by tables inlaid with ivory and tortoiseshell. This room, this house was hers for the whole of the next year. Monsieur Freret's man of business had taken the draft on her bank and given her the key not a half hour ago.

She had escaped. She was truly free for the first time in her life. Never again would she be otherwise; this she swore with fierce determination. To be forced to bow to the will of others, to accede to unreasonable demands, to hide how she felt and thought, had been a kind of death. Now after much travail she had come into her own. From this day, she would live well and without fear. Holding out her arms, she spun in a slow circle. This euphoria must be what it was like to be tipsy. If so, she could become used to the sensation.

Suddenly she stopped so her skirts swirled around her ankles before falling into place again. She should not, perhaps, have disregarded the advice of Caid O'Neill. His objections had been valid; she was not such an *imbécile* that she could not recognize that much. Given the task of providing for her safety, he was simply attempting to make the task as certain and easy as possible. She didn't fault him for it, but she had

had enough of being told what she could and could not do. She would be her own mistress, no matter the cost.

Oh, but the look on his face when she had said she had no use for the *ton* but preferred intelligent discussion. Amazement and disapproval had chased themselves across his handsome features. Had there also been the faintest hint of being intrigued? She could not tell. But how dare he disapprove of anything she might say or do? He had not become her keeper by his agreement to what she had asked.

The sound of a carriage rattling to a halt outside caught her attention. She walked quickly to one of the French doors which opened onto the balcony overlooking the street and pulled it open. Stepping out onto the canvas-covered floor, she peered over the wrought iron railing.

A hackney carriage sat just below her. Alighting from it was a lady of angular, upright form dressed in somber brown-and-taupe-striped merino and with a cheap straw bonnet covering her hair. Her movements were brisk as she turned and directed the driver while he handed down her baggage.

"Agatha! You're here already," Lisette called down from her balcony perch. "I can hardly believe— Wait there! I'll be right down to pay the fare."

"Nonsense, my dear," the lady began.

Lisette didn't stay to listen. Whirling around, she ran back into the second-floor salon then across it to the gallery that hung above the inner courtyard. The staircase descended from the far end where it met the wall of the house next door. She took it with flying skirts, almost tripping in her haste. The coolness of the *porte cochère* greeted her as she passed quickly along its brick-lined length beneath the upper floors of the house. At its end, she pushed open the wicket gate for pedestrians set into the larger wrought iron barrier and emerged onto the street.

The hackney was already pulling away. Agatha Stilton

stood beside the meager pile of her belongings consisting of a scuffed portmanteau, a well-stuffed carpetbag and a capacious woolen knitting bag. Her hands were clasped loosely on her reticule and a quizzical smile lit her narrow face. "Well, my dear?"

"Oh, Aggie," Lizzie cried, giving her the *petit nom* she had used as a child as she stepped forward and encircled the thin figure with her arms. "I've missed you so."

"And I, you," the older woman said with twin spots of color on her cheeks and a hint of moisture in her eyes as she returned the hug. "How long it seems since last we were together."

"Too long," Lisette said. And indeed it had been several months and more. Agatha, originally from Boston, had been Lisette's governess from the age of five years until her marriage. A lady of decided opinions on the rights and abilities of females, she had educated Lisette in the classical manner suited for young men instead of as a female who must inevitably marry. They had grown to be friends rather than teacher and pupil. Lisette had kept nothing from her dear Aggie.

Her governess had opposed the betrothal arranged by Lisette's mother, primarily because she considered her charge too young at eighteen, but also because she felt the groom lacked the proper husbandly ardor. Though a practical woman in most areas, a predilection for the romantic poets had given her an idealistic outlook which deplored the French Creole habit of contracting marriages based on assets and antecedents.

Agatha had taken a position with a family in St. Francisville after Lisette's wedding. She had been there well over a year. When she returned to the city, Lisette had wanted to invite her to the Moisant town house, but Eugene's father had forbidden it. He had disliked the woman intensely because of her independent ways that she had passed on to her pupil, and had no inclination to allow her to become Lisette's ally. If she wished to see Agatha, she had to slip away unattended. That had been difficult before Eugene's death and impossible afterward.

"Come inside at once," Lisette urged now. "I do apologize, but there is no one to help with your baggage since I have just this instant taken possession. Here, give me the portmanteau while you take the other bags, and we will soon have you settled in your room."

A short time later, they were ensconced at a small table in the salon. Lisette had gone into the street to buy rice cakes, known as calas, and coffee from one of the vendors who plied their wares on nearly every corner. The hot beverage had been poured into a Sevres pot she had found in a cabinet, and the cakes arranged on a matching plate. That she had found something to offer was a great relief, since nothing was more embarrassing than an empty cupboard when a guest arrived.

She would have preferred tea rather than the coffee. The habit was one that Agatha had brought with her from the northeast and Lisette had acquired by emulation. There had been a time when her governess had been her model in all things from deportment and dress to her manner of eating. It was not surprising, perhaps, given that she had been closer to Agatha in many ways than to her own mother. So many children died in childhood that babies were often ignored until the age of five or six to prevent the pain of loss from being so devastating. The marriage to Eugene had actually brought Lisette closer to her parent, that and the illness that had taken her life. In those months before the wedding, she had realized that her mother's concern for her and fear of leaving her alone in the world were the true measure of her love. They had spoken of many things in the long nights when pain made sleep impossible, had crammed a lifetime of remembrances and advice into the hours while Lisette had sat holding her mother's frail hand. She had agreed to marry Eugene, in the end, to allow her a measure of peace.

"I'm delighted that you could come to me so quickly," Lisette said as she pushed her empty plate aside and reached for the rose-painted china coffeepot to replenish their cups. "It makes matters so much easier."

Rosy color stained the thin skin of Agatha's cheeks. "I had only to throw my few belongings together, which I was heartily glad to do. I tell you frankly that I've had no glimmer of a new post since leaving my last. My own fault, of course, for not keeping my tongue between my teeth—my employer refused to give me a reference, you know. But I could not allow without protest that his dear daughter, only five years old, should be fastened into a corset with applewood slats up the back, even at night. I was never more incensed in my life, particularly as she was such a little thing already. This business of looking as if a strong wind might blow one away is most unhealthy."

"It's common enough these days."

"Indeed, but that doesn't make it right." Agatha shook her head. "Next, we will hear that they are plying children with vinegar and arsenic in emulation of their mothers. But, as I was saying, my prospects were few and the little boardinghouse for women I frequent between positions comfortable enough but hardly…convivial. Your kind invitation was a godsend."

The boardinghouse, Lisette knew, was in fact a dreary place with sad, timeworn furnishings and a strong smell of the cats. Visiting her old teacher there had always pained her. "Well, we shall be much livelier here, I assure you."

"While you are in mourning? I know well that you are not precisely overcome with grief, still…"

"Yes, some concession must be made." Lisette sipped from her cup. "New Orleans is not as strict as Boston in such observances, you know, so I do not repine. It's perfectly acceptable to attend the opera in the rear of a box or behind the protection of the loge grille, and no one will think it at all unusual if I receive a few friends of an evening."

"You must do as you think best, but a young widow should always be more circumspect, if only because everyone will be watching for indiscretion."

"Let them watch. I care not at all."

"You must care, my dear, if you wish to remain in society."

"A vastly overrated distinction."

"Oh, I quite agree. Still, what else is there? And it's very necessary if you are to find another husband."

"Why is it that everyone thinks I should remarry? I am quite content as a widow."

"For now, perhaps."

"You have made a life for yourself without a man," Lisette pointed out with what she thought to be unanswerable logic.

"The single state requires fortitude and a decided taste for one's own company. Besides, I am not so sure I would have refused a proposal if it had chanced to be from the right man. I should have liked having a daughter like you, my dear." Agatha's face was pink again, a sign of how affected by emotion she was at the moment.

"What a lovely compliment," Lisette said softly. "Oh, it's going to be such a grand thing, having you under the same roof again."

Agatha met her gaze across the table for a long moment before taking refuge from emotion by sipping the last of her coffee. Clearing her throat then, she said, "Yes, well, but you mentioned a gallant rescue in your note. I am consumed with curiosity. Was it from the home of your dead husband? How did it take place and when? Come, give me every detail."

Lisette was happy to comply. By the time she finished, Agatha sat staring at her with her mouth open. Then she drew an audible breath through her aquiline nose. "My word, but I can hardly credit such an adventure."

"I assure you every word is true."

"Oh, I didn't mean to accuse you of falsehood, my dear, only—how extraordinary! And to place yourself in the hands of a *maître d'armes?* What possessed you?"

"Desperation, in a word. Few men will dare cross such a one as Monsieur O'Neill."

"They are a law unto themselves, these swordsmen. Why, I've heard the most scandalous tales, as you must have yourself. Some become rich from extortion paid to assure that no cartel is offered, a few accept payment to remove a man's enemies. Then there are those who choose their paramours at will, even from the highest of the *ton* or so it's whispered, for what lady can gainsay them when it might mean a challenge for her husband, father or brother? They can be quite unscrupulous when it comes to such matters."

An odd frisson, half fright, half pleasure, moved down Lisette's spine at the idea, though she suppressed it at once. "Such stories can hardly apply to Monsieur O'Neill as he has been in the city such a short while."

"It only means that none can say what kind of man he may be," Agatha pointed out. "Now you have this close acquaintance, and I can't imagine what may be the result of it."

"You need have no fear. Monsieur O'Neill has agreed to help me because he feels guilty for depriving me of a husband, or so I believe. In any case, he has merely agreed to give me his protection."

"Yes, and he may easily protect you into an extremely compromising situation. Beware of the altruism of gentlemen, my dear. They often expect something in return."

A trace of bitterness colored Agatha's voice. It was not to be wondered at, Lisette knew. As a young woman left alone after her parent's death, she had been offered a place as governess to the young children of a Beacon Hill gentleman who had lost no time in taking shameful advantage of her. To escape him, she eloped with the chauffeur, a man who boasted of relatives in the West Indies. The couple had set out to join them, stopping in New Orleans enroute, and here Agatha had been abandoned. She had never really recovered.

"I doubt very much that Monsieur O'Neill has any such thing in mind," Lisette said with a dismissive gesture. "He has his duties at his *salle d'armes* and far more entertaining amusements to occupy his time."

"For which we must be thankful."

"Indeed. We need not trouble ourselves then, but should consider practical ways and means." Lisette picked up a rice cake and began to break off pieces, popping them into her mouth.

"Such as?"

"Servants, for one thing. This house is far too large to keep up ourselves."

Agatha arched a brow. "Are you quite sure? I do not at all mind turning my hand to scrubbing and dusting."

"I do appreciate that, but did not invite you here to become a maid-of-all-work. What do you feel is the minimum we may require?"

"Well, if you mean to entertain, even on a limited basis, you will need a cook and also a butler to announce visitors, serve meals, shop for the kitchen and see to your gentlemen guests," Agatha said, counting them off on her fingers. "A woman or boy to wash up in the kitchen is essential, as is a housemaid to keep the salon and bedchambers presentable. Then there should be a man to do the same for the courtyard and banquette. I count five, at the very least—unless you intend to keep a carriage?"

"I think it likely."

"A coachman must be found, then, and a boy for the stables, as well. Say seven, unless you'd care to have a personal maid. Then it would be eight."

"So many," Lisette murmured with a frown.

"You could naturally get by with fewer, but there are standards to be met."

"Yes." Lisette pressed her lips together. "I'm not sure I care to have the responsibility of owning so many, or buying them."

"Far better you as a mistress than some I could name, my dear. And if you are disposed to be humane, you may allow them to work for wages to be credited against their purchase price, or else permit them to become peddlers of garden vegetables, pralines and the like in their free time. As an alternative, of course, you could seek suitable persons among the immigrants of the Irish section."

"An excellent suggestion, Agatha. I can see we shall be formidable together!"

"Will you indeed?"

That deep-voiced comment came from the doorway. Lisette whipped her head around to see Caid O'Neill lounging there with his arms across his chest and one shoulder against the frame. How long he had been there and how much he had overheard was impossible to guess, though the grim set of his mouth made her think he had heard her speak of his countrymen as possible servants.

"Monsieur O'Neill," she began as she rose to her feet.

"Assuredly, it will be pleasant," he continued, cutting across what she had meant to say as he straightened and came toward her. "Just think, two females alone in this fine house that is as drafty as a sieve from the eight pairs of French doors set into the walls so any intruder may walk in by the simple expedient of knocking out a pane of glass."

"How do you come to be here?"

"Madame Herriot sent me after you since she expected your return an hour ago. I assume the meeting with your friend detained you."

"It did. Forgive me, Agatha. As you will have guessed, this is…"

"Monsieur Caid O'Neill," Agatha said, rising and extending her hand. "How very convenient. I have been wishing to meet to you."

"Have you now?"

Caid's voice was grim, the look in his eyes appraising as he sketched a bow. Agatha did not seem to notice. "It seems best that we become acquainted without delay, given that we have much the same task ahead of us. I speak of keeping Mademoiselle Lisette from the clutches of her former father-in-law."

"I rather thought you were equally concerned with keeping her from *my* clutches."

Lisette could feel the fiery heat of her blush mount from her chest to her hairline. Agatha also turned rose-red, but faced him with admirable sangfroid. "You did overhear then. I feared so, but can't be sorry for it. To come to an understanding on the subject must have been necessary at some time."

"So it may as well be now? Very well, Madame Stilton."

"Mademoiselle."

He inclined his head in acknowledgment of the correction. "Permit me to tell you that I have no designs of any variety on the virtue of Madame Moisant."

"None at all? You are quite sure?"

Lisette discovered within herself a great disappointment in his answer. No woman, she thought, enjoyed hearing that she roused not an iota of desire in a man's breast.

"She is here because of my actions in the death of Moisant. It would be unbelievably crass to take advantage of that circumstance."

"So it would," Agatha said, folding her hands at her waist. "Still, that doesn't answer the question."

Anger flared in Caid's eyes for brief seconds like lightning reflected on ocean waves. Then it died away, leaving a glimmer of something like respect overlaid by amusement. "I have sworn to see that she comes to no harm. I keep my word. Better than that, I cannot say."

"I suppose it will have to do then," Agatha replied with a grudging nod. "For now."

The two of them studied each other for long seconds. Then Caid inclined his head in what seemed ironic acknowledgment of the agreement between them.

"There," Lisette said as she released the breath that she had not realized she was holding. "Are you both satisfied? If so, perhaps you will remember that I am present and may have some small stake in this arrangement?"

They both turned to look at her, their faces so blank that she felt a ripple of mirth inside her.

"My dear," Agatha said in quick concern, "I meant no offense, but spoke only from attention to your welfare."

"I know," she said with a wry smile before turning to the sword master. "And am I to suppose from your comments, *monsieur,* that you have looked over the premises already?"

"In a manner of speaking." His gaze was shuttered, his manner withdrawn.

"Then I expect you have inspected the windows, as well, also the locks and the security of the wicket gate in the *porte cochère.*"

His frown was magnificent in its way, especially as she had no cause to fear it. "Not yet, but I have the fullest intention of doing these things and more."

"Excellent. I will accompany you since I have not seen all the rooms. Agatha?"

"Yes, I will come also."

They marched from the salon with Lisette in the lead. Her former teacher strode along with her stern expression mirroring her determination to see that nothing untoward occurred in the empty rooms they must enter. Caid brought up the rear.

To have him there where he might watch the sway of her skirts made Lisette feel extremely self-conscious and not a little warm across the back of her neck. Would she have been so aware of him if Agatha had not been so frank just now? She thought it likely. He had a most disturbing ability to destroy her serenity.

Passing along the upper gallery, they wove their way in and out of rooms, sometimes moving from one to the other by way of their connecting doors, sometimes returning to the long covered gallery that acted as an exterior hallway. Caid tested locking mechanisms, pointing out the upright lengths of wood placed between the sash and the upper frames of the windows to wedge them shut and the long iron bar that swung from the wicket gate set in the iron grillwork that closed off the *porte cochère,* fitting into a loop on the near wall to prevent it from being opened from the outside. The main house seemed in reasonable order, as did the kitchen and laundry located on the bottom floor of the two-story *garçonnière* wing.

"There," Lisette said as they emerged from the coolness of the laundry with its stone floor. "I fail to see how you can find fault with the premises, monsieur."

"They are well enough," Caid agreed, though his attention was on the courtyard that he searched with a narrow glance, particularly the walls with their covering of creeping fig.

"Well, then?"

"I still don't like it."

She allowed herself an exasperated sigh. "Because it was not your first choice."

"Because you will be alone here."

"Not at all. I have Agatha."

"Who is a worthy lady with the courage of a lioness, I'm sure," he said, barely glancing in her companion's direction. "But she can hardly serve as a defender."

"The same could be said of Madame Herriot."

"She has her guards, as I've said before. I am also known to have *entrée* at her house, while this one must be closed to me."

"You are here now," Lisette pointed out with all the patience she could summon.

"A visit that must not be repeated except, possibly, in the company of others and on extremely rare occasions."

"I fail to see why."

"Because you prefer to be obstinate instead of listening to reason."

She gave him an incensed look. "I prefer to have my own place. Is that really so difficult to understand?"

"Not at all, but it makes my pledge to guard you damnably hard to keep."

"Then you are relieved of it," she declared, setting her hands on her hips. "Forget that I asked. Forget that you found me two nights ago. Forget that I exist."

"Impossible."

How did he mean that? She wished that she dared ask, but could not quite find the nerve. "Then you must do the best you can, for I have no intention of imposing on Madame Herriot for a second longer."

His frown was daunting in its blackness. "You will be here tonight?"

"I will indeed," she said with a lift of her chin. She had not made the decision until this moment, but suddenly it seemed imperative.

"Without servants in the house? With no protection whatever?"

Put like that, it did not seem the wisest of moves. Still, she refused to back down. "That situation will soon be remedied."

"And who will provide you with suitable people? You can hardly visit the slave mart yourself."

He was perfectly correct. It wasn't done. Females were assumed to be too sensitive to undertake such transactions, or too inclined to make purchases out of pity instead of practicality.

Just then, a door creaked open some few yards from where they stood. A dark face peered out. Then a tall, spare-shouldered man emerged and came toward them. "Beg pardon, monsieur, madame," he said diffidently. "I could not help overhearing. We are here." He waved toward where a number of other slaves hovered in the dim interior of what appeared to be a storeroom just this side of the three or four rooms that would ordinarily have been designated as servant quarters.

Caid eased in front of Lisette as if to shield her. She gave him a sharp glance, but did not object. The dark-skinned man who faced them stopped as he saw Caid's protective gesture.

"Who are you and what are you doing here?" Caid asked with exactitude.

"I am Felix and we live here, Monsieur, if it pleases you. This is our home, at least for now."

"It isn't me that you must please, but this lady." Caid spoke in brusque tones as he nodded in Lisette's direction. "How is it that you failed to show yourselves before now?"

The manservant glanced away for a moment. "We were not sure…that is, it seemed best to wait until someone sent to tell us we were needed."

What he meant, Lisette saw, was that they had been hiding until they could find out what manner of person had taken possession of the town house. Surely they could not have been afraid of Agatha and herself?

Caid seemed to have the same difficulty with that idea. "The ladies had no idea you were here, that anyone was here."

"We meant no harm."

The smile the man gave them was placating but not servile, uncertain but not sullen. The real anxiety that Lisette saw in his liquid brown eyes made her step around Caid. "I take it that you belong to Monsieur Freret who owns this house. I am sorry, but his agent failed to mention your presence. Have you been left here for long?"

"Near three weeks, since the master and his family took ship for France."

"And you have fared all right in his absence?"

"Well enough, *madame,* though it is most kind of you to ask."

The words sounded halfhearted. Lisette could only surmise that little in the way of food or funds to purchase it had been left with them. "You depend on your services being engaged along with the town house. Am I correct?"

"But yes, *madame.* That would be an even greater kindness. We have prayed to *le bon Dieu* for it. The master can't afford the expense of keeping idle slaves. If you can't see your way to taking us on, then his man of business will have to put us all on the auction block before the week is out."

Agatha exclaimed under her breath. Lisette put a hand to her throat. "That seems severe."

"A firm man, Monsieur Freret, but just. He said we must see to it that you have need of our services."

It was a great responsibility. Lisette could feel the weight of it settling on her shoulders. "How many are you?"

"Not so many, truly, only a dozen. Oh, but kind *madame,* four are small so eat very little, and one is Tante Magda who can barely see anymore but tells marvelous tales of ghosts, goblins and *chats-haunt,* the hoot owls, you know, to keep the little ones quiet. You will barely know she is here."

Caid spoke then, his voice authoritative. "And you? What is your position in the house?"

"Butler and valet to Monsieur Freret, *monsieur,*" Felix said, straightening his shoulders.

"You hunted with him when he went into the country, perhaps? You know how to handle a pistol?"

Interest rose in the manservant's eyes. "But yes, to both questions. I hunted often with the master."

Agatha, at Lisette's shoulder, spoke then. "It seems we may have our staff."

Lisette nodded, but spoke to Felix. "Perhaps we could see the others, if they would come forward."

"Immediately, *madame*." The manservant turned and waved in a gesture of command. The others trooped from the darkened storeroom, blinking as they stepped into the light. With the men coming first and women behind them with children clinging to their skirts, they formed a ragged line, as if for inspection. A somber, defensive air clung to them, and they stared at the ground. Regardless, they were neat and clean in appearance, and showed no sign of being physically ill-treated.

"A better solution than trafficking in slaves," Agatha said, "even if it does mean that you will relieve Monsieur Freret of their upkeep for a year."

"Yes, assuredly." It might also be better than hiring servants from Ireland.

"Madame Moisant," Caid began.

Lisette paid him no heed as she ran an expectant look over those ranged in front of her. "Is there a cook among you?"

A man of impressive girth, easily the largest among them, stepped forward. "I am Cook, *madame,* trained in the kitchens of Monsieur Alvarez. I am a cook most extraordinaire!"

"I am sure you are," she said with a smile for the man's evident pride. "It will be my pleasure to sample your art. And is there a chamber maid?"

"I have been trained so, *madame*." A sturdy woman with her hair tied up in a white kerchief came forward to drop a quick curtsy.

"Excellent." Lisette turned to Caid. "You see? I shall not

be alone after all, but will be well served and surrounded by defenders."

He shook his head. "It isn't enough."

"How can you say so when we are so many here now?"

"To have people on the premises is better than nothing, but still won't prevent you from being molested if someone is determined enough."

"Molested? That's a strong word."

"Would you prefer I had said murdered? It isn't impossible."

She gave him a narrow look. "Nothing of the sort is going to happen. You are trying to frighten me."

"Too bad I haven't succeeded."

Lisette spared a glance at Agatha's concerned features before turning back to the sword master. "I can appreciate your concern, *monsieur,* and even share it in some sense. Still, I refuse to allow fear to rule my life. I will send Felix or one of the others for my few belongings. We will be at home here from this evening onward."

Caid said nothing for long seconds. Then he gave a short nod. "As you prefer." Hard on the words, he swung around and walked away toward the dark, tunnel-like mouth of the *porte cochère.* The wicket gate clanged shut behind him.

A shiver caught Lisette unaware as she listened to that ringing echo. Odd, but she suddenly felt much less safe than before. The presence of Caid O'Neill had been like a bulwark against all evil. With his removal, the sense of invincibility was gone. It was not a comfortable thing to realize, particularly now when it was too late.

The evening slipped past into night. Lisette's belongings arrived from the Herriot town house, her freshly laundered nightgown, the day gowns provided by Maurelle, and a few conveniences in the way of dentifrice, hairpins, ribbons and stockings that had been provided by the modiste along with a new corset and petticoats stiffened at the hem with *crin,* or horsehair. A sketchy meal of thin soup was made with the few odds and ends remaining in the kitchen, and a list prepared for the markets near the levee where Felix would go next morning. Bedchambers were made up using linens found in a press with herb-scented vetiver roots among their folds. Felix went around checking doors and windows for the night before reporting that all was secure. Lisette and Agatha sat talking for some time after he descended to his quarters, discussing the past, planning their activities of the next few days. Finally, the sound of carriages and foot traffic ceased, the barking of dogs died away, and there was nothing left except to go to bed.

Lisette lit two night candles from the whale oil lamp in the salon, then handed one to her new companion and took one herself. Dousing the lamp, she followed Agatha out onto the gallery and along to her room where she said goodnight. Moving two doors farther along, she stepped into the bedchamber she had chosen as her own. She turned at once with her skirts belling out around her to secure the lock.

Abruptly, she was caught from behind by a hard arm about her waist, snatched into a rough embrace. The candle was plucked from her hand, snuffed and flung aside. As darkness closed down, a voice, deep and melodic, whispered, tickling, against her ear.

"I have come to molest you, *ma chère*. What will you do now?"

5

*C*aid.

The identity of her assailant swept into Lisette's mind on a tide of relief and wrath. Yet beneath it ran febrile awareness of the rock-solid wall of his body against her, the smoothly sculpted muscles that lay beneath his linen and broadcloth and the tempered strength of his arms that were wrapped, one around her waist and the other across the softness of her breasts. Heat gathered inside her, pulsing at the center of her body. It was a moment before she could force words through the constriction in her throat.

"Release me! At once."

"Not until you admit that you are at risk here. Not until you see that I or any other men can reach you if they try, could do anything at all to you."

She knew full well to what he referred. The idea of that ultimate, penetrating intimacy with this man made her heart leap against the bones of her rib cage while her blood coursed through her veins in torrents as wild as the Mississippi in flood. She jerked against his hold, but it only tightened until she could not move, could barely breathe.

She could scream, but what would be the point? Agatha was no match for him, nor was Felix. In any case, she was certain—fairly certain—that Caid O'Neill meant only to make her face her vulnerability here alone in the town house. Once she had acknowledged that, he would let her go, just as he had said. Yet something unyielding inside her refused to give him that satisfaction in spite of the insidious languor creeping over her, confusing thought, threatening purpose.

"If this is your idea of protecting me," she said as acidly as she could manage, "I don't think much of it."

"It's my idea of seeing that you understand what can happen."

"What makes you so sure I don't realize it? I am not so foolish, believe me." The words were half strangled by the tightness in her chest.

"How can I when you won't see reason? What will make you fully understand?"

"Nothing will make a difference," she began.

He wasn't listening. Before she could guess his intent, he swung her around with dizzying speed and pressed her back to the wall. Catching her wrists, he held them on either side of her face while the lower half of his body pinned her like a captured butterfly. Then he dipped his head, hesitated, and covered her mouth with his own.

His lips were firm, warm and flavored with honeylike sweetness. They demanded her capitulation and something more that tugged at her sensibilities but defied understanding. His tongue traced the curves of her lips that were closed against him, tasting her, learning her, seeking to delve deep into her secrets. The smooth glide of his explorations, the faint roughness of late-evening stubble at the edges of his mouth, his throbbing firmness and the thud of his heart against her breasts were incredibly tantalizing. His hot male power surrounded her, compelled her; the scents of starched linen, bergamot-scented hair tonic and clean male skin mounted to her head, subtle yet intoxicating. Heat stirred deep inside, welling upward with exquisite pressure. Her nipples puckered, becoming so sensitive that she could identify the small bumps of his shirt studs, the lengths of his gold watch chain, even the broadcloth weave of his frock coat. The need to press closer, leaning into the hard, muscular length of him, was so strong that she flexed her wrists in his grasp with a stifled moan.

He took instant advantage of her parted lips, sweeping inside as if the intimate recesses of her mouth were his to possess. His flavor was a sweet enticement, rich and warm on her tongue. The assault on her senses was elemental, enthralling in a way she had never imagined. His tempered steel strength and her inability to control it should have frightened and repelled her. Instead, it made her feel overheated and boneless with acquiescence, as if only the force of her will prevented her from opening to him like some exotic flower under tropical rain. If he should only whisper of surrender, then…what then?

She stiffened and drew a sharp breath before turning her head away. For long seconds he remained rigid against her. Then he whispered a soft curse against the softness of her hair. Releasing her with a sudden, openhanded gesture, he stepped back.

The rasp of their breathing was the only sound for interminable seconds. He shifted with a quiet rustle of clothing then, moving farther away as if in need of more distance between them. His voice sounded strained, almost disembodied, as he spoke.

"Forgive me. I didn't intend the lesson to be so…drastic."

"No." She stopped, cleared her throat of its huskiness. "No, I would imagine not." She smoothed her skirts, touched her hair while saying a small prayer of thankfulness for the darkness that hid her hot face. "I quite see…that is to say, I know that it must appear irrational of me to remain here against all your good counsel, but I assure you it isn't from stupidity or mere willfulness."

"I never thought so."

"Most men would have assumed it, I think. But it's more than either of those things. You don't know, can't imagine what it's like to be confined against your will, to have your every movement controlled, guarded, watched against any escape. I have sworn never to put myself in such a position again. I refuse to submit to it, be it ever so benevolent. I refuse even if I must die for it."

"You are wrong."

"I do assure you…"

"No," he said in harsh interruption. "What I mean to say is that I do know what it is to be imprisoned, that I understand the craving for freedom very well."

His voice had a compressed sound, she thought, as if it was not easy for him to say those words. "Then why can you not accept my need to have a place of my own?"

He was quiet for an instant. "I was not listening to what you were saying before, or so I must suppose."

"And now?"

"Now I'm beginning to," he said with a clipped sound in his voice.

Some small part of the tightness in her chest eased. She moistened her lips before she went on. "I realize it makes what I asked of you a much harder task. It has come to me, as well, in my few hours here, that it was unfair of me to expect it. I really think I must release you from your pledge."

"I beg you will not."

She could not have heard him correctly. "Pardon me?"

"You had every right to recompense from me. If my protection is your choice, then I give it willingly."

"Just not without question," she clarified, her gladness at the possible reprieve filtering into the words along with a shade of humor.

"I have always been certain I know the right of things. It's a fault that has caused a deal of trouble."

"Such as…prison?" It was extremely rude to ask such a question, but they had moved past such things, she thought, at least for the moment.

"Does that shock you?"

"It depends on the crime."

"Sedition, treason against the crown…though it wasn't the crown of any king I recognized or accepted."

"You were not guilty of murder or theft or…"

"Or rapine?" he finished for her in hard tones. "No. It happened in Eire, the land where I was born."

"You must have been quite young."

He turned toward her, a shadowy movement against the light that filtered through the closed jalousies behind the French doors of the bedchamber. "Meaning?"

"Something Madame Herriot said in passing about your long sojourn in France where she first met you."

"You spoke of me?"

"Briefly. She wished to make certain I understood your position."

"And do you?"

"I believe so. But you must know that many in New Orleans can count a condemned man or woman among their ancestors. We like to think we are descended from innocent young orphan girls sent by the French crown as brides for the colonists or families escaping the Terror. For some it may be so. Yet it's also true that the prisons of Paris were emptied to populate the place in the earliest days. My own great-grandmother, or so my *grand-mère* whispered to me once, was taken from *Salpêtrière* where she had been confined after being accused of poisoning her husband's mistress."

He said nothing for so long that she thought he would not answer. When he finally spoke, the words were abrupt. "You have a soft heart."

"You think I spoke of my old family scandal to make you feel less alone in yours? You give me too much credit." She was not even sure the story was true. Her mother, a woman of great elegance and imperious will, had scoffed at it when it had been brought up during the betrothal negotiations with the Moisants.

"I think not. Regardless, I must go before the gossips have something to spread about this generation."

He took a step in her direction. She moved aside, clearing the way to the door. As he reached it and pulled it open, however, she spoke quickly. "Wait."

"Yes?"

"How did you get in? I know very well that everything was locked and barred, for I watched Felix do it."

"It wasn't difficult, a matter of using my cane to reach through the grille of the wicket gate and lift the latch pin. I'll see to the defect in the morning."

"And until then?"

"You won't be able to sleep knowing it may be repeated? It will not, I promise you."

"I didn't think, that is, I know you would not enter again."

"Despite the temptation, no," he said. "Nor will anyone else. You may sleep easy knowing that I am keeping watch."

"But you will need to sleep, as well," she said in protest.

"Tomorrow. Perhaps."

What did he mean? That he wouldn't be able to sleep even then or would not require it? She could not guess, and he didn't linger for questions. Passing through the doorway, he continued along the gallery and disappeared down the darkened stairwell. Though she followed him as far as the gallery, listening for his footsteps grating on the slate paving stones of the *porte cochère* or the creak of the wicket gate closing behind him, they did not come. Either he had gone silently out into the street, or else he had not gone at all.

She stood for some time, staring into the dark, but heard no further sound. Finally, she turned and went back into her bedchamber.

"Great heavens, my dear," Agatha exclaimed next morning as Lisette entered the dining room. "You look like something the cat dragged in and the kittens refused. Are you quite well?"

Lisette summoned a smile. "I couldn't sleep. The excitement, you know, over the move into this house." The excuse might be rather lame, but she could hardly admit that the midnight invasion of the Irish sword master was to blame, or rather the shatteringly vivid memory of his kiss. Lying wide-eyed in the dark, she had relived the moments when his hard form had been melded to hers, his lips upon her lips, time and time again. With each revisit, she was more disconcerted by the commanding power of his touch and her fervid, almost wanton response to it. Yes, and by the lingering effects that left her restless, unsettled, aching for something more. Had he noticed her moment of weakness or, noticing, did he care? She was nothing to him except a reluctant obligation. His sole aim in entering her house by stealth had been to prove a point. Nothing remotely personal had moved him to embrace her and it was foolish to imagine otherwise. She knew these things very well, and yet…

Oh, but she must attend to what Agatha was saying before her companion guessed something of her distraction and demanded the cause. Already, she was looking at her with concern pleating her brow.

"I know we spoke of a round of the shops this morning, love, but if you don't feel up to the exertion, we can just as well postpone the foray."

"No, no. We must order a few things made at once, otherwise the season will be over before they are delivered."

"Plenty of time remains, you know. No other city has a winter season as long as New Orleans. I wonder at the stamina of these French Creole ladies who seem hardly able to lift a finger for themselves but manage to dance until dawn virtually every night from November until well after Easter."

"Perhaps it's because dancing is our main occupation," Lisette said with a smile, "Or at least for those who are young and unattached. Besides, Lent gives us a respite."

"Oh, Lent." Agatha sent her a sardonic look. "I was quite shocked by the lack of observance when I first arrived."

"And now?'

"I have allowed myself to become corrupted, I suppose, in part because I know that piety in the Creole fashion has more to do with inner faith than outward appearances. In any case, I should miss the Sunday evening theater outings and parties if I returned to Boston."

"But surely you aren't thinking of leaving?"

"Not any time soon, in all events."

"Not at all if I have anything to say in it," Lisette told her in firm tones. To object immediately to the departure of a guest was the Creole way, but she could not bear the thought of losing Agatha when she had just rejoined her. With no one else could she ever feel so comfortable, so assured of perfect understanding regardless of whether she wished to be solitary or have company.

Felix arrived then bearing a tray of croissants still warm from the *boulangerie* across the street and pots of hot coffee and milk for café au lait. The smells that wafted forth as the linen cover was removed were enough to distract a saint. Afterward, she and Agatha spoke of gowns and headpieces, and also the *canezou* blouses and colors in shades of gray, pink and pale yellow that were so fashionable this spring. They were still engrossed in such important matters an hour later when they donned bonnets, veils, and gloves and left the house.

Their footsteps took them from Madame Crevon's millinery establishment where Lisette purchased a fetching bonnet of Italian straw, to Scanlon's where Agatha had seen advertised in *L'Abeille* the arrival of a shipment from Le Havre of spring and summer headpieces from the celebrated establishment of Madame Goeneutte of Paris. These being more for evening wear than expected, Lisette bought a charming *capotte* of batiste, organdy and lace for Agatha but nothing for herself.

As they emerged on the banquette again, she noticed a man sitting at a café just down the street, where the French doors stood open to the morning air and tables had been moved out onto the paving stones. He was tall, well dressed, handsome in a romantic fashion; still he drew her attention mainly because of the intent glance he sent in their direction. Immediately, he drank down the last of his coffee and took out his purse to drop a few coins on the table. Then he rose to his feet with athletic grace, tucked the news sheet he had been reading into an inside coat pocket, picked up his cane and sauntered along, paralleling their progress on the opposite side of the street.

The gentlemen seemed vaguely familiar, Lisette thought, though she could not quite place him. As it was both impolite and unwise to stare, she faced ahead. She was still aware of him, however, as he strolled along, twirling his cane, bowing to acquaintances and tipping his hat to the ladies as he stood aside to let them pass.

She and Agatha stopped briefly at a small shop on Bienville where fine-gauged English hosiery was to be found, then came at last to the dry goods firm of Bourry d'Ivernois, on Chartres. There, they picked over French merinos, fine *Mousso de Laine,* printed challis, merino shawls, Italian embroideries, draper's muslins and jaconet for cravats, as well as mantilla, tartans and Swiss goods of every variety.

The lightweight fabrics were beguiling, and Lisette found several in black which might suit her purpose. Still, the item that took her breath was a length of black velvet. Never had she worn such sumptuous fabric. Velvet was prohibited until after a woman was wed, but Eugene had not approved of it even then. Anything which drew attention to his wife was inevitably vulgar and unbecoming in his opinion, so he forbade it. It was the jealousy of possession which moved him, she thought, rather than any passionate interest. He preferred her in subdued colors and styles so he need not trouble himself over her attractiveness. The velvet was not the least vulgar, however. It flowed and rippled, catching the light like the shimmering pelt of the fabled swamp panther. It was a fabric fit for a queen.

When she and Agatha left the shop, Lisette was the proud owner of the velvet which would be delivered to the town house with the remainder of her purchases. What she required now was a seamstress suited to the task of making a gown from the goods, something suitable for mourning but not overly severe, unique but still demure. The woman employed for such work by her father-in-law had been capable enough but without flair or artistry. Someone else was required, but where to find her?

"From what you tell me of Madame Herriot," Agatha said as they weaved their way past an organ-grinder and his monkey on the banquette then nodded to a gentleman who made way for them, "she must surely know such a person."

"You have no acquaintance with Maurelle?"

"I've never had the pleasure, though one hears things as a matter of course."

Lisette gave her an inquiring glance before stepping over a puddle left where someone had recently scrubbed the banquette stones. "Of what nature?"

"Her eccentricities, in the main. They say she is more Parisian than the Parisians."

"A great fault," Lisette said dryly. Most of French Creole New Orleans looked to Paris for all things. It was the center of their world, source of their food, fashions, household furnishings, literature and most of their ideas. Ships from England and the east coast of the United States landed at the levee docks every day, but had little effect compared to those from Le Havre.

Agatha pursed her lips. "The lady trips along very close to the edge of what is acceptable."

"She was kindness itself to me."

"Then she is all heart and my very dear friend." Agatha sent Lisette a twinkling smile. "Shall we cross to the shady side? The sun is quite strong this morning."

It was an understatement. Spring was advancing at a great pace, and the sun's heat already carried the sweltering promise of summer. The fragrance of the sweet olive blooming in courtyard gardens was amplified to almost overpowering strength by the increasing warmth. Trees along streets and in the woods outside the city were in bloom, as well, producing clouds of pollen. Every breeze brought drifts of it so thick that it sifted into the folds of their clothing and coated the banquette where it lay tracked with footprints like yellow snow.

Lifting their skirts, Lisette and Agatha stood waiting for a dray to rumble past before attempting to reach the far side of the street. As they watched it approach, Lisette noticed the tall dandy she had seen earlier, strolling along across the way. She wondered what had occupied him while she and Agatha were busy at the dry goods emporium, also if he was aware that he had a motley group of small boys mocking his insouciant stroll as they crowded at his heels. Then the dray rattled past and she turned her attention to threading the obstacle course of horse dung, straw and moldy vegetable refuse that littered the roadway.

Arriving on the opposite banquette without mishap, they proceeded only a few steps before their way was blocked by what appeared to be a drunken sailor. He swayed, his feet set as if on the deck of a rolling ship, holding the center of the paving. Lisette made as if to go around him, but he shuffled to block her way.

"Ah, now, me foine mam'zelle," he drawled in the accents of the London stews. "Come on, gi' us a kiss."

Lisette stepped well back, lifting her chin. "Permit me to pass, *monsieur*."

"Oi can't be doin' that, dearie, no wi'out ye pay the toll."

"My good man," Agatha said at her most severe. "Remove yourself or I shall call for the gendarmes."

"You do that, ye ol' cat, and oi'll box him good." The sailor swerved his head around and nearly tripped as he reached tar-stained fingers toward Lisette. "Now then, me loively…"

"Enough." The hard, slicing command came from behind them. At the same time, the gentleman Lisette had noticed earlier came forward with swift strides and halted at her side. Placing the ferrule of his malacca cane against the seaman's chest, he pushed hard enough that the Jack-Tar fell back a stumbling step. "Begone, fool, or regret the failure."

"'Ere now!" The sailor swatted the cane aside and staggered forward again.

The malacca cane flashed up, across and back, with solid whacks. The drunken man howled, bending double as he clutched at his midsection with one hand and a bleeding ear with the other. "Aw, now, gov'nor, I meant no 'arm to the laidy. Just havin' a bit o' fun."

"The lady does not appear to be amused. Take yourself out of her sight at once."

"Aye, Cap'n." The sailor sketched a drunken salute, rocked back on his heels, then turned in clumsy haste and made off across the street.

Lisette drew her first deep breath in minutes and turned to her savior. "Thank you, *monsieur*, your arrival was most timely."

The gentleman, showing no sign whatever of his swift exertion, tucked his cane under his arm. Bowing, he lifted his hat of fine beaver. "It was my pleasure to be of service."

Seen at close quarters, he was a vision of grace and sartorial splendor in a flared frock coat of golden brown that reached to his knees, brown trousers and an intricately tied cravat of brown and black plaid. His hair waved over his head with one errant curl falling onto a noble brow and his eyes held imminent laughter in their black depths. With the halt in his progress, a small dog of distinctly plebeian lineage had come to rest at his heels along with his retinue of ragged street boys in every color from pale grey-white and café au lait to bluish-black. The dog yapped and the boys muttered among themselves in the patois of the slaves known as gumbo, but the gentleman seemed deaf to the noise, blind to everything except her presence.

Just then, one of the boys a little taller and rangier than the rest spoke up. "*Sacré,* Monsieur Nick, you showed that bugger!"

The compliment, such as it was, caught the gentleman's attention. "Mind your tongue, Squirrel, my little wharf rat. There are ladies present."

The entire group of boys fell as silent as if a power from on high had spoken.

The gentleman's French had the suggestion of an Italian accent. Lisette studied him an instant while suspicion grew in her mind. "May I know your name, *monsieur?* I should like to say to whom I owe my gratitude when I speak of this incident."

"Of a certainty, Madame Moisant." He bowed again. "I am Nicholas Pasquale, *à vôtre service.* Permit me to say that I am honored to make myself known to you and your excellent lady-companion."

It was just as she thought. Nicholas Pasquale was a *maître d'armes* of some fame despite arriving in the city from Rome only this season. That explained his following of boys, since they trailed after all the sword masters like mice after Pied Pipers. For the small dog, patched with white and brown and with one flop ear and a tattered excuse for a tail plume, there was no ready explanation unless he was a stray that had attached himself to the street urchins. There were many such homeless ones in the city, both orphans and animals. Almost at random, she said, "You know my name."

A smile tilted the generous curves of his mouth. "I have the honor to be a friend to Caid O'Neill."

"He spoke of me to you?" Her eyes narrowed as she put the question.

"Not lightly, I do assure you!" He pressed his fingers to his furrowed brow. "*Mon Dieu*, the mad Irishman will have my head for giving you such an impression."

"I assume he spoke with purpose then."

"He was concerned for your safety. Granted, he could hardly have envisioned the circumstances of the moment, but the intent was everything of the most correct."

"You were following me."

"Yes, well, as to that…"

"You need not trouble to deny it. Monsieur O'Neill requested that you look out for me."

"Lisette, calm yourself, my dear," Agatha said. "You are attracting notice."

Pasquale lifted his gloved hands in a helpless gesture. "A man, even one of O'Neill's great stamina, must sleep sometime."

"But to involve you, someone with no connection whatever…it's infamous."

"I am his friend," the sword master said simply. "And now yours, *madame.*"

"We must be heartily glad of it, too," Agatha said with more warmth than was her habit. Holding out her hand, she continued. "I am Agatha Stilton, *monsieur.* Please accept my gratitude, as well."

The fine, crepelike skin of Agatha's cheeks was pink and her smile bright. Lisette, watching her, felt her irritation receding as amusement took its place. Who would have guessed that her companion would be so susceptible to a handsome rogue of polite address and doubtful repute?

The noise of quick footsteps on the banquette brought her head around just then. Coming toward them was a striking couple. The gentleman was of a height with Pasquale and of the same lithe physique. The lady was soignée, dressed *à la mode* in gray and lavender from her bonnet to her kid boots, and quite lovely in a serene fashion.

"Monsieur Pasquale," the lady in gray called out. "Well done. Rio and I caught sight of the contretemps as it began. I thought he should come to your aid, but he said it would be over before he arrived. That he is right again is beyond enough. He will be insufferable."

"His confidence unmans me," the Italian said, his gaze quizzical.

"I'm sure," the saturnine gentleman called Rio murmured with apparent irony.

"We are well met, anyway," the lady said. "I am expecting you for my little Mardi Gras soirée in two days' time, if you remember. Please say I may count on your presence."

"Assuredly, *ma belle.* I would not miss it for anything."

The Italian bowed with an informal flourish that had been missing from the courtesy he had shown to her and Agatha, Lisette thought. It was obvious he knew the couple well. A brief spasm of something like envy constricted her chest. To have such a friend and be so easy with him must be something quite unique.

Nicholas Pasquale turned to her. "Forgive me for my neglect, Madame Moisant, and permit me to make known to you Mademoiselle Celina Vallier, if you are not already acquainted? And this gentleman is Damian Francisco Adriano de Vega y Riordan, Conde de Lérida," he continued, rolling the syllables off his tongue with relish. "Though he is better known by his nom de guerre of Rio de Silva."

"Mademoiselle, *monsieur,* a very great pleasure." She exchanged a bow with Celina Vallier, but offered her hand to the man at her side. He took it, brushing her gloved fingers in a salute that would not have been appropriate if she had been unmarried.

"Madame Moisant is a recent acquaintance of our Irish friend," Nicholas went on with a brief glance under his lashes for his friends.

"Ah," Rio de Silva said. "I thought the name was familiar."

Lisette suspected that he had known it all along. Something in his voice suggested that he not only had heard of her from Caid O'Neill, but was well aware of the duel that had preceded their meeting, and its consequences. She gave away nothing of her thoughts, however, but turned to present Agatha. When that formality was done, an awkward pause fell over them.

The little dog filled it by choosing that moment to leap up on Lisette's skirts, reaching with his nose for her hand. She bent a little to allow him to sniff it, then smoothed her gloved fingers over his scruffy head. There was something of the poodle in his ancestry, she thought, judging from the shape of his nose and springing curl of his hair. "What a charmer you are," she said, noting the dog's piquant face which looked as if he were smiling. "I wonder if you have a name?"

"He is a rascal," Pasquale said, frowning at the mongrel who gave him a look of slavish devotion. "Don't encourage him, or I promise you he will become your shadow."

She glanced up at him as the little dog, attracted by the sound of Pasquale's voice, ran back to cavort around his ankles. "As he is yours?"

"By no means, *madame*. I would never lay claim such a hopeless specimen. He is a dog of no discrimination, one who follows me when I leave my atelier but otherwise plays with that rabble over there." He waved a hand toward the street boys whose attention had been distracted by a pickle barrel one of their number had discovered outside a shop.

"I believe," she said gravely, "that he claims you."

"She has you there, La Roche," De Silva said with a grin, even as Celina Vallier's silvery laugh echoed his words.

"Are you engaged for the evening in two day's time, Madame Moisant, you and your companion?" the lady asked.

Lisette shook her head, fondling the silky ears of the dog which had returned to fling himself at her skirts again.

"It is short notice, I know, but we should be happy, my father, my brother and I, if you would also care to give us your company for our Mardi Gras soirée. We plan nothing very grand or that might compromise your mourning, only a family party with a few friends. We shall dance a little, talk much and have a light supper before watching the night parade from our balcony."

"It's very kind of you, but…"

"Please don't say no! I have been trying to persuade Caid to honor us for an age, and I'm sure he must if he is to escort you." The laughter in Celina Vallier's sherry-brown eyes faded. "That is…I thought he might do so, but realize it may not be quite the thing."

"I see nothing wrong in it," Lisette said distinctly.

"Brava, *madame*. I will expect you also then."

Celina Vallier's enthusiasm was contagious, her coaxing tone impossible to resist. More than that, it had been months without end, long before Eugene was killed, since Lisette had ventured out to an evening party. Quite suddenly, she wanted to go, longed to be among people who smiled and teased and were lighthearted, was curious to know more of the bond between this lady and the sword master to whom she was betrothed. She straightened as she said, "Since you put it that way, how am I to resist?"

"Excellent!" The charming hostess turned to the Italian. "Nicholas, I charge you with acquainting Caid with his engagement. Inform him that he must not fail."

"It will be as much as my life is worth, you know," he replied with mock resignation. "Still, for the sake of two such beautiful ladies, the risk must be taken."

A few more pleasantries were exchanged, after which *au revoirs* were spoken and Lisette and Agatha moved on, making their way toward the town house. They had gone scarcely more than half a block when Lisette heard a clicking sound behind her. She glanced back. It was the small dog, his toenails tapping on the banquette stones as he followed them.

Coming to a halt, she turned in a whirl of skirts. "Go away now," she said with a herding motion of one hand. "Return to your master."

The mongrel sat on its haunches and looked up at her, tipping its head in an expression of comical interrogation.

Agatha, who had kept walking, glanced over her shoulder then retraced her footsteps. "Shoo," she said, waving her beaded reticule. "Shoo, now."

The dog flopped over onto one hip, lifted a hind leg and began to scratch behind its ear with vigor and a total lack of regard for modesty or their commands.

Thinking he might not notice they were leaving in his preoccupation with his fleas, Lisette faced forward and began to walk again. She had taken no more than a half dozen steps when she heard him coming after them.

"Go away," she said, facing the small mongrel once more.

He sat, tilting his head for all the world as if he were laughing at her.

"Go at once, before your little friends run away and leave you."

The dog leaped up to paw at the fullness of her skirts, attempting to reach her hands. Lisette turned to Agatha with a helpless shrug. "What shall we do?"

"You can't let him follow you home."

"I don't see how I can stop him."

"The little beast is eaten alive with vermin. I mean, only look at him."

He was certainly scratching again. "Poor thing, I expect he needs a bath. Perhaps he could stay a short while, after which I could send a message telling Monsieur Pasquale where he is and asking him to come take him away."

"You must do as you think best," her companion said in foreboding tones.

That much was true. Certainly, there was no one to stop her. "He shall come," she said firmly. Turning, she walked on again with the dog trotting along behind her.

At the town house, Felix appeared to take their bonnets and gloves, suggest a refreshing beverage, and tell them that their purchases from the milliner's and dry goods emporium had arrived. Lisette thanked him and turned the stray mongrel over to him for a bath in lye soap. Felix did not seem best pleased. The small mongrel thought it was a great game, however, and scampered about the courtyard, mouth agape and eyes bright, daring the butler to catch him.

Lisette watched from the upper gallery, laughing over the antic battle of wills, but finally took pity on her new butler and descended to call the stray to her. He came, wiggling all over at the attention, licking her hand as she swooped him up into her arms. It was a wrench to hand him over to his fate. Feeling like a traitor, then, she went quickly back up the stairs.

In the two days that followed, she and Agatha were busy with their needles, taking up another of the gowns Maurelle had given her for the Vallier evening party since there was not time to have anything else made. This evening costume of black silk had a surplice bodice with dropped shoulders, closely fitted sleeves, and skirt gathered to the narrow waist with cartridge pleating but left open at the front in an inverted V-shape. A cambric chemisette and underskirt, both with lace-edged ruffles, created a *demi-décolletée* neckline and a waterfall of white from the center waist to the floor that relieved the gown's severity but were still respectable for a widow. The altered gown might not be the first stare of fashion, but Lisette thought she would embarrass neither her hostess nor herself.

It was Tante Magda, the elderly woman who looked after the servant children, who conveyed the suggestion, by way of Felix, that she send for a hairdresser on the afternoon before the soirée. She knew one that her absent mistress, Madame Freret, often used. The new lady of the house would be *ravissante,* Tante Magda said, if Marie Laveau did her hair. Besides, the hairdresser might also bring with her a potion which would assure every man she met that evening would find her ravishing, as well.

Lisette knew the name, and had no objection whatever to being thought ravishing. It would be a refreshing change from appearing merely presentable, as her late husband had always styled her. The stable groom was duly sent off with a request for the hairdresser's aid.

Marie Laveau was young and attractive, with gleaming brown skin and luxuriant black tresses worn in a cloud on her shoulders. She praised the fullness, length and fiery color of Lisette's hair while drawing it back from a center part, then braiding the length in an intricate design and leaving the ends free to make a coronet of curls.

"You are very talented," Lisette said, smiling at the woman in the mirror as she watched the deft movements of her graceful hands.

"If you say so, *madame.*"

"I feel fortunate that you could come to me on such short notice."

Marie Laveau nodded without conceit. "It was most unusual for a Mardi Gras evening. One of my other ladies fell ill, or it would not have been possible. These things are in the hands of the gods."

"I was told that you have another talent."

"Were you, *madame?*"

"One involving prayers, spells and wishes?"

"You have a prayer, perhaps?"

Lisette gave her a rueful smile as she met her eyes in the mirror. "Not precisely. What I have, I fear, is curiosity."

"There's naught wrong with that." The answer was carefully noncommittal.

"Suppose I did? Suppose I wanted to interest…someone."

"A man, perhaps?"

"Perhaps." She didn't, of course. How could she when the very last thing she wanted was another husband? She was only talking to pass the time and because it was better than sitting in awkward silence, or so Lisette told herself. Still it was interesting that it might be possible to effect a change in her situation.

"You know something of the Voodoo?" Marie Laveau asked.

"Who does not?" The religion, or the more sensational aspects of it, pervaded New Orleans from top to bottom, as Lisette well knew. African in origin, it had been brought to the city by slaves during the past century, then reinforced by those who came with their masters and mistresses from Saint Domingue during the uprising there some forty years ago. Though once quite pagan in form and purpose, it had mixed with the rites of the Catholic Church to become something not quite one or the other. Fascination with its more perilous aspects, and use of them, was not at all uncommon.

"I could make a potion for you, if you wish." The large, almond-shaped eyes of the hairdresser were darkly hypnotic in her reflected image.

"Could you really."

"It would be for whatever you choose, to make your man desire you, to ensure his love, to keep him from straying— or to punish him if he leaves."

"I have no man."

"Then it will make certain that you do."

A low laugh caught in Lisette's throat.

"You mock me?"

"No, no," she said, reluctant to hurt the woman's feelings. "Only, you seem so certain."

"Because I am, *madame.* Do you want the Irish sword master?"

Lisette was perfectly still. "What do you know of him?"

"Everything," Marie Laveau said, her voice deep, almost sultry. "I am a priestess. Nothing is hidden from me."

"I thought…that is, I had heard that you were an acolyte for the priesthood of Doctor John."

"For now. But not for long."

The woman's features with their light mahogany highlights were inscrutable. The gossip actually said that she and Doctor John, a huge black man with a tattooed face who claimed to be the son of an African king and the premier Voodoo priest in New Orleans, were lovers. Was Marie Laveau ambitious to be more? If so, it was none of Lisette's affair, none at all. She said, "It could be dangerous to entrap a *maître d'armes* with a spell."

"Being alive is a treacherous thing, *madame.* What is one small risk more?"

It was all too true, Lisette thought. Only look at Eugene, alive one day, dead the next. "Would it cost a great deal? I may or may not use it, you see."

"For you, very little, because you are one who has taken the hungry into your care and given shelter to one who had none." She tipped her head toward the servants' quarters beyond the outside courtyard, and then down at the small dog that lay curled at Lisette's feet.

"It was nothing." Lisette glanced away, obscurely embarrassed. She had only done what seemed necessary at the time.

"Nothing to you, but it counts. Look for your potion soon."

"And the payment?"

"You know where to find me."

Lisette should not have gone so far with the idea, she knew. Still, she disliked recanting, could not bring herself to say that she did not believe in this power of Marie Laveau's after all, or fling the offer back into her face. It was best to accept the thing when it came and then pour it away. Certainly, she would never use it. She was a civilized female, carefully educated by the nuns. Such things were beneath her dignity.

No, she would never, ever use it. She wanted no man, certainly was not so desperate as to try gaining one in that manner.

No, indeed.

6

A small gathering, Mademoiselle Vallier had promised. Family and friends, she had insisted. Caid snorted as he counted off at least five dozen people in the house. If this was a small gathering, then he was a twice-damned British Grenadier.

The rooms glowed with candles in girandoles and whale oil lamps on tables since Monsieur Vallier was opposed to the American affectation of gas lighting. Cool night air flowed through the French doors that stood open to the balcony overlooking the street and also to the courtyard that was bright with pine pitch torches. The aromas of wood smoke and food wafted up from the courtyard kitchen, vying with the scents of massed bouquets and perfumes from Paris. Ladies sat like overblown flowers on the settees and small gilt chairs, half submerged in their billowing skirts of silk and satin in pastel hues. Some few waved fans edged with lace and ribbon, while others had plucked *éventails lataniers,* the ubiquitous woven palmetto fans, from the vases weighted with sand that sat about on tables. The evening was warm enough to require that relief, but a fan was also useful to wave away the occasional mosquito that joined the gathering. A few attentive gentlemen stood wafting the insects away from their ladies and themselves, fanning so vigorously that shreds of palmetto drifted down to litter the carpet.

It was a pleasant enough affair as such things went, but Caid was in no mood to be pleased. He felt distinctly out of place among these Creole aristocrats with their airs and graces, easy assurance of plenty, and glances askance at the sword masters circulating among them. How he had allowed himself to be talked into attending, he couldn't imagine, any more than he could understand how he had come to escort Lisette Moisant when he had sworn to stay away from her.

The lady was having a fine time, or so it appeared. She had danced once with Rio and once with Nicholas, which seemed to be acceptable conduct even for a recent widow. Currently, she was flirting outrageously with Denys Vallier, the son of their host, a young pup with an earnest face decorated by a silly *mouche* of a beard, as the flylike bit in the middle of his chin was called by the Romantics, and alley cat tendencies.

But no, that was unfair. Lisette was merely talking to the boy, and young Vallier was no more a libertine than any other young Creole of his age and generous allowance. Caid liked him ordinarily, but found the sight of him practically drooling over Lisette Moisant more than a little annoying. The young gentleman had taken her gloved hand and was fondling it at the moment while declaiming some flirtatious nonsense, most likely a paean to the brightness of her smile. That was indeed brilliant and a real pleasure to watch.

"A great pity, isn't it?"

It was Nicholas who spoke as he sauntered up to join him in the window embrasure that Caid had made his own for the evening. The glance Caid gave him was wary. "What is?"

"That one is not allowed to mark a lady as taken until the vows are actually spoken. A tablecloth thrown over her head as a covering would do the trick. They handle these things better in other countries."

"I have no notion what you're blathering about."

"I speak of Madame Moisant, the lady you have been glaring at for the past half hour," the Italian said, ignoring the scathing look cast in his direction. "Take care, my friend, or someone other than my harmless self may notice."

"You may go to the devil."

"Such a way with words," Nicholas lamented. "Why can I never achieve such heights of eloquence?"

"Because you're forever using ten good words where one will do," Caid said frankly. "Speaking of which, I'd like to hear how you managed to talk Madame Moisant into taking that ugly mutt that you've had trailing around after you for the past week."

"Not my doing, I promise you. Like any male animal of normal instincts, the poor little bastard fell head over tail in love at first sight and went crawling in her footsteps." The Italian pursed his lips. "Of course, it may have helped that I sneaked away while his head was turned."

"I thought so."

"So she really gave him a home?"

"He was lying in her lap, fast asleep with all four feet in the air, when I arrived to offer my escort," Caid said. "If you don't believe me, you have only to notice the scattering of his hairs still decorating her gown. The ungrateful little cur jumped up and barked fit to wake the dead when I came into the room, at me who just last week bought a bone for him at the rue de la Levee market."

"An animal of keen discernment, I always said it. So she has another protector."

Caid inclined his head. "There is that advantage."

"For which you may thank me in any manner you deem suitable."

"So I will, if no one else notices the transfer of Figaro's affections or questions how a dog from the Passage de la Bourse gained the lady's bedchamber."

"Figaro?" The Italian sword master winced as if with pain.

"Yes, well, you never named him other than calling him a rascal and imp of Satan for chewing your boot tops, and so I told her."

"I had thought of Casanova, for his habit of…"

"I know that particular habit, and can only hope he doesn't display it in front of Madame Moisant until after he has solidified his position."

"What position is this?" Celina, arriving beside them just then, looked expectantly from one to the other.

"Houseguest," Nicholas said suavely.

"Who, Denys?" Celina glanced toward where they still watched Lisette in conversation with her brother.

Caid could not resist. "Figaro."

"You can't be serious," she said severely. "Madame Moisant has no one with her by that name."

"A recent arrival, I believe." Nicholas's face was perfectly straight.

Celina's eyes gleamed sherry-brown behind her narrowed lashes. "I believe you are both inebriated."

"Not yet," Caid said. "But it's an idea."

"First you must do your duty by the ladies who have not yet taken the floor," she said with precision. "Immediately. And both of you."

"Your wish is my command, fair one," Nicholas said, executing a graceful obeisance as he departed on his errand.

Caid refused to follow suit for fear his own bow must suffer by comparison. He called after the Italian, "A thousand thanks for the sacrifice, La Roche."

Nicholas Pasquale acknowledged the courtesy with a wave over his shoulder but did not answer. It was possible that he had been more attached to the little dog than he or anyone else had suspected.

"You have not danced with Madame Moisant," Celina said.

"Is that a command?"

"A suggestion." Rio's betrothed gave him a quizzical look. "Though I must say it seems an odd oversight."

"I have been promised the next dance, though I expect she would be better off if I stayed well away."

"Are you sure it's for her protection?"

Celina was far too sharp, which was one of the things Caid liked about her. However, he thought his best defense at the moment was to appear dense. "Who else? She requires a respectable alliance, or at least the prospect of one."

"Her first requirement, I should think, would be a friend."

"She has you," he said, slanting a smile down at her. "I saw the two of you discussing weighty matters with your heads together in a corner."

"Oh, yes, extremely weighty if you consider modistes, seamstresses and hairdressers in that light."

"I'm sure she has need of those, as well."

Celina gave an abstracted nod. "But I fear she may need friends more. I have heard whispers."

"Such as?" Caid could not keep the grimness from his voice.

"Flightiness, attempted suicide, even a touch of madness."

"You can't believe that nonsense."

"It matters little what I believe. Others are far more careful, you know. Our mad ones are hidden from sight since it's felt these maladies run in families. To harbor such a strain in the bloodline is nearly as detrimental as having a drop or two of the café au lait."

"So any suitors will shy off."

"Just so, and any allies."

"But she's an heiress."

"Which means the fortune hunters may court her, but with the full intention of shutting her away after the wedding."

Caid suppressed an oath that was best kept from feminine ears. "Moisant's doing, of course. If he can persuade everyone she is unstable, it will counter any claim she may make that he himself had been keeping her shut up."

"Or make it reasonable if he manages to do it again, yes."

Celina touched a finger to the point of her chin. "I think the more people who see her out and about, behaving in a natural fashion, the better it will be. A veritable whirlwind of engagements should be arranged."

"The opera, the theater?"

"At the very least. Perhaps an outing into the country, as well, if someone like Madame Herriot can be persuaded to arrange a house party. Lent will narrow the scope somewhat, but it may be managed easily enough."

"It's good of you to concern yourself when you have a wedding to plan," Caid said with grave appreciation.

"Not at all. Lisette has my sympathy since I have some experience of men who will go to any extreme to acquire a fortune."

That much was certainly true. A scoundrel and fortune hunter of the worst stripe had conspired with Celina's father, their nominal host for the evening, to force her into marriage and gain control of her dowry and future prospects. Only Rio and her own common sense had prevented it. "Still," Caid said with a lifted shoulder.

Celina smiled warmly up at him. "Added to that, you are Rio's good friend, which means you are mine. If it will ease your conscience to see the lady settled and safe with a new husband, then that is how it must be."

"She wants none, or so she says."

Celina gave him an appraising look. "But you intend she shall have one whether she wishes it or not. Why is that, *mon ami?*"

Rio must have said that to her, for Caid certainly had not. "It will put the most effective end to Moisant's persecution."

"It will also put her beyond your reach."

"She was always that, *mademoiselle.*" Caid bent his head briefly, then began to move away as the waltz that was playing came to an end, signaling the advent of his duty dance with Lisette. "Always."

The music struck up by the ensemble of violin, harp, pianoforte and French horn was another waltz. Why it could not have been a quadrille or something else with less physical contact, Caid did not know. The Fates were against him, that's all there was to it. These harpies wanted to see how miserable they could make him.

They were doing a fine job of it. Lisette came into his arms as if she belonged there. She required her free hand to manage her heavy skirt, however, and had no cord to the fan she held. Caid took it from her and secreted it in the pocket of his tailcoat. Her smile of gratitude was his reward for that bit of practicality before he swept her among the swirl of dancers.

Her movements matched his to perfection; she floated like thistledown in his arms. She was lovely this evening with white camellias tucked into the braiding of her shining auburn hair and the dark color of her gown turning her eyes to silvery moonstones. The silk fabric was an enticement of softness that triggered an almost irresistible impulse to strip off his gloves and slide his fingers beneath it's billowing fullness. Would she be as soft and yielding at the warm center of all the layers? The need to know burned in his brain, making it difficult to think, much less make conversation. Yet that distraction seemed essential.

"Madame Stilton seems tolerably amused this evening," he said, plunging in with the first topic that occurred to him.

"She discovered a former pupil in one of Mademoiselle Vallier's cousins and has been catching up with the family. Nothing is more gratifying to her than to be remembered, and to remember others."

"I would not have thought her a sentimentalist."

"Those who have the most tender hearts often don't appear so, I believe, keeping them guarded as a matter of self-protection."

That seemed a subject fraught with pitfalls. Caid sought for another. "You have a conquest in Denys Vallier."

She gave him a look from under her lashes. "He's young and gallant, and must practice on someone."

"You should not encourage him."

"That wasn't my intention."

"You will have him camped on your doorstep if you aren't careful, and I doubt you will relish that. His father may consider it unacceptable, as well."

She frowned a little at the prospect, Caid was glad to see. Then she shook her head with a sigh. "Why must everything be so complicated?"

"It isn't. Have you looked around you for more acceptable candidates?"

"As a husband, you mean? It's far too early."

"Not at all," he insisted. "How are we to plan a campaign if you have no objective?"

"That is the last thing on my mind."

"Then shall I choose for you? What say you to Monsieur Soubit? He is only a few years older and has a nice piece of property at Algiers across the river."

"He squints and his given name is *Zulime*." She gave a theatrical shiver. "I could not face either at the altar."

"Monsieur Thierry?"

"He has buried two wives. I feel he is unlucky…for his brides!"

"Latour?" he asked in resignation.

"He uses snuff."

"An execrable habit, I agree, but he has a strong physique."

"So does an ox, which is exactly what he puts me in mind of now that I consider it."

"Duchaine, then. You can hardly find fault with him." Caid tipped his head toward an exquisite young man presently dallying with the young wife of a doddering older gentleman. Good-looking in a refined manner, possessed of excellent address, he was a cousin to the Comte du Picardy, a nobleman who had left the city earlier in the *saison des*

visites, returning to Paris. Neville Duchaine had been abandoned after some disagreement with his exalted cousin over
an actress at the St. Charles Theater, or so it was whispered.
If he was a fortune hunter, he was at least a well-connected
one.

"Hmm, yes," Lisette said with speculation in her gaze as
she allowed it to rest on this prospect.

It was irrational, but Caid took an instant dislike to the
Frenchman. "No, forget him. He will probably sail for home
in a few days, as soon as he can raise the fare. In the meantime, he is unlikely to be interested in anything beyond mere
flirtation."

"Perhaps I might change his mind."

"Unlikely. He has libertine written all over him."

"I cannot see it," she answered lightly. "Of course, if
you're sure, then I must look elsewhere. Why is it, do you
think, that none of those who may be eligible have the least
pretense to attraction. You would suppose they might be at
least a little like your friend La Roche."

"Nicholas?" Caid was startled, though he could not have
said why.

"Devastatingly attractive, of superior strength, slightly
dangerous, a charming accent—and the look in his eyes? La,
so very like a caress."

"Also as prohibited as I am, and for the same reason." His
voice was grim.

"Such a stupid proscription, really. Who can have made
it? Yes, and why is it that Mademoiselle Vallier and Madame
Herriot may receive such men in the hallowed sanctity of
their homes but I should not?"

"Nicholas and I are friends of the man to whom
Mademoiselle Celina is betrothed. More than that, this is a
private soirée, not a public ball or other entertainment. Also,
unlike you at this moment, the ladies mentioned have no
need to be as Caesar's wife."

"Above suspicion, I do see. Though the question is, suspicion of what. I've done nothing wrong."

The bitterness that tinged her voice pained him. She was correct. He was the guilty party, the man who had placed her in her current awkward position when he killed her husband. The knowledge did nothing to lighten his mood.

The dance ended. Caid returned Lisette's fan to her then led her back to her companion. Shortly afterward, they heard the clanging of the cowbells that was the signal of the approaching parade which was a part of the evening's entertainment, though maskers had been strolling the streets all afternoon. Everyone immediately crowded out onto the balcony. They lined the railing, straining to catch a glimpse of the procession. Caid stood back near the door since he had an advantage in height not given to others.

The noise grew louder as the marchers heaved into view. It was a mummer's fancy, with the masked participants looking surreal in the leaping glow of a few torches carried alongside by holders dressed as Nubians. Most of those parading were on horseback though some few rode in carriages. Fanciful and grotesque masks covered their features, with the usual dominos, or long capes, concealing their clothing. All were men naturally, since such public display was not suited to females. Dogs barked at their heels. Street boys ran alongside, laughing, calling and being liberally splattered by the flour thrown by the people on adjoining balconies as well as the men on horseback. Ignoring all attempts at discouragement, these urchins scrambled in the gutters for the *dragées* that were also tossed by the riders. These candy-coated almonds, usually bought at the pastry shop in a paper cone, had become a tradition of the mounted parade, or so Caid had been told. This was his first brush with the spectacle.

There seemed no protocol and little organization. Each man had decorated his mount or carriage in keeping with his sense of style and the depths of his pocketbook. Streamers abounded, as did cockades and paper flowers. The masks were a personal choice, as well, with Harlequins, pirates and chanticleers, though the main theme was Satanic with nightmarish beasts running a close second. The men behind the disguises were solid citizens, for the most part, Creole gentlemen of leisure with a taste for frolic and merriment. Most were young and unmarried, though that seemed not to hold true for all.

Talk of the parade had been bandied about for weeks by men lounging around Caid's *salle d'armes*. He had been invited to join them, but declined as he lacked both horse and carriage, and to buy either for such a frivolous purpose went against the grain. He tended to side with the more staid, older Creoles who were vocal in their disapproval, characterizing the whole business as a vulgar display that must surely die a natural death.

Servants bearing trays of champagne glasses moved among the guests on the long balcony. As the main body of the mummers paused below the balcony, everyone cheered and applauded, and Monsieur Vallier gave them a toast to which all drank. Then they moved on with the last of the torch bearers trailing behind them. A horseman, masked as a fearsome wild boar and covered by a cloak bearing a cross of the Order of Saint John, cavorted in the semidarkness at the tail end of the parade, though straggling revelers were strung out down the street, many of these women of less than pristine virtue.

The wild boar high-stepped his mount to a position below the balcony, standing in his stirrups as he scanned those at the railing. He seemed to be looking for someone, perhaps a friend he knew to be among the Vallier guests. Then his gaze narrowed. He reached into the sack that hung at his side in the manner of those tossing *dragées*. Those on the balcony surged forward, intent on catching the candy as it was tossed. For an instant, Caid's view was obscured.

The air was suddenly filled with missiles. White, pink, yellow and green, as hard as rocks, they swept toward those on the balcony like windblown hail. A few rattled against the wall, but most struck the ladies who had been given first place at the railing with their escorts behind them. Women shrieked. One cried out, spun around in a swirl of dark silken skirts.

Lisette.

Caid pushed toward her without ceremony, shoving aside those escaping the hail of *dragées*. He caught Lisette's shoulders and bent his head as he tried to see into her face that was covered by her hands. "What is it? Are you hurt?"

"My eye," she said in muffled tones. "He hit me in the eye. It felt like a brick."

It was a brick, or at least a piece of one that must have been thrown with the *dragées*. The evidence lay at her feet.

Caid took her wrists and drew them aside. Her right eye was red and beginning to tear, and she could barely hold it open. Blood seeped from a small cut just under one brow. "Can you see?"

"I can, yes, but your face is blurred."

He whispered a curse, and then glanced around him. "Anyone know that rider?"

Few paid any attention as men led their ladies back inside. For the rest, head shakes and shrugs were the only answer. Caid turned to Nicholas who stepped to his side at that moment. "See to her, will you. I want to speak to this Knight of St. John."

"Here is Mademoiselle Vallier to take her in charge. I'll come with you."

Caid didn't answer. Turning, he strode back into the salon then out again and down the stairs to the *porte cochère* and from there to the street. He stopped a moment to scan the last of the maskers, looking for the horseman. He had not gone far, being held back by the remainder of the parade. The cross on the back of the man he sought showed plainly in the next block.

Caid set off at a run, threading through the crowd with more force than finesse. Nicholas pounded after him. Men yelled curses, but they didn't stop or look back.

The Knight of St. John must have heard the commotion. He turned his masked face in their direction for a brief second then faced forward and spurred his mount toward a side street.

A man in his path went flying. Another leaped aside, stumbling before falling to his knees. Then the knight was gone, clattering away down the near-empty roadway. Caid sprinted after him for half a block, but it was useless. He jogged to a halt and put his hands on his hips in disgust while he practiced invective learned in the hold of a prison ship.

When he had run out of breath, if not imagination, Nicholas spoke at his side. "You think the attack was deliberate?"

"Looked that way to me."

"Who might have done it is obvious, why is less so."

"Pure malice would be enough."

"Yes," Nicholas said thoughtfully. "In that case, I would advise against eating any of those *dragées* or allowing Lisette to partake."

For a single instant, Caid felt as if his heart had stopped. Then he turned his head slowly to stare at his friend and fellow sword master. "We will find that horseman. Tomorrow."

"And then?"

"He will regret his choice of costume makers."

"It was a rather distinctive choice. What if it belongs to Moisant?"

"I don't believe it was him," Caid said slowly. "This man was taller, more agile, or so it seemed to me."

"Younger?"

He nodded.

"So more of an opponent."

Caid met the keen, dark eyes of his friend. "What you are saying is that it may be a trap?"

"It isn't impossible."

"You have a devious mind, Pasquale."

Nicholas lifted one shoulder. "Machiavellian, I fear. It's in the blood. But people are not simple, my friend. No more are you."

Surprise shook a short laugh from Caid's chest. "You think not?"

"I know it."

"Then we must hope that it's enough."

They returned to the soirée. Supper had been served in their absence. That was according to plan, no doubt, but almost certainly as a diversion, as well. It was not a formal repast. Guests indicated their preference from the table laden with Westphalian hams cooked in champagne, wild turkey, roast venison, calves's feet à la vinaigrette, *pâté de foie gras,* macaroni *au fromage gratte,* red snapper court bouillon, lobster salad, crab soup, roast of sirloin, shrimp, oysters on the half shell, soft-shell crabs, Lyons sausages, Gruyere cheeses and all manner of desserts, tidbits and relishes. The centerpiece was a huge nougat confection representing the Alhambra Palace in deference to Rio's country of birth, and everyone was urged to taste it. Filled plates were carried to a series of small tables covered with white cloths and twined with ivy. The musicians continued to play.

Lisette was not at any of the tables. She emerged from a side room soon after Caid entered, however. She held a wet cloth pressed to her eye and her cloak was over her arm. She had a headache, she said, and her eye hurt. Would he mind escorting her home at once?

"You aren't hungry?" He searched her face and that of her companion who stood beside her. "Mademoiselle Celina will be upset if you go before eating at least a little something."

Lisette gave a quick shake of her head. "Monsieur de Silva would let no one eat the *dragées,* but ordered them swept up and burned in the kitchen fireplace. That quite destroyed my appetite."

"And mine," Mademoiselle Agatha said with a shudder.

At least they understood the danger. "We'll go at once." Caid looked around for Rio or Celina, but they were not close by.

"I will make your goodbyes, if that's your worry," Nicholas said quietly from behind him.

"Yes, I would be grateful." Caid took Lisette's cloak and began to drape her in its folds.

It was then that he heard a braying laugh from a group of men gathered in the near corner. He turned his head in time to see one of them tip his head in Lisette's direction as he spoke with a curl to his lip. "Poisoned *dragées?* Such nonsense. Eugene Moisant was a friend of mine, you comprehend. He always said his lady wife was as lacking in the head as she was in bed."

The anger that simmered inside Caid flared into rage. His voice deadly quiet, he said, "Your pardon, *madame, mademoiselle.* I will be with you in a moment."

"Monsieur O'Neill, please," Lisette put her gloved fingers on his coat sleeve.

He didn't answer. Stepping away, he moved toward the trio of men. They turned at his approach and the face of the one who had spoken blanched. Caid did not allow that to weigh with him. He had seen the gentleman in the *salles d'armes* of the Passage, knew him as one of the most notorious womanizers in the city and a graceless oaf who bragged of his conquests in the bedchamber as well as on the dueling field and was seldom mute on any other subject.

"Monsieur Vigneaud," he said evenly, as he executed a bow so brief as to be an insult while proffering his calling card taken from his tailcoat pocket. "My seconds will call on you in the morning."

Vigneaud gaped, making no answer. Caid waited an instant as a matter of form, then nodded to the man's companions and walked away. Returning to the ladies, he escorted them from the house and into the street.

"You intend to meet that man over a few bits of candy?" Lisette asked, her voice barely audible.

"He may issue a public apology if he so chooses."

"Not without being branded a coward. Oh, *monsieur*…"

"It was necessary. You heard what he said. He can't be allowed to repeat it as he wishes, or perhaps as Moisant wishes."

"So this is your idea of protection? To have it said, instead, that you will challenge any man who speaks ill of me?"

He gave her a sharp look. "Isn't that what you wanted?"

"No indeed! I thought to discourage one man, my father-in-law. I never meant that you should risk so much."

"Don't concern yourself. You aren't to blame for Vigneaud's stupidity or lack of manners, both of which have needed correction for some time."

"That isn't the point!"

"And what is?" he inquired with trenchant precision. "Should I have allowed him to insult you in public? Do you not mind being labeled as daft, among other things? Did you really think there would be no consequences attending on your defiance of Moisant? The whispers have begun, and fools like Vigneaud will build upon them unless convinced that doing so will cost them. I see no other way to stop it."

"If you are killed…" she began, then faltered to a halt.

Caid stopped so abruptly that his cloak flapped against his heels. "Yes?"

"Nothing." She looked away from him, sharing a brief glance with her silent companion. In the quiet could be heard distant laughter and someone with a decent tenor voice singing an aria from *Le Domino Noir*.

"I won't be killed," he said more gently. "Vigneaud is hardly a match for any *maître d'armes.*"

"You won't kill him?"

Her concern was for the death of any man, not for his personally. He should have expected as much. "It isn't required. First blood should be enough, or second if he proves obstinate."

"Yes," she said, a mere breath of sound. Turning away abruptly, she moved on again.

Caid saw her and Agatha Stilton to the wicket gate of the town house where he gave them into the care of their butler and the guardianship of the little mongrel, Figaro. Then he said a polite good-night above the noise of the dog's delirious welcome and went quickly back out into the street.

As he stepped out onto the pavement, the bells of St. Louis Cathedral began to toll. Mardi Gras was over and Lent had begun. For long seconds, Caid stood listening, his face set in grim lines while the melodious clanging soared above the city, resounding among the stars.

He wondered what he should give up for this season of contrition.

Other than *dragées,* of course, and women with soft gray eyes.

7

The seamstress, Madame Fortin, was at the town house within an hour after the note from Lisette was carried around to her. She was delighted to be of service to a lady acquainted with the so-gracious Mademoiselle Vallier, for whom she had been commissioned to make the loveliest of wedding gowns. How very gracious of the lady to recommend her. The entire complement of her small atelier would be at the disposal of Madame Moisant; she had three ladies who were superior artisans with the needle. Between them, they would see that Madame Moisant was beautifully outfitted as suited her circumstances.

Ah, but Madame had the very great desire to attend the theater that evening? She was a most fortunate lady, for there was an evening costume, the very thing, languishing in her atelier at that moment. It had been ordered from Paris early in the season by a lady who had lost her father just before Christmas but not realized she was enceinte and so would be unable to wear it before the season ended. The lady had asked if Madame Fortin might attempt to dispose of it for her, since she despaired of being able to fit into it later. A bride of the season before, the lady had been at that time much of a size with Madame. It could be sent for, if Madame wished?

Lisette did wish it, very much. The offering, when it arrived, was highly satisfactory, being a gown of black silk that was the latest word in fashion, with a bell skirt minus the usual split front and trimmed with wide horizontal bands of embroidery at the shoulders and hem. With its headdress of a nodding black aigrette in a silver filigree holder, it would be just the thing. Lisette would have preferred a gown made from the black velvet purchased a few days before, but there was no time. At least she would not be forced to wear the same evening costume she had worn to the Vallier soirée. Accordingly, she sent to accept Maurelle Herriot's kind, if unexpected, offer of a seat in her box at the *Théâtre d'Orlèans* that evening.

The program featured the Ravel family, in New Orleans for only a week. Billed as "The Night of Surprise," it was to begin with a pantomime ballet, a form of high wire performance enacted on a bar some twelve feet above the stage. To follow was a changing tableaux with actors posing as famous sculptures and a ballet performance, after which would be a drama entitled *Madame Siddons* or *Une Actrice Anglaise*, and based on the life, presumably, of the famous actress who had died some ten years ago. The entertainment promised to be adequate, which was to say suitably diverting without being too great a distraction from the real purpose of attending the theater, which was to see and be seen.

The evening began much as anticipated. Gabriel Ravel, the leader of the family troupe, was tolerably handsome and possessed a fine physique as displayed in the close-fitting costume of his ballet pantomime. However, most of the opera glasses in the house were trained on the occupants of the boxes that mounted in gilded tiers above the stage or else on the orchestra seats. The parterre, where sat those who could not afford a more exalted view, was not of so much interest except for the occasional young gentleman who preferred to remain seated. These were few, for the majority of the young blades prowled the theater like alley cats, seeking out acquaintances or else jockeying for position at the rear doors of the boxes occupied by the belles of the season. Those first in line would be assured of a visit during the intervals, an enviable position. And of course the *mamans* of marriageable daughters kept careful count of the visits received in the family box as proof of the girl's status.

Lisette would have preferred the privacy of a *loge grille,* one of the boxes set back behind a carved wooden screen and created expressly for women in mourning such as herself, ladies near their lying-in or else those in the company of men not their husbands. Behind its protection, she could have surveyed the house while knowing she was safe from similar inspection or conjecture over the small sticking plaster she wore above her injured eye. She might well procure such a box for herself and Agatha, she thought, should one be available this late in the season. As it was, she was glad their seats were in the rear of the Herriot box.

"A sparse crowd," Agatha commented from where she perched on the edge of her chair, dressed in a plain gown of lavender satin with a blond lace collar, a cap of blond on her hair, and with mother-of-pearl opera glasses held to her eyes. "One must suppose that some few in the city still observe Lenten restrictions."

"Or they are recovering from the excesses of last night, no great surprise."

"If you expected to see no one of consequence, then why were you so set on coming, my dear?"

"Because there is no one to prevent me," Lisette answered with a wry smile. "Eugene did not care for the theater, you know, so saw no reason that funds should be wasted on such staid entertainment."

Agatha gave her a brief sympathetic glance but made no direct comment. "You know, my dear, I wish you had sent a note to Monsieur O'Neill saying we would be here tonight."

"Now why would I do that when he must only have disapproved?"

"Surely you don't believe he would have forbidden it?"

"That is beyond his power. Besides, if he is as conscientious as I believe, he will know where we are."

"You are relying rather heavily on his sense of duty, are you not?"

"We shall see," Lisette said in dry tones.

She began to think her confidence misplaced when the only gentlemen to visit the box after the pantomime were a few friends of Maurelle. She was sure of it when the curtain closed upon the last of the tableaux and still Caid had not appeared. Was he otherwise occupied, or had he lost interest in looking after her? Either seemed possible.

The advancing evening seemed sadly flat. She had little interest in the *Danses de Corde* promised next, and could easily have forgone the final play. Only the fact that Agatha seemed to be enjoying the entertainment kept her from suggesting that they go home. The town house was close by, only three blocks away. They had walked to the theater with Maurelle, led by one of her menservants carrying a lantern and a heavy staff, and could easily return in the same manner.

Maurelle Herriot shifted in her chair to face Lisette and Agatha as the gaslights in the theater were turned higher. "Thank heaven that is done. I usually delay my arrival until after the pantomime, and would have done so this evening had I not thought it might appeal."

"How kind of you to go to the trouble for us, then," Lisette said at once. "Though I hope we are not so difficult to please, Agatha and I."

Agatha leaned forward. "So kind of you to include me in the invitation, *madame*. That was most gracious of you."

Maurelle made a dismissive gesture, but had no time for more as a light knock came at the curtained doorway behind them.

"Your pardon, ladies. May we join you?"

Lisette turned on her chair to see Denys Vallier hovering at the rear entrance. Given permission to enter, he came forward along with his friends whom Lisette had met at his sister's evening party, Hippolyte Ducolet, Armand Lollain and Francis Dorelle. The gentlemen seated themselves in the extra chairs provided, chatting amiably about the performances and certain of the actors, or rather the actresses, since the female members of the troupe seemed to have occupied most of their attention. They also inquired after her hurt eye, expressing their gladness that it had not been serious and condemning the man who had caused it.

"I had expected that we might be left to make tapestry, as the saying goes, during these intervals," Lisette said at the first lull in the conversation. "How is it that you found us?"

"Celina told me you would be here," Denys answered. "She heard it from Rio, I think, who was told you were here by Pasquale, who almost certainly had it, in turn, from Monsieur O'Neill. I trust you have no objection?"

"None at all," she said, and could not refrain from sharing a flash of amusement with Agatha for the fact that she had been right about Caid. "We are all glad of the company."

"And we are in transports at our good fortune in coming upon such charming company." Denys smiled on all three ladies with sunny flirtatiousness before turning back to Lisette. "Permit me to say that I dread when you are out of your black, for then everyone will realize what beauty it covers and I will be lost in the crowd around you."

It was prettily done in the fulsome manner in vogue at the moment. This young man, though hardly out of his teens, would be a dangerous rogue one day when he reached his full growth. His waving hair, earnest eyes and square chin showed much promise. Lisette was sure any number of young girls fresh from the schoolroom had lost their hearts to him before now.

"It is time to step aside already, *mon vieux.*" This deeper voice spoke from behind them as another gentleman strolled into the box. "Behold, I am here, and have reinforcement behind me."

"Monsieur Pasquale, at last. I wondered what kept you. But now that you are here, I shall go in search of refreshments for the ladies, thereby earning their undying devotion. See that these three fools, Francis, Hippolyte and Armand, don't usurp my place while I am away."

Hardly had Celina's brother vacated his chair than a good-natured shoving match sprang up between Denys's friends over who should have it. Nicholas settled the argument by the simple expedient of grasping the back and pulling it away, then taking it for himself. Even as he was seated, his place in the doorway was filled by a mulatto in a rust-colored coat and ruffled shirt with cameo studs and another gentleman of slender build and good-humored countenance whom Lisette recognized as Gilbert Rosière, the sword master known affectionately to all as Titi.

None of these men were Caid O'Neill, but their presence was enough to persuade Lisette that the time spent on her toilette for the evening had been worth the effort. In any case, there was something heady about being attended by two of the most notorious of the city's masters at arms in addition to a trio of young men of worshipful mien. Armand, Francis and Hippolyte seemed as conscious as she was of the honor being bestowed. Their horseplay ceased the instant they recognized the company they were in, and they stood back, keeping a respectful distance from both the visitors and Lisette's chair. That state of affairs lasted less than five minutes however, only until Titi and his companion had paid their compliments then excused themselves, lounging away to their next call in order to relieve the congestion in the box.

"If I may, La Roche, that is, Monsieur Pasquale," Hippolyte Ducolet said. "What news is there today concerning this tournament of sword masters? One hears such odd things, you know. Some say more clashes are occurring in the preparation for the meetings than will ever be accommodated on the strips. Is it true that Bernard insulted Llulla yesterday, and that Llulla poked holes in him for it at dawn this morning?"

"I believe so," Nicholas said, his attention on a microscopic piece of lint that he was removing from his coat. "Bernard will survive. Just."

Armand Lollain leaned forward eagerly. "Dauphin is supposed to have had words with Captain Thimecourt…"

"Settled without bloodshed."

"For which we thank God," Agatha said in colorless disapproval.

"Yes, otherwise Dauphin would have eliminated the Captain. And then there is the affair of Monsieur O'Neill and Vigneaud, though I hear it did not originate over the tournament…"

"Have done, my good child," Pasquale said in tones of steel. "You will upset the ladies, and then we shall all be ejected from this quiet haven."

"N-naturally," Armand said, turning wine-red while tripping over his tongue in his haste to redeem the error. "Your pardon, *mesdames, mademoiselle.* I wonder where Denys can have…"

"You owe me no apology, Monsieur Lollain," Lisette said. "In fact, I have an intense interest in this subject. Tell us, Monsieur Pasquale, what, precisely, did happen with the meeting between Messieurs O'Neill and Vigneaud?

"Not a great deal," he answered shortly. "It takes place in the morning."

That explained why they had heard no results. The knowledge did nothing to ease the tightness in her chest.

"Everyone will be there," Armand said, his eyes bright. "It isn't every day that a master at arms faces two opponents in succession."

"Quiet!" Hippolyte hissed with a strong nudge in his friend's ribs.

"Yes, you were saying?" Lisette asked with determined pleasantness, her gaze fixed on the young man.

"Your pardon, *madame.*" Perspiration appeared on Armand's forehead as he sustained a hard stare from La Roche even as he apologized to Lisette. "I misspoke."

"I don't believe so." She turned to the Italian sword master. "Has Monsieur O'Neill more than one appointment under The Oaks?"

Nicholas sighed. "He will kill me, without a doubt. My friend the Irishman will run me through when he has finished with the others. But yes, he meets two men in the morning, first Vigneaud, and then one Philippe Quentell, a *maître d'armes* of more ego than skill, one who paraded in a cloak with a St. John's cross."

"And this Quentell has perhaps a fondness for *dragées?*"

"He did, though I believe he may have lost his taste for them, or soon will."

Two challenges, two meetings on the field of honor. Caid would face the naked swords of two men at dawn tomorrow, and there was nothing she could do to stop it. Quentell was apparently a fellow sword master which would make the second match far more dangerous than the first, and it would come when Caid was already fatigued, perhaps, from the encounter with Vigneaud. A shiver moved over Lisette's skin, leaving gooseflesh in its wake.

In the brief silence, Maurelle cleared her throat with a discreet rasp. "And just where is Monsieur O'Neill this evening?"

"Sleeping, I hope," Pasquale said dryly. "Though I doubt it."

"His *salle d'armes* was open today, yes?"

Pasquale nodded. "And he rested little last night."

He meant that Caid had been awake guarding her town house the night before, Lisette thought. Then it had been his day to give fencing lessons to his clients at his atelier. If he was not on his best form, it would be her fault, just as he would face both men on the dueling ground for her sake.

Denys returned then, followed by a manservant bearing a tray laden with lemon drinks. By the time they had been distributed, they were joined by Neville Duchaine, cousin to the Comte de Picardy. Lisette was quite eclipsed, she thought with amusement, her gaze on the Frenchman's mournful splendor in a coat and trousers of the same deep black shade worn with a waistcoat of silver brocade.

"Why, Madame Moisant," he exclaimed with a caress in his dark, expressive eyes. "I do believe we are a match."

"Indeed." The single word was repressive out of dislike for the double entendre. "But not, I trust, for the same reason."

"No, no, if you mean to ask if I have had a bereavement. It's only that black has become *de rigueur* for evening in Europe, almost a uniform. I mean to say for men, naturally. So practical in cities where coal smoke and ash take their toll on one's attire."

"Very true," Madame Herriot said amiably. "I saw it myself while I was there. Tell me, *monsieur,* will you be with us for long? Everyone I know asks this question and no one seems to have the answer."

"My plans are not fixed, *madame.* I had considered continuing my adventures by traveling up the Mississippi and then overland to New York." He expanded on this statement with more of his itinerary, segueing from there into his various travel adventures as a part of his favorite subject, which seemed to be himself. The opinion was not hers alone, she thought, for she caught the exchange of an expressive grimace between Denys Vallier and his friend Hippolyte.

Duchaine had just embarked on a tale of a carriage accident in Mobile, where he had first landed, when Agatha reached to touch Lisette on the arm. Lisette glanced at her companion with a raised brow. Agatha said nothing, but handed over her opera glasses and nodded toward a box just across the way.

Lisette searched the figures in the boxes one by one with the glasses to her eyes. Then she saw what had attracted Agatha's attention.

Henri Moisant.

Her father-in-law stood staring across at her, his face a mask of fury. No doubt he had paid a visit, as was customary for gentlemen, to Monsieur and Madame Plauchet, who occupied the opposite box. That he had not expected to see his daughter-in-law was abundantly clear.

A strong urge to flee the theater surged up inside Lisette. Pride alone held her in her place. She would not allow this man to make her run away, refused to let him see her disturbance. Lowering the glasses, she gazed back at him with cool self-possession, or as near a fabrication of it as she could summon. At the same time, she could not help but wonder if her father-in-law was, perhaps, acquainted with one Monsieur Quentell.

At that moment, she felt a warm touch on her bare shoulder revealed by her décolletage. Caid's low voice came from above her head, as if he had moved to stand behind her as bulwark and shield. "Steady. He means to intimidate you, but cannot do so if you refuse to allow it."

"No," she whispered. Caid must have just arrived, with the influx of more gentlemen into the box. Glancing over her shoulder, she recognized one or two more of the fencing masters who had been at the Vallier soirée, one of them with the intense air and slender athleticism of a matador who went by the name of Eduoard Sarne. Just behind him was Gustave Bechet, a gentleman for whom she'd felt a certain pity before her marriage because his mother had pushed him into dangling after her. In the hubbub they created in greeting Maurelle and each other, no one seemed to have noticed her preoccupation or Caid's quiet advice.

"You don't believe Monsieur Moisant will come here?" she asked with a brief upward glance that did not quite meet his eyes.

"I doubt it. If he did, he would find no room to stand. A popular place tonight, Maurelle's box."

"It was kind of her to invite us." Lisette suspected it had been at his instigation. Her comment had been an oblique attempt to discover if she was right. It was also an unsuccessful one.

"The lady can be very kind," Caid said lightly, "when it suits her."

Maurelle turned in a whisper of taffeta and swirl of bird of paradise feathers, as if she had antennae for discovering when she was under discussion. "What is that you're saying, *mon ami?*"

"That you are ravishing tonight, *chère,*" he answered without pause. "And that you richly deserve the homage of those gathered around you."

"I do not believe you, my rogue, but accept the sentiment in the spirit that it should have been given." She touched the chair beside her. "Come, sit next to me and let me know what you have been doing since we last parted. I hardly see you at all these days, I do swear."

Caid displayed no sign of reluctance as he moved to obey. Lisette could only suppose he was used to being ordered in that way. She was hardly in a position to complain, though she was aware of an exposed feeling at her back where he had stood moments before.

"Finally, a chance to speak to you, *madame,*" Denys Vallier said as he moved into the place Caid had held. "I had despaired of it."

"And now it is yours," she said with a smile. "I trust your sister has recovered from her exertions as a hostess?"

"She goes along very well, forever doing something," he answered with brotherly disregard. "But I must tell you at once, before we are interrupted. You have inspired me."

"I? Surely not."

"But yes, of a certainty! We spoke of poetry last evening, if you recall. Your kind encouragement caused me to sit down and pen a poem after the guests had taken their leave. I wonder…that is, might I call upon you soon to read it to you? I would value your opinion most highly."

"I am no expert, I promise you."

"You have read much and have a refinement which suggests elevated taste and ideals."

"Oh, no, you are mistaken."

"It's quite plain to those who know how to see," he protested, his expression earnest. "These things indicate superior judgment on your part, particularly in matters of style which must encompass the literary."

"You're very kind, *monsieur,* but…"

"My good friend Francis is a poet, as well, though few know and fewer still would believe it of such a scapegrace. He would like nothing better than to sit talking of his idols in the world of words, Monsieur Byron and Keats and also of those who pen novels like the latest by the Englishman, Scott."

"A Scotsman, I believe," she said in gentle correction.

"What? Oh, yes, of course. You have it all at your fingertips, you see. Please say you will allow the visit?"

"Well, if you truly wish it. I shall be interested to see what you and your friend have written."

Denys turned, raising his voice as he called out. "You hear, Francis? We are invited. You owe me a bottle of champagne."

"You shall have it, lackwit," Francis Dorelle said, his face flushing dark red as he looked around. "But must you let everyone know of our wager?"

"What is this?" Duchaine asked. "A venture and I missed it? What was it about?"

"A poetry reading at the salon of Madame Moisant," the

young poet said, turning darker still while a moist sheen appeared in his large, dark eyes. "Vallier said Madame Moisant would be gracious enough to agree, while I was sure she must decline because of her mourning as well as unwillingness to bother."

"And a bottle of champagne hung in the balance." Duchaine turned to Lisette. "I have no part in this wager, but the reading sounds delightful. Please say I may be added to the number attending, kind lady?"

"And I!" Armand Lollain called over his shoulder.

"I, also." That ponderous request was made by Bechet, though the portly fellow looked rather mournful about it.

"All are invited who wish to be present," Lisette said in bemusement.

"Then I shall be there of a certainty," Duchaine declared. "It will be as if I had not left Paris, enjoying a literary salon where those of like mind may meet and talk of something other than politics, which horse is running at the Métairie, or who has impaled himself on which sword master's blade. I can hardly bear to wait."

"A literary salon," Lisette repeated, much struck by the idea. "I have heard of such things. I believe the hostesses are at home for them one night each week?"

"You could set a fashion, *madame*. Does that please you?"

It didn't displease her, though she was not certain Caid felt the same. When she glanced his way, he was frowning. "Perhaps, I shall have to see," she said. "How would it suit to meet on Friday evening, two days from now?"

The renewed chorus of acceptance was pleasant to hear. Lisette could feel the slow rise of excitement in her veins, as if it was she who had won the champagne. Almost, she wished that she had suggested the following evening, but there were the small matters of arranging refreshments and waiting for the modiste to deliver another evening costume. Even two days was little enough time.

In her concentration on this new prospect, she had almost forgotten Monsieur Moisant. When she looked across at the opposite box again, he had gone.

It was inevitable, perhaps, that Caid would remain to act as escort for the walk homeward when the evening ended. Since Maurelle complained of a headache, they took a route which carried them to her town house first. Caid did not linger inside, but returned to the entrance where Lisette and Agatha waited. They continued on their way, turning at the next street for the short journey to the rue Royale.

Very little was said as they walked along, primarily because of the manservant with the lantern which Maurelle had insisted on sending with them. Something was on Caid's mind, however; Lisette was sure of it. His manner was watchful yet grimly forbidding. When not scanning the area ahead or behind them, he gazed at the pavement, slashing with his cane tip at bits of refuse or spent flowers that had fallen over garden walls. Allowing the few comments exchanged by Agatha and herself to flow around him unheeded, he answered only queries directed specifically at him.

Lisette had supplied herself with a key for the wicket gate so that Felix need not wait up for them. Figaro began to bark the instant the wicket squeaked open, however, though he was apparently inside somewhere behind a closed door. Agatha turned to Caid. "I shall say good-night, Monsieur O'Neill, since I must go and see to poor Figaro before he scratches the paint off the door. I feel sure that dear Lisette will say everything necessary to express our appreciation for your escort."

Caid murmured politely and inclined his head as she left them. Lisette turned to him then, holding out her gloved hand. "I do thank you most sincerely for this escort. I should also like to say that I…"

"A moment, if you please," he said abruptly. "There is a matter we should discuss."

His grim request interrupted her little speech. It was just as well, since she had been about to reveal her knowledge of the two duels he would face at dawn, so short a time from now. Instead, she said, "It's very late."

"I assure you that what I have to say won't take long."

How could she refuse when it might concern her father-in-law and his presence this evening? Still, she hardly knew how to proceed. To speak of private matters here in plain view of anyone who passed by in the street seemed awkward, yet to invite him upstairs was clearly unsuitable.

The thought raised images of the last time he had been in her private rooms, the moment when he had actually been closeted with her in the bedchamber. A flood of heat suffused her mind and body. Her breasts felt full and heavy and her lips tingled. Could he have another such lesson as he had imposed then on his mind? She glanced at him, staring at the width of his shoulders, the shape of his head, the fullness of his bottom lip an instant, before looking away again.

He watched her while the strained silence vibrated between them. Then he turned away, bracing one hand on the upright iron spokes of the open wicket gate. Over his shoulder, he said, "This literary salon of yours, it won't do."

She should have known. "I beg your pardon?"

"It's much too odd an undertaking. People will have a great deal to say, little of it complimentary. The *haut ton* of New Orleans may read in private, but to be bookish is no more expected than among the aristocrats of the British Isles I call home. No man wants to marry a bluestocking, a woman with her head stuffed full of strange ideas, strange knowledge of a worldly sort. It would be too uncomfortable."

"Uncomfortable?" she inquired. "Uncomfortable, to sit across the table from a female who can talk of something other than food, babies and the latest scandal?"

"You know very well what I'm trying to say."

"I know I care little what a man may prefer in a woman since I have no use for one."

"It isn't that alone."

"What then? A woman with an idea in her head may frighten the population? You think the oddity of a salon would lend credence to the tale that I'm unstable?"

"Now you have it."

"Well, I don't care. I can't sit at home and do nothing!"

"No one expects it. There are plenty of other things—the theater, the opera, normal morning calls, excursions to Tivoli Garden or walks on the levee. You should not lack for entertainment."

"Thank you so much. Perhaps you may add attending duels to your list. Though I must say that I cannot see how you can fight any number of duels in a single morning for my sake without it being considered the least unusual while I may not have intelligent guests without being thought insane."

"No lady would think of appearing at the dueling field. It isn't done."

"I am well aware," she said, incensed. "The point I wish to make is that you aren't reasonable."

"I am perfectly reasonable. You won't listen to what I'm trying to tell you."

"Because I don't care to hear it."

"Anyway, who told you of the second duel… No, permit me to guess. La Roche."

"Not deliberately." She would not for the world do anything that might damage the friendship of the two men.

"He is entirely too soft where women are concerned. I am not."

That sounded very like a warning but she was in no mood to heed it. "I had not fully decided to make a regular thing of this salon, but you convince me that it is a brilliant idea. Toward that conclusion, I should like to point out that neither Messieurs Pasquale, Vallier, Ducoulet, Lallain nor any of the others seemed to think it anything at all out of the way, or that I must be mad to contemplate it."

"I didn't say that," he said with a growl in his voice.

"I think you did. I believe you said that you would be repulsed by a woman of bluestocking tendencies. Let me tell you, *monsieur,* that I shall scour the city for blue stockings and wear nothing else. I shall have my literary salon, invite whom I please and discuss anything and everything I please. I shall do this, and nothing you have to say will stop me."

A white line appeared around his lips while the tips of his ears grew red. "You will regret it, *madame.* And once everyone learns of this *outré* little gathering of yours, it will be too late to alter how they think of you."

"If that is so, then I will have nothing to lose, will I? I may then behave exactly as I choose."

His brows snapped together in a frown. "What are you saying?"

She faced him with her hands placed on her hips so the shawl she wore draped from her elbows. "I am saying that I may as well abandon living quietly. I shan't mind, you know. If being unusual will convince you and everyone else that I don't wish a husband, will not take one, can hardly stand the thought of one, then it is all to the good. I think, in fact, that it means I should do something more, something else to shock and amaze, something…something…"

"What?" he demanded as she paused for inspiration.

"Something completely outrageous!"

8

Caid stood waiting, sword in hand. Vigneaud was still fussing with the sleeves of his shirt, folding back each cuff just so. All else was in readiness, the strip marked off, the surgeons waiting to one side with their instruments laid out on ground cloths, the seconds standing by, including Vigneaud's man who held the handkerchief he would use to signal the beginning of the duel. A fair crowd had gathered, but they were reasonably quiet. Few wagers seemed to be taking place, perhaps because the outcome of the contest was so little in doubt. Vigneaud was known in the salons along the Passage de la Bourse, at least according to Bastile Croquère. He possessed no natural aptitude for the swordsmen's art, and was unwilling to do the hard work that might build craft as a substitute.

Caid adjusted the handkerchiefs that wrapped his wrists, tucking the ends more snugly into place. The one on the right served to protect the vulnerable blood vessels behind his sword hand, while that on the left was a mere affectation. Both also covered his scars left by rusty manacles. Not that he was particularly ashamed of them, but he saw no use in flaunting them, either.

He thought somewhat pensively that he should feel some remorse for the fact that he was clearly the superior with a blade. He did not. Fairness was not the object here. It was, rather, to illustrate the danger in speaking ill of Lisette Moisant.

The day looked to be a pleasant one. The sun was rising, sending spears of light striking down through the trees. Birdsong drifted on the cool morning breeze, led by the repeated two-note song of a cardinal. Dew lay heavy on the grass, which could make for uncertain footing. Caid made a mental note to have a care for it.

He wondered if Lisette was awake yet. Yes, and if she'd given even a second's thought to how he was spending this early-morning hour.

Vigneaud was finally ready. Caid walked forward to take his place on the strip of grass marked off with lime. He swept up his sword in the expected salute, inclined his head, and then crossed his blade with that of his opponent.

Vigneaud was watching him, his gaze narrow. Did he think that made him look menacing, Caid wondered? If so, he was mistaken. He looked, instead, as if he had bad eyesight. It was to be hoped that was not the case. A man flailing around at random could sometimes be more dangerous than one who knew what he was doing.

The signal came. Caid launched a measured attack designed to test his opponent's skill before essaying any rash moves. Vigneaud countered it with clumsy bravado. The effort seemed to wind him. Sweat appeared on the man's forehead while the animal smell of it fouled the air around him. A hunted look appeared in his eyes.

It was a quite different expression from the sneer he had worn when speaking of Lisette. With any other man, Caid might have prolonged the match long enough to allow a modicum of pride. For Vigneaud, he felt no such compunction. He only wanted to have done with it.

He attacked again in glittering competence and a flurry of wrist-tingling blows. Steel beat and clanged, raked edge to edge for a nerve-cringing instant. Caid's blade met linen and the warm flesh beneath it. Abruptly, all was silent.

Vigneaud groaned and dropped his sword. He clutched his upper arm with one clawlike hand while blood seeped through his fingers. Caid stepped back, waiting for the man's seconds and surgeon to gather round.

"Nice bit of work," Nicholas, his chief second in this affair, said in low tones as he walked up to stand beside him. "Though not of any duration for adequate judgment."

"I saw no reason to prolong the agony."

"I doubt Vigneaud has the same view of the situation, particularly at this moment."

"He should be grateful I didn't choose to put my blade through a lung."

"Meaning you could have, but refrained? Forbearing of you."

"I promised I wouldn't kill him."

"Ah."

Nicholas sounded as if he understood completely that it was at Lisette's request. Perhaps he did. The Italian was damned knowing about women.

"Come now," Titi Rosière, his other second, said with a crooked grin as he joined them. "You would not have us believe you intended to end his existence."

Would that Lisette had shown a similar trust, Caid thought. But then she had known him mere days rather than weeks. "No."

"So I thought. It wouldn't be like you at all." Titi glanced over his shoulder toward the other end of the dueling ground. "We should have a decision at any moment as to whether their principal can continue. I assume you are satisfied, should they ask?"

Caid gave a curt nod.

"Excellent. Nicholas and I will be back in a moment then."

He watched his two friends as they walked across the trampled grass to confer with Vigneaud's seconds and surgeon. From where he stood, it appeared the medical man felt it was impossible to resume the duel, that his patient's arm was too badly wounded to allow adequate handling of his sword. Caid wasn't surprised since that was his intention.

Rosière stood talking a moment longer, while Nicholas returned to where Caid stood. "You heard?

Caid indicated his agreement.

Nicholas reached for the sword, pulling it from Caid's hand in spite of his momentary resistance. Taking a folded cloth from his tailcoat pocket, he wiped the blade clean, polishing it to a brilliant sheen again. "I don't see Quentell," he said, glancing around the field. "Perhaps his courage failed him."

Caid scanned the gathering in his turn. It was true. By all rights his next adversary, Quentell, should have been standing by with his attendants, waiting for his turn on the field. That he was not was a clear breach of the code. A relaxed attitude toward time was common in New Orleans given the city's Latin heritage, but not for an affair of honor where tardiness might be seen as a deliberate insult or else a reluctance to appear. Quentell must be allowed a few more minutes in case of an accident, but after that a default would be declared.

Pray God for it.

That instant flash of hope that his second opponent might not appear caught Caid by surprise. Fear had no part in it, though the outcome of a match between fencing masters was always in doubt. Rather, it was his very real reluctance to shed more blood today.

Was he losing his nerve? It could happen, the sudden revulsion for the entire concept of personal honor and the need to defend it at extreme risk, the striving while seeing sick horror in an opponent's eyes, the knowledge that he held incipient death in his hand. Yes, and the accusation and condemnation that he recognized in the eyes of those who might have known his late adversary.

For instance, in the angel eyes of Lisette Moisant.

To have that crisis of doubt creep up on a man, particularly a swordsman who lived or died by the strength of his resolve as much as the temper of his steel, could be a catastrophe. Nothing, in fact, could be more deadly.

"Vigneaud is done," Rosière said as he lounged back toward them.

"Done?" Caid's voice was sharp. "I thought… How can that be? I only pierced his arm."

"Calm yourself, *mon ami*. Not done *for,* as you suppose, but done for the day."

The relief Caid felt spreading through him was the most frightening thing he'd known that morning.

Waiting did not produce Quentell. A rumor began to circulate that he had been seen boarding a steamboat heading upriver. Finally, the two men who were to have acted as his seconds appeared to announce that their principal could not be located. They made the required offer to take their man's place, but it was naturally declined.

Caid donned his coat and waistcoat again, and he and his party drove back into town. After a celebratory breakfast for all parties, he and Nicholas made their way to the Place d'armes where the militia was drilling under the command of their senior officer. They had joined just the day before, and this was to be their first taste of quasi-military discipline. The mindless marching to shouted orders could be a useful, if somewhat demeaning, antidote to Caid's fit of the megrims.

Two hours later, they were released with written instructions regarding the ordering of their uniforms. Reading the details was the first he and Nicholas knew of their appointments as sergeants with units of their own to command. Since to tarry might mean other new officers might get in ahead of them, exhausting the supply of gold braid and gray worsted, they set out at once for the tailor chosen by their commander. An hour of being measured at every single limb and angle, and they were finally free to make their way, exhausted, to Alvarez's for a well-deserved drink.

"Here," Rio de Silva called, waving them toward a table he shared with Titi Rosière. He kicked a chair around so Nicholas could be seated to his left, then swung out another for Caid. "I understand it's Vigneaud whose health we must ask after."

"He will recover."

"The best possible outcome, as always. And Quentell failed to come up to scratch? An unhappy man, but I suppose his atelier will now be available."

"Not so," Rosière corrected him. "It's taken already, and by an Englishman of some skill, or so one hears. Blackford is his name, Gavin Blackford."

"I heard something of the gentleman. Arrived on the steamer from Liverpool last week, yes?"

"A man who lets no grass grow under his feet," Nicholas said casually, as he signaled the waiter.

"He beat out several who have been waiting all season for space to fall vacant. Still, such a devil with a blade as they say he is, no one will be too inclined to dispute his lease on the premises."

"You can't be serious," Caid said with a frown between his brows.

"Not entirely. But I hear Madame Tallant, who owns the building was charmed by his address and manners." Rosière shrugged. "He has the face of a fallen angel or so I was told by my darling wife who chanced to meet him on the banquette."

"Should we beware of drawing his name for the tournament?" This came from Nicholas, who looked not at all concerned.

"He may not enter. I've heard he disdains such displays."

Caid grimaced. "Indicating that he's so well off he has no special care for his pocketbook, I suppose?"

"The story is that his family is an old one and not without influence, though using his father's name is another thing he disdains. He's a younger son, so forced to make his own way. If he refuses to enter the competition, then it will likely be as a matter of principle."

"An excellent thing," Nicholas said. "If one can afford it."

"In short," Rio said, leaning back in his chair as he surveyed them, "you had best take care, all of you, or you may be thoroughly eclipsed."

"But not you?"

"Oh, I shall be far away in Spain, where my path and this English swordsman's may never cross."

Caid gave him a frown. "Let's hope the rest of us are as lucky."

"Unlikely," Rio said, his voice with its slight Spanish accent languid with amusement. "He has made the acquaintance of my future brother-in-law and Denys did not hesitate to extend an invitation to accompany him tomorrow evening to Madame Moisant's literary salon."

Caid swore. It was all he needed, to have Lisette's town house invaded by yet another man, and an Englishman at that. He was torn between a strong wish that her literary evening should be a failure and the fear that it might. To see her disappointed was not something he relished, still he could not think attracting every poseur and artistic pretender in town, not to mention a swarm of swordsmen, was the way to convince the *ton* that she was a lady of perfect respectability. There was little he could do about it, however, short of standing guard at the entrance and turning away all who were unsuitable.

Arriving for the affair on Friday evening, Caid had every hope of finding the company thin and conversation languishing. Instead, he heard the rumble of talk and laughter before he reached the stairs. Felix took his hat and cane at the door, but he could barely edge his way into the salon and could not see his hostess for the crowd of men gathered around her chair.

This was worse than Maurelle's salons, which had at least some pretense of balance between the gentlemen and the ladies, youth and age, sporting gentlemen and intellectuals. Caid could feel the hair on the back of his neck rise as he realized that except for the presence of Maurelle, Celina Vallier and Mademoiselle Agatha, it was solely a male gathering. If he had the right, he would clear the room forthwith, sending every grinning jackanapes who did not belong out into the streets. Any who was slow to go would be ejected by force, and he would take pleasure in doing it.

A frown gathered between Caid's brows at the violence of his reaction. Could he be jealous? No, that made no sense. He had no right, none whatever. By his own criteria, he should be the first man put into the street.

A break in the crowd allowed him a brief glimpse of Lisette. She sat on a rose brocade settee with Madame Agatha beside her and Figaro on a velvet cushion at her feet. Gowned in sumptuous black velvet, she wore a vaguely medieval headdress of some kind that featured beads of jade, rose quartz and citrine with an amethyst drop falling to the center of her forehead. The sticking plaster she had worn at her eyebrow was gone, along with the eye's redness. She appeared exotic and enticing, not at all the staid, heartbroken widow.

The small dog, Figaro, lying near her slippered feet, watched her every movement, his black eyes swimming with adoration. He was not the only one. Denys Vallier hung over the arm of her seating place, obviously in the throes of infatuation, while his friends Armand and Hippolyte appeared only slightly less enamored. He recognized a judge, Reinhardt by name, who had been a lawyer but was recently elevated to the bench, a portly gentleman who smiled down on Lisette with fatuous and unwarranted familiarity. La

Roche lounged in a tambour chair on her left hand while several others—Dorelle, Sarne and even the stolid and mother-ridden Bechet—stood around in attitudes of studied nonchalance and ill-concealed lust. Or so it seemed to Caid, though he had to admit that he was less than objective.

He really was becoming obsessed with the lady. It was an uncomfortable feeling, an uncomfortable thing to recognize.

Lisette seemed unaware of his presence, or so he thought. She did not so much as glance in his direction, much less make him welcome or inquire after his health as a means of discovering his fate on the dueling field. That studied obliviousness became suspect after a time, making him believe she preferred not to acknowledge him. She was still angry then. It mattered little; he had no need for her smiles as long as she was safe. Still he could not help wondering what form her displeasure might take later, also what method he might be forced to use to counter it.

A man bowed then turned to go, relinquishing his place in the magic circle. With the shift, Caid was able to see more of the coterie around Lisette. A stranger came into view, one of average height with the muscular grace of a swordsman, sandy hair bleached to silver-gold at the temples by the sun, regular features, a mobile mouth bracketed by grooves of amusement, and blue eyes vivid with intelligence. His manner carried the assurance of those born to high position married to an air of ease and relaxation. The last was mere pretense, however. That the gentleman knew to a precise degree every move that was made around him was something Caid would wager upon without hesitation. He didn't know him, but it wasn't difficult to guess his identity. This must be the new English swordsman, Gavin Blackford.

Caid disliked him on sight.

"Mexico has an enormous land mass and her capital is

many leagues from the Texas border," an older gentlemen standing behind Lisette was saying. "Why in the name of *le bon Dieu* should the Mexican government care what becomes of this so-young republic of Texas, much less extend itself to take it?"

"A large majority of its citizens are of Spanish blood," Nicholas observed. "No doubt the Mexican leader expects a popular uprising to swell the Mexican army and so bring victory."

"And swell the coffers in Mexico City with their taxes later," another murmured with a cynical smile.

"A nice point," Nicholas agreed. "Texas is a land of potential wealth."

"Nevertheless, pride is the real culprit in the affair," Blackford said, his voice quiet, almost reflective. "The territory was once Spanish, had been Spanish for generations. That it was taken away after it became Mexican is a stain on the national honor. To be forced to concede that it can never be regained, and by such an upstart of a nation, must be a painful thing."

"I'm sure you are correct, *monsieur*," Lisette said, her gaze thoughtful as she raised it to the Englishman. "Still, to be willing to die for such a cause seems unreasonable."

"War is but the continuation of politics by another means, or so it's been said, Madame Moisant. No reason for it exists that can be acceptable to those of a contemplative turn of mind. If more men thought before taking up arms, war as a concept might well fall into disuse."

"And what a tragedy that would be," Hippolyte said with a grin. "I would then have no opportunity to wear my uniform and strut before the ladies."

A rumble of laughter greeted that quip, but Lisette did not join in it as she turned her gaze on the young man. "You have joined the militia then?"

"Of a certainty, as have Denys and Armand. It's quite the

thing, you know. It must be, since so many of the sword masters have been before us in enlisting, even Messieurs Pasquale and O'Neill."

"Have they indeed?" She lifted a brow as she looked toward where Caid stood.

He met her eyes without flinching, though it was an effort. "It seemed politic."

"This business between Texas and Mexico isn't your quarrel."

"I have a prejudice against those who may use force to curtail the freedom of others."

A brief expression, quite unreadable, came and went across the Englishman's too-handsome face, for Caid caught it from the corner of his eye. Before Lisette could speak again, Blackford intervened.

"I should think New Orleans would sympathize with Mexico, given that its citizens were Spanish themselves a mere—what, forty years ago or less?"

"We were always more French than Spanish, even when ruled by the dons," Denys Vallier said with a trace of heat. "Now we are Americans. We fought a similar tyranny here, you know, as recently as 1814."

"English tyranny, I believe, or so you would style it. Touché, *monsieur*." Brightness that might have been laughter shone in Blackford's eyes before he inclined his head. "You make me glad my sire was not in that battle, else I might not be here now."

"I didn't mean…" young Vallier began in confusion.

"No, I'm sure of it. Rest easy, my friend. I issue no cartels over affairs long past or unintended disparagement."

The softness of the Englishman's voice grated on Caid's nerves. So did the brief smile of approval Lisette sent in that gentleman's direction. If Blackford was, by chance, here in search of fortune in the person of a wealthy bride, then he appeared to be making progress.

"So you will fight, then?" Lisette asked the young Creole.

"That is my hope." Vallier's manner was stiff.

"Why, there being no tyranny directed at you this time around?" Blackford's voice held mild curiosity, nothing more.

"Louisiana shares a border with Texas, *monsieur.* Only the narrow Sabine River separates us. In the fullness of time, so everyone assumes, this Republic of Texas will enter the union, after which the frontier of the United States will be pushed that much farther west. It seems a more fitting development than having Mexico just across the river, preventing further expansion."

"But surely your country is large enough as it now stands?"

Politics could be a dangerous subject, especially when men of different nationalities came together, Caid thought. He glanced at Lisette, wondering if she held enough sway in this salon of hers to lead the conversation into a safer subject. She made no attempt, however, but merely waited with every appearance of interest for what Vallier might answer.

"It isn't a question of size, *monsieur,* but of purpose. England has no need for Ireland, yet will not let it go."

"A matter of tradition, I believe."

"Which cannot be the case here, you mean? Perhaps not, but there are those who believe it's our destiny for our sway to reach from one sea to the other across this continent."

"Destiny," Blackford repeated in musing tones. "One must not fight that. Or fail to fight for it."

Vallier frowned, as if suspecting an unacceptable degree of irony. It was then that Lisette chose to intervene. "What brings you to New Orleans, Monsieur Blackford? And will you be with us long?"

"A small matter of business occasions my visit," he answered. "As to its length, that is uncertain."

"At least until the end of the season, I imagine?" Nicholas said, resting his elbows on the chair arm and steepling his fingers, observing Blackford over their tips. "Otherwise, you would not have taken an atelier on the Passage de la Bourse."

"You know much of my affairs, *monsieur.*" There was a question in the Englishman's voice.

Nicholas smiled. "I will be your neighbor, as it happens."

"I see. An interesting prospect."

"As you say."

The polite exchange told them nothing, which was doubtless the purpose, Caid thought. That secretiveness raised more questions, which someone among the gathering, curiosity being what it was in the city, would see settled eventually. He wouldn't mind hearing the answers himself.

"I believe, Monsieur Vallier, that you promised us a poem," Lisette said, changing the subject again with a shade of desperation in her voice.

Denys Vallier gave a self-conscious laugh. "The idea of a public reading so alarmed my muse that she has deserted me, alas. I pray you will allow Francis to read his instead."

"*Monsieur?*" she inquired, turning toward that young man. "If you will be so kind as to favor us."

Dorelle turned an alarming shade of olive-purple but did not lose his innate politeness. "I may have mentioned a poem, *madame,* but truly, it isn't worthy. Perhaps another time."

"Nonsense," she said, giving him her most persuasive smile. "Every poet must have his audience, and you are among friends here. Please, for me?"

The poor lad had obviously intended his literary effort for the lady's ears alone. Watching him with sympathy thick in his chest, Caid wondered if he'd ever been that callow, that tender and desperate for the regard of a lady. It didn't seem so, but he had also never been a pampered heir to wealth and breeding. The urge to help the boy avoid this embarrassment was strong. But then it was too late. Dorelle pulled a sheaf of papers from inside his coat and began to declaim.

It wasn't that bad, actually, a narrative poem of a man caught in an arranged marriage with a wife who cared more for frivolity and fashion than for him, but who loved her in silent desperation, silent acceptance of her flirtations with other men. Like all such epics, it ended in tragedy and a grand gesture of the sort beloved by the romantic and impressionable. When it was done, the applause was politely enthusiastic, enough so to bring a flush of pleasure to Dorelle's olive features. The discussion afterward was spirited, with several quotes from the better couplets. The conversational value of the work was soon exhausted, however.

"I am thinking of buying a carriage," Lisette announced. "Perhaps some of you gentlemen may advise me. What type should I look for, supposing I thought to drive myself?"

"How dashing of you," Maurelle said, from where she had reclined, languid and silent in her chair, until that moment.

"Not especially, I think. Many ladies in other cities drive themselves." The words were cool.

"But not in New Orleans."

"I shall set a precedent then."

"It's quite true that ladies drive in London," Blackford said. "Most are of a sporting bent, however, so on familiar terms with horses. You seem a more fragile creature, *madame,* if I may speak so boldly."

"You may not, *monsieur!*" Lisette snapped open the fan that hung on her wrist and used it to cool her cheeks. "There is nothing of the fragile about me. I would swear you have been conniving with Monsieur O'Neill to say so."

"I assure you…"

"That he has not," Caid finished in decisive tones. "Though I agree with the assessment."

Vallier, seeing a chance to earn favor, spoke up then. "I believe Madame Moisant would make an excellent whip, given the proper horse and vehicle."

"My point exactly," Lisette said with precision. "I have no wish to set myself up as a jehu of the reins, driving some great freight dray with an eight-mule team, but it isn't as if I've never been in the driver's seat—I drove many times with my father, before his death. A light equipage, perhaps a phaeton with a single fine animal, should suit me perfectly."

"If you require an escort, I should be more than happy to be of service," the young sprig said at once.

"You are all kindness, *monsieur,* but what I require is expertise."

Caid thought that one or two of the men gathered around the settee sent covert glances in his direction. It was not surprising, since he could feel the scowl that sat between his brows. He smoothed it with a forefinger while swearing beneath his breath.

"That a lady's need should go unanswered is a breach of my personal creed," Blackford said easily. "I am thought to have a fair knowledge of horseflesh. In this cause, Madame Moisant, or any other near to your heart, I am at your service."

The offer hung in the air like a too-sweet perfume. It was both gauntlet and truth wrapped in politesse, Caid thought, and impossible to resent without incurring Lisette's disfavor or starting something he had no right to finish. Pressing his lips together, Caid waited to see how she would answer.

"How very obliging of you, *monsieur,*" she said. "I shall not hesitate to take advantage of your experience—with horses, of course."

That slight innuendo was accidental Caid was sure, mainly because of the light flush that mantled Lisette's checks as she corrected it. Still, it annoyed him. With no intent whatever to interfere, he heard himself speaking. "I re-land is known for its fine horseflesh and I was brought up on a horse farm. I request the honor of joining this expedition, if I may."

"As you please, *monsieur.*"

Lisette veiled her eyes with her lashes as she spoke and her tone was lukewarm, still it was an acquiescence. It was also, Caid saw plainly, a defeat for him, since he was as certain as a man could be that a horse and carriage were the last things Lisette needed.

He did not take such setbacks lightly.

The evening wore on. Some few men left for more lively entertainment, but others arrived to take their places. It was the novelty, perhaps, for these were men who had seldom picked up anything more weighty than a news sheet since leaving their tutors. The conversation was animated, nevertheless, as the Creoles could always find subjects for discussion, and tongues were kept well lubricated by Felix who circulated with trays of claret and tafia. Intimations of a late supper in the offing drifted up from the courtyard and through doors thrown open to the mild night. Since the cook left behind by Freret, now halfway across the ocean on his way to France, was known for his skill with seafood, that may have been part of the draw. Yet Caid had to allow that much of it was purely Lisette.

She was not a managing type of hostess. Sitting at ease, she seemed simply to be enjoying her guests and the many conversations going on at once around her. Her silvery laugh came often, and now and then she engaged in quick repartee which revealed a deep vein of humor in alliance with an agile mind and wide knowledge of many things. She allowed others center stage, however, preferring subtle direction from the sidelines. She dominated no single discussion but added to many.

Her literary salon looked to be a success. Caid had been afraid of it.

"What are you looking so sour about now, *mon cher?* One would think you would be pleased to see Lisette attracting attention."

It was Maurelle, magnificent in green silk shot with gold and accented by a parure of emeralds that included necklace, earrings and a matched pair of bracelets. She strolled to his side, coming close enough so her wide skirts pressed against his half boots. He glanced down at her, suspecting mockery, but her limpid gaze was edged with something close to impatience.

"This isn't quite what I had in mind."

"I failed to see the difficulty."

"She requires a respectable alliance, not a hurried betrothal to some gamester or *fainéant* in need of a rich wife."

"Even if she enjoys their company? You must allow her to know her own preference."

"She has no preference at the moment other than to snap her fingers in my face." The words had a savage edge that he did not even try to soften.

"Then leave her alone. You are under no obligation to settle her life."

He gave a short laugh. "Unfortunately, you are in error."

Maurelle tipped her head. "You could marry her off to someone like Armand Lollain. I'm sure he would have her."

"So am I, but he's much too young. He would be her slave in less than a week."

"Not a bad thing in a husband, in my opinion." Maurelle tapped her chin with her fan. "What of Gustave Bechet?"

He gave her a pained look.

"He isn't so bad, only a little stout."

"The only way he will ever bring himself to propose is if his mother writes out a script for him."

"Which she may, considering the state of the family coffers. She is looking for a mouse of a girl who will give her a clutch of grandchildren then fade away so she may rear them as she pleases. I could always drop a hint that Lisette is the biddable sort."

"If the lady believes that then she deserves to be fooled."

"But yes," Maurelle said in tart rejoinder, "which leads me to wonder why you think she'll marry to please you."

"I don't." He had thought to exert some influence over her choice, but that wasn't the same thing. Was it?

"Whatever you expected, you will do much better at getting her off your hands and your conscience if you'll stop glowering at every man who goes near her."

"I'm not."

"Then you're doing a very good imitation."

He made no answer, in part because the comment deserved none, but also because La Roche made it unnecessary by sauntering over to join them. His arrival, as it happened, was hardly a reprieve.

"She's right, you know," the Italian sword master said. "If the look on you were any more cutting, our English friend would be bleeding now from a dozen wounds."

"That's a different matter," Caid said distinctly. "His kind put my family off their land and carted me away to prison. They are the reason my mam died sooner than need be and my sister took the ship that brought her here to her death. If I have no love for his arrogant self, it's with reason."

"None said otherwise, *mon ami*," La Roche told him, putting a hand on his arm. "But you might consider that he was elsewhere when these things happened, and most of us have our tragedies."

That was probably true, but Caid was in no mood for logic. He only shook his head.

"Let it go, *cher*," Maurelle said in an undertone audible only to the three of them. "This is nothing you can control, nor should you. It's Lisette life, her future that is being decided. You're a fine man, but you can have none of either."

He could not argue with a lady in public, so he did the only thing left to him. He turned and walked away. Still, her words settled, a hard, burning knot, in the center of his chest.

It was a short time later that Caid, half attending to an argument between Denys and his friends over the merits of the rival gaming houses, noticed a flurry among the ladies. He turned in time to see Lisette, with Maurelle and Celina, rise and make her way from the salon. Their destination, he suspected, was the bedchamber set aside as a retiring room for female guests; it seemed the custom for such withdrawals of the ladies to be made en masse. Bowing out of the circle of youngbloods, he moved in their wake with unhurried purpose.

He reached the gallery in time to see a skirt flounce disappear into the bedchamber at its far end before the door closed, leaving him in darkness. A post wrapped in leafless wisteria vines made a black shadow at the corner just beyond, where the *garçonnière* was joined to the main house. Caid eased into that concealment, put his back to the post and waited.

Maurelle and Celina emerged after some few moments. So engrossed were they in a story involving two Mississippi planters, their wives and mistaken hotel rooms that they failed to even glance in his direction. Lisette was not long behind them. Caid gave a silent grunt of satisfaction as he saw her appear with a maid trailing behind her while she issued instructions over her shoulder. He had depended on Lisette to take this opportunity to oversee the conitinued comfort of her guests.

As the maid started off down the gallery to carry out orders, he stepped out of the darkness. Lisette swung toward him in a swirl of black velvet. She caught a sharp breath then stood perfectly still while the lamplight behind her shimmered in the folds of her gown, gleamed with pearl-like luster across the gentle curves at the low neckline of her gown, caught the jewel that dangled in the center of her forehead.

"Yes?"

Her calm self-possession was convenient, since he had no wish to draw attention, but obscurely annoying all the same. For long seconds, Caid could not recall what had been so important that he must seek her out. Then he stepped around to close the bedchamber door. Grasping her elbow, he drew her deeper into the shadows before he spoke in low demand. "What do you think you're doing?"

"I beg your pardon?"

"Are you trying to set up as a courtesan? If so, you're making a fine job of it."

"Thank you," she said in tones breathless with either anger or amusement, or possibly both. "Am I to assume that you don't care for my guests? Or can it be my gown?"

He had not intended to be so blunt, but something about the evening and her manner drove him to it. With a swift but comprehensive glance at her velvet, he answered, "There's nothing wrong with what you're wearing."

"Yet you find it provocative?"

"I didn't say that. In fact, it's quite becoming. So is this bauble." He reached with a hard finger to flick the ornament on her brow. "What I object to is the number of men circling around you."

She was quiet for an instant. Then a smile flitted over her face. "I am quite alone here with you."

"You know what I mean." He waved an arm in the direction of the salon.

"I can't help who attends, you know. An evening such as this isn't by invitation alone but allows friends to bring others of like mind. Besides, it's your fault."

"Mine?"

"Most of those here are your friends or their connections." She tipped her head. "If there is a dearth of ladies, it must be because you number so few among your acquaintance."

He could hardly argue that point. "You don't have to be quite so…so forthcoming."

"With the gentlemen, you mean. Who else am I to talk to, if you please? You, perhaps?"

"Hardly. I am no suitor."

"I must sit in the corner waiting like a spider for an eligible *parti* then. I suppose I may be as active as I like in ensnaring him."

"Don't be ridiculous." The words were an exasperated growl.

"Then I see no alternative except to go on as I've been doing."

"You may wind up in a situation you won't relish. Most men are predators behind their smiles and bows. They require only minimal encouragement to act the part."

She lifted her chin. "You included, I suppose."

"Especially me."

Hard on the words, he reached for her, pulling her against him. Her velvet softness, her warmth and scented splendor, acted like flame to tinder. He took her mouth with a hungry sound deep in his throat, drowning in the rich, wine-sweet intoxication, the honeyed depths. He wanted to plunder her like a flower's heart, to drink her like nectar. And he would, this once.

He had been looking for an excuse, he saw with distant self-knowledge. Anything would have done.

She leaned into his grasp so her breasts pressed against his chest. The sensation was maddening. Without thought or intention, he slid his hand to her waist then upward to close it on the velvet-cushioned resilience of one soft mound. She jerked with a gasp that feathered across his lips and tongue before he captured it, swallowed it. Mindless with the need to possess, he cradled her flesh, found and kneaded the hard nipple beneath its cloth covering. Releasing her mouth, he bent his head, nuzzled the tender line of her throat with his lips, trailed hot kisses over her collarbone before brushing his eyelids and eyelashes over the straining fullness he pushed above the edge of her bodice. Then he buried his mouth in the fragile and delicious valley.

The gratification was so intense that it was a second before he realized she had shifted to slip her hand inside his evening coat, burrowing under his waistcoat. She spread her fingers, pressing her palm to the ridges of muscle that covered his rib cage, sliding higher to those padding his chest. She smoothed over his skin covered only by thin linen, flexing her fingers, drawing together a fistful of his shirt as she curled them into a knot. And it seemed she captured the center of his being, gathered the very essence of him and made it hers to the last, shatteringly violent beat of his heart.

The shock of it brought his head up, cleared the fog from his brain. He released his hold and stepped away from her grasp. Taking her hand as it slipped free, he carried it to his lips, closing his eyes as he brushed the skin in wordless contrition.

From the salon along the way came the murmur of voices, the clink of crystal and melodious chime of a clock. A night breeze rustled the dry twining of vines on the post close by. Somewhere, a night watchman called. Caid sighed and released her as he put several feet of distance between them.

"Accept my most abject apologies," he began.

"Not at all," she answered, her voice brittle and not quite even. "Am I to suppose this is another of your lessons?"

"Rather, another of my mistakes."

"I do see the point of it."

What she meant he was not sure, but he did not intend to risk finding out. Inclining his head, he answered, "As long as we understand each other."

Her short laugh held an edge of pain. "Unlikely."

What could he say that would not make matters worse?

Caid bowed again. She gazed at him for long seconds there in the dark, then turned abruptly and swept away down the gallery. He watched her until she reached the salon and stepped inside. And with every click of her heeled slippers that echoed back to him, he whispered a curse.

9

Lisette sent the lightweight phaeton spinning along the top of the levee while elation bloomed inside her. The carriage was beautifully balanced, with its wicker body lacquered dark blue and tufted seat upholstered in soft velvet. The top used to protect against sun and rain could be folded back when not required and there was a small groom's seat in back. The gray gelding that she had chosen with the help of Caid and Gavin Blackford was a sweet-tempered animal with a stride like satin. Everything was exactly as she had pictured it, in fact, and she was immensely grateful to Blackford for his help in finding the rig. Well, and to Caid, also, though his aid had been so grudging that it hardly counted.

What an uncomfortable excursion to the carriage maker and stables that had been, even with the addition of Maurelle to their company. The two gentlemen had been so determined to disagree on what she required that she had finally accepted Blackford's choice of carriage and the horse Caid suggested, simply to keep the peace. Not that either was a bad bargain; she was ecstatic with her purchases.

Thank heaven she was finally away from the promenade area of the levee and the docks where she'd had to weave in and out among drays with their mule teams and stevedores rolling barrels while avoiding the gangplanks and bowsprits of vessels. She needed untrammeled space in which to grow accustomed to handling the reins and also to get the feel of the rakish little phaeton. The equipage she had driven in the country had been much more staid, an ancient mare and a heavier phaeton that had been a relic from her father's salad days. Not that there was a tremendous amount of room for error here. The yellowish-brown Mississippi in near flood stage made a mile-wide millrace along one side of the levee track, while the other was lined with warehouses, long sturdy brick buildings sitting cheek by jowl with log and mud structures that must have been standing since the last century. These were slowly giving way to shacks and shanties that would eventually cease, fading away into swampland.

She was alone, which was rather daring. The occupants of the shanties were not known for abiding by the law or even recognizing that it existed. The swamplike woods harbored runaway slaves and those who followed Doctor John and his Voodoo practices. Still, she had not cared to put Agatha or even Felix at risk by taking either of them up with her for this practice drive. To overturn them, cracking a head or a limb, would be too awful to contemplate. She did not intend to go far, so should be safe enough. And it was wonderful to be completely alone. Agatha was a lovely person and she enjoyed her company, but these few minutes of privacy were precious.

The gray was so well trained that she need only hold him steady on the levee roadway and watch for anything that might serve to distract him. Her mind wandered to her salon of a few nights ago. That it had been a success gave her a warm sense of pride. She had feared no one would put in an appearance. Whether they would continue to attend was another question altogether, of course, but she had hopes that they might. For this, she was indebted to Caid and his friends, she knew. The partisanship of the sword masters, the fact that she was deemed worthy of their attention, had made her the fashion for the moment, at least among the faster set. The more staid would no doubt look askance at this sign of favor.

Lisette didn't care. Circumspection was not something that concerned her overmuch at present. That fact seemed to disturb Caid, which would be amusing if it weren't so frustrating. She could not seem to make him understand that she cared nothing for the social censure of the *ton*. Why should she when those in its inner circle had abandoned her once she entered the Moisant household? If she preferred to live now as if they scarcely existed, it was only to be expected. As for proving that she was competent to handle her own affaires, surely the establishment of her household should be sufficient?

How very interested Caid had been at her Bohemian airs and especially the male attention she had garnered. And that attempt of his to bring the dangers home of them to her? She felt a little light-headed at the mere thought.

Surely there was something more than a lesson behind his kiss in the dark—a man did not behave so recklessly unless driven by strong emotion. She would not deceive herself that the sword master was in love with her, of course, but it was plain that he felt some modicum of desire. Such a conquest was the kind women whispered of behind their fans before using them to cool their cheeks, a liaison of unusual excitement. Not that it was a cause for pride in it, she knew, since it had no discernible future.

Caid O'Neill rejected the title of gentleman, yet must have more of that quality in his makeup than he claimed. If not, he would assuredly have encroached further during those moments in the gallery. That she would have stopped him was unlikely. Or was it really? She hardly knew. What she was sure of was that she had felt no inclination in that direction. His touch seemed to banish thought, replacing it with purest sensation; he swept aside her defenses with scant effort. The strength and the power he wielded so deftly in his chosen sphere were fascinating to a troubling degree.

It would be dangerously easy to become infatuated if she weren't careful.

Abruptly, the gray shied as a cat dashed across the road

in front of him. Lisette reined him in with precision and care while chastising herself for a lack of wit. It would be far better if she reined in her wandering thoughts, as well, concentrating on the levee track.

The day was somewhat overcast, which made it pleasantly cool. The breeze off the river was fresh in spite of its smell of mud and decaying vegetation, and brisk enough to make the veil that protected her face lift and flutter around her shoulders. From the woods came the tantalizing fragrance of yellow jessamine along with the calls of birds and occasional chatter of a squirrel. The rhythmic thudding of the gray's hooves was calming, lulling Lisette into a near trance.

Ahead of her lay a rutted track leading down from the levee. She was moving so quickly that it was impossible to tell if it offered room to turn her rig. Hauling on the reins, she slowed the gray but not in good time. The phaeton swept past the lane before she could pull him to a halt. To back the gray on the narrow roadway was not something she cared to undertake at this stage. There seemed nothing for it except to go on.

She had not intended to come so far, would not have if she had realized how quickly the swampy growth would encroach once the town disappeared behind her or how scarce would be the places wide enough for her to swing the rig around for the return journey. Apprehension began to seep into her bloodstream. Possibly Caid had been right, and driving herself was a foolish notion. Irritation and the urge to be individual could well have led her into a chancy situation.

Rounding a bend which followed the sweep of the river, she saw well ahead of her another worn dirt track leading down from the levee. She held her breath as she closed the distance. With luck, it might lead to a plantation which would have a front drive planned for turning carriages. She slowed the gray to a walk, searching the waterlogged wood-land, hoping for the glimpse of a dwelling.

She could see nothing. With little idea of when the next opportunity might appear, however, she took a deep breath then guided the gray carefully down the steep levee bank and along the ruts which lead into the trees.

The still dankness of the swampland closed in around her. Few sounds could be heard beyond the rattle and squeak of the carriage and thud of the gray's hooves in the soft dirt. The rutted track seemed to be following a slight ridge from which spread a muddy bog shaded by giant cypress, gums, maples and willows, with here and there a spreading oak on an ancient shell mound. A rank growth of vines and palmetto mixed with fern and moss lined the edges to present an al-most impenetrable barrier. As she drew farther away from the river with no sign of a house, Lisette began to fear that she might have made matters worse instead of righting them. There was certainly no way of turning the carriage with the woods crowding so close around her.

All manner of thoughts flitted through her head, from the action she might take if a wheel dropped into one of the holes in the road and splintered an axle, to what she would do if the gray took it into his head to bolt. The horse seemed a lit-tle unnerved by the deserted byway, or else sensed her trepidation. He shied at a butterfly that swooped near his nose and pulled away from an uprooted dead tree that swung, creaking, in a tangle of wild grapevines draped halfway across the miserable excuse for a road. He tried to balk at crossing a fetid stretch of water that was half creek, half slough then had to be urged up the far side.

Abruptly, he reared in the shafts, neighing in shrill terror. Lisette braced her feet on the footboard as she wrestled with him. Her arms felt as if they were being pulled from their sockets. Her bonnet was knocked askew as she was jerked from side to side. She called to the gray, trying to keep her voice steady and even. Finally he began to calm, coming to a standstill. Glancing ahead then, she saw the long black shape of the water moccasin in the roadway that had spooked the horse.

From her seat, it was impossible to tell if the snake was alive or dead. There was no one to hold the gray's head while she got down to see, and he was too fractious to risk it otherwise. Looking around, she sought something, anything, to fling at the reptile to try moving him from his place. There was nothing. Her only weapon was the small whip that stood in its socket with its lash tip wrapped around it.

Reaching for the whip, she snapped it with a loud crack. The gray reared in the shafts once more, startled by the common sound in his nervous state. She dropped the whip and grabbed the reins with both hands, calling, fighting him again. In the same moment, she thought she caught a flicker of movement in the woods to her right.

The carriage rocked, jibing back and forth. The gray reared again and again, trying to bolt. Lisette's hands and shoulders burned, aching as she held him. The snake had not moved in spite of the gray's hooves trampling around it. It was dead, without doubt. She feared that its presence in the road was part of a trap, was afraid that a man, or even more than one, might appear from the dense undergrowth at any second. She could just catch a crackling sound among the mats of dried leaves under the trees, and vague movements like shadows shifting.

It was then that she heard the rapid tattoo of hoofbeats. They came from behind her, traveling fast. She flung a quick glance over her shoulder, and then gasped in mingled relief and vexation.

It was Caid on a tall bay stallion, riding as if a part of the great animal. His mount dropped from a fast canter to a walk as he came nearer, picking his way across the slough before Caid pulled him up beside the phaeton. "Trouble, Madame Moisant?"

"Obviously," she said through set teeth. "And if you dare to say I told you so, I shall…I shall scream."

"I don't advise it, not unless you want to pick yourself up out of that mud hole back there." He glanced at the gray. "Your horse seems disinclined to go on. Shall I turn him for you?"

"If you are able." The words were ungracious, she knew, but all she could manage at the moment.

"Nothing easier."

He stepped from the saddle and tethered the reins to a handy sweet gum sapling. Moving to the gray's head, he caught the headstall and stood speaking to the animal in low tones with the musical lilt of Ireland while he smoothed a hand down his neck. After a moment, its shivering stopped and its ears pricked forward. Then Caid backed him bit by bit, led him forward and backed him again until the phaeton was facing the way Lisette had come.

She half expected Caid to tie his stallion to the back of the vehicle then swing up onto the seat beside her to take the lines. Some part of her would have been glad of it, regardless of the blow to her pride. He did nothing of the kind, but merely remounted and moved up even with where she sat.

For long seconds he said nothing, but only stared at her with a dark, assessing gaze. Lisette was suddenly aware of how isolated they were here, miles from any sign of habitation. She recognized, too, how tall and broad he was as he sat his horse, the strength of his hands on the reins and the flexing of the powerful muscles of his thighs under the smooth cloth of his pantaloons as he controlled the bay.

Heat invaded her midsection, leaving her breathless and achingly vulnerable. She could not look away from the dark blue of his eyes, was unable to move or marshal coherent thought. Some distant portion of her mind accepted that if he should reach for her, touch her, kiss her at this moment, she would not resist him.

And she was abruptly reminded of the small bottle of love potion from the hairdresser Marie Laveau which had finally been delivered to the town house the evening before. What would really happen if she should find the chance to use it? Would he call a halt to his kiss, or anything else, then?

"Shall we?" he asked, his voice a low rasp in his throat.

She was at a loss as to his meaning for a fleeting instant. Then she saw that he was waiting for her to set the phaeton in motion. She gave a swift nod and gingerly slapped the lines on the gray's rump. They started off.

Regardless, the fine trembling of reaction coursed through her. She was forced to take several deep breaths to calm herself and prevent her unsettled state from communicating itself to the gray again.

A short while later, when they had recrossed the slough and almost reached the main road again, she turned in her seat to stare back the way they had come. Nothing moved among the trees. Facing forward, she called to Caid above the rattle of the carriage, "Did you see anything in the woods back there just now?"

He sent her a narrow glance. "Did you?"

"I believe so, though it may have been my imagination."

"Unlikely."

It was gratifying that he accepted her word. "You think it possible?"

"You are an attractive woman who appeared to be alone on this deserted road. Easy prey is hard to resist for the kind who make their home here."

It was a reminder of his comment about predators that night on the gallery. A shiver rippled down her spine, though she did her best to conceal it. "Then I must be grateful that you came after me."

"Must you?" he asked with the ghost of a smile, as if he knew full well how difficult it was for her to acknowledge her appreciation.

"I am indebted to you." Having forced herself to speak the words, she discovered that they were profoundly true.

"Not at all. I swore an oath to look out for you."

"I suppose you were watching me, so knew where I had gone."

"I prefer to think of it as watching over you. To protect you adequately would be difficult otherwise."

Dull color had appeared under his sun-bronzed skin. Was it from anger or embarrassment? She could not tell, but was unlikely to misconstrue his interest in spite of the fact that he had called her attractive. "I suppose I should be glad you had no dawn encounters arranged."

"I wondered when you would come to that point."

"What point is that?"

"Taking me to task for the challenge to Vigneaud."

"And Quentell. You should not forget him, even if he did decide that flight was the better part of valor. Though I cannot think how you could fail to see that the serious injury or death of either man would be forever on my conscience."

He reined in closer so she need not raise her voice so much above the noise of phaeton and horse hooves. "It would not rest on yours, but on mine."

"Your own injury or death, as well?" she asked with waspish exactitude. "That would be difficult."

"Now why do I have such trouble believing you would care?"

"I cannot guess, unless it's that you know me less than you believe."

He turned his head to stare at her an instant before facing forward again. "Indeed, and that is how it must stay."

This was becoming rather too personal, even she recognized that. "Perhaps your protection isn't necessary after all. What I mean to say is, Eugene's father has given no sign that he means me any harm other than spreading falsehoods. Could be he is resigned to my departure."

"What if he isn't?"

"You can't be thinking of today? He could not have known I would come this way or take that particular track. To have someone intercept me…"

"Would be improbable, yes," he interrupted. "That wasn't my meaning."

She gave him a quick look while guiding the gray around a particularly large mud hole. "Then?"

"Moisant's lack of activity doesn't mean he's no longer a threat. He could be simply playing it close to his chest. When you are lulled into a feeling of security, then he may strike."

"A pleasant thought," she said with a grimace. "I wish there was some way to be sure what he intends."

"No more than I do, I assure you."

They had regained the levee. Lisette encouraged the gray up the incline, acutely conscious all the while of Caid sitting his horse at the top, watching her performance. At least he seemed to find nothing to criticize. It was only when they were moving back toward town at a steady clip that she spoke again.

"I did not realize what a wearisome duty it would be for you when I requested that you keep me safe."

"Think nothing of it."

"But I do. To know that you are going without sleep while I'm tucked up in my bed weighs heavily, I assure you."

"It's the least I can do after…your loss."

To speak of Eugene's death as if it were a true bereavement was more than she could manage just now. What was required was a diversion. "Does it never trouble you, the results of your duels?"

"Are you asking if I have regrets, particularly concerning your husband's death?"

"If you will."

It was a long moment before he answered, then his voice

was abrupt. "It seems to have been somewhat unfair in retrospect."

"Because of your greater skill?" She risked a glance at Caid where he cantered beside her. His face was set, his expression guarded.

"Some would call it legalized murder, I suppose. The news of Brona's, my sister's, death was too fresh, too... painful for me to see it that way at the time."

"And now?"

"Now I wonder."

She had suspected it. It was nothing he had said or done but only a fleeting shadow seen once or twice on his stern features. The urge to alleviate that ritual guilt was a hard lump inside her. She could do it with a few words if she cared to take the risk.

"Eugene...my husband..." she began.

"Yes?"

How could she speak? She could not afford to have Caid turn from her, not yet. "He...was not without fault," she continued almost at random. "But why put yourself in the position where the injury or death of an opponent is inevitable unless you fall yourself?"

"It's required."

Like her, he seemed to have several things he was unwilling to discuss, but that did not mean she was required to refrain from questioning him. "More so for a sword master than for any other?"

"Possibly, yet what else am I to do?" he asked with a rough edge to his voice.

"I'm sure I don't know, but there must be some other occupation suited to your skills."

"Name one."

She applied thought to the problem, then smiled. "You are good with animals, particularly horses. I suspect you know something about farming methods, as well."

"So I should seek a position as an overseer?"

"Or borrow the money to establish your own plantation."

"I would hardly be considered a sound investment risk. Besides, I have an engrained dislike for profiting from bondage."

The sentiment did him credit, certainly, but would be deemed impractical by most, if not impossibly idealistic. Men of strength and wealth had used the labor of others from the beginning of time. The worker who toiled for next to nothing was hardly less exploited than the slave who at least had a roof over his head and food in his belly. "They say there is land to be had for the taking in Texas, and you were brought up on a horse farm for you said as much yourself."

"Years ago, when I was but a lad. We had hunters, in the main, though a few were bred for the racetrack. But I'm no longer a horseman."

"I wouldn't say that," she answered with a brief glance at his seat on the bay, so easy that he seemed at one with the beast like some centaur of old. "What changed matters? The Corn Laws?"

"The very same, that took away the open grasslands common to all and turned good horsemen into potato farmers. But what do you know of Irish matters?"

She gave him a sardonic smile. "My studies included a bit more than embroidery and penmanship. Agatha was hired to give an elegant appearance to my letters but had ever an interest in European events and favored Aristotle's teaching methods of discussion and debate."

"An interesting woman, Mademoiselle Stilton."

"Indeed, but you are avoiding the question, I think."

"That being?"

She was not to be put off by a pretense of obtuseness. "Why you persist in living by the sword if you don't care for the results?"

"I am that mad for the feel of my sword sliding into the vitals of another human being. Who would not be?"

She was now supposed to be shocked into silence by his crudity. The distressing thing, however, was the real pain in his voice. "How do you force yourself to it if it disturbs you so much?"

"Self-preservation and a strong dislike for being taken for a coward."

"And if the time comes when these goads are not enough?"

He met her intent gaze, his own dark. "That's the question, isn't it? A swordsman without nerve is nothing."

She returned her attention to her driving as she considered it. She had thought him callous, or at least inured to the pain of others as well as his own. To suspect that he might be the exact opposite was strange.

After a moment, she said, "It does sound a bit chancy, to be reluctant to make the home thrust when someone is trying diligently to kill you."

"You have it exactly," he said, then kicked the bay into a gallop and rode on ahead.

In the event, he did not go far, but only to where a break showed in the trees. Returning, he pulled up beside her, and Lisette drew the gray to a halt, as well.

"I must leave you. It's bad enough for you to be seen returning from an outing with no female companion or groom, much less adding my presence. You will be all right from here?"

"I know my way very well, thank you."

"I meant," he began, then stopped, closing his lips into a tight line before he began again. "We shall meet again soon, I expect. In the meantime, take care. Don't let down your guard for an instant."

Swinging the bay back toward town, he rode away at a brisk trot. Lisette stared after him with a frown between her brows. Then she lifted the reins and bowled into the dock area and the Vieux Carré with as much élan as she could bring to the performance.

Felix met her at the foot of the town house stairs, watching with an anxious frown as she guided the gray gelding through the *porte cochère* and into the courtyard. She passed her reins to the stable boy who came running and got down, then began to tug off her driving gloves. "Well?" she asked with a trace of humor in her voice. "What calamity has befallen now?"

"You have a visitor, *madame*." He paused to take her gloves, bonnet and short driving cape. "Mademoiselle Agatha is entertaining her in the salon."

"Her?"

"Madame Herriot. I tried to tell her you were not at home, but she insisted she would wait."

"Thank you, Felix. Please say I'll join her as soon as I make myself tidy." Lisette tarried a few seconds to give instructions to the stable boy about caring for the gray then went quickly up the stairs.

"Madame Herriot, what a pleasant surprise," she said as she entered the salon moments later. "I would have remained at home had I known you would pay us a visit."

"Not at all, *chère*," Maurelle replied with a wave of her hand. "Mademoiselle Agatha and I have passed the time quite comfortably."

A tea tray sat on a table near the settee, along with another holding *eau sucrée*, or sweetened water, and a plate of small cakes topped with candied violets. Without asking, Agatha poured an extra cup of tea for Lisette. She took it with gratitude, then seated herself on the tambour chair. An awkward pause fell that was broken as they all three began at once.

"I trust you have been…"

"Your salon was most…"

"Madame Herriot was just saying…"

They all stopped at the same time, as well. After a small exercise in mutual politeness, Madame Herriot, as the guest, was left with the floor.

"I only meant to say that I've heard nothing except the most glowing compliments for your salon. I believe you may consider it to have been a success of the most formidable."

"How very kind of you to say so." Lisette sipped her tea to hide her gratification.

"No, no, I assure you. There are always those who disparage anything new, calling it too *outré*, but they were not there, did not experience this so charming evening."

"You don't feel with Monsieur O'Neill that I am teetering on the brink of social ruin?"

"La, that Caid." Lisette's guest shook her head so that the plumes on her hat swayed back and forth. "As with most who have scant respectability, he exaggerates its value. He is concerned that you should do nothing which might cause those who matter to give you the cold shoulder or prevent you from contracting a suitable alliance when your mourning is at an end."

"Scant respectability?"

"As he would be the first to tell you."

"I understand from Caid that his family bred horses in days gone by. I should think that would suppose considerable acreage and a certain amount of leisure."

"Indeed?" Agatha put in. "I heard him mention horses but thought his family might have worked upon some squire's estate or for a landlord."

"Apparently not."

"That doesn't make him of the gentry, of course."

"Or prevent it."

Maurelle Herriot frowned as if she disliked the idea that Lisette might know more than she about the sword master. "Still, I believe they had turned to growing potatoes by the time Caid was old enough to remember, so suffered reverses during bad years for the crop. These mounting losses eventually caused confiscation of their land by some English milord as well as the burning of their home. Caid was hardly more than thirteen at the time, and active with a group of men who sought to resist the encroachment of English interests. He was arrested and sent away to prison."

"So he told me," Lisette said quietly, while Agatha made a small sound of distress.

"A great barbarity, is it not? Yet these things happen."

Speaking of Caid's past was fascinating, but it felt strange, almost a betrayal, to be discussing him behind his back. "Nonetheless, I fail to see why he should have such concern for what is said about me when I do not."

"If he had not taken the life of your husband, then you would not be in your present position. Then something of it may come from the fate of his sister, a woman alone in the world and fallen from grace. He failed her, or so he believes, though he was half a world away at the time and without means of coming to her rescue until it was too late. And he is also cursed with extreme notions of responsibility which lead him to feel that he must protect all women, but especially those with some connection to him."

Agatha gave their visitor a straight look. "A fine thing in a man, as I'm sure you will agree?"

"Of a certainty, but uncomfortable at times."

"You knew his sister perhaps?" Lisette asked.

"Unfortunately not." Maurelle lifted a shoulder. "She was not…that is to say, she moved in circles other than my own."

"Circles?" Agatha asked, her voice as cool as her New England homeland.

"She arrived on a packet boat some three years ago, I believe, like so many other of her kind. You realize that the Irish have been pouring into the city for twenty years and more, recruited as laborers for the digging of the Basin Canal. They come, they work, and they die like flies from fevers and sunstroke, being unused to our climate."

"I am aware," Agatha said austerely.

She would be of course, Lisette thought, since she had been in the city nearly twenty years herself, since being abandoned there by her lover. But Maurelle was not to know that.

"But surely women like Caid's sister were not put to work with pick and shovel?" her companion went on.

Lisette barely registered the question. Figaro had suddenly begun to bark like mad downstairs at the wicket gate. Rising to her feet, she paced to the window to glance out. It took only a second to find the reason. The gang of street boys that she had seen while shopping had congregated across the way. It was not the first time they had taken up a position there, sitting on the lintel or lying on the flagstones in front of the *boulangerie* that occupied the ground floor. It was odd, since that side of the street was in the sun at this hour, though she thought the attraction could be the day-old bread the baker gave them on occasion.

"By no means," Madame Herriot said with horror in her voice as the conversation continued behind Lisette. "I suspect she came with a man who died, leaving her alone to make her way. Caid prefers to think otherwise, that she came intending to hire herself out as a laundress or seamstress, perhaps. Whatever her reason, she met a gentleman instead, one who made her his mistress."

"My husband," Lisette said without inflection as she turned to rejoin the other two women.

"*Vraiment.* He cared for her as long as she was fresh and no trouble to him, but put her out of the house he had bought for her when the situation altered."

The version of the story told by Maurelle was not strictly accurate in its details but Lisette saw no point in correcting it. Time enough for that later, when things were settled and she felt a little braver.

"It's quite understandable that Monsieur O'Neill would be incensed when he learned of it," Agatha said as the silence stretched past what was comfortable.

Their guest sipped her sugared water. "Moisant was made to pay for his misdeeds, yes, but that fact did nothing to relieve the weight of guilt Caid feels. This has bearing on your circumstances, you see, Madame Moisant. He feels you also suffered at the hands of your husband. He was too late to save his sister, but it has become a necessity with him, and a point of honor, to make everything right for you."

What Madame Herriot was saying, Lisette suddenly realized, was that there was nothing personal in Caid O'Neill's concern for her welfare. This was probably quite correct and as it should be. However, the two of them were bound by the past and the fact that he had saved her from the less than tender mercy of Henri Moisant. She owed Caid something for that and for what had been done to his sister. She paid her debts.

"How noble," Agatha was saying, a flush riding high on her thin cheekbones. "One is always surprised to discover such sentiments when so often the emotions which animate the breasts of men are quite…quite otherwise."

"You have much right, Mademoiselle Agatha," Maurelle said with a sigh. "But it appears that someone has begun to redress this imbalance between men of honor and those of more animalistic tendencies. Have you heard? Monsieur Lamotile was found severely injured from what appeared to have been an impromptu duel with an unknown assailant. In the dirt next to him was slashed the letter *V* and a short phrase."

"And the phrase was?" Agatha asked as the lady stopped and gazed at them expectantly.

"Wife beater. Amazing, *n'est-ce pas?*"

"Certainly it's odd," Lisette said as she took her seat again.

"Oh, we have all heard of a woman's father or brother taking the husband to task in this way, but to make it so public? La, what can it mean?"

"Perhaps it wasn't meant to be public but only a warning for the gentleman that was discovered before it could be erased?"

"Yes, but why was the affair not carried out like a normal meeting?"

It was Agatha who answered, a thoughtful look on her thin face. "It underscores the nature of the meeting as a punishment, or so it seems to me."

"But yes," Maurelle said. "Not that other such affairs of honor are conducted on a high moral plane."

They exchanged rueful smiles then sat quietly for a moment. Lisette, driven by curiosity and an odd presentiment, said then, "Nevertheless, one wonders who the other duelist may have been."

"Someone of more skill than is usual, obviously, since Monsieur Lamotile was known as quite a competent swordsman."

"How came you by these details?" Agatha asked.

Maurelle shrugged. "The news passes. A man's valet speaks of it to another servant. It is overheard by a ladies' maid who speaks of it to another that she sees while attending her mistress at some ball, then that one regales her lady with the tale while brushing her hair. So it goes."

"Yes, I see. But a man of skill, you said. Might it not be a sword master?"

"Anything is possible." Maurelle lifted thin, high brows. "But not every *maître d'armes* has Caid's tender conscience. More likely, it was someone who knew the woman but had no particular right to take her husband to task. Or else he took Monsieur Lamotile by surprise so prefers not to acknowledge the deed."

"What does this Lamotile say about the matter?"

"He isn't talking. I believe he has left town on a visit to his country plantation, leaving his wife in possession of the town house."

"Not precisely a permanent solution," Lisette said with a shake of her head. "Such men are not reasonable in their anger. What if he blames the wife for his pain, not to mention his embarrassment? Can she expect this Good Samaritan to continue to protect her?"

"You believe the man who intervened should have made a final job of it?" Maurelle's gaze was direct as she waited for an answer.

"I didn't say that."

"You implied it, *chère.* One might almost suppose you did not object to the fate of your husband."

What was she to say to that? Lisette wondered. To deny it would be a lie, to admit it a solecism which might be repeated until it echoed in every salon in New Orleans.

Before she could fashion an answer, Agatha spoke up. "I'm sure every woman has wished at some time or other to be free of her marital ties. It's human nature to chafe at restraint in any form."

"Even I have felt this impulse," Maurelle said with a wry smile. "But we must take care how we go about it, you understand. For a woman, only a fine line lies between freedom and ruin."

"Are you suggesting—" Lisette began in some irritation.

"I am saying that to chance ruin for sufficient reason is well enough, but to achieve it might have the opposite effect from the one intended."

Behind the woman's indolent manner lay surprising shrewdness, Lisette thought. "I will endeavor to remember that, should the need arise."

Maurelle lowered her lashes, making no reply as she sipped her *eau sucrée.*

It was then, as silence descended upon them, that they heard the jangle of the wicket gate bell.

10

"Monsieur Pasquale, *madame*."

Felix, having announced the new arrival, stepped aside so he might enter the salon. Lisette rose to greet Caid's friend, giving him her hand. She felt the brush of his lips across her knuckles as he bowed, then straightened with a smile calculated to melt the most hardened of hearts. Agatha sat forward in her chair, coloring warmly as she was greeted in form in her turn. Maurelle put aside her glass as she beamed upon the newcomer, acknowledging his obeisance.

"How fortunate it is that you are here," Lisette said, indicating that La Roche should take the larger chair where she had been seated while she moved to perch on the edge of a spindle chair with a woven cane seat. "You are just the man we need."

"I live to be of service to lovely ladies," he said, though a wary look appeared on his face. Brushing aside the full skirt of his deep green frock coat, he seated himself with lithe grace.

"I don't mean in a personal way, of course."

"Such a disappointment."

That lamentation, as with much of what the Italian said, was mere flirtation by rote; he did it because it was expected. He lacked the self-consciously salacious air of a true womanizer, or so Lisette had come to think. His manner was too tender, with too much concern. Once or twice, she thought she had seen the shadow of past pain in his eyes in repose, though it vanished quickly enough when one spoke to him.

"We were just discussing this mysterious duel in which a certain gentleman was chastised for mistreating his wife," Lisette went on. "Have you knowledge of it?"

"I've heard the rumors." Taking the glass of claret that Felix poured for him, La Roche merely held it without sipping from it.

"But you have no firsthand knowledge?"

A smile flickered over his handsome countenance. "You are direct, *madame*. Do you suspect me of the deed—but no, you would not ask me if you thought I was this gallant."

"We did wonder if he might be a *maître d'armes*." She looked to Agatha and Maurelle for support before she went on. "It seems he must have similar expertise, else how could he be certain of exacting a lesson instead of receiving one."

"Let us hope others are not of the same turn of mind," Nicholas said with irony. "Or we may have the gendarmes visiting in the Passage. It's my opinion that your man must be a gentleman of leisure. It's the only way he could get around to the number of duels he's said to have fought."

"There have been others?"

La Roche struck his head with the heel of his hand. "My accursed tongue. Forget I said anything, if you please."

"Impossible, and you know it. How many of these meetings have occurred?"

"No one is putting notices of them in *L'Abeille,* you understand, but I've heard tell of three or four."

"A daring gentleman," Maurelle said thoughtfully. "What can have set him off?"

"Who can say?" The Italian shielded his gaze with his scandalously long lashes as he sipped at his wine.

Agatha pursed her lips. "So we are left to guess. How very disappointing."

"Yes, but if he is a gentleman of the *ton*," Lisette said with a frown, "then it stands to reason that he cannot be a family man as he would hardly risk leaving a wife and family without his support. And he must be seasoned at the duel, or a veteran of the fencing strips at the very least, else he would lack the necessary skill. He can hardly be above forty years, either, as excellent physical trim must be a prerequisite."

"You seem to have spent considerable thought on the subject." Humor twinkled in the darkness of the sword master's eyes.

"It's the puzzle of it, you see," Lisette said, "one much too fascinating to be left alone."

"Take care. Next thing you know, people will be saying that you enjoy thinking."

She gave him a wan smile as she reached for her teacup. "That would never do, now would it?"

Sitting forward a little, Agatha said, "I have every sympathy for those whom this savior with a sword would avenge, but the business seems underhanded to me. Most gentlemen prefer an audience for these affairs, if only to make certain there are no charges of unacceptable behavior."

"The very thing the *code duello* with all its rules was designed to prevent." La Roche gave a nod of agreement.

"What does it say that it's all done in secret then? I fear this gentleman is taking the law into his own hands."

"What law would that be, Mademoiselle Agatha?" the Italian sword master inquired in soft reason. "For the crimes which have been addressed so far, there are no enforceable prohibitions and few rules except those of common decency, which are easily ignored."

Agatha took refuge in her teacup as if unconvinced but disinclined to argue.

It was then that Figaro, who had been visiting in the kitchen, came trotting into the room with his toenails clicking on the polished cypress floor. He started toward Lisette, then swerved to head straight for Nicholas Pasquale. Rearing up on his hind legs, the small dog put his paws on the sword master's knees while wagging his tail so hard it very nearly turned in circles. A beatific expression came over his canine features as Nicholas reached to scratch behind his ears. He dropped to the floor where he rolled to his back in utter abasement, looking up at the tall Italian with his eyes glazing over with satisfaction.

A brief suspicion crossed Lisette's mind, but she did not voice it. "Figaro, you rascal, have you no discrimination?" she scolded in wry tones. "First you fraternize with that gang of street boys and now you fling yourself at the feet of the first man to enter the room."

Nicholas glanced up from where he was rubbing Figaro's belly. "He has had visitors?"

"In a manner of speaking. He barks like a wild thing at the street boys when they chance to appear across the street. Were they not there when you came in?"

"They may have been. I didn't notice."

"I believe he must have been attached to one of those boys since he seems so excited to see them."

"It's possible, but they must see how much better off he is here with you."

"A child's affection is seldom practical. I should not like to think that I've deprived someone of his pet, particularly when these boys have so little else to call their own."

La Roche looked up, his smile warm. "Your compassion does you credit, *madame*."

"Compassion without action is of little use," Lisette said. "I wish I might do more."

"You would find it difficult, I fear. It isn't that there is no place for these young hellions to go. St. Joseph's opened a new orphanage not so long ago, and there are others. This bunch refuses to be shut away behind walls. The hooligans have roamed the streets for as long as most of them can remember, and are unwilling to sacrifice the freedom of movement for a full belly and a place to lay their heads."

She lifted a brow. "You seem to know a great deal about them."

"I have a fellow feeling, I suppose, having been one of a similar gang in Rome some time ago."

"Forgive me," she said at once. "I didn't mean to pry into what is none of my concern."

"You didn't know, and how should you?" La Roche went on to tell them of his birth to a respectable woman who was disowned by her parents when they learned she was to have the child of an English sailing man. He made a story also of his rejection by the man she had eventually married, the birth of a younger brother, the brother's suicide and his own journey to Spain, Cuba then on to New Orleans on the trail of the man who had caused it. Lisette had heard something of the rest, the aid that Nicholas Pasquale had given to Rio de Silva in his defeat of the Spanish count who was both the sworn enemy of one and the usurper who had stolen the title and birthright of the other.

"You stay on in New Orleans though the task of avenging your brother is over," she said when he fell silent. "Is it a permanent move then?"

He spread a graceful hand. "Perhaps I am waiting for a sign. At the very least, I will remain for the wedding of my friend De Silva and his Celina."

"Till after Easter then, I suppose?" The Lenten season, being a time for contemplation of death and redemption, was not considered propitious for such a happy event.

"Just so, though Rio would have had it earlier if he could." He smiled. "They both swore at first to make it a small affair to be held at once, but then Celina's father had friends who must be present or feel themselves slighted, her brother was the same, and the priest must make certain that they are ready for this important step. The thing grows and grows and seems ever further away. It's so frightening that I have sworn never to be wed, or else to steal my bride away in the dead of night."

She could not help smiling at the droll look in his eyes. "You will make a Gretna escape then?"

"Pardon?"

"Gretna, the small town across the river, you comprehend. The judge there is a Scotsman known these many years to be accommodating in the matter of hasty marriages since he is most happily married himself. Because of it, the town was named for the Gretna Green in Scotland, haven of eloping lovers. It takes more than a blacksmith to perform a marriage there—at least a judge or notary public is required. But if a couple can only make it across the river without being stopped, then they can be husband and wife in a matter of minutes."

"How very convenient," he said on a low laugh. "I'll have to keep it in mind."

The *maître d'armes* rose to take his leave a short time later, and Maurelle decided to depart at the same time. As was the custom in New Orleans, where to allow guests to leave was viewed as a great hardship, she saw them out, going as far as the banquette where she watched Pasquale tuck Maurelle's hand into the crook of his arm and stroll away. Finally, Lisette turned back into the *porte cochère*.

Instead of going upstairs again, however, she made her way to the kitchen beneath the *garçonnière* wing where she spoke to Cook about dinner then was persuaded to sample a bread pudding he had just taken from the oven. On her way back along the lower gallery a few minutes later, she chanced to glance down the tunnel-like *porte cochère* in passing.

Nicholas Pasquale may have escorted Maurelle to her town house, but he had certainly not lingered there. He stood across the street, talking to several of the street boys. They gathered around him, listening with rapt attention to whatever he was imparting to them.

An interesting man, the Italian, she thought as she moved on again. He seemed to collect the affections of animals and children as well as the ladies. She wondered if it was deliberate.

The day wore on. In late afternoon, at least two hours after the dinner hour, Lisette walked out onto the front gallery overlooking the street for a breath of air. Below her, she saw the street boys still in their places. It was barely possible that they had departed for a time and now returned, but she didn't think so. They sat on the banquette, or lay on it in obvious lassitude, as if performing some wearisome duty.

Her appearance on the balcony across from them had a galvanizing effect. One or two leaped to their feet. The taller lad who seemed to be their leader kicked the sleepers awake. Then they all turned to stare up at her.

Feeling somewhat self-conscious, Lisette lifted her hand in a small wave. Just then, Figaro, who had taken to following her from place to place, came trotting out onto the balcony. He lunged for the railing, barking in sharp, short bursts of sound and trembling with eagerness as he greeted his former cohorts. He pushed his head through the wrought iron bars then leaned against them as if trying his best to follow with the rest of his small body.

It was heartrending. The dog wanted to see the boys. More than that, the motley gang had apparently had little to eat or drink for most of the day. On impulse, Lisette turned and made her way down to the wicket gate. She swung it wide and called out to the boys, waiting while they exchanged glances then straggled across the street to where she stood.

They were seven in number, ranging in age from about five or six to no more than thirteen. Their nationalities were as mixed as their skin color. They shuffled their feet, darted quick glances here and there, anywhere except at Lisette, and did their best to hang back at least two arms' length out of reach. Figaro leaped and cavorted around them, beside himself with joy. A few patted his head, but seemed too wary of her to actually play with the small dog.

The leader was the oldest among them, a boy with a rangy build, a rough thatch of brown hair and a permanent frown between his eyes. His manner was wary, as if he mistrusted her invitation, fearing a trap.

"How are you called?" she asked, singling him out and motioning him forward.

"Squirrel, *madame*. We done nothin' wrong." The boy's face was set in lines of sullen obstinacy.

"Your full name, I mean."

He looked at the banquette, scuffed at a clod of mud there. "All I got."

Lisette felt a pang as she realized that if this boy had ever had a real first name, much less a surname, it had been forgotten. "And your friends?"

"That's Faro, and this is Weed. Over there's Cotton and behind him is Buck and Molasses and Wharf Rat."

"I'm very pleased to make your acquaintance," she said, after clearing her throat. "I don't mean to accuse you of anything, I promise. It's only that you have been there across the street for some time. Aren't you hungry?"

"No, *madame*."

One or two of the other boys looked at each other as if less sure of that answer, but they didn't contradict their leader.

"I believe this little dog must belong to one of you," she said as she turned and walked toward the kitchen, motioning for them to follow. "Is that true?"

"No, *madame*," Squirrel answered. "He don't belong to nobody."

"You're certain?"

A shrug came and went so quickly that she almost failed to see it. "He come along with us sometimes, that's all."

It was a fine distinction. If he didn't belong to them, then they had no responsibility toward him. "Nevertheless, he seems lonely without you. I hope you will feel free to come and visit him from time to time."

They looked at each other with varying degrees of skepticism, making no answer. Those at the rear of the group slowed, and then began to edge back toward the wicket gate.

"I'm sure you're thirsty, even if not hungry," she went on as an inducement to follow her deeper into the house. "Come and have a cool drink. Then I think Cook has a few leftover tea cakes…"

"*Mon Dieu!* What passes here?" Felix asked in concern as he trotted down the outside stairs with his face like a thundercloud. "Are these little thieves troubling you, *madame?*"

The boys scattered, racing back down the *porte cochère*.

"Stop!" Lisette cried. "Come back. Oh, Felix, look what you've done."

It was too late to halt the flight. The wicket gate flew open and the boys scattered into the street like dry leaves before a hurricane wind. Seconds later, there was neither sight nor sound of them.

Lisette clapped her hands together in vexation before turning on the butler. "I invited those children inside, Felix. I wished to speak to them, to question them."

"I am sorry, *madame,* but no, no, surely not. Such dirty little beggars? They will have more fleas than Figaro before his bath, yes and body lice, too, or worse. Monsieur Freret would never want them in his house, I promise you. Allow it once, and you'll never be rid of them."

"They are children, not animals."

"They are wild ones, *madame,* not fit to touch the hem of a fine lady such as yourself."

His gaze and his voice were firm. No doubt he believed every word he spoke. That conviction failed to move Lisette. "If they should return…"

"They shall not, *madame.* I will see to it."

"If they should return," she said louder, overriding his words, "you will give them food and water."

"You know not what you do," he insisted. "You will never be rid of them."

He was, she thought, taking a little too much of the running of her life upon himself. It could not be allowed. "Banish that notion from your mind, if you please. I know very well what I am about and also what I want. If you care to continue here with me, you will listen carefully. I wish to speak to those boys. You will see that this is possible. Do I make myself clear?"

"Yes, *madame*." He drew himself up stiffly and inclined his head.

Lisette, hearing the subdued tone of the man's voice, felt an uncomfortable twinge of conscience. Perhaps she had been too harsh. She would not retract the words, however. She was mistress here and must act the part, one way or another.

Her frustration was extreme. She was almost certain the boys had been set to watch her. The question was by whom. Nicholas seemed the obvious choice, but it did not follow that it was his idea. It could as easily have been her father-in-law. Or it might have been Caid. She had underestimated the Irish sword master before, but would not be guilty of that again. One thing was certain. She would have a few questions for him when next they met.

It was three days before she saw either Caid or Nicholas again, and then it was quite by accident. She and Agatha, with Figaro trotting at their heels on a leash of cordovan leather, were on a quest for silk stockings and hair ribbons. While making their way to Avinenc's on Chartres, they heard the rattle of snare drums. Soon, they came upon the old parade ground before the cathedral, the Place d'Armes. A crowd had gathered there, standing about in the shade cast by the sycamore trees that edged the open plaza. Gossiping, fanning languorously in the spring warmth, they watched the men who drilled behind the low wrought iron fence. It was the militia, marching back and forth, sweating in the heat and dust that rose from the bare ground.

The sight was not unusual; the militia had been drilling there for decades. Still there was something different about it this morning.

"I believe there are more of them," Lisette said to Agatha as she paused at a point where she could catch a glimpse through the crowd. "Don't you think so?"

"And how well they move. Though it pains me to say so, I believe they are superior to such groups where I come from."

"I've heard it said the Louisiana Legion is formed on the French pattern as established by Napoleon." They appeared superb to Lisette's untrained eyes, as well, garbed in their splendid uniforms, moving together with steady precision, as responsive to the called commands as though guided by a single instinct.

"Oh, look, there is Monsieur Nicholas!" The high color of excitement tinged Agatha's cheeks.

"Where?"

"In the front rank near Monsieur Caid. How splendid they are."

They were indeed. With their fine bearing and muscular forms, they were easily the most striking men on the field.

An odd sensation began under Lisette's breastbone, rising to her throat where it took her breath. Made up of febrile excitement and a strange warmth that settled in her lower body, it had also an element of distress. Until this moment, the possibility of war with Mexico that was spoken of so easily had seemed a threat without substance, one that might be resolved in good time by diplomacy or a mere show of force at most. The men in their marching ranks made it distressingly real. They could die, these brave men with their smart steps and heads held so high. They could go away to war and never come back again.

Any one of them could be killed on the dueling field tomorrow, next week, next month or next year. It was the way of their world. What courage, what pride it took to be a man. The urge to cry out against the need was so strong that Lisette lifted a hand to her mouth as if to hold back the useless sound.

At that moment, Figaro gave a low growl. Hard on that warning came the scuff of a footstep behind her. Gooseflesh prickled along her arms and the hair rose on the back of her neck even before she spun around.

Her father-in-law stood within arm's reach. He appeared less healthy than when last she had seen him. His features had a ravaged look that somehow mirrored the odd illness with which his wife had died, and his smile was thin lipped as he spoke. "I might have guessed I would find you here where so many in trousers are to be seen all in one place."

Lisette refused to dignify the slur with an answer. "I can hardly conjecture what brings you here."

"Best not. You might dislike the answer."

He spared not a glance for Agatha while staring at Lisette with cold malevolence. It was pointless to bandy words with him, she thought. He was not reasonable, and she no longer expected otherwise. "You must excuse us, *monsieur*," she said, gathering up Figaro's leash.

"On the contrary. You have hidden yourself away these many days, sheltering behind the murderer of my son. Now that we meet face-to-face, you will listen to what I say."

"I think not. Come, Agatha."

She made as if to brush past him, but he put out a claw-like hand to clutch her arm. Figaro leaped to attack, grasping the hem of one trouser leg in his sharp teeth and worrying it while snarling deep in his throat.

Moisant released Lisette at once, staggering back. Lisette dragged the dog away by main force though he twisted and turned on the end of the leash, trying to get at his adversary once more. She bent to pick up the little mongrel, and thought for an instant that he might turn on her. Finally, he was still as she held him against her, though the low rumble of his growl shook his small frame.

"Nasty little beast," Moisant said, swatting at the tear in his trousers with the tip of his cane. "I shall need repairs."

"Be glad it's no worse."

"Yes, well. That I remain on this spot in spite of such an unprovoked attack…"

"Unprovoked?"

"Very well, I should not have laid hold of you. I admit it. You should understand from this how determined I am to speak. I wish to say to you that I was wrong and offer my sincere apology."

Lisette glanced at Agatha to see the same stunned look in her companion's eyes that she could feel on her own face. "Your apology."

"For my uncertain temper which seems to have driven you from my house. I plead the natural grief of a father for his only son. Should you return, as I hope you will, I promise to adopt a more calm humor as suited to your sensitive nature."

"You cannot be serious?"

"Only tell me how I may convince you. When I think of how you were when you first came to us, so young, so sweet and like a trusted daughter, I am bereft that things went so wrong. I thought you would always be a part of my family, would bear our proud name to your grave. That we have come to this separation of households…it is devastating to me."

"I have no doubt of it, if you mean devastating to your pocketbook," Lisette said in low indignation. "Need I remind you of your threat to shut me away as a madwoman if I did not sign over my fortune to you? No, I thank you. I am no longer so young and trusting. You and your son saw to that."

"You have never had a care for your husband's family or for me as its head. You abandoned us as if we had no value or had never been a part of your life."

"We, *monsieur?* You speak as if your son is still alive."

"He will always be alive in my heart, always!" His black eyes with their yellow whites glittered with hatred at that reminder of his loss.

"Perhaps, but you can't expect me to live as if he is still here among us. It's unnatural."

"What is unnatural is for a female to have charge of her fortune or to remove herself from the care of her husband's father like a snake sloughing off its skin. You were a Moisant. You must always be a Moisant."

In some odd manner, Lisette could almost feel sorry for him. With less heat in her voice, she said, "I am myself, *monsieur.* Widows are allowed to leave off their mourning, eventually. They even remarry in time."

"Remarry? How can you speak of such a thing? It profanes the memory of my son."

Agatha stepped a little closer, moving to block the view of two women who had turned to stare in their direction. "*Monsieur,* please. Only listen to what you're saying. They burn widows alive on the funeral pyres of their husbands in India, or so I've read. You sound as if you would approve of that practice."

"And why not, pray? What use is my son's wife now? I accepted her because she was biddable and soon to be alone in the world, because of what she could bring to my house and my name. She failed to produce an heir, refused to permit my rightful control of the property she brought to the marriage and my family, failed to honor me…."

"For which sins, you think she should die?" Agatha appeared aghast, as if she could not believe what she was hearing.

"I tell you, she denied to me the immortality of my name.

Because she would not be bedded by my son, I will die the last of my line."

"Would not be…you cannot mean what I understand you to be saying!"

"Can I not?" Moisant asked in a fierce undertone even as he flashed a glance toward nearby groups of people who were moving away, distancing themselves from the small scene. "I told Eugene it was a mistake to delay his possession. He laughed. She did not attract him, he said. Her maidenly shrinking gave him a disgust for her. He swore he would bed her, eventually, and in the meantime, the threat of it was a fine lever to pry money from her."

Agatha drew herself up. "If that is true, *monsieur,* then it appears the fault lies with your son."

"Do not say such a thing to me! My son was a man with the virile appetites of his father, more manly than you can ever know, poor spinster that you are. He fathered children…."

"Indeed he did," Lisette said with a curl to the corner of her mouth. "And because of it, Caid O'Neill's sister died as certainly as if he had stabbed her through the heart. She carried his child for a time, your grandchild and heir, had you shown more responsibility or even a modicum of compassion."

"Bah! What good was a little bastard to me while Eugene was wed to you for life—you who could not do this simple thing that was accomplished easily enough by an Irish peasant?"

"You have no idea what I can do, nor will you ever."

His eyes narrowed to venomous slits and he lifted his cane to shake it at her, though he kept his voice to a hissing whisper. "We shall see, my fine daughter-in-law, we shall see. There are other ways to have from you what was promised. You will return to my house, one way or another, and I shall have from you my due wealth and my heir. This is as it should be, and will be yet. I swear it!"

Did he intend that threat as it sounded? Lisette was by no means sure she wanted to find out.

Turning on the heel of her walking shoe, she strode away with Agatha at her side. Moisant made no attempt to stop her, perhaps from respect for Figaro's sharp teeth or because he had vented his spleen and preferred to make no further spectacle.

"The man is quite mad," Agatha said with precision when they reached the next block and their footsteps slowed.

Lisette gave her a wan smile. "Now you understand why I was forced to apply to Monsieur O'Neill."

"Something more must be done."

"I quite agree."

"Yes, but what it should be is more than I can see. You can hardly keep this sword master with you night and day."

Was that strictly true? Lisette was silent while her thoughts moved in rapid calculation. After a moment, she said, "There might be a way."

"Whatever do you mean?"

"I'm not sure."

A frown clouded Agatha's face. "My dear…"

"You will know soon enough if it turns out," she said. "And if it does not, then I will have some small shred of pride left to me."

"Good heavens. I shudder to think what you can mean."

So did she, Lisette thought. So did she.

11

Caid watched the confrontation between Lisette and Moisant from a distance while anger burned in his belly. The old man had chosen his moment with nice attention to malice. It was impossible to leave the military formation, a fact Moisant knew well. Doubtless, he had intended to prove that Lisette was vulnerable in spite of everything. That he had managed it was more galling than his effrontery in accosting Lisette in public.

The need to know what had transpired between the two of them so occupied Caid's attention that he missed the command for a left turn and was jostled by the man next to him. He cursed softly, torn by a strong need to walk off the parade ground. Exertion of the intense concentration he normally brought to swordplay allowed him to get through the remainder of the drill, but it was a close thing.

"You saw?" Nicholas asked, the moment they were free.

Caid was hot, tired and in need of a bath and change of linen before he was fit to appear before anyone, particularly a lady. He barely glanced at his friend as they strode in the direction of the Passage. "I did."

"What now?" Nicholas ran a hand through his dark curls, flinging away droplets of sweat.

"A discreet visit, of course."

"Of course. How kind of Moisant to give you an excuse."

"At least I will make some attempt not to compromise the lady."

"Meaning?"

"I hear you paid her a visit in broad daylight."

"My presence is so contaminating?" The Italian's voice held an edge.

"You know very well that ladies of high respectability such as Madame Moisant do not receive private visits from the likes of us. It's bad enough that we pass through her door while in the company of others."

"Ah, men like us, we *maîtres d'armes*."

"Did you think I spoke personally? Don't be a nod-cock." Caid's voice was rough, but his intention polite enough. He should have remembered that Nicholas was defensive on the subject of his birth and position.

"Allow me to point out that Mademoiselle Stilton and Madame Herriot were with the lady in question while I was there. Above that fact, my friend, she is not some innocent schoolroom mademoiselle who can be seduced in an hour."

"Seduced?" Caid's voice had the ring of steel in it.

"You understand what I mean to say, or should. She has been married, thus is a woman of the world now, and she has no male relative to decide for her whom she will or will not receive. She is at liberty to make her own choices for her friends—or, if it comes to it, her lovers."

Caid whipped his head around. "Lovers?"

"Forgive me," Nicholas said with a wide grin. "I could not resist."

"Try harder." Caid gave his friend a sour look. "And I will remind you that she does have someone to scrutinize her visitors."

"You, I suppose."

"You have it."

"And I am warned away?"

"It would be best." The Italian was the soul of honor in so far as Caid could tell, but he was also a magnet for gossip and much too charming for his own good.

The Italian gave him a speculative look. "Take care, my

friend. You are becoming obsessed, and it is hopeless by your own admission."

"I'm not obsessed." The words were grim.

"You give an excellent imitation."

"Don't be ridiculous."

"Let us review, shall we? You spend your nights lurking outside her house. You set your friends and half the wandering boys of New Orleans to watch her. You question her, follow her movements, and came close to getting yourself thrown out of the Legion for her sake just now. Your conversation has a lamentable tendency to revolve around the lady, and you are like to murder any man who lingers too long at her side. If these are not the actions of a man enthralled, then I know nothing whatever of love."

"I thought the subject was obsession."

Nicholas grinned. "Same thing, with the addition of unrequited lust and other noble fancies."

"Don't be an idiot."

"Not I, *mon ami*."

Caid gave him a black scowl. Of course he felt desire for Lisette; what man would not? But he was too well aware of the differences in their stations to permit it to affect him. As for nobility, what a load of manure. There was nothing noble about him, and particularly not about his fancies concerning the lady. Those were as carnal as any man's, as were his dreams. But he knew well the difference between them and reality.

They crossed a street, threading their way through the offal, then stepped under the welcome shade of an overhanging, iron-grilled balcony once more. The scent of fresh-baked goods assailed them from the *patisserie* on the corner. Nicholas turned his gaze toward the window display, then came to an abrupt halt.

"What say you to a taste of something, my friend? My morning coffee is but a faded memory. Yes, and my sweet tooth is calling."

Caid grunted. "It will be the death of you."

"But not, please our good God, before it has been satisfied many times. Shall we?" He did not wait for an answer, but stepped into the cool interior of the shop.

Moments later, they were seated at one of a trio of small tables that had been pulled out onto the banquette. Napoleons sat before them, a treat made of almond cookies sandwiched with whipped cream and arranged in the shape of a tricorn hat, then drizzled with chocolate and dusted with powdered sugar. Cups of hot black coffee were in their hands. Nicholas sipped, then made a face. Setting down his cup, he began to ladle sugar from the bowl into the inky brew.

"I don't know how you can do that," Caid complained.

"With a spoon," the Italian said flourishing that instrument that he had plucked from a spooner beside the sugar bowl.

"You will be abysmally stout and toothless one day."

"But a happy man." Nicholas sipped his amended coffee then gave a contented sigh. "So. You have heard the latest about the tournament, this *assaut d'armes?*"

"If you mean that it's to be held at the old St. Philips Theater."

"An abominable pile, from what I can see, at least thirty years old, drafty and moth-eaten. The boards usually installed over the parquet section as a dance floor for the quadroon balls are amazingly warped, I hear. They are sure to trip the unwary."

Caid grimaced. "Duly noted, with thanks for the warning. You have made your application?"

"In form. And you?"

"Likewise. I hear the order of combat has been decided."

Nicholas nodded, but they did not pursue the subject. Implicit between them was the knowledge that they might have to face each other on the fencing strip during this tournament. Neither shrank from it; they had met once or twice in friendly competition and had a healthy respect for each other's ability with a blade. Still, there was no point in delving into what could become a sensitive subject.

Caid finished his napoleon in a few bites and followed it with a healthy swallow of coffee. As he wiped his hands on the napkin provided, his idle gaze fell on a figure progressing down the street. Impeccably turned out in a coat of rich blue worn with a white cravat, light blue waistcoat and gray pantaloons, he strolled the banquette as if he owned it, twirling his ebony cane, bowing deeply to the ladies, less so to the priest he passed, and according a lounging shopkeeper a cordial nod. Between times, he whistled a melody in a minor key and with perfect pitch, one Caid recognized as "Greensleeves." Passing from shade to sunlight, his presence seemed to glint with the polish of fine silver.

"The Englishman," he said with a nod in that direction.

Nicholas turned to follow his gaze, then a crooked smile appeared on his lips. "Blackford was the name, I believe. Will you warn him away from the fair Madame Lisette, as well?"

Caid saw no humor in the idea. "If necessary."

"I doubt he feels himself ineligible."

"Then he should learn the etiquette of his chosen locale."

"My friend," Nicholas said, his smile fading, "I advise you to moderate your tone. Not everyone is willing to make allowances for your concern."

As a warning, it was probably deserved and Caid knew it. Heeding it was a different matter altogether.

Blackford, approaching with loose-limbed grace, had to either detour around their table or stop and pass the time of day. "Gentlemen," he said as he came nearer. "Well met."

"Join us, if you please," Nicholas said easily.

The invitation had to be offered as a matter of courtesy, though Caid regretted the necessity. "Take a chair," he added.

"No coffee for me, but I will pause for a moment, if you don't mind." Blackford swept the tail of his long coat aside and sat down. Stacking his hands on the head of his cane, he went on. "There is a matter I would discuss with the two of you, here where we have a small amount of privacy."

"And that is?" Caid exchanged a quick look with Nicholas, but the Italian's face was as blank as he felt his own to be.

"Stories, implications, suppositions—in a word, circumstances that could be an outright lie."

"But not attributed to either of us?" Caid queried softly.

"I hope I have more intelligence than to suggest such a thing." An amazingly warm smile came and went across Blackford's aristocratic face.

"Then?"

"A facility at reading faces can be an excellent thing in our profession, as I'm persuaded you will agree. It's a small talent I have developed."

"Laboriously, I expect?"

"Painfully." The smile appeared again. "And you share it, I imagine, if you understand that much. Yet it's something that often proves useful in other arenas."

"Such as?"

"You have no use for indirection, I see. Odd, in an Irishman. But I can, if pressed, speak plainly. I was at Alvarez's last evening when someone mentioned a peculiar duel fought in an out of the way place minus seconds or witnesses but for exalted reasons. The conde was there, which is to say your friend Rio De Silva. As the story unfolded, he looked around him. I rather thought that he was searching for you two, and perhaps checking to see if you had prior knowledge of the tale."

"We were not there." The hand with which Nicholas held his cup was granitelike in its steadiness, but the ends of his fingers had little color.

"No doubt you had business elsewhere. The pastime of men in this city, or so I'm told, is women."

"Surely the pastime of most men everywhere?" Caid said.

"The difference being that here they admit it, even glory in it. Refreshing, isn't it? Only that was women in the plural and you deal in the singular, I believe."

"You were going to speak plainly?

"It gives the brain little exercise, but as you will. Whatever guardianship you pursue along the petticoat line is your own affair. My interest is in your more Quixotic adventures."

"As if we had any such thing," Nicholas said, draining the last sugared drop of his coffee.

"I believe you do. The recent victims of summary justice have been handled with such neatness and dispatch that it fairly shouts expertise. And one of their number seems to have run afoul of a left-handed swordsman." Blackford looked pointedly at the coffee cup La Roche still held in his left hand. "I suspect a triumvirate of masters."

"Not just one?"

"Not unless he has the ability to be in two places at one time. A pair of these reprimands-by-steel seemed to have been held on the same night."

Caid looked at Nicholas who gave a fatalistic shrug. To Blackford, he said, "And your interest in these affairs would be?"

"A strong urge to add my sword to the cause."

"Why? Supposing there is such a thing?" Caid added the last with sardonic humor, knowing that his first question was as good as admittance.

"Boredom?"

"Excitement is not necessarily included among the articles of formation."

"Neither, I suspect, was relieving past pain, but tell me such action has no efficacy."

Something in the Englishman's face stilled the thought in Caid's mind, allowed him, suddenly, to see into his being as if his eyes were glass windows stained blue. And what he saw was agony and desperate grief, with something more that seemed to hold only a small grasp on being alive.

"*Monsieur,*" Nicholas began, "I regret to disappoint…"

"No," Caid interrupted, making one of the few decisions based on impulse that he had made since he was torn, swallowing tears, from the sight of his mother, his sister and Ireland's black-green shore. "If you care for righting the occasional wrong, we shall be glad to have use of your sword. If we are to be four, however, we require from you a single oath and watchword. Can you supply it?"

"Fashioned on those already sworn? Repeat them, and I will attempt it." The gold-tipped lashes of the other man came down, hiding whatever sins had been committed by or against him. It felt like a loss.

"Vengeance," Nicholas said softly.

"Valor," Caid added. "And lastly, for De Silva, Vigilance."

Blackford smiled. "Without question then, mine should be Verity."

Verity, *vérité* in French, the meaning was the same either way. What Blackford had added was a pledge for truth. It would do. Caid looked at Nicholas who gave him a nod, then he turned back to Blackford.

"We will meet later this evening. There is a small ceremony, melodramatic but such things have their uses. A message will be sent."

Blackford rose to his feet. "Ceremonies," he said gently, "are life's punctuation marks. Without them, few things have meaning." He touched the brim of his hat. "Until later."

Nicholas, frowning after the Englishman as he walked away, asked, "Was that wise?"

"I have no idea," Caid said, "but it was necessary, or seemed so at the moment."

"I have known men—we both have, I think—who became *maîtres d'armes* as a convenient means of suicide."

Caid gave a grim nod. "I'm not sure it's the case here."

"It isn't an obvious thing."

"No. But some simply have a great need to right the wrongs done by others, or by themselves."

"And so should be allowed? It's a point."

"We must hope it's the only one."

Returning to his atelier, Caid bathed and changed into another of his two dozen linen shirts, a ritual which would need to be done more and more often, as many as three and four times a day, as the weather grew warmer. While replacing his shirt studs, he tried to think how he was to speak to Lisette without being guilty of the same too-particular attention of which he'd accused Pasquale. In the end, he decided to visit Maurelle and throw himself on her mercy.

The lady was inclined to be kind. She sent a groom around to Lisette's town house with a note at once.

Lisette appeared with her duenna within the hour, entering Maurelle's salon in a rustle of silken skirts. Her face was alight with laughter as she and Mademoiselle Agatha divested themselves of bonnets and shawls. "We barely made it before the rain! Have you noticed how dark it has become? I hope you will allow us to take shelter until the downpour is over."

"But of course, *chère,*" Maurelle said comfortably. "I would have it no other way. And yes, it grows darker outside even as we speak. Is that thunder I hear? Perhaps Monsieur O'Neill will do us the honor of lighting a few candles against this storm?"

"My pleasure," Caid said from where he stood with one elbow resting on the marble fireplace with its empty coal grate.

Lisette swung so quickly that her skirts spun around her like a top. "*Monsieur!* I didn't see you there."

"Madame." His bow was both an acknowledgment and a cover for the fact that he had been staring. She seemed so fresh and unaffected, laughing a little as she brushed a few raindrops from her cheeks with a gloved hand. To watch wariness replace the animation in her features made the muscles of his stomach clench even as he fought a sudden need to taste the raindrops on her face.

The room felt suddenly overwarm and far too stuffed with bric-a-brac and spindly furniture. Turning, he took a sulfur match from the vase on the mantel and scratched it until the flame caught, then proceeded to touch it to the wicks of the girandoles that flanked the marble mantel.

"Caid has been with me for a while," Maurelle said, her tone dry. "Could the two of you entertain each other for a moment, do you think? I must see that the windows have been closed in the remainder of the house, also that dinner preparations are underway."

Their hostess did not wait for an answer, but rose with languid grace and moved from the room. At the door, she paused and glanced back. "Mademoiselle Stilton, would you mind very much giving me the benefit of your opinion on a new recipe for chowder made with crawfish? We will not be gone above a moment or two, I assure you. In any case, a widow can hardly require the presence of a chaperone in the same way as a young girl. Don't you agree?"

It was more than Caid had expected. He flashed Maurelle a look of appreciation to which she returned a moue that might have indicated either amusement or displeasure or both. An instant later, he was alone with Lisette.

"You might have saved yourself the trouble of this charade by simply appearing in Royal Street." She glanced around as if trying to decide whether to sit or stand, but apparently decided on the mobility provided by remaining on her feet.

"You know why that is ineligible."

"I know why you think so."

"Then to the devil with it," he said bluntly. "What did Moisant say to you?"

"A great deal of nonsense. What is more pertinent is what I said to him."

He barely blinked. "And that was?"

"Quite simply, no."

"No?"

"No, I don't care to return to his house. No, I don't wish to bury myself, figuratively speaking, with Eugene. No, I don't intend to submit to his wishes concerning my fortune, and never, ever intend to…"

Her voice failed her, Caid thought, or perhaps her nerve. "To what?"

"Nothing."

She turned away from him, but not before he saw the color that surged into her face. He was beside her in two strides. Catching her arm in a firm grip, he turned her face him. "What insult did he give you?"

"I'm sure I misunderstood him."

Caid was sure she had not, especially as she refused to lift her gaze to meet his. "It was something more that he wanted of you, or so I imagine. You had best tell me, because otherwise my guess may be more insulting than his intention."

"It could not be."

Caid felt the breath leave his chest as his brain supplied the answer. "He could not have given you such insult in public."

"It was obliquely done, of course, but Agatha heard him."

"Then he's mad."

"I did try to tell you."

Caid shook his head, not quite willing to accept what he suspected was the truth. "He actually suggested to you…"

She snatched her arm from his hold. "He seems to feel that I owe him an heir, one way or another."

The urge to annihilate the perverted monster who had been, still was, her father-in-law was like a black cloud filling Caid's head. For long seconds, he could neither move nor think. Then reason returned. "There are laws against such marriages."

"I doubt he intends a legal union. It would be enough to call it a posthumous birth."

"At eleven months, minimum? I hardly think that would pass without comment."

"There are ways to hide the exact birthdates of children who are inconsiderate enough to come earlier or later than expected. Extensive wedding journeys to the northeast or France seem to be a favored method, particularly those that stretch to cover the child's second birthday."

It was true enough. Caid whispered an expletive as he turned away, pacing a few steps before he swung back again. "You must take special care never to go out without an escort."

"I will not be a prisoner in my own house. Besides, Figaro was quite the hero. He put the gentleman to rout before he could do more than threaten me."

"I've no doubt he was as fierce as a lion, but that doesn't make him adequate protection."

"Are we back to my supposed need for a husband?"

"You must admit the advantage. Not only would he have the right to protect you both day and night, but the vows between you must spell the end of any pretensions Moisant might have."

"Since any child I conceive must belong to him," she said softly, finishing his thought. "That is a formidable incentive. I have come to the conclusion, recently, that there may be others."

At last, she was willing to see reason. The evidence of it should have made Caid happy, but seemed instead to have the opposite effect. "You have a candidate in mind?"

"I do."

He waited, but she spoke no name. Finally, he asked, "And he is?"

She tilted her head and clasped her hands behind her back as she moved to the fireplace then turned to face him. "It's a question to which I've given some thought since this morning. No ordinary man will do, I think—that is say, no simple gentlemen of easy habits and courtesies, the kind who enjoys his family circle and the usual entertainments without ever venturing further afield. My next husband must be a man of strength and watchfulness, one used to guarding his back and also exhibiting a certain facility with sword and pistol since he may be called upon to protect himself as well as my honor. I believe it would be best if he had some repute as a man whom it could be dangerous to cross, since this should serve as a deterrent against my father-in-law's machinations."

"Is that all?" Caid asked as she came to a halt in her list of qualifications. His temper, so carefully banked for this meeting, threatened to burn through the restraints he had placed upon it.

She looked judicious. "It would be nice if he could be tolerably handsome and pretend to be desperately in love with me, since otherwise it will not seem reasonable of me to throw off my mourning on his account."

"A sword master, in other words. Are you quite sure he should not be a European, as well, so able to plead ignorance of normal social behavior among the Creoles?"

"Now why didn't I think of that?" she murmured, looking much struck by the idea.

"Pasquale, then."

Her lashes flickered, and then she gave him a sharp look. "The Italian? I think not. Nor the Englishman, either. I hardly know them."

Caid could hear the rain falling outside, splattering from

the roof into the street at the front of the house, rattling into the drainpipes that led to the cistern in the rear. Its moist breath seemed to seep into the room, bringing with it the smells of wet dust and flowers. His voice held a rough edge when he spoke. "You don't know me, either."

"Are you proposing yourself?" she inquired.

He shook his head, in large part to rid it of confusion. "I thought you—"

"An interesting suggestion, I will admit. You do possess the proper qualifications."

"It's impossible." He could feel his heartbeat thudding against his ribs. The half intrigued, half amused expression on her face was fascinating.

"Is it? I fail to see why, when a marriage was your idea in the first place?"

He watched her a moment longer while he weighed her tenacity and daring. Her gaze was steady, the only sign of her agitation the quick rise and fall of her breasts under her bodice with its deep point at the waist. She would require something explicit in the way of rejection. With a mental shrug, he said evenly, "Then I will show you."

He did not wait for more, but pushed up the coat sleeve on his left arm, slipped the plain gold link from the holes of his shirtsleeve and turned back the cuff of white linen. He quickly served his other arm the same, setting the links on a side table. Then he closed his hands into fists, turned the undersides up and held them together as if they were connected by manacles and thrust them toward Lisette.

The old, rust-red marks of shackles were like bloodstains in the dim light of the candles. Embedded in the skin, they were overgrown with thick ridges of scar tissue. The pale streaks of healed sword cuts earned in practice slashed across them. A glazing of golden brown from the sun, gained in outdoor practice matches, merged with their red-orange shading, but they were permanent marks, a part of him that could never be erased.

"Oh, Caid," she whispered, reaching to lay gentle fingers across the twin places where his pulse throbbed under the skin. "What did they do to you?"

She had used his given name. He wondered if she realized it. "I told you when we first met."

"Yes, but I didn't know, didn't understand."

"It's what happens to felons." He attempted to withdraw his wrists, but she circled them with her fingers, holding tightly. He stood quiescent, though the effort to remain that way brought a glaze of perspiration to his forehead.

"And this is the reason you consider yourself unfit to be a husband?"

"For a lady."

"Even if the lady wishes it?"

"I refuse to inflict my disgrace on another along with my name. Put it down to pride."

"Suppose I put it down to arrogance instead?"

"It makes no difference. Like the bald fool who had himself sewn into his belled cap, I prefer to wear my shame rather than attempt removal and expose it for all to see."

She stared at him a long moment. Then she snatched her fingers away as if she had been burned. "You should understand, then, why I want no husband unless it is one who already knows my sad tale. To be the object of pity to any other would be insupportable."

She was saying, he thought, that there had been nothing personal in her preference. As if he could have thought otherwise. "Pity is not the thing most men would feel."

"Nor do I want anything else."

He tipped his chin a fraction. "Nothing? No admiration, no affection, no…passion?"

"Passion, least of all," she said in cool denial.

"Am I to understand," he asked deliberately, "that you had little pleasure from your marriage?"

She hesitated, and he thought she was about to deliver

some point of significance. Then her lips curved in a wintry smile. "None."

"So you expect to find a similar lack of excitement in the next venture into parson's mousetrap? I must point out that one disappointment doesn't always follow another."

"That is gratifying to hear but doesn't make me inclined to take the risk."

"In other words, you don't believe me."

"Oh, I believe it may be true enough, for a man."

"Suppose I could prove it to be true for a woman, as well." He wasn't sure where that had come from, unless from the fevered arousal of dreams.

"What, another lesson?"

"Since it seems required." He kept his gaze steady though his chest felt hot and tight.

She gave him a clear look.

"And how valuable would such an experience be if it occurs only once? Or do you suggest that I test all prospects to make certain the chosen one meets the standard you would set?"

It was an outrageous suggestion. Anger that she could even think it, much less speak it aloud, thrummed with the blood in his brain. He stepped toward her, reaching to grasp her arms and pull her against him. Staring down into her upturned face, letting his gaze rake her parted lips, he said, "That would be your affair, *madame*. I only promise the first fulfillment."

She stiffened in his arms, but he barely noticed. He touched his mouth to hers in a questing caress, brushing his lips over hers as he absorbed their smoothness, their gentle contours, delicate edges and moist, inviting corners. He savored the taste of her, her sweetness, invading her soft and luscious depths. He found and touched her tongue, seeking its alliance, engaging it in sinuous play that was a foretaste of rapture.

The resistance left her. She seemed to flow toward him,

fitting against the hard angles of his body with grace and precision, matching her breathing to his in natural aptitude. His hold tightened and his chest expanded in a breath of wonder. Blindly, as once before, he smoothed his hand from her waist to capture the fullness of her breast pressed up so enticingly by her corset stays, and sensed the tightening of her nipple through layers of cloth. Pure, unrestrained joy surged through him with the force of a lightning strike. Lost in the woman he held, he felt as if he had regained everything that had been taken from him, everything that had once been home to him.

His mind was on fire; his body seemed to have slipped his will. He wanted Lisette, suddenly and completely, as he had never desired another woman in his life, needed her with a heart-stopping power that verged on madness. If he had been anywhere other than Maurelle's salon, he might have taken her there on the floor while the rain fell beyond the window, lifting silk and muslin petticoats, pushing aside laces and ribbons and other silken barriers to reach the molten hot center of her body. She was temptation armored with whalebone and acres of white linen, enticement scented with violets and vetiver. She was everything he had ever wanted and could not have, the forbidden placed forever beyond his reach.

She was the widow of the man he had killed.

He released her so abruptly that she stumbled a little before regaining her balance. Almost, he reached out to her again. Instead, he swung around and braced his hands on the cool marble of the fireplace mantel while he dragged air into his lungs and sense into his brain.

"I'm sorry," he said after a moment. "It would be infamous to remove your husband then take advantage of his absence."

"His absence. An odd way to put it."

"I could be considerably more crass, but adding insult to injury doesn't seem useful."

"Suppose I said there is no injury?"

Her voice sounded distant, as if she were moving away from him, removing herself from his orbit. He straightened and pushed away from the mantelpiece. Turning, he saw her near the window, her face melancholy and pale in the gray light that filtered through the thick pane as she watched the falling rain.

"No injury?"

"Do I appear in the guise of a grieving widow to you? Have you not noticed that I am quite able to control my tears?"

"I assumed yours was not a love match and knew, certainly, that Moisant had little care for your happiness. But such marriages are hardly unusual, and widows still mourn."

"I do not," she said, her voice flat.

"You can't expect me to believe that you rejoice. I murdered your husband in something akin to cold blood. His death at my hands caused you to lose your status as a respected member of a noted family, with the direct result that you were shut away in the attempt to wrest control of your dowry from you. These losses must affect you."

"They do, of course."

"And because of it…"

"They also allowed my freedom, for which I owe you unending gratitude."

Stringent thought scoured his mind like acid, leaving behind a single conclusion. "So you feel I deserve a permanent place in your household because of it? Gratitude is only a small step above money as a basis for a marriage."

She turned to face him, though one hand still clenched the drapery beside her. "I gave you my reasons, none of which touched on my very real appreciation."

"So you did. Let me see if I recall. You placed me in the role of your savior and think it should become a permanent position."

She lifted a brow. "Only if you desire it."

Oh, he desired it. He desired to snatch her up and take her somewhere private where he could strip her naked and shatter the cool composure she wore like a cloak while making nonsense of her careful plans and specious arguments. He desired to bind her to him, taking for himself the right to keep her from all harm, all fear while sleeping beside her through countless aeons of nights. He desired to sit across a table from her or in the same room of an evening, watching the play of light upon her skin and in her hair, watching her breathe, and knowing that he could, at any chosen instant, touch her as he pleased, where he pleased. But none of these desires were practical or of lasting importance compared to her welfare. So they must come to nothing.

"To rescue you was never my intention, Madame Moisant. I am no one's knight in armor. I owe you restitution, or so you once said, and on that head agreed to your demand for my protection. The debt is reasonable and will be discharged. More than that is beyond my ability to perform."

She watched him, her gaze fathomless. Then her lips curved into a smile and she moved to retrieve her bonnet and cloak where they had been placed on a side table against the wall. "Not quite."

"I don't understand you," he said, the words stiff.

"You offered a demonstration of…of passion, I believe?"

Caid said nothing. He could not have spoken if a single word from him might have saved the world from tumbling to fiery death. His eyes burned as he watched her place her bonnet over her hair and begin to tie the wide apple-green ribbons that served as bonnet strings.

"Since you have removed yourself from consideration as a husband, it seems I may benefit from the comparison your offer made just now will provide." She picked up her cloak and held it out to him, her smile too bright and a little fey in its defiance. "Unless, of course, that is withdrawn, as well?"

It was a challenge of the most flagrant kind, something Caid had been conditioned never to refuse. Still, he tried. Oh, he tried valiantly while his brain simmered in the hot cauldron of his skull and his heart swelled, aching, to match and surpass the painful tumescence concealed by the long skirt of his coat. He damned himself for ten kinds of fool for ever touching her, wished in desperation that he had never voiced the asinine suggestion she now used to taunt him. He told himself she did not understand what she was saying, could not mean it, certainly would not follow through with it.

Yet he had said the fatal words, and it was all too clear that she might well understand, might mean it, might follow through with some man, if not him. That uncertainty was his undoing.

He dare not risk it.

"By no means, *madame,*" he said in soft promise as he paced forward and took her cloak, swirling it around her shoulders as she turned her back to him. "For that, as in anything short of the most holy of unions, I am yours to command."

12

There was no time for more as Maurelle and Agatha chose that moment to return. It was just as well. Lisette was by no means certain that she could have found words to answer such a stunning declaration.

What had possessed her?

She had seized the chance presented by being alone with Caid to implement her semiformed plan. That had been difficult enough, to propose that he extend his protection to becoming her husband, at least in name. She had thought he might require to be persuaded, but had not expected a refusal of such finality or one so distressing. It was disappointment and chagrin that had led her to say more than she should, she was sure.

Curiosity was a part of it, as well, along with the rebelliousness that had gripped her of late. Yet the kiss he had pressed upon her, and her reaction to it, had, perhaps, been the final goad. More than that, she could not, or preferred not, to comprehend.

Lisette and her companion took their leave as soon as politeness and the rain allowed. Hurrying homeward over the rain-slick banquettes, they spoke little, each busy with her own thoughts.

"I am yours to command."

Had there ever been a more fascinating or exciting concept? That the muscular strength, coordination and the skill of a master swordsman such as Caid O'Neill was hers to call forth at will caused a secret shiver to flow along every nerve ending of her body each time it came to mind. That was often, for she could not get the words, or the idea behind them, out of her head.

When would he come to her? Would he wait for her invitation, her command as he had phrased it? And what would happen then? What did she wish to happen?

She had not told him that she was still a virgin. It had crossed her mind that she should but seemed, on second thought, such an inane thing to say, as if she was sure it must make a difference. Would he notice or, noticing, care? She had no idea. Such a thing might be of importance to a husband, but what could it matter to a—how was she to identify him? Lover, instructor, perhaps chance-met acquaintance who might render a particular service?

How very detached such descriptions seemed. It was beyond strange when she did not feel detached at all.

Lisette and Agatha reached the town house ahead of another shower of rain. Climbing the inside stairs, they removed their wraps and bonnets and gloves, then went into the salon where a small fire had been kindled to combat the dampness. Lisette moved to hold her hands to the blaze, feeling unaccountably chilled. Figaro, who had greeted them at the door, curled up beside her and promptly fell asleep. Agatha seated herself and picked up the mending that currently occupied her leisure time.

As she set her first stitch, Lisette's companion said, "So you had the answer you expected."

"Not precisely."

Agatha raised her brows. "But you and Monsieur O'Neill seemed in such charity with each other when Madame Herriot and I rejoined you."

"Charity had little to do with it."

"Don't be so provoking, my dear. Had you the promise of Monsieur O'Neill to prevent further threats from Moisant or not?"

"I'm not sure it is within his power, or that of any man."

"Then what, precisely, did you two find to agree upon?"

A faint smile touched Lisette's mouth. "Methods, perhaps. We have finally agreed that a husband would make an effective barrier to the plans of my former father-in-law."

"You actually approve the concept?"

"I indicated at least some small interest."

"Not that I disapprove, of course, but why the change of heart?" Agatha held her sewing suspended in her hands.

"Necessity." That was truth, but not the full extent of it. Lisette thought the fathoms-deep blue eyes of the Irish swordsman might also have a part, and the way he sat a horse. She was, she was discovering, a more sensual creature than she had believed possible.

"Who will be the groom? Surely not Monsieur O'Neill?"

Lisette straightened, turning to face her. "He declined the honor."

"Lisette! You didn't… I can't imagine that you would…" Agatha was nearly incoherent, though whether for the fact of her protégé's proposal or the man she had chosen to receive it was impossible to tell.

"Why not? Can you deny it would serve very well?"

"You don't choose a husband for his ability with a sharp weapon, my dear!"

"Not even when it seems to be my greatest need? I can't imagine that a popinjay with a fine name and no fencing skill would be of much use to me."

"There are other considerations, other requirements."

"None of which prevented me from being married to a man who cared only for his own comfort and outside interests. You need not worry, however. It's all in theory. I shall not marry Monsieur O'Neill. It's doubtful that I will marry at all."

"Doubtful," Agatha repeated, her eyes narrowing. "That is a notable change from a few days ago when you swore never to marry."

"So it is," Lisette said, her voice compressed in her throat. "So it is."

It turned warm the next morning, following the rain. The sidewalks steamed, sunlight glittered on damp railings and rooftops, and the air was so thick with moisture that it was like a tepid bath. It was a hint that the winter season, the long *saison de visites,* would soon be over and summer was fast approaching. Lisette rose and dressed early. Agatha was not yet up, so she asked that her breakfast be served to her on the gallery overlooking the courtyard. Felix brought it to her on a tray table which he placed in front of her chair.

A folded note lay on the tray. She reached and picked it up while Felix poured coffee and hot milk in twin streams from different silver pots into her coffee cup. The perusal did not take long.

Lisette sat staring at the paper while the blood drained from her face. Looking up at Felix, she asked in strained tones, "How did this arrive?"

"It was brought by a boy, *madame.* He said he had been given a picayune to deliver it."

"And naturally you saw that I received it. Have you read it?"

"I regret," he said with great dignity as he stepped back, still holding the pots, "that such a feat is not within my power, even if I would take the liberty."

He spoke so well, in much better French than the gumbo patois composed of French, Spanish, African, Choctaw and odd combinations of all four that was used by most slaves. It was difficult to realize he could not read. "I do beg your pardon," she said at once. "This paper is a most scurrilous broadside, one concerning the death of my late husband. If there should be more…"

Concern clouded his features. "Shall I destroy them, *madame?*"

Lisette hesitated, strongly tempted to order it. Then she

shook her head. "Only make certain, please, that I am not with company when you give them to me."

"As you say, *madame*."

"Thank you, Felix." She lowered her gaze to the sheet again as the butler left her to the breakfast for which she suddenly had no appetite.

Printed like the death notices edged in black which were attached to lampposts and other uprights in the Vieux Carré to broadcast funerals, the broadside announced the murder of a gentleman in a duel with the connivance of his widow and a *maître d'armes* of deadly skill. Rife with innuendo, the thing gave no names, but included enough detail to be a public accusation of collusion between her and Caid in the death of Eugene Moisant. It suggested Eugene had died because they wanted to be rid of him so they could be together.

Lisette's first impulse was to send the sheet to Caid, but she thought better of it at once. No doubt this terrible notice had been posted everywhere. He would see one soon enough.

Or perhaps not, if she acted quickly.

Rising, she hurried down the stairs to the *porte cochère*. At its end, she opened the wrought iron wicket gate and crossed the street to where the street boys had already congregated that morning. Showing them the sheet, she promised a reward for every one like it that they brought to her. Seconds later, the boys had scattered into the street with zeal in their thin faces. She soon heard the sound of ripping paper from up and down the block.

It was the most she could do for now. Lisette closed her eyes for a brief instant, then went slowly back down into the town house.

By midday, she had thrown thirty-six of the broadsides onto the fire in the kitchen fireplace, for which privilege she had paid a picayune per sheet. She provided a feast, as well, for the seven boys who had come to her aid, one served at the big wooden table in the courtyard and consisting of slices of ham, bowls of savory gumbo, several loaves of bread—which they tore into as if they were the lightest of cakes—and sticky molasses cookies. Her only requirement for partaking of this repast was that they wash their hands and comb their hair before commencing. Varying degrees of grumbling accompanied their compliance, but at least she was able to tell what they looked like under their grime.

The result of her inspiration concerning them, and her bounty, was something other than expected, however. When she chanced to cross the courtyard some time later, she saw that the boys had moved their post. They sat or lay just outside the wicket gate, and every one of them was fast asleep, overcome by the unaccustomed size of their repast.

Lisette stopped short while an odd constriction swelled in her throat, followed by a prickling behind her eyes. What a terrible world it was where children like these had no one to care for them or about them. Something should be done about it, and would before she was much older. Turning quickly, she went to find some task, any task to occupy her hands while she considered possibilities.

No one called during that interminable day, no one sent word. Not that the company she had received before had been numerous, but there had been one or two of her particular friends who had called, along with a few of the more determined fortune hunters and of course Nicholas Pasquale. Now the entrance bell was silent. It was proof enough, if any were needed, that the posters has served their intended purpose in spite of all she could do.

Lisette could settle to nothing. Her needlework had no appeal, the book she had been reading no longer held her interest, and the plan she drew up for fresh summer plantings in the courtyard seemed insipid. She considered running away, perhaps taking ship for France. Agatha would accompany her, she was sure, and they might outdistance the slurs and her father-in-law's machinations for a while. The idea was rejected while only half formed. France would soon be full of Creoles from New Orleans, families escaping the fevers of summer, couples on wedding trips or young men stopping to visit distant relatives while on their Grand Tours. There would be no escape. In any case, she would not steal away as if she had done something wrong when she most certainly had not.

She half expected to receive a visit from Caid before dark. Matters between them had been left in such an indefinite state, and now this new quandary made it even more imperative that they talk. Surely he must know by now what had occurred and realize she would be concerned?

How stupid it was that she could not walk the few blocks between the town house and the Passage de la Bourse and rap on his door. Such restrictions were annoying at the best of times, but now they irritated her past bearing. It might be useful to pen a note to the stubborn sword master, after all. A gentleman could hardly ignore such a summons.

She was seated at the small secretary desk in the salon, mangling paper and wasting ink, when the commotion began in the street. Putting down her pen, she rose and moved to one of the French doors that stood open to the mild evening. There was nothing to be seen, but she could hear the street boys yelling and screaming. Hurrying out onto the balcony, she looked over the railing.

She drew a sharp breath. Directly below her in the street, the entire gang of boys danced around a gentleman in a frock coat and tall beaver hat, darting at him with shrill cries. The man had Squirrel by the arm and was thrashing him with his cane.

Anger boiled up inside Lisette. She leaned over the railing, calling out in sharp command. "Stop that, *monsieur!* Stop it at once!"

The man glanced up, but did not stay his arm. It was Eduoard Sarne, the sword master who had hovered at the edges of the Vallier soirée and put in brief appearances at the theater and her literary salon. His face was twisted with angry intent. As he turned back to his task, his cane whipped the air, rising and falling.

Squirrel dodged and skipped, trying to avoid the blows. A few he escaped though most landed with too-solid whacks. His face was white, his features pinched and grim, but he did not cry out. Several men and women passing on the banquette turned to stare. A few gathered closer but did not intervene.

Whirling, Lisette ran across the salon and down the stairs. At the end of the *porte cochère,* she flung open the wicket gate and burst into the street. She did not stop but flew at Sarne, grasping his arm in one hand and a fistful of his coat and the flesh underneath with the other.

The sword master swung his head, his eyes wide with irate astonishment. Squirrel stared at her in shock. The other boys fell silent.

It was then that a tall figure appeared beside her. Caid, his face set in hard lines, reached to wrench the cane from Sarne's hand. Then he took Lisette's arm, breaking her grasp on Squirrel's attacker and drawing her to his side.

Sarne turned on Caid. Squirrel seized that moment to jerk free of the saturnine sword master's grasp and stumble out of reach. He could have run then, probably should have, but he did not. Standing his ground, he stared from one man to the other.

The two men faced each other, their feet planted and shoulders back. Words were exchanged that seemed lethal in their quietness though Lisette did not quite catch their meaning. Then Caid took a card from his waistcoat pocket, proffered it with a stiff bow. Collecting the street boys around him with a brief movement of his head, he escorted

Lisette to the town house entrance then turned and walked away with the motley gang trailing behind him.

Turning, Lisette went slowly back up to the salon. She stood for long moments just inside the door, staring at nothing while seeking to accept what she had just witnessed.

One gentleman did not strike another except under extreme provocation; that was not the way of the code. A soft word, the presentation of a card, and the cartel was issued. A man's seconds would call. The affair would be settled between them. The gentlemen would meet with the dawn.

Caid intended to fight Eduoard Sarne as he had Vigneaud.

He would meet on the field of honor the man who had struck Squirrel, but he would not speak to her on a public street, would not enter her house alone to offer comfort, discussion or even an explanation. It was, she supposed, another form of protection. If so, she didn't care for it.

The boys had no doubt been seen tearing down the posters. The man who had commissioned them had been incensed, so sent a hireling to punish them. Squirrel must have been singled out as the ringleader. Caid, who had posted the street gang to watch her and, beyond doubt, had a soft spot for them, had hastened to protect them. And the rest was as she had seen.

The whole affair was her fault. The man who sent Sarne had to be Henri Moisant.

For an instant, she wondered if Sarne had danced attendance upon her of late at her father-in-law's request, had carried tales back to him of her activities, her guests and her movements, including her purchase of a carriage and first foray in it without an escort.

She should have been surprised at Moisant's chosen instrument. Somehow she was not. A gentleman who had hovered on the edges of the *ton* for some years, Sarne had opened an atelier after running through the modest fortune left him by his mother. Before that, he had dangled after an

heiress or two without avail, mainly because his family was
not the best. Everyone knew that his great-grandfather had
been a felon hanged for beating a man to death. People
whispered about the untrammeled temper and bad blood in
his family. Such things mattered in the Vieux Carré.

Caid had also been a felon.

She refused to think of that, much less allow it to matter.

It sickened her to realize that Squirrel had received a
beating because she had made use of him and his friends.
Beginning the instant she saw them again, they would all
have plenty to eat and a safe retreat at night and any other
time. A room would be set aside for them in the *garçonnière*
wing, if they would accept it. It was the least she could do
and a beginning for her future plans.

But was it true that Caid had extended his protection to
the street gang? Might his challenge not have been in answer
to Moisant's aim rather than the beating itself, so another effort to protect her? If the man her father-in-law chose to do
his bidding, Sarne, could be seen to pay for it, then Moisant
might think better of any further attempts to blacken her
name. Though what more he could find to do, Lisette could
not imagine.

She could not bear it if Caid—or any other man for that
matter—should be killed because of her. It might be unlikely
if the weapon chosen was a sword, still the challenged party,
in this case Sarne, had the right to choose the weapon and
might opt for pistols, rifles or any such thing. She had heard
of duels fought with Bowie knives, harpoons and even shot-
guns, murderous weapons with little honor in their use or
pretense of anything more than the urge to commit murder.

Lisette paced up and down, trying to think of a way to
stop what had been put into action. There was nothing that
she could see, nothing at all.

She calmed down enough, finally, to finish her note to
Caid and send it around to the Passage. No answer was

forthcoming though she waited up past midnight. He was either away from his atelier or determined not to appear on her doorstep. At last, she went to bed.

News of the outcome of the duel came with her morning coffee. The chambermaid brought it, her eyes wide with its import. Lisette, hearing it, thought it incredible, and did not scruple to say so.

"*Mais, oui,* I am sure! People talk of nothing else this morning. The Irish sword master has been arrested. This Monsieur Sarne would have been, as well, except he was nimble enough to evade the gendarmes as they descended upon *pauvre* Monsieur O'Neill. So now the big Irishman will be tried for fighting the duel."

"But that never happens!" Laws against dueling had been on the books since Spanish days, Lisette knew, but were seldom enforced. Even when arrested, a man's peers always found him innocent of wrongdoing since they might well appear on the field of honor themselves at any time.

"It is a great injustice, very great. Four other duels were fought this morning. They line up to hack and thrust, these gentlemen, waiting their turn under The Oaks as others wait to buy opera tickets. But only Monsieur O'Neill was taken to the calaboose."

She meant the jail, of course, calaboose being from the old Spanish *calabozo,* so yet another hold over from that colonial era.

"Something must be done." Lisette said, flinging back the covers and sliding her feet from the bed. "Help me to dress. Quickly, now."

Within the hour, she was striding along the banquette with the ends of her lightweight shawl fluttering around her and Agatha hurrying in her wake. She knew few people in her own right, rather than as the wife of Eugene Moisant, but one of them was Judge Reinhardt. He had been a friend of her mother's and also the lawyer before his elevation to the bench, who had drawn up her will and the marriage contract containing the terms of Lisette's dowry. Knowing Henri Moisant well, since they were of an age, the judge had made both documents as explicit and binding as possible. It was to him that Lisette owed much of her present independence.

The judge was at breakfast. Already dressed for the day, he rose as Lisette and Agatha came into the room, expressing his pleasure at their unexpected visit, his enjoyment of her salon some few days ago, and offering café au lait, and breakfast. Lisette was not at all hungry, but accepted the hot drink so the judge might continue with his own meal instead of letting it grow cold from politeness.

"You must wonder what brings us here so early," she said when the butler had been dismissed. "It is presumptuous of me to rely on past friendship, but I have a small favor to ask."

"Consider it done, *ma belle,* for the sake of your sainted mother." Judge Reinhardt gestured magnanimously with a well-buttered roll. "Though I cannot imagine anything it's in my power to do for you."

"It isn't for me personally, but for one who has run afoul of the gendarmes for my sake," she said, then launched into the tale.

"This is hardly a small matter," the judge said when she had finished. He sipped his café au lait while watching her with shrewd eyes.

"I believe it to be at the instigation of Henri Moisant and from spite. Surely there can be no fairness in allowing it to go further."

"It's been a terrible seasons for duels, you know. One hears of two or three or more every day. Young Jourdain died of his wounds last week, and the fiancé of my niece will walk bent over at the waist all his days because of a bout with a man he barely knew. Talk of this tournament of sword masters stirs the blood of young men so they are ready to slash at each other at the first hint of an excuse."

"I agree that it's senseless and should be discouraged, yet why should one man be singled out for the crime?"

"These professionals get above themselves."

"Is it their fault others see them as targets? Should they not defend themselves?"

"It's more than that, *chère*. I have heard rumors of demands made by some for money under penalty of a meeting."

"Not by Caid O'Neill. He sought only to protect a defenseless boy. But someone knew of the duel and arranged for the gendarmes to be there, so using justice for his own ends."

The judge looked thoughtful. "If this is true, it cannot be allowed. I will have to think on it, particularly in light of a certain odd notice which appeared lately."

"You do know of it," she said in suffocated tones. "I wondered."

"Someone made certain of it."

"But surely you can't believe…"

"Relieve your mind on that score, *chère*. I have nothing except contempt for such a crude ploy. But is it the reason you defend the bloodletting? Or is it that it pleases your vanity to know that men are willing to fight for you?"

"Most certainly not! I despise it for any reason."

"Yet I am told that no fewer than four duels have been fought in your honor by this O'Neill during these days just past. This one with Sarne would have made five."

Shock took her breath so it was an instant before she could speak. "Four? You are quite certain?"

"Such things cannot be kept quiet, *chère*. Soon everyone will know. You must have a great care that such ready defense doesn't give rise to the question of what could cause such desperate measures."

"I have told you the answer to that."

The judge shook his head so the morning light filtering through the dining room windows slid over the silver waves of his hair. "So you have. Still."

"You must see why it's more imperative than ever that Monsieur O'Neill not be brought to trial, even if he is likely to be acquitted."

"You make a good point," the judge said, frowning as he pulled at his lower lip.

Lisette, taking heart from these signs of agreement, continued to plead. Her reward was a promise to look into the matter. By the time she and her companion left the judge's house, she could be fairly sure that the charge against Caid would be dismissed.

"You amaze me," Agatha said as they turned toward the town house at a pace very much slower than when they had set out for the judge's residence.

Lisette gave her a wary glance. "I don't see why."

"You charge forth without hesitation, using your acquaintance with the judge to secure the freedom of a sword master who is a virtual stranger, but have not applied to this family friend for aid in your own situation."

"You know the judge is ineligible." Judge Reinhardt was a widower, and no unmarried man could sponsor an unattached woman without it being assumed that he had an interest in her of a personal, even intimate, nature. Lisette had accepted that fact long ago, just as she had recognized that her mother's friend would not necessarily approve of her actions of late.

"There must be other acquaintances of your mother's who might invite you to their entertainments, provide escorts to parties and balls, give you some semblance of a social life."

"There may have been, though who can say now? Truly, I prefer to remain as I am, at least until I leave off my black."

"If your mother's friends knew the truth about these ridiculous rumors and accusations, they might rally around you."

"Possibly. But I can't help hoping that my father-in-law will grow weary of his game when he sees that I will not be forced into compliance. Or that Monsieur O'Neill's efforts will convince him to give it up."

"I fear you are too sanguine. The man is beyond reason."

"I pray you are wrong, Agatha."

"So do I," her companion said, but she did not sound hopeful.

The day turned out fair in the afternoon, with a balmy softness to the air. The rain had washed some of the noisome debris from the gutters which ran down the middle of the streets, and a prison crew in their striped uniforms came along in good time to remove the rest. The pastel colors of the buildings seemed washed clean, merging their soft shades with the springlike ambience. The scents of garden pinks and sweet olive and jasmine drifted on the warm breezes, along with the perfume of wild azaleas. As the sun canted westward, throwing shadows of wrought iron across the galleries like black lace, it seemed much too nice to stay inside.

Lisette and Agatha ventured out, strolling in the direction of the levee. To promenade there was traditional in fair weather, and the numbers of family groups and young bachelors wending their way in that direction suggested that they had chosen a fine evening for it. After a block or two, Lisette chanced to glance back. The street boys had appeared from nowhere to trail after them. She was amazingly glad to see them, and to know that she had not been deserted after the furor of the evening before. On closer inspection, she noticed that one or two of their number were missing, though it was impossible to say whether they had grown bored and wandered away or if they had hared off to report her movements.

That question was answered in short order. They had progressed no more than a few dozen yards along the low, grassy river embankment when they saw a pair of gentlemen ascending it some distance farther along.

It was Caid and Nicholas, ambling along as though they had nothing on their minds other than taking the air. Bowing to the occasional lady with the inimitable grace that came from excellent physical condition, pausing now and then to speak to other gentlemen, they seemed oblivious to the presence of Lisette and her companion. Still it seemed unlikely that their appearance was an accident.

Lisette hoped that it was not. She still had much to discuss with Monsieur Caid O'Neill.

"It seems your efforts to have the gentleman released were not in vain," Agatha murmured.

"For which, the saints be praised."

"Do you think he is aware?"

"We shall soon see."

Lisette felt a small frisson of apprehension even as she spoke. Surely he would not mind her intervention? Men could be most peculiar about such things, as if pride and lack of obligation were more important that life. That was idiotic, and she had never been more certain of it than on hearing how many times Caid had put himself at risk for her sake.

"How delightful to see you here, Monsieur Pasquale," Agatha said as the four of them came even and bows were exchanged.

"It's a distinct pleasure to be out and about this evening," the Italian answered with laughter in his dark eyes. "You heard, I suppose, of our acquaintance with the new jail, O'Neill's as principal in a duel and I as his chief second?"

"And what a mercy it was so brief." Agatha's color was high, perhaps because she had the complete attention of the sword master with his meltingly soft eyes and dark hair that insisted on falling forward on his forehead in a curl.

"The mercy, *mademoiselle,* as we know well, is owed entirely to you and Madame Moisant. It's the kind of debt one despairs of ever repaying."

"Unnecessary, *monsieur,*" Lisette said, speaking to Nicholas though her gaze was on Caid. "Since the difficulty came about on my account, it was incumbent on me to remedy it."

"For myself, I prefer to think otherwise," Caid said with an edge to his voice. "May we now have done with the pleasantries? Other matters need settling before we begin to attract attention."

It was a little late for that, Lisette thought, noticing the heads of passersby turning in their direction. Still she spoke with as much composure as she could assume. "Such as?"

"Madame Herriot has taken a sudden decision to gather a house party at her upriver plantation. You and Mademoiselle Stilton will receive invitations in the morning, I believe. It would be convenient if you could accept."

"Convenient?"

"As a reason to remove from the city until the unpleasantness created by the posted notices and the Sarne duel has died down."

"An excellent scheme," Agatha said.

"The informality of the country should make a welcome change," Caid went on as he met and held Lisette's gaze. "More opportunity may be afforded to discuss the matter broached at our last meeting."

Lisette felt her heart leap against the wall of her chest. He meant the matter of her instruction in the art of love. "A…pleasant prospect." She paused to clear her throat of an unaccountable obstruction. "Is the plantation a great distance from town?"

"A matter of twelve or thirteen miles, I believe."

"Then there can be no objection to me driving myself."

His expression grew darker. "You will require an escort."

"I feel sure the problem will arrange itself."

"No doubt," he said as he tucked his cane under his arm and touched the brim of his beaver hat in farewell. "Madame Herriot's invitation will detail the arrangements. Until the house party then."

She had expected Caid to volunteer as her escort. That he had not left her annoyed and nonplussed. Watching him and the Italian as they strolled away alongside the river, Lisette said to Agatha, "Monsieur O'Neill was in an odd mood, did you not find it so?"

"It's often the case with gentlemen, particularly when they find themselves in an uncomfortable position."

"Uncomfortable?"

"They dislike being under an obligation to a female. Moreover, he has been made to feel unfit for respectable company, accused of dishonorable murder under the guise of a duel, forced to conduct private conversations in public and prevented from acting publicly as your protector by a raft of rules and prohibitions that have the end result of leaving you in danger. It's enough to try the patience of any man."

"Yes, I suppose." It seemed to Lisette, however, as she watched the Irish sword master stride away, that his grim mood did not encourage anticipation of this house party as a lover's tryst.

The day set to depart for the Herriot plantation dawned cloudy and afflicted by sultry heat. Not a breath of wind stirred as Lisette bowled out of town with Agatha up beside her on the seat of the phaeton and Figaro sitting upright between them. For outriders, she had Denys Vallier, Armand Lollain, Hippolyte Ducolet, Francis Dorelle and, as a nice addition, Judge Reinhardt. Bringing up the rear was Gustave Bechet, in a decrepit carriage that he shared with his mother.

Not a single swordsman kept her company.

The entourage was so respectable that it set her teeth on edge.

It was odd how used she had become to the company of

dangerous rakes, artistic types and other social outcasts. The stimulation of being a part of their circle was beyond anything she had ever known. It made her feel alive, feel included in something perilously close to family. To have the pleasure of the house party before her, with long hours spent in such company, was lovely; she could feel her spirits rising with every mile she put between her and town. Soon, soon, she would see Caid and Nicholas, perhaps Rio de Silva and his Celina, and even the Englishman, Blackford. She would be able to talk in a casual manner with those who shared her feelings and her interests, and without the need to be forever looking over her shoulder or worrying about the proprieties. It was, perhaps, a sad commentary on her character that this excited her much more than the promise of whatever entertainment Madame Herriot might have thought to provide.

They were a type, these masters at arms—powerful, aggressive, fearless, in many ways a law unto themselves. As a masculine ideal, they were peerless, and it was this to which she responded rather than to a particular man. Of course, that was it. Her skin burned at the mere thought of being touched by such as they were, her body ached for the perfect security that closeness must bring. She sometimes thought, waking in the night from feverish dreams, that she was hopelessly wanton in spirit if not in deed, so disturbing was her reaction to these fantasy encounters. That the swordsman of her nighttime fantasies always had Caid's face was an accident, because it was he whom she knew best. That was all. Well, and, more recently, because of his promise. Yes, that was enough to make any woman's mind wander in her sleep. A perfectly reasonable explanation, after all.

She slapped the reins on the glossy rump of the gray gelding and drove toward the Herriot plantation with her heart beating high in her chest, smiling and tossing laughing comments to the gentlemen who rode at the wheels of her vehicle. And if she was barely aware of what they answered or even that they existed, the secret was hers alone.

13

At the Herriot place, Maison Blanche, the season was advancing into spring, the trees lush with growth and cane fields a checkerboard of rows in various stages from just planted to ankle and knee high. Named for its West Indies style house whose wide eaves and galleries shaded white-washed walls built of heart cypress over a whitewashed raised basement of stuccoed brick, the estate was sizable.

Caid, standing with his hands braced on the railing of the upper gallery, looked out over the prospect. A parklike area, spotted with live oaks and marked by a winding drive, stretched from the front of the house to the Mississippi River with its low levee that was maintained by the planters who lived along it. To his right lay the outbuildings: the carriage house, chapel, blacksmith and coppersmith shops, school and nursery, doctor's office and, farther back, the diary barn, corncribs and tree-shaded track lined with white-washed slave cabins. Beyond these were the fields. On his left was a flower garden with shrubbery borders, beds, arbors and winding paths which directed strollers toward a natural, wooded area encircled by the river. The daffodils and jonquils were almost gone along the garden walks, he saw. Maurelle's favorite flowers, the camellias, littered the ground with their petals so thickly that a gardener was gathering them into drifts with long sweeps of his broom made of dogwood saplings. The China roses, along with the gallicas and Bourbons brought from Italy and France, were already opening their buds so their sweet perfume wafted across the gallery.

It was really too warm today, even for this semitropical latitude. The atmosphere was oppressive and so thick with moisture that fitful sunlight refracted the green of grass and trees from it to give the light an emerald sheen. An occasional cloud covered the sun, lending a general air of gloom.

Few of the guests invited by Maurelle had arrived as yet. It was early; still Caid was restless. In order to be here these few days, he had closed his atelier. He would normally be crossing swords with pupils, calling instructions and admonishments at this hour. His muscles felt stiff with tension, as if missing their usual work on the strips. It was to be hoped that the change in his routine had no lasting effect. He could ill afford to lose clients.

The sound of quiet footsteps on the planking of the gallery brought his head around. It was Maurelle, gliding from the sitting room by way of its open French doors, moving to his side with studied languor as if she had nothing better to do. Possibly she didn't. Her house was filled with servants, each with a specific task. He was certain their management was more strenuous than it seemed, but if the prospect of two dozen or more guests descending within the next few hours troubled her in the slightest, she gave no sign.

His mam had always been thrown into a dither by company, Caid remembered. That was the difference having servants made. He wished with sudden fierceness that he could have given his mother the same leisure that he saw here, the same freedom from work and worry.

"Alors, mon ami," Maurelle said with a smile. "What a sentinel you make. Is there anything to be seen?"

"A dust plume on the river road." He turned to face her with his back to the railing, moving aside to make room for her skirts which seemed likely to polish the yellow dust of tree pollen from his boot vamps.

"I hope it is Madame Moisant at last, for your sake. Or your friends at the very least."

"Have I been unbearable?" he asked with a wry smile.

"Like a caged tiger waiting for its dinner." Maurelle opened the fan which dangled from the chatelaine at her waist and waved it gently before her face.

"My apologies. It's not something I do well, waiting. But while I have the chance, permit me to tell you again how obliged I am to you for arranging this party."

"Please, it's less than nothing. A few days of rest in the country had great appeal, I promise. I had become quite *fatiguée,* you know. The entertainments of the *saison* grow more burdensome every year."

"Then why bother? Why not remain in the country?"

"One is reluctant to become known as a rustic." Her smile was brief. "Besides, I quite enjoy the gossip, the new gowns, new faces. I am easily bored, you perceive."

"And honest, with it."

"Oh, always that." The words were light enough, but she looked away from him, out over the fields from which came the wealth that she seemed to enjoy so much.

"Tell me," he began then stopped, uncertain how to put what he wanted to know.

"But yes, *mon ami?*"

"Have you never thought of marrying again?"

"You are proposing, perhaps?"

He gave a short laugh. "I think you know the answer to that, and the reason."

"Ah, yes, your lack of prospects."

"Among other things."

"Such a pity. But in truth, I have no great regard for matrimony, so no intention of embarking upon it again at present."

"You are satisfied as you are?"

"*Précisément.* Is it so difficult to believe?"

Caid shook his head, thinking of Lisette and a similar declaration. "This lack of regard…" He stopped, uncertain that

Maurelle was actually sophisticated enough to permit the question he had in mind.

"You wish to know why? Is that it?"

"In part. I wonder if it's the restrictions, the fear of the pain of childbirth, or simply distaste for the physical obligations."

She drew away from him a few inches. "You have no right to be so particular."

"No. I do apologize."

"Why were you? Or no, allow me to guess. Madame Moisant has expressed such reservations."

"Yes, if you must know."

"So you wish to understand the objection in order to overcome it? A praiseworthy aim, if misguided."

He folded his arms over his chest while a frown sat between his eyes. "Misguided in what way?"

"Must I point out the obvious? No two women are alike in this matter. Some may object to one thing, some to another."

"I asked about you."

"So you did." Her smile had a twist to it. "Very well, then. It was not the physical obligation that troubled me, though I had no great appreciation for it. Rather, my nature was too independent, some would say too proud, to submit easily to the will of a husband. I was not born to be the servant of any man, and object to being ordered about in the thousand and one small ways that men find to command their wives."

"A small thing, surely, one that could be cured by frank discussion."

"If you think so, then you have no understanding of the situation. Most gentlemen have been reared to feel their every wish should be instantly granted, their every need filled, every comfort seen to by the females around them. They think nothing of lounging in their chairs and waggling their wineglasses to signal for a refill, or thrusting out a leg and grunting as a signal that they wish their boots removed."

"Surely there should be others for such tasks."

"Servants, you mean? That would require that they ring for them and wait on their appearance. Why bother when they have a convenient person ready to hand in their wives."

The bitterness in her voice gave Caid pause. He wondered if he had ever been so carelessly certain that the females close to him owed him servitude. He remembered, in a vague way, his mother's attention to his comfort, but didn't think he had taken it for granted. "Such egotism might be expected to extend to the marriage bed. If so, then a certain lack of…enthusiasm there on the part of a wife becomes understandable."

She raised a graceful brow. "You seem unable to turn your mind away from that subject, *cher.*"

He had the honesty to admit it, though he still possessed the grace to be embarrassed. It had, in fact, been with him for days, since the moment he realized something of what lay at the root of Lisette's reluctance to accept a husband.

"But from what else should such a lack be derived except resentment over imperious demands?"

He shook his head. "Failure to reach the pinnacle of shared pleasure of a certainty. Failure to share the generous impulse and the satisfaction of receiving as well as giving."

Maurelle gave him a considering glance, though her voice was light when she spoke. "Such novel concepts, *mon ami,* though they are sure to endear you to the woman you eventually marry."

"Or ideas that may never see practice."

"What a shame."

Maurelle's warm brown eyes met Caid's for long seconds. In the quiet between them lay a wealth of possibilities and implications. If he lifted a hand, Caid thought, he could probably draw her to him, kiss her, perhaps more than that. She was a woman of experience, independence and curiosity. He was a man of compassion, normal appetites and little to lose. It would be easy to make love to the lady, and perhaps even to mean it to some small degree. Not so long ago, he might have taken up the challenge without a thought or backward glance.

Now he couldn't do it. What had changed, he wasn't sure, but it seemed fundamental and, quite possibly, permanent. He didn't move, nor did his hostess. Then beyond the screen of live oaks, a carriage turned into the drive with a crunching of the oyster shells that filled its ruts. They turned toward the sound.

"A veritable cavalcade," Maurelle murmured, her expression droll as she surveyed the phaeton with its escort, also Madame Bechet's traveling carriage and the baggage wagon that followed with a pair presumed to be her maid and Gustave's valet. "I do believe Madame Moisant has arrived."

Relief and satisfaction welled up inside Caid, though irritation threatened to overcome them. Entirely too many men rode with Lisette. One or two would have been sufficient for her safety, three might have added to her consequence, but six made her grossly conspicuous, the one thing he had hoped to avoid. Where had they all come from, and, more importantly, what the devil was he going to do with them over the next few days?

Turning stiffly from the railing, he offered his arm to Maurelle. Together, they descended to the front of the house to greet the new arrivals.

Lisette appeared in high spirits as she brought the phaeton to a halt with a flourish before the wide front steps. Her driving costume was black of course, but piped in a soft gray that matched her eyes and finished with a jaunty shoulder cape. She wore a hat rather than a bonnet that might restrict her side vision, one in the stovepipe style that was swathed in gray veiling with ends that fluttered behind her. Her eyes sparkled with gaiety, her smile was brilliant, and her seat on the driving bench ramrod straight with no hint whatever of tiredness from the drive. As she turned to descend, she was abruptly surrounded by the men of her escort who had dismounted and now clamored for the honor of helping her down.

Caid stood perfectly still while his eyes burned with the intensity of his gaze and his heartbeat increased to the heavy Bamboula rhythm of a Saturday night in Congo Square. His first inclination was to hand out mass cartels to the entourage or, failing that, drag Lisette down from the carriage and make passionate love to her in front of the assembly. That she could arrive this way while knowing the reason she had been invited here incensed him beyond reason. Or maybe she didn't understand. Maybe she had no inkling of the burning impatience and ferocious need that gripped him. Could she possibly believe their discussion of her experience with love, or lack of it, had been mere conversation without point? Certainly, she seemed unconscious of any special reason for his presence.

In truth, she hardly seemed to notice him at all. Handing the reins to a stable hand who had come running, she surveyed the group of men who waited to learn which one she would chose.

It was too much.

Caid strode down the steps and shouldered his way through the group of gallants. Reaching the phaeton's near side, he gazed up at Lisette. It occurred to him to lift both hands and catch her waist, holding her an instant in that one semiacceptable instance of closeness. He decided against it at once—far better, under the circumstances, to err on the side of staid respectability. Schooling his features to impassivity, he held out his hand.

Lisette's smile faded as she met his eyes. For long seconds, she regarded him, her expression searching. Then she reached to accept his support. Her grasp was tight, and he thought he felt a tremor in it. That one small indication of her awareness had to suffice him, for then she was on the ground and murmuring her appreciation in prosaic tones before turning to greet Maurelle. Caid was left to take Figaro and then hand down Mademoiselle Stilton, accompanying her into the house. It did little for his feelings to note the look bent upon him by Lisette's companion, one of crisp irony overlaid with sympathy.

Before Lisette and her party were settled, Rio de Silva arrived with his fiancée, Celina, and her father, Monsieur Vallier, plus Nicholas Pasquale and Gavin Blackford. Caid feared too large a percentage of the company would be made up of *maîtres d'armes*, but was reassured by the arrival of Governor Roman and a half dozen other notables to aid Judge Reinhardt in lending respectability. A few astringent glances were cast in the direction of the sword masters, but politeness, or perhaps self-preservation, forestalled any complaints. Maurelle, with great foresight, had made certain no *jeune filles* were invited for the weekend. The lack of such innocents may also have contributed to the attitude of laissez-faire.

The original suggestion for the house party had come from Celina, or so Caid thought, one quickly put into play to allow Lisette to retreat from town after the affair of Moissant's insulting broadside. She had suggested, as well, that other guests be added to prevent the ploy from becoming too obvious. Caid hoped that she and Maurelle between them hadn't overdone it.

Country hours were kept at Maison Blanche. This was primarily because there were no formal evening entertainments such as the theater or balls to require rearrangement of the evening hours, but also due to the early hours kept by male guests intent on pursuits such as shooting, fishing and riding. As introduction to the regime, an early luncheon was served at noon, after which some members of the party repaired to chairs on the gallery to chat or nap in the warmth.

Several couples descended to Maurelle's garden to view her prized roses. Caid was among these, in large part because Lisette and Mademoiselle Stilton expressed keen interest. Rio and Celina joined them, as did Nicholas, who gave his arm to Maurelle, and also Gavin Blackford. By chance, Caid found himself partnered with Lisette's companion on the brick walkway where only two could stroll abreast. The two of them brought up the rear, behind Blackford and Lisette, as they wandered along the paths edged with lemon thyme and violas that wafted their fragrance into the air when the skirts of the ladies brushed against them.

"It was kind of you to have me included in this outing along with Lisette," Agatha Stilton said as she moved with upright posture at his side.

How much did she know? Caid could gain no idea from her expression. "It was Madame Herriot's idea, I assure you."

"Indeed? I must remember to thank her. But how lovely to be here! The pleasures of town are considerable, yet I am drawn to the country. There is nothing like it in spring."

"Are you a gardener, *mademoiselle?*" The question was occasioned by her halt to pull an errant weed while sniffing an odd rose blossom made up of green petals.

"An enthusiast only, *monsieur,* since I have never had a plot of land on which to try my skill. Perhaps one day."

"You must apply to Maurelle when the time comes. I'm sure she would be happy to supply you with rose cuttings."

"That would be a kindness, but then I should not be surprised. The lady has been more than generous with her town house, theater box and now her plantation. It means a great deal to Lisette, I can tell you. I am grateful, for her sake, that you put her in the way of the friendship."

"Madame Moisant gathers friends easily, particularly gentlemen friends."

"You refer to her retinue this morning, I believe? It was

not planned, you know. We set out with young Vallier, but were soon overtaken on the road by the others. Dear Lisette was attempting to maintain a sedate pace to avoid mishaps, and that in itself allowed still others to catch up to us. Before we knew, we were a parade."

Was the lady attempting to reassure him? It was impossible to tell from her prim expression. "I have no right to question her choice of company."

"I should think not. Still, I would not have you think that she intended to make a spectacle of her arrival. Nor, I venture to guess, would she wish you to believe it. She is fully conscious of her indebtedness to you."

"No such thing," he said with revulsion. "Any effort of mine has been in repayment of the wrong I did her."

"If you mean the removal of Eugene Moisant, I cannot consider it anything other than a release."

"So Madame Lisette suggested, but that may have been mere politeness."

Agatha Stilton's footsteps slowed so the two of them fell farther behind. "I assure you, it was not. I dislike betraying a confidence, but you should know, I think, that the man— I cannot give him the title of gentleman—was quite unscrupulous in his methods of extracting funds from her. It was not what she had been led to expect. A lonely young woman living alone with her mother who was in ill health the last years of her life, she longed for a wider family circle, friends and acquaintances, acceptance and belonging. Instead, Eugene Moisant ignored her presence except as a convenient source of funds. She can hardly be blamed for thinking twice before entering any similar alliance."

"All men are not cut from the same cloth."

"No, but how is one to tell? A husband's true character, and that of his relatives, may be revealed only after the vows have been spoken."

"I agree it's a gamble."

"For a female who has never known the true union of souls in or out of the marriage bed, it can seem too great a risk to undertake. If she had more experience of that nature, the venture might not seem quite so desperate."

Her gaze was narrowed upon his face, Caid saw, as if she hinted at some meaning not immediately obvious. Was she saying that Lisette had not reached fulfillment in the marriage bed, or that she was truly untried, a virgin in fact? The last was a stunning possibility. But even if correct, Agatha surely could not be suggesting a remedy that he might supply. Could she?

"Experience," he said slowly, "is not normally considered an advantage in a prospective bride."

"In the view of the groom, no. We are not concerned with his advantage, however, but my dear Lisette's. Such experience must be unexceptional in a widow."

Impatience with such roundabout discussion flooded over him. "Are you suggesting that she may never marry again unless she receives this experience?"

"Or some intimation of the true meaning of conjugal happiness."

The back of Caid's neck grew hot as he wondered if Lisette might have discussed his intent in this direction with her companion. "Something of the sort may be seen by paying close attention to De Silva and his Celina. They are highly compatible, from all appearances."

She looked away from him, though high color rode her cheekbones. "To be sure, and yet I doubt that is sufficient to the purpose. Something more physical may be necessary."

"You mean…"

"I leave it to your imagination, sir. And your kind offices."

Kind? The word was not one that he associated with the intense heat he felt at the thought of any service of a physical nature that he might perform for Lisette Moisant. Still it was oddly gratifying to know that he was thought capable of it.

They said no more, for the party ahead had stopped to make out the inscription on a corroded sundial set in a diamond-shaped bed around which the path diverged, and he and Agatha caught up with them. It was just as well.

Leaving the rose garden, they gathered on the lower gallery where drinks were served. For the ladies, there was sangaree, or spiced and watered wine, as well as mint tea cooled with cracked ice and flavored with orange flower water, and for the gentlemen, Madeira or Palmes Margaux wine along with chilled *bière* Creole. With these came a collection of nibbles to stave off any suggestion of hunger, including bowls of olives and almonds, dishes of brandied cherries and trays of macaroons.

Cards were produced for those inclined in that direction, primarily the older ones among them who quickly became immersed in games of *bourée*. An impromptu group gathered around the pianoforte in the music room just off the gallery, from which the mellow notes eddied out to the others. One or two couples danced their way out through the open doors, whirling completely around the main structure of the house while weaving in and out among the chairs and tables that cluttered the galleries. Caid was inveigled into singing, giving them an Irish air or two before being joined by Rio, Nicholas and Blackford for a quartet of voices blending to the strains of "The Rose of Tralee."

Toward evening, when cards, music and dancing palled, playbooks were brought out and pored over with the idea of an amateur theatrical to be given on Sunday evening, a proceeding greeted with cries of delight by the ladies and groans from the gentlemen. The decision fell on Sheridan's perennially popular *School for Scandal*. A salon comedy with a small cast and few scene changes, therefore suitable for their relatively small group, it was a tale of cross-purposes and hidden agendas among members of a malicious circle of gossips. Caid suspected irony on Maurelle's part in the choice, but would not give her the satisfaction of accusing her of it. The ladies set to work, copying out the various parts, though none were yet assigned. So the afternoon and evening wore away until it grew dark and the whine of mosquitoes drove them inside.

Supper was a less elaborate meal than dinner, consisting merely of redfish chowder and rice and tomato soup, followed by broiled pompano in a stewed sauce and removed in succession by turkey with oyster sauce, beef tongue, warm meat pies, Lyons sausages, chicken salad, oysters baked in the shell and a selection of custards, cheeses and nuts, all served with various wines and followed by *café brûlot* and cordials, particularly a nice Dantzig. Enthusiasm flagged afterward, and the guests began to yawn and wander off, one by one, to bed.

Caid, who had taken possession of a corner of the upper gallery, was joined by Rio and Nicholas. Rio offered his special cigars, prepared to his order by Madame O'Hara's tobacco shop on Saint Pierre. Blackford, when he arrived a few minutes later, declined one of the smokes, but carried a brandy bottle by its neck and a bouquet of glasses in his other hand.

"So, how goes things?" Rio asked when they were all supplied with refreshment.

Caid lifted a brow. "In general or…?"

"With the Brotherhood, I should have said. Some few incidents are known to me, but I feel sure I've missed others."

"The two meetings I've had, you know about from acting as second," Nicholas said from where he lounged against the railing. As always, he appeared elegantly put together in some indefinable fashion, as if knowledge of manly style was in his bones.

"One only for me." Rio contemplated the end of his cigar with a rueful smile. "My time is not my own, you know, but at Celina's service."

"And you would have it no other way," Caid said.

"Agreed, being no man's fool."

"I've had two myself," Caid said, "and also paid a visit to a certain printer to discuss the inadvisability of printing further broadsides concerning Lisette. He seemed to see the force of my argument, particularly after I told him to refer to me anyone who sought to engage him for a similar task."

"This is in addition to the various official challenges issued to protect Madame Moisant's good name, I suppose," Rio said. "Speaking of which, what became of Sarne?"

"I've seen nothing of him since he left the field ahead of the gendarmes, but his seconds presented his apology for his conduct toward Squirrel."

"Which you accepted, I suppose."

Caid lifted a shoulder. "It seemed best since I had made plans to be out of town."

"And you had exhausted your temper by then, let us hope."

"You could say that." Caid took a mouthful of the mellow brandy in his glass.

"And you?" Rio asked, turning to the Englishman.

"I fear I'm behind times compared to the rest of you. I've only issued a warning."

"To anyone we know?"

"Possibly." Blackford dipped his head. "You are acquainted with an American named Haughton, Jubal Haughton?"

The others shook their heads, as did Caid as he studied the Englishman, noting his neatly tailored frock coat and pantaloons, more loosely styled than was favored by the French Creoles.

"I met him myself at a quadroon ball where I witnessed his boorish behavior." Blackford swirled the liquid in his glass, his gaze on the iridescence that coated its crystal interior. "He seemed to believe that he had the right to a public sampling of his chosen *placée's* charms before committing to her upkeep. The young woman was…upset."

The entertainment Blackford mentioned were relatively staid affairs, in the main, but with definite sensual undercurrents. Attended only by white men of wealth or some degree of social standing, they were dances where young women born of white fathers and more than half white, half black mothers were displayed for selection as concubines. The girls, chaste, exotically attractive, many of them as carefully reared and educated as their Creole sisters of the same age, might be selected on their first appearance held at the old St. Philip Theater ballroom. Binding negotiations ensued forthwith between the gentleman and the girl's mother, or sometimes between the mother and the young gentleman's father who might provide the girl as an essential part of his son's education. A settlement would be made which covered purchase of a house in the girl's name on Rampart Street at the rear of the Vieux Carré, also an allowance and provision for the support and education of any children. A few such unions lasted a lifetime, or so Caid had been told, though most ended with the man's marriage.

Caid had attended one or two such balls out of curiosity, but soon learned to avoid them. He could not afford to keep a *placée,* for one thing, but the arrangement turned his stomach, as well, being too much a reminder of Brona's situation.

"Your sympathies were engaged, I suppose," he said to Blackford in deliberate tones. "Or did you want the girl for yourself?"

Blackford gave him a straight look. "Haughton was drunk. The girl was frightened and embarrassed, and no one else seemed likely to come to her aid. I recalled my oath and took the gentleman aside to remind him of his manners."

It was entirely possible that he had misjudged the Englishman, Caid realized. "He abandoned his pursuit?"

"And sobered enough to take his leave in some haste."

Blackford shielded his gaze with lowered lids. "It was rather a disappointment. I'd have liked to bleed him a little."

"Well done," Rio said with a small salute of his brandy glass.

Nicholas followed suit.

"There is another thing," Blackford added, "though on a matter other than The Brotherhood."

Rio lifted a brow. "We are done with that, I think. What is it?"

"I spoke to the head of the tournament committee. He allowed me to know the identity of my first opponent as well as the projected order of subsequent bouts."

"And that would be who?"

"Thimecourt, for the first round."

Caid whistled. The man was a French cavalry officer, and no mean swordsman.

"Quite," Blackford said in sardonic agreement. "For the second, should I be the victor, of course, I am to fight the winner of your first bout, O'Neill."

"Something to look forward to," Caid said with a ready grin. "Let's hope we both survive to a second round."

"As you say."

It had been inevitable that some of them, Blackford, Nicholas and himself, must meet on the strips, Caid thought—Rio would be out of it, of course, from consideration for his bride and his looming journey to Spain. He'd as soon not have to face La Roche while others jeered and hooted in the background and both vied for the golden prize of Best of the Best. Pray God it didn't happen, since he was well aware of his quality. Blackford's, on the other hand, was unknown. In addition, he was aware of an unspoken rivalry pulsing between them, one based on ancient resentments and traditions as well as some undefined antagonism. It behooved him to learn more of the man's style, his strengths and weaknesses, in the days before the tournament began.

Apparently, Nicholas's mind was running along the same lines, for he spoke up just then. "We should keep our hand in during these few days, don't you all agree? A bout now and then wouldn't come amiss, with the proper padding and buttons."

"What of the ladies?"

"Ladies?" Blackford inquired with a frown.

Nicholas shrugged. "I had not thought of their attending, but it might be difficult to prevent them from catching wind of it."

Blackford lifted a brow. "Hardly an edifying sight for them, I'd say. Their delicate sensibilities must keep them away."

Rio gave Blackford a pitying look. "You don't know Creole ladies. Their sensibilities are as fine as any woman's, but their curiosity, not to mention their daring, is honed to a far keener edge."

"Then let them watch," the Englishman said with a glimmer of bright speculation in his eyes. "I've no objection."

It went against the grain with Caid. Practice would be a much stiffer and inconclusive affair if they could not strip down to shirtsleeves. "I think we should keep it as quiet as possible, and hope we are done before they rise from their beds."

"You have no inclination to provide additional entertainment for Madame Herriot's house party? You are most uncooperative, *mon ami*," Nicholas said with a lazy grin.

"Taking a part in her damned play will have to be enough."

A rumble of laughter greeted that heartfelt complaint. Caid shook his head and looked away.

He was just in time to catch sight of a shadow falling from inside a room farther along the way that he thought was the study used here by Maurelle's late husband. The glimpse was fleeting, but he required only a second to recognize the

domed shape of a woman's full skirts and the distinctive
lines and silhouetted profile of Madame Lisette Moisant.
Then the shadow retreated and the light was closed off as
the jalousies were pulled shut over the opening. A rattle of
brass rings and further dimming of the light told of the
draperies being pulled for the night.

The hunger of desire hit Caid like a blow to the solar
plexus. Every sense strained toward Lisette's retreat. The
need to seek her out in that room was so strong that he felt
perspiration break out across his forehead.

Still, he waited through several more minutes of desul-
tory conversations, waited until he had finished his brandy.
Then tossed his barely tasted cigar into a handy brass cuspidor. "Time to call it a night, I think," he said casually. "I'll
see you all at dawn."

Grumbling mixed with calls of good-night followed him
as he turned away. He answered over his shoulder, but did
not look back.

Caid made his way into the house, then crossed with
noiseless treads the salon from which the study opened. He
listened a moment outside the door, but heard no voices to
indicate that Lisette was not alone. The knob turned without a sound under his hand. He eased inside, then closed the
door and leaned against it. If Lisette heard, if she knew he
was there, she did not turn.

The writing table where she sat was hardly a yard square.
Above it, a mosquito *baire* of ivory gauze was suspended
from a hook set into the paneled ceiling, forming a diapha-
nous canopy that wafted gently in the rising heat of a single
tall candle. Half-hidden within this bower, seated on a small
chair cushioned with watered silk, Lisette was safe from ma-
rauders of the winged variety, if nothing else. A glass pen
tray and inkwell sat before her, and she drove a pen over a
sheet of thick paper. From the way she glanced at a sheet
lying in front of her, he thought she might be copying out

lines from the play, but she could as easily be answering a letter.

She seemed oblivious of his presence, continuing to write with steady purpose. Yet something in the hunch of her shoulder and tilt of her head hinted that it was a charade. The notice of him taken by Figaro, who thumped his tail in brief acknowledgment where he lay almost hidden behind the window draperies, should have alerted her. Caid wanted to think so, wanted to believe that Lisette waited for him. Otherwise, his intentions, honed by fervid imagination and rampant need, were too dishonorable to be borne.

A hard shape at one side of his lower back told him that the key for the study was in the door. He reached back, grasped and turned it with a single, deliberate twist of his wrist.

14

Lisette lifted her head like a deer scenting danger as she heard the quiet click of the door lock. Swinging around on her chair, she saw Caid moving toward her. His footsteps had the silent glide of a panther. His features appeared grim and watchful through the tent of gauze that had been the refuge of Maurelle's husband while he wrote in his plantation journal each night. Her breath caught in her throat as a thousand fears and impressions tumbled along her nerves. The knowledge of his purpose bloomed in her mind with suffocating heat.

He had come to answer her challenge. At last.

Her heart shuddered in her chest. Anticipation burned like acid coursing through her veins. She moistened her lips as her chest began to rise and fall as if she was about to enter a race. Instinctively, she flicked a glance around the room, seeking escape.

There was none. To run away now would be cowardly, the end of all her plans. All that was required was the courage to survive the next few minutes.

She wasn't sure she could muster it. To invite one of the most dangerous men in New Orleans to make love to her was one thing, to sustain the experience quite another. Yet, why else was she here?

The challenge was hers, but the time and place was of Caid's selection. That made it different. Somehow, at this instant, she felt herself to be at his mercy. And she had no idea if he could be, or meant to be, merciful.

Barrier or protection, the mosquito *baire* hung between

them. To remain behind it was discourteous, but she could not quite make herself step outside it. She expected Caid to stop as he reached it, but he did no such thing. Lifting a hand, he laid his fingers unerringly on the slit where the hemmed edges came together, parted them and stepped inside.

She came to her feet in instant alarm. It was a mistake, since instead of towering over her, he was mere inches away, far too near in the enclosed space. His eyes were vivid sea-blue, the pupils wide in the dimness, reflecting the candle-light as twin golden flames as he watched her. Then with a swift, almost negligent, gesture, he reached to pinch the candle flame from its wick.

His warm breath fanned her cheek as he straightened, bringing to life senses she scarcely knew she possessed. The aroma of leaf tobacco, the headiness of brandy, night freshness and warm male assailed her. Without conscious thought, she put out a hand to touch the satin lapel of his evening coat, though whether to ward him off or draw him closer, she could not have said. Taking her fingers, he raised them to his lips then placed them on his opposite shoulder as he circled her waist and drew her against him.

A shiver moved over her, shaking her from the bemused trance that held her. "What…what if someone tries to open the door? What must they think?"

"Nothing, except that the lock was turned for a purpose. Far better they should wonder what someone may be doing on the other side than they walk in and find out exactly."

"Yes, I suppose." The words were no more than a whisper.

"Is this a change of heart? Tell me now, *chérie*, yes or no? Say it while I have the mind and strength to release you. Delay more than a moment, and it may be too late."

"It was too late days ago."

"Then you accept what is to come?"

The faint trembling that ran along her nerves entered her voice as she answered, "I require it."

A soft sound left him. Then he lowered his head, paused. His lips hovered above hers for a lingering second, as if he still allowed her the chance to turn aside. She slid the fingers of her hand that was caught between them higher, smoothing them along the lapel until she touched the taut column of his neck. Then she pushed her fingers into the crisp silk of his hair that grew at his nape. The gentle pressure she applied there was permission and invitation.

He took her lips, melding their tender surfaces to the smooth warmth of his own. His strength surrounded her, supported her. Swaying against him, she gave herself up to the taste and texture of him, to the power he held in such stern control. Amazement filtered into her consciousness along with vagrant gratitude and sheer, effervescent pleasure. The urge to press closer, to blend with him, into him, was so powerful that she felt light-headed with it. The restrictions of clothing, place and societal expectations were so frustrating that her lips parted to release a low moan.

His grasp tightened and he deepened the kiss, invading with a satin sweep of his tongue. Making free of the warm recess of her mouth, he savored its depths at leisure, as if discovering its textures, its taste, before engaging her tongue in sinuous play. She thought he smiled; it had that feel. Or perhaps it was a sign of pleasure. Then by degrees, he withdrew, encouraging her pursuit, her explorations.

His mouth was sweet, the flavor as heady as the finest cordial. She traced the molded edges of his lips, felt the faint prickles where his beard grew, enjoyed the delicate throb of the pulse there as he held himself in abeyance, though the steel-hardness of the muscles under his coat testified to the effort required for that restraint. Her heartbeat quickened. It was difficult to breathe against the constriction of her corset.

She was hot, so hot inside that the very core of her being seemed to turn to molten liquid.

He cradled her face with his hand, smoothing along the hollow of her cheek as though memorizing the bone structure beneath, brushing the high cheekbone with his thumb. Carefully, he threaded his fingertips into her high-piled hair even as he feathered a path of kisses from the corner of her mouth to the point of her chin and along the turn of her jaw to the sensitive hollow behind her ear. Then he held her against him as he rested his face against her hair, swinging her gently.

Maître d'armes, master at arms. Caid Roe O'Neill was that, a master of concern and skill at love, endlessly controlled.

She didn't want him to be in control.

His heedful tending of her responses while showing little of his own was disturbing. She needed to know that she moved him just as his nearness, his physical strength and incalculable aura of masculinity affected her. She wanted him at the mercy of the swift rush of the blood in his veins, wanted him to let slip the tumult she sensed behind his stern facade and join her in sweet and wild abandon. To be the pupil for a lesson in love was a lovely and fascinating thing, but lacked some essential ingredient. If the object was to instruct her in the joys of the marriage bed, of what use was a passionless demonstration?

With a soft murmur, Lisette pressed closer against him. She could feel the raised stripe pattern of his waistcoat under her hand, sense the rock-solid wall of his chest underneath. To slide her palm under the edge of his open coat, sensing the musculature, enjoying the warmth and resilience of his flesh, made her heart swell inside her. What freedom there was in it, what incredible pleasure in the knowledge that no one could forbid it.

If she had thought to encourage his active participation,

she must accept disappointment. He allowed her unimpeded access, but seemed scarcely to notice her incursion as she smoothed her way to his silk-clad back, testing the play of muscles there as he shifted slightly to splay his fingers at the slender indentation of her waist.

"Is this always how it goes?" she asked in a fretted whisper while resting her forehead against his lapel. Her fingers itched to release the elaborately tied knot of his cravat but she stifled the impulse.

"Not always."

Was his voice a little rough? She couldn't be sure. "What else is there?"

"Many things, beginning with this," he said, and skimmed his hand upward to cup her breast. Finding the nipple beneath the silken layers of her bodice, he brushed it with his thumb. "What do you think?"

"Very…pleasant."

"Only pleasant? Nothing more?"

"Enticing," she allowed. "Or it could be, I think."

"And what prevents it?"

"An excess of covering and…and the need to know it was more agreeable to you."

"Believe me when I tell you that it's no hardship," he answered with a slight quake of his chest.

"But no delight, either."

His movements stilled. "What makes you say so?"

"You don't seem particularly moved."

"Moved."

"Excited, enthralled."

"You mean to indicate that I'm not panting with desire."

The edge in his voice made her uneasy, but she refused to retreat. "Something of that sort. Should there not be at least some small show of feeling?"

Silence held him for an instant. Then he circled her waist with one tempered-steel arm, lifted her and moved forward a single stride to set her on the writing table. Immediately, he stepped between her spread knees, easing them wider even as he pushed his hands under her skirts and flipped them up into her lap.

"Is this more what you had in mind?" he demanded, his breath hot against her ear.

"Yes…no…I'm not sure." She retrieved her wits with an effort. "It could depend on…on what comes next."

He seemed to take her answer as a challenge, and why not? What else was it indeed? And the result was satisfactory in the extreme as he skimmed the low neckline of her evening gown off one shoulder, exposing a breast, then lowered his mouth to hers again in heated possession.

It was overwhelming, an unerring sensual onslaught against which she had no defense, and desired none. His touch was magic as he sought the areas of her body where lay the most intense, shivering reaction. His strength surrounded her, supported her. His expertise stirred untapped longing, bringing it to sentient life.

Nor was he immune, now, to her hesitant caresses, her small attempts to return a measure of the incredible feeling that he roused inside her. His heartbeat increased, his skin, his clothing, his touch radiated vital heat, his chest rose and fell as if he could not find enough air to breathe under the confining net of the mosquito *baire*.

And still, as he kissed the soft, blue-veined curves of her breast and laved with his tongue the sensitive, berry-tight nipple he had uncovered, he refrained from leaving her too exposed. He disturbed not a single, high-piled curl of her upswept hair as he cupped the back of her head for his kiss. Her skirts were folded back out of his way but not crushed. Not an inch of lace was torn or ribbon crinkled by his ministrations. She could not have been handled with more deference and assiduous care if she had been made of spun glass.

Lisette wanted to protest, wanted to rip open the buttons

and studs of his waistcoat and shirt, to press her naked flesh to his while inciting him to ungovernable transports of love or at least the lust that was a semblance of it. She longed to throw off clothing and constraints in equal measure and tumble to the floor, naked and unashamed, in his arms.

It was impossible.

Manners instilled over long years, reinforced by his gentlemanly forbearance, prevented her. These and also the fear that it was not respect alone that caused his high courtesy but rather her inability to inspire anything more.

Then came the moment when his long, swordsman's fingers, questing with delicious deliberation between the split half legs of her silk pantaloons, among the moist, satin folds at the apex of her thighs, pressed deep, deeper, then paused. He stiffened, and his arm that held her semireclining against him, closed tightly upon her. He was still for interminable seconds, his heartbeat thundering near her ear as though he had ceased to breathe.

A soft imprecation left him, one she couldn't fully decipher in her delirious, slumberous trance. She stirred in distress, hovering in the crucible of unappeased longing and the need for something that had always been just beyond her reach.

He soothed her with soft words that had no meaning, apologies and promises and quiet condemnation of arrogant, ignorant men, not excluding himself. She didn't listen, couldn't think, was beyond caring as his strong, supple fingers invaded and withdrew, tantalized and stroked in clever, insidious rhythms that matched the frantic beat of her heart.

It came upon her then like a dark tide edged in phosphorescent joy. It closed in on her, catching her for a frozen instant of mindless, shattering pleasure. It was transfiguring, the breath-stopping contraction of time and mind, a ravishment of the heart that threatened soul and sanity. She cried out, though Caid captured the sound in his mouth, swallowing it as he turned her against him and held her close.

Minutes later, as her breathing slowed and her skin began to cool, she grasped at reason and dignity and tried to get her bearings. She had not known. She could never have guessed that what had just happened was remotely possible. The knowledge that Eugene had cheated her of it was something that she could not bear to contemplate. Not that she could feature such intimacy, such implicit trust, with the man who had been her husband. Nor could she imagine him exerting the degree of consideration required.

As devastating as had been this upheaval of the senses, however, she knew instinctively that there was more to it than she had been shown this night. She felt the loss, and regretted it with fervor in exact proportion to the pleasure she had been given.

Moving with care, she eased away from Caid and sat up straight. Then she pushed down her skirts and slid from the table. Caid put out a hand to steady her. She accepted that support for a moment before stepping aside and batting her way out of the confines of the mosquito *baire*. With her back to him, she shook out her petticoats and gown, made sure her bodice was back in place.

"You were quite right," she said over her shoulder, her voice distant even to her own ears. "Marriage may possibly have its compensations."

"Am I supposed to applaud this agreement?"

"Why not? It's what you set out to prove."

"Perhaps."

She turned to face him, though he was no more than a tall shadow against the pale sweep of the mosquito netting. "What else? Or was it simply a game?"

"If the last, it seems I am the loser."

"Because you failed to finish what you began, you mean. That was your choice."

"Forgive me. I rather thought the purpose was to protect you."

"From what? From you?"

"Rather, from the risk of bearing a child a good year after the death of your husband. But then—that would have been as nothing compared to the miracle of its apparent immaculate conception."

She had given no thought to the possibility of conception of any variety. Not surprising, perhaps, since there had been no cause to do so during her marriage. To dwell on the subject at this juncture did not suit her, however. With a lift of her chin, she asked, "You objected to being the first?"

"By no means, but I do balk at the surprise. If I had known… But you are a widow. How could I begin to believe that you might be a virgin wife?"

"You feel I should have told you, I suppose. So I might, if I had realized the store you would put in it. No doubt an appropriate moment would have presented itself, at the theater, say, or on a public street. A casual comment dropped into a conversation about the weather, perhaps? Oh, by the way, my husband was insufficiently interested in my charms to perform his marital duties. Could you see your way to remedy the matter along with your other responsibilities?"

He took a swift step toward her. "Lisette, don't…"

"Never mind. That you were not sufficiently ardent, either, makes no difference. I don't blame you at all. In fact, I suppose I should thank you. Only consider the joy of the man I eventually wed on discovering that he has gained an enormous fortune and a chaste bride without kith or kin to care which he despoils first."

Her voice broke a little on that final word. Before Caid could form an answer, before she was forced to say something more in return that might show how badly she was hurt, she whirled and ran to the door. Its lock would not turn at once, but finally she managed it. Then she was on the other side, pulling it shut behind her with a decisive click. She set off for her room at a stumbling run, then stopped, drew a deep breath and went on again at a stiff walk, her head held high.

As a precaution, the sedate pace proved useless. No one passed her in the hall. Caid did not come after her.

In her bedchamber, Lisette dressed for bed like a zombie, and was grateful that a strange maid attended her, one who did not know her well enough to talk. Afterward, she lay staring into the darkness.

What did she want of Caid? She hardly knew, yet was positive beyond doubting that it was not what she had received.

That he had given her pleasure while remaining so little affected himself offended her. It should be different, she was sure of it. She would like to make him lose his iron control, make him respond to her touch as she had responded to his caresses. He thought she required a lesson in love, did he? From where she lay, it seemed it was he who needed a lesson in surrendering to the heat of the moment. And yet, what was the purpose of that when there was no future for them?

How very confusing it all was, being on her own. She had thought while a virtual prisoner in her father-in-law's house that to be free of his presence, his influence and dictates was all that she required. She had been sure that perfect happiness lay in following her will alone. Now she had that benefit, at least for the present, and something was missing. She wasn't lonely, exactly; she had Agatha, after all. She had friends, acquaintances, servants around her. And yet, she felt unconnected, as if she were floating through life without purpose or anchor and might easily drift away into nothingness.

Was Caid right? Was marriage with its staid routine and obligations what she required, the making of a family what she needed to ground her? It seemed far too simple. She had expected something more, something different.

That it must include a means of final escape from Moisant, however, could not be denied. His pretensions to her fortune could be foiled best by her taking a husband, as Caid had said. Many women married simply to become the mistresses of their homes, did they not? They did it even knowing that they must inevitably become subject to the wills of their husbands and to the rigors of frequent childbirth. There was no real bar to that course; widows and widowers had been known to ignore the prescribed two years of mourning. The sensation created was usually forgotten by the time the first child was born of the union.

Yet what man could give her a semblance of freedom while still standing as a bulwark between her and Moisant? She could think of none who would suit her, none she could trust so far. That was, of course, with the exception of Caid. In all truth, he was still the best choice as a husband.

It was impossible; he had said so himself. He cared far more for the proprieties, Lisette thought, than she did. In the meantime, he had all the obligations of the office of husband without any of the benefits.

He also had the special danger that she had brought to him.

She could remove that danger—indeed, remove the necessity of marriage altogether—by simply forfeiting to her father-in-law the estate she had inherited. But how would she live then? She had to have her wealth as her livelihood and source of independence. The other alternative was to marry one of the men who danced attendance upon her, so removing the necessity of being guarded. So it came down to a devil's choice: to remain unwed and allow Caid to risk his life, or to choose a husband and accept a marriage that might or might not be better than living as Moisant's pensioner.

Or there was one other way.

She still had the small bottle of potion given to her by Marie Laveau.

Under influence of the voodoo concoction, Caid might forget the barriers to a marriage between them. By the time the effects wore off, it would be too late; the deed would be done.

It would not be too late for him to despise her for it, or to repudiate her. Only imagining his rage made her feel cold to the heart. She would like to think she might have the power to overcome such a reaction, but there was no guarantee of it.

No, it would not do.

Lisette lay under the tent of mosquito netting which covered her bed, staring at the moonlight falling through the slats of the jalousie blinds. She pushed her hand beneath her pillow and clasped the small bottle of potion brought with her and secreted there. Smoothing its glass side and cork stopper with her thumb again and again, she thought of many things, but she did not sleep.

Figaro woke her just before dawn, scratching on the door to be admitted. She crooned to him in apology for leaving him behind in the study the evening before, all the while wondering if he had perhaps remained with Caid for the night after her desertion since he usually slept under her bed.

The little dog seemed to want to go out and she was tired of tossing and turning. Dressing in a walking costume designed for the country, with a loose fit and front closure which made it possible to dress herself, she found Figaro's lead and left the room by the French doors that opened onto the upper gallery. It was a pleasant morning, with sunlight already warming the gallery railing and beginning to glint on the dew-wet grass of the front lawn. She closed her eyes for an instant, enjoying the gentle heat on her face, the glow penetrating her eyelids. Turning then, she made her way to the stairs which led down to the ground at the back of the house, with the dog hopping down them at her side.

She strolled through the garden they had visited the day

before while reaching now and then to deadhead a rose. As she came to the far end of its brick path, she stood for a moment in indecision. A walkway of sorts continued from where she stood, though it was little more than a rabbit track winding through tall grass and into a woodland area, heading in the general direction of the river. The dew on the grass would dampen her skirts to the knees, but what did it matter? She could hardly become lost with the great white bulk of the house to guide her return, and Figaro showed eager interest in what had last passed down the trail. She set out with a determined stride.

The area was apparently tended as a variety of wildwood garden where it entered the woodland, with huge, arching live oaks forming a high ceiling overhead. Masses of ferns unfurled tender green fronds along its edges, and tangles of yellow jessamine vines dangled from above, shedding fragrance and yellow blossoms onto cushions of green moss in which nestled white and lavender violets. Wild azaleas and dogwoods spread their perfume on the air, intensifying as the sun's warmth increased, blending with the mustiness of decaying leaves.

As she neared the river, the dampness grew more pronounced and she lifted her skirts above small pools of stagnant water while guiding Figaro around them. She could hear the rush of the great stream, though the levee prevented her from seeing it. Now and then, she noticed a scuffed spot in the moss and a boot tread in the mud. Others had come this way before her, perhaps the gardeners or some of the house staff. She recognized an animal track or two, as well, but thought they belonged to raccoons and opossums, or possibly the mouser from the plantation kitchen. Certainly, they weren't large enough for the swamp panthers or feral boars known to populate these woods. She pressed on, intrigued by the turnings of the path, half expecting to see a summerhouse or picturesque ruin hidden away in the Gothic tradition that had become so popular.

A faint sound came from somewhere behind her. Figaro spun to look back, growling low in his throat. Lisette stopped a moment to listen, wryly aware of the leap of her pulse and the knowledge that she had half frightened herself with thoughts of swamp panthers and other creatures. It served her right for venturing away from the main house, though the glimpse of its roof above the trees was enough to let her know she was still no great distance from it.

The noise ceased. No doubt it had been a bird rustling among the fallen leaves or a squirrel or rabbit scuttling for safety after her passing. She moved on again.

For long moments, she heard nothing except bird calls and a light breeze in the treetops overhead. Then the noise began again. She stopped once more, staring back the way she had come, while Figaro did the same. Had that been a foot tread? Surely there was no danger, here, no threat from Henri Moisant?

How foolish of her to even think it. It was just that someone had risen early, as she had, and was strolling along behind her. Perhaps it was even Caid.

Yes, but why didn't he call out or attempt to come up to her? It could be done easily enough; she had been idling along, not making a race of it. Figaro would not have growled at him, either.

What if it was not Caid or one of the others who made up the house party? What if it was someone sent to seize her and take her back to the Moisant house, after all?

How very easy she had made it for him by coming out alone. She had been lulled into complacency by the distance from town, yes, and by her dependence on Caid. It could well become a fatal mistake.

The urge to run surged into her mind. But run where? She was unfamiliar with the acreage, had no idea what lay ahead. Though the edges of the path were clear, beyond them now was a dense undergrowth of saplings and briars that would be almost impossible to get through in her wide skirts. Besides, the only certain safety lay behind her, at the house.

She couldn't go back, not now. Her only course was to go forward.

Picking up her skirts, she hastened toward the curve in the path ahead of her. Her breath rasped in her lungs. A stitch began in her side. Her lips curved in a grim smile as she thought how fortunate it was that she had not taken the time to don a corset this morning, since her boned bodice was constriction enough. Jumping a mud puddle, she felt her hair begin to slide from its pins, but had no time to worry with it. She could hear the regular thud of booted feet behind her. They seemed to be gaining.

Then an odd sound, almost like the clang of a bell, reached her from somewhere around the next bend. A work party, she thought in relief. Anything, anyone, should be sufficient to end the pursuit if she could only reach them in time.

Now she could hear the metallic tapping and clanking in swift tattoo interspersed with calls of complaint or encouragement. She frowned, her mind teased by vagrant familiarity. It was a noise heard in town now and then, while walking along the streets adjacent to the Passage de la Bourse. Not a blacksmith's hammering, no, nor even a coppersmith's, but something lighter and more lethal.

An open area lay before her in sun-dappled brightness beneath the high canopy of a pecan grove. The grass beneath the trees had been scythed the fall before for the gathering of nuts, leaving flat terrain that now burgeoned with spring green. A group of men lounged there while two of their number faced each other with blades in their hands. The clacking and clanging she had heard was the beating of swords against each other. She had come upon a duel.

Caid and the Englishman, Gavin Blackford, were engaged on the field. They flailed at each other with concentration and glittering steel. Moving back and forth, in sunlight and shadow, they courted death in the fresh, sweet air of the morning.

Or did they?

There was nothing formal about the contest, no rigid observation by those gathered around, no sign of attending surgeons. The men watching stood in casual groups, exchanging laughing comments or bombarding the competitors with bits of raillery. The pair themselves, while giving every indication of intent to commit mayhem, grinned at each other in good cheer and exchanged an occasional breathless quip. The swords they held appeared blunt on the tip, the result of applied buttons that prevented any mortal thrust.

It was a practice match, not a duel.

For a single instant, Lisette forgot her possible pursuer, forgot Figaro tugging on the lead while wagging his tail like mad, forgot everything. The display she watched was beyond anything she had ever seen before, a forbidden glimpse of that most manly of pursuits, a friendly fencing match. Caid and Blackford had discarded their coats, waistcoats and cravats to fight in their shirtsleeves. Their open collars and sleeves rolled to the elbows gave them a disheveled, rakish look that was seldom revealed in public. Exertion flushed their features and left the sheen of perspiration on their skin. Their damp hair clung to their scalps and their linen shirts molded taut across their wide shoulders as they lunged, while their knit pantaloons adhered to the muscular lines of their lower bodies with utmost fidelity. Well matched in height and prowess as they faced each other on the carpet of green, they were ferociously handsome, and stunning in their virile strength.

Caid, in particular, fought with such intently controlled power that it sent a frisson along her nerves. It seemed, in some indefinable way, a reminder of his restraint of the night before, his restraint to which she had responded with such a lamentable lack of it.

A slow flush began somewhere in the center of her body and moved upward with debilitating heat. In the same instant, she realized she was viewing something she was not meant to see. Caught between dread and chagrin, she hardly knew which way to turn in that particular moment.

"As good as a play, isn't it?"

Lisette whirled around in a flurry of skirts as the insouciant comment came from near her right shoulder. Even as she moved, she knew the voice, could feel relief breaking through her apprehension.

Maurelle stepped from the undergrowth and stopped beside her. Her voice low and throaty, she went on, "You also heard that they were practicing this morning?"

"No, not really. I was just…walking." She indicated Figaro's lead as she forced a smile. "How glad I am to see you. I thought someone was following me."

"Just now?" Maurelle's brow creased in a frown and she glanced back along the path that lay empty behind them.

"Silly, was it not? As if your guests would do such a thing."

"But I did not come after you, *chère.*"

"You were here before me?"

Her hostess gestured toward a small stand of sumac just back from the path. "There, where I would not disturb the gentlemen at their amusement. My maid chanced to hear of the session from the woman who looks after Mademoiselle Vallier, and she had it from the manservant of Monsieur de Silva, I believe."

Irony was strong in her voice, though whether directed at the swordsmen, the efficiency of the servant's grapevine or her own curiosity was difficult to say. Lisette gave a small shake of her head. "But then who…?"

"One of the gardeners, perhaps, in case you had difficulty finding your way back, or even to warn you away from fencing session. Or it may have been a gentleman with scant interest in swords who thought to speak privately with you. Don't alarm yourself, *chère*. He is surely gone now. And we have other problems."

As Maurelle spoke, she tipped her head in the direction of the mock duel. Lisette did not have to turn around to tell that it had been interrupted; the abrupt cessation of sound was more than enough to alert her. Caid and Blackford, swords disengaged, were standing shoulder to shoulder, gazing in their direction, while the others also turned to stare.

"Your pardon, gentlemen," Maurelle called. "We did not mean to intrude, and will go away at once."

Blackford, grinning, swept up his sword in a salute then rested it on his shoulder. "You are most welcome to stay."

Lisette thought Caid was not entirely in agreement with that invitation, for he glanced at his opponent with what appeared to be annoyance. That small reaction irritated her overstrained nerves for some reason, or perhaps it was mere embarrassment at being caught where she should not be. "No, no, we would not dream of it!" she called in her turn. "Please carry on."

She did not wait for more, but swung around again to return to the house, tugging Figaro along as she did so. Maurelle turned, as well, falling into step beside her. Lisette thought she could feel the stares of the men following them. The very idea made the act of walking feel awkward, though she moved with as much grace as possible. There seemed no point in turning the retreat into a clumsy rout.

It was only when they were out of sight that she suddenly realized she should have noticed exactly who had been present back there under the pecan trees. If she could recall, then she could eliminate them from the list of those who might have been following her. Monsieur de Silva, Celina Vallier's fiancé, had been there she was sure, as was Nicholas Pasquale. She had paid scant attention to anyone else, however, in truth had hardly looked at them at all in her discomfiture. They had been simply a group of males.

"Well now, that was exciting," Maurelle said with amusement strong in her voice.

"A little too much so," Lisette answered.

"Oh, agreed. But stimulating, I must say. I wonder what we may find to do for the rest of the time to equal it."

15

The amateur theatricals planned the evening before occupied that afternoon. The ladies entered into the project with enthusiasm and no small amount of talent. The gentlemen were slower at taking part. Caid was not enchanted at being given the role of smitten lover opposite Lisette's ingenue, and strongly suspected Maurelle of allowing her sense of irony to overcome her when she made the assignments as stage director. Though he refrained from grumbling in front of Lisette and the other ladies, he had no such reticence before his fellow sword masters.

"Don't be such a sorehead," Blackford said, bright blue lights of amusement dancing in his eyes as he watched Caid with the safety of one who was not a member of the cast. "It's a classic piece with witty, even intelligent, dialogue and much opportunity for playing up to the ladies. You have only to unbend and enjoy it."

"Not bloody likely." Caid almost added that the Englishman could take the part with his blessing, but stopped himself in time. Playing opposite Lisette could be something Blackford might enjoy entirely too much.

"You could prevail upon young Francis to take your part, if you're set against it. I'm sure he would be delighted."

"Probably," Caid answered with a dark look. "He apparently doesn't mind making an ass of himself."

"That doesn't please you, either? I suppose you're stuck then. Shall I help learn your lines? My voice may lack the proper maidenly falsetto, but I could make the attempt."

"Go ahead, amuse yourself at my expense," Caid drawled

with a threatening glance from under his lashes. "Next time, I'll make sure Maurelle gives you a part to play."

"I have one, my friend," Blackford returned without noticeable alarm. "I have the arduous task of prompter."

They sat on the gallery with their feet propped on the railing and glasses of claret in their hands. It was that twilight hour known as *l'heure bleu,* though in this case the scant few minutes between the time when the sun had set and before the mosquitoes came out to plague them, between the siesta hour and the evening entertainment. Most of Maurelle's guests were in their rooms preparing for the play rehearsal that would be followed by a late supper.

Blackford leaned back in his chair and laced his fingers together behind his head. "There is something I've been meaning to ask you, O'Neill. Just what is your role vis-à-vis the lovely Widow Moisant? I come to the situation late, you understand, and can't quite make it out."

"I have none. To think of such a thing while she is still in black would be inappropriate."

Blackford looked judicious. "True, still, those who make themselves most agreeable now may have front positions when grief has run its course. So they buzz like flies around a honeypot while you stand by as if prepared to swat any who get too close. One could be forgiven for thinking you are saving her for yourself."

"Banish the idea," Caid advised in hard tones. "I am merely a very temporary guardian of the lady's welfare."

"Against the threats of her father-in-law, yes, so I understand. But are you certain you have no feelings for her?"

"My feelings don't come into the matter."

Blackford gave him a considering look from the corners of his eyes. "You err, I believe."

Caid returned the Englishman's stare but made no answer. Blackford faced forward again, pursing his lips. "If you can't remain impartial, how are you to see that she makes the right choice, old man? Or any choice at all?"

"Are you, by any chance, thinking of trying your luck?"

"Tempting, but I'd rather face you on the fencing strip than the dueling field."

"I wasn't warning you off," Caid said in exasperation.

"Weren't you?" Blackford paused a moment, then answered himself. "Possibly not, though my qualifications are no better than yours."

"You at least have breeding."

"For that, I thank you, though my elder brother might disagree, not to mention my father. In any case, I see little to choose between us."

"A modest English aristocrat, something I thought never to see," Caid said in marveling tones.

"A realistic one, rather. Few things are lower than a younger son."

Caid, watching Blackford, thought he caught a brief flicker of pain in his eyes. "I thought younger sons were usually destined for the army. How did you escape that fate?"

"A sickly childhood and the complete lack of discipline which attended it, or so some would say. I prefer to call it the disinclination to take orders."

"Particularly those of an older brother?" Caid asked on a guess.

"You have it. But we were not discussing my failings, I believe. What, precisely, do you intend toward the lady in question?"

"Only what is right and honorable. And you?" Caid waited with hard patience for the answer.

"Oh, I have no pretensions whatever, but only wondered which man's suit to push forward."

"None," Caid said shortly.

"That's what I thought," the Englishman said, his smile gilded with complacency.

Caid sent him a disgusted look there in the gathering dusk, but made no answer for fear of revealing more than he had already.

Practice for the play went much as might be expected. They walked their way through the thing while reading their lines from pages held in their hands.

Regardless of his reluctance to join the theatrics, Caid took perverse pleasure in the scenes performed opposite Lisette. To court her in public was perfect torment, while Lisette's blushing replies and difficulty in looking him in the face made him both randy as a ram and doubtful as the most callow of adolescents. He would have given much to know the source of her apparent blushing confusion, whether acting ability, too vivid memory of what had transpired between them the evening before or maidenly shrinking from the fencing practice she had witnessed that morning. The opportunity to discover her state of mind came after supper.

The meal began with turtle soup and ended with syllabub, with a cold collation in between them and all served on the white Parisian china rimmed in gold that was a hallmark of Maison Blanche. Maurelle kept to the old French style at meals, so the gentlemen did not remain sitting over their brandy and nutmeats but rose with the ladies from the long table, making their way to the salon. There, their hostess seated herself at the pianoforte which occupied a corner of the long room and allowed her fingers to wander over the keys in a sonata. After a time, when she considered that the meal just past had settled enough for digestion, she swung into a sprightly waltz and a few couples got up to dance.

Here in this informal atmosphere, there could be no objection to a man such as himself inviting Lisette onto the floor. Caid rose to his feet and moved to bow before her.

She came into his arms readily enough, which led him to believe that she might not hold him in too much disgust on any of the possible accounts. While they circled the floor, he watched her face, the tender curve of her cheek, the fan pattern of her lashes as she kept her eyes downcast, while trying to think how to put what was uppermost in his mind. To approach it head-on was the only way that he could see.

"I'm sorry that you had to come upon us at practice this morning."

"Sorry? Why?" She drew back a little to gaze up at him with surprise in her eyes, though a soft flush bloomed across her cheekbones.

"It wasn't our intention to offend the sensibilities of any lady."

"And you think I must have been offended?"

"Most women would pretend so at the very least."

"I am not most women."

Caid allowed his features to relax into something close to a smile. "So I'm beginning to believe."

"What part of the spectacle was supposed to be offensive, the swordplay or merely the…the informal dress?"

"Both, I would imagine, as well as the prospect of violence that is always attendant on the meetings of two men with lethal weapons in their hands."

"But this was mere practice, hardly an occasion for bloodshed."

"It can happen, even so. A loose button on a foil or rapier, the flare of tempers and there you are." He lifted a shoulder, too immured to the prospect to be troubled by it.

"Well, I witnessed nothing of the kind," she said with precision. "Nor was I there long enough to see anything of a truly disturbing nature. To be perfectly truthful, I am glad to have had a glimpse of this mysterious occupation of yours."

"Why might that be?"

"Most women are curious to know what draws men to it so strongly."

"I'm not sure I follow."

"How else to explain the amount of time and effort required to become proficient? It's my belief that it's part and parcel of this Romantic fascination with the macabre. Young men pretend to familiarity with death to banish its sting, and swordplay is but another manifestation of that idea."

"So I teach them to welcome death? Is that what you're saying?"

Her brows drew together in a frown. "That would be going too far. Rather, you teach them to face death and look it in the eyes, to meet it without fear."

"Yes, but is that always a good thing? A healthy fear of death is what keeps most of us safely away from dangerous pursuits of all varieties."

"That should be my argument, I think," she said seriously. "Do you doubt the value of your chosen profession or the code which requires it?"

"All men of any intelligence do so."

"Then why do they continue?"

"Life would be brutish without it, given over to the vulgar and obscene and those who run roughshod over their fellow men—and women. It will stop when it has served its purpose. It's the threat, you see."

"Even when it's the innocent and gentle who die?"

"It's my job to see that they don't pay that penalty."

"Then it is worthwhile, what you do."

Caid knew in that instant, if he had not known before, how very hard it was going to be to give up Lisette Moisant to another man when the time came. The glimpse of that future pain took his breath and made him wonder in despairing fury just what he thought he was doing. And so he whirled her in a fast turn that sent her skirts flying out behind her and brought her breasts in tingling contact, for a single instant, with the difficult rise and fall of his chest. Then he slowed, thought of the distance prescribed for holding a lady, and put her exactly that far away from him.

Lisette seemed to accept the gesture at face value, but watched him as if weighing in the balance the effect of what she wanted to say. It was a long moment before she spoke. "I was followed this morning, or so I believe."

"Followed," he repeated, trying to rearrange his thoughts, to see past her reserve to whatever annoyance or trepidation had caused her to broach this suspicion.

"It sounded like the footfalls of a man though I never saw him, perhaps because of Figaro's growls. Then I am almost certain he was deflected from whatever purpose he may have had when Maurelle appeared."

"She didn't catch sight of him?"

Lisette shook her head so decisively that the bunches of curls that had been drawn forward on either side of her face in the latest style swung freely. "She said not."

"So you have no idea whether he was simply prevented from joining you, an attractive lady out for an early stroll, or was actually up to no good?"

"Not really. I thought…that is, I wondered if you had taken notice of all the men who were there at your practice session."

Caid saw at once what she suggested. "They came and went as their mood and need for breakfast moved them. I can identify those who sparred with me, of course."

She looked a little disappointed but not particularly troubled. That was good, because he was troubled enough for both of them. The house party was turning into a nightmare for keeping track of the guests' movements. No one seemed to stay in place for more than a few minutes, and it was impossible to tell who was off on nefarious activities and who had only retreated to their bedchambers to rest.

More than that, it was almost as difficult to be alone with Lisette as it had been in town, primarily because so many were after the same advantage. Everywhere he turned, Francis, Denys, Neville, Gustave with his mother and a half dozen others seemed to be there. She could not have arranged a more effective *garde du corps* if she had tried. At least no one else among them was likely to have any better luck at being private with her. He had that much satisfaction.

Maurelle brought the waltz to an end with a tinkling flourish. As it happened, a set of French doors were nearby as Caid halted. Noting the delicate flush on Lisette's face and the way she unfurled and applied her fan, a somber thing of black silk and ebony sticks, he asked, "Shall we walk outside for a moment?"

"By all means." Placing her hand on the arm he offered, she strolled beside him, as self-possessed as the society matron she would doubtless become one day.

"A warm night, like Paris in the summer," he murmured, gazing out into the darkness as they left the brightly lit salon behind them. At least it was fresher here than inside, with a soft breeze to cool their faces.

"Too warm. I keep expecting it to rain."

"A situation which would keep you inside with your suitors."

"What a thought." She gave a theatrical shudder. "I shall pray that it cools off tomorrow."

He sent her a wry glance in the dimness. "Come, is there no one among them you find agreeable?"

"They are all agreeable enough, but I can't picture spending the rest of my life with them."

"Not even Duchaine?"

She tipped her head to gaze up at him. "What makes you ask that?"

"I don't know. He seems the most suitable, I suppose."

"As he would be the first to tell you."

It was all he could do to hide his smile at her tone. "His cousin, the Comte de Picardy…"

"Please! I've heard more than enough about his cousin

the comte and his estates, his position at court, income, carriages, wardrobe and mistresses."

"Mistresses?"

"Being a married lady, I am apparently knowledgeable enough to find such subjects titillating rather than shocking."

Caid made an undetermined sound in his satisfaction that Duchaine had not discovered her essential lack of experience in that regard. "He said as much?"

"Implied it rather. Monsieur Duchaine is too discreet to put anything into words which may be repeated."

The surge of anger Caid felt was out of proportion to the crime, and he knew it. Still, the very idea of Duchaine whispering salacious innuendos in Lisette's ear made his hand itch for his rapier. "Well and good, that disposes of Monsieur Duchaine. What of Dorelle?"

"Sweet, but too young and too much the sensitive artiste. He spent the afternoon composing another poem for me."

"A wholesale condemnation, if ever I heard one. And Monsieur Bechet?" Caid could not prevent a trace of humor from rising in his voice.

"His mother would be an interesting woman if only she had no son." Lisette flung him a quick look. "What is so amusing?"

"Nothing."

"I'm sure. You may think it hilarious that I am forced to avoid the addresses of half a dozen gentlemen in an evening, but it doesn't suit me at all. A little more and I may steal away back to town."

"What, and leave Maurelle to entertain them all alone? You wouldn't be so cruel."

"It would not be cruelty but self-preservation."

He stopped, turned her to face him and reached to touch her cheek with his hard swordsman's fingertips. "Is it really so bad?"

"Intolerable." She caught his wrist, and her fingers closed

on it for an instant, the sensitive tips lingering in exploration. Then she lowered his arm between them and pushed his cuff higher.

Caid made an abortive movement, as if to snatch his arm from her grasp, but was still as her fingers tightened. "Don't," he said in gruff protest.

"Why?" She glanced up at him even as she brushed over the rust-embedded scars that circled his wrist bones. "You covered these marks with wrappings of cloth this morning, I believe. Are they so terrible?"

"The bindings are only to prevent accidental slicing of an artery. They had nothing to do with what you see." It wasn't the exact truth, but the best he could manage at the moment. Her gentle touch sent involuntary shivers up his arms and across his shoulders, igniting a heat inside him that seemed to spread to every inch of his body.

"You came by them while on the prison ship when you were so young. What shame can there be in them?"

"I never said there was shame."

"Yet you hide them, don't speak of them, would rather no one knew of them."

"They mark me as being of a class that can be locked away without cause and little recourse to the law," he said in harsh tones. "They brand me a felon."

"Former felon, surely? And through no fault of your own."

"It makes no difference. They are indelible."

"And if they could be washed away, they would still be imprinted on your soul, I think," she said in tones of quiet reflection. "I wonder what it would take to make you forget they are there."

As her voice trailed off, she released the cuff link that held his sleeve, then pushed aside the stiff fabric and lowered her head to press her lips to his scars. He stood like a statue, unable to move, think or even to breathe. His heart pounded in his chest until he was sure she could feel the basso drumming. The need to touch her hair, to feel her cool lips on the hot surfaces of his mouth, to sweep her up in his arms and carry her away into the dark, was so profound that he felt its throb deep inside him. He wanted to hold her, make her his, bind her to him with ties so strong they could never be broken. He wanted her, period, anyway he could have her, for as long as time allowed.

He was not here to fix his interest with her in any manner. His promise had been to protect her rather than take advantage of her position. To even dream of anything different was foolish; to carry through with it would be criminal. He should pull free and set her firmly away from him.

It was impossible. And so he stood and waited until she lifted her head.

She stared at him in the gray gloom relieved only by distant lamplight, her eyes like pools of soft, dark magic. Then her lips curved in a smile that trembled a little at the edges. "Nothing a mere woman can do will take them away, is that it? What will then? Sweat and blood and, finally, death by the sword you hold so dear? I shall pray that it doesn't come to that, for your sake."

He made no reply. What was there to be said, after all? In any case, his throat was too tight to speak without giving himself away.

At that moment, a sound came from behind them. Caid turned his hand and caught Lisette's waist, swinging her behind him even as he turned. A bulky figure hovered a short distance away. It was an instant before he recognized Gustave Bechet.

"Beg pardon for the intrusion," he said stiffly. "Didn't see you there. Wouldn't interrupt your tête-à-tête for the world."

Was there a note of peevish, even snide, resentment in the rotund suitor's voice? If so, it was no doubt because he thought Caid was stealing a march on him and the others. "No, I'm sure you wouldn't."

"Excuse it, if you please." With a curt nod, the other man turned and retraced his footsteps until he ducked back into the salon. Caid stared after him for long seconds, a frown between his brows.

"I suppose he will go straight to his mother to report," Lisette said unhappily.

"Without doubt. The question is what she will make of it."

"We were doing nothing wrong."

That, Caid thought, was only by the grace of God. "It's my fault for taking you away from the others."

"Oh, yes, always your fault."

"What do you mean?" he asked, his gaze searching her face as he heard the weary defeat in her voice.

"Never mind." Stepping away from him, she turned toward the French doors of her bedchamber which lay some few yards down the gallery. "I suddenly have a headache. If you will convey my apologies to the others, I will say good-night now."

He inclined his head but made no answer. After a moment, she moved on, the heels of her slippers making a hollow, clacking sound on the gallery flooring. He waited until she had reached the door, until her hand was on the latch, before he spoke. "Thank you," he said softly. "Thank you for the prayer."

If she heard, she didn't answer. She stepped into her bedchamber and closed the door behind her.

Caid returned to the salon. There, he delivered Lisette's message and remained long enough to prevent it from appearing that the two of them were leaving the company at suspiciously near the same time. After bidding the others good evening, he took a turn in the garden while enjoying a last cigar. Everything was quiet except for the separate kitchen building where the washing up from supper was in its final stages. A few night birds called. One of the roosters in the chicken run near the slave quarters crowed with a croaking, sleepy sound. Taking up a post under a live oak, Caid watched as the kitchen maid threw out the dirty dishwater then locked the kitchen and trundled off to bed. He saw Maurelle's guests disperse for the evening, their night candles bobbing along the galleries, then the lamps in their rooms going out one by one behind their closed jalousies.

Agatha Stilton had left the salon as soon as she heard of Lisette's headache, so her lamp was one of the first to fade away. Lisette's, next door, burned bright even after most of the others had darkened. Either the headache she complained of had been a ploy or else she had been more ill than she seemed.

Caid debated finding a maid and sending her to ask, but decided against it. Agatha would most assuredly have stayed up if there was cause for concern.

A half moon rode the night sky. High clouds chased across its face, now hiding, now revealing its light. Mosquitoes whined around Caid's head so he turned up the collar of his coat to protect his ears from their bites. Nothing was happening or seemed likely to happen. He was beginning to think of his own bed when a flicker of movement at the side of the house caught his attention.

A man eased from the shadow cast by the house wall. In his hand was clutched something white. He stopped to stare up at the gallery above him, turning his head as if seeking a particular set of doors before moving on again. Reaching the end of the house where lamplight gleamed through the jalousie slats of Lisette's bedchamber, he stopped. He moved back until he apparently had a clear view, and then stood staring with his face turned upward like a mooncalf.

Love-struck fool or Peeping Tom hoping for open draperies, it was impossible to tell. Caid was taking no chances. Moving with stealth, he circled to within a half dozen paces of the new arrival, close enough for recognition.

The clouds cleared the face of the moon at that moment, illuminating this section of Maison Blanche in a soft white glow. It delineated the man who stood there, picking out his features with the utmost fidelity.

Francis Dorelle.

Caid allowed himself to relax a fraction. The poet hardly posed any difficulty.

Such confidence was misplaced. Dorelle not only could be difficult, but fully intended it, as Caid saw a moment later. The white object in his hand was a sheet of paper. Raising it so the moon shone full on it, he began to declaim his poetic effort at the top of his lungs.

Even if the thing had been of a perfection to rival The Bard himself, no one wanted to listen to such racket at this hour. Caid started forward, intending to collar the poet and shake some sense into him.

A jalousie several doors farther along the gallery swung open with a bang. Blackford stalked out into the moonlight. He was swathed in a dressing gown of Oriental splendor and apparently nothing else. Leaning to brace his hands on the railing, he called down, "Stifle it, Dorelle. People are trying to sleep."

The poet broke off in midspate, turning toward his detractor. "I am love-inspired, *monsieur!* Stop your ears if you don't care to hear the message of my heart!"

It was plain to Caid in that instant that Dorelle had fortified himself for his performance with liberal applications of spirits. He swayed a little as he stared upward at Blackford, and his words were not as clear as they should have been. From inside Lisette's bedchamber could be heard the sound of Figaro barking in canine displeasure.

"I don't care what inspires you," Blackford said with menace shading his tone. "Nor, I would imagine, does the object of your affection. Cease the caterwauling or you will regret it."

"You are a boorish critic with no romance in your heart!"

"I am a man with no patience. Take your miserable excuse for poetry and be off."

Dorelle drew himself up. "You are offensive, *monsieur*."

"I'll be violent if I have to listen to you a moment longer."

"You may be as violent as you wish on the field of honor. My seconds will call on you in the morning."

The young fool didn't know what he was doing, could have no idea of the caliber of the swordsman he had just challenged. The Englishman was a true master, blending finesse with intelligence, heart and something more that might be called nobility. Caid had begun by disliking the man, but his conduct on the grass strip of the clearing this morning, where it was impossible to hide one's true nature, had gone far to change that. The two of them had not continued the match between them after Lisette and Maurelle appeared. Caid was still curious to know how it might have ended.

Blackford stared down at the poet in what appeared to be amazement before giving a hard nod. "As you please, if it means silence from you tonight."

Dorelle bowed, a somewhat unsteady performance. Turning, he stalked off into the darkness.

The exchange had taken no time at all. Most of the guests had not roused, judging from the darkness of their bedchambers, or else had concluded that the affair was no business of theirs.

The jalousies leading to Lisette's room had swung open, however. She stood framed in the doorway, with her dressing gown hanging from her shoulders in elegant folds and her hair like a waist-length cape around her, shimmering red-gold in the lamplight from inside the bedchamber. Caid, drawing back into the shadows, watched her with his breath suspended in his chest while wondering if she had heard enough to know what had taken place, wondering if she realized the gravity or if she cared.

Then she turned and went slowly back inside, closing the jalousie behind her. The clouds covered the moon once more, and he was left alone in the dark.

16

First Caid and Vigneaud, Sarne and others unknown, and now Francis Dorelle and the Englishman. Lisette, counting them off, wondered in despair what she had done that men must fight because of her. She knew of nothing that might warrant it, still the duels continued.

It wasn't as if she was an acknowledged beauty or some theatrical actress with a fanatical following. She was just a woman trying to live with decorum and a small degree of independence.

What a ridiculous thing it was, this affair of the poem. Who could have imagined it might lead to the spilling of blood? That was, of course, if it did not end in worse.

She would stop it if she could. In fact, she had scarcely slept for trying to think of some way to manage it. It had not helped. The business had moved beyond her involvement to the sphere of manly pride and ferocious honor. Francis Dorelle could withdraw by applying through his seconds, if he so desired, but the possibility the Englishman might suspect lack of fortitude as the reason made that unlikely. Blackford could certainly not be accused of cowardice if he accepted such a withdrawal, but might well feel that the young man deserved a lesson in consideration.

Lisette dreaded to think how it would end, but knew the seconds for the two men must be in conference even as she sat at the breakfast table. Nicholas and Caid, Blackford's most likely seconds, were absent, as were Denys Vallier and Armand Lollain who might be acting for Francis. Those left tried to appear unconscious of the empty

places. Conversation was stilted and separated by awkward silences.

Lisette's headache of the evening before was worse this
morning. She rested her temple on the heel of her hand as
she took an occasional sip of café au lait but fed most of her
roll to Figaro who sat beside her chair. She could feel the
curious stares that rested upon her. Maurelle was all compassion, her manner solicitous, and Celina Vallier met her
gaze with grave sympathy. Madame Bechet, however,
seemed to emanate condemnation, as if she blamed Lisette
for the flare-up. Her son, Gustave, watched Lisette with his
close-set eyes narrowed in apparent speculation. He opened
his mouth once or twice as if to speak, but closed it again
each time after a glance at his mother.

A pall was cast over the house party. Several of the guests
packed up and departed with hastily concocted excuses.
Judge Reinhardt was among them, since he could not afford
to be a party to the affair. Lisette considered leaving herself,
might have if it had not seemed such a desertion. Besides,
waiting for news of the duel's outcome to reach town would
be intolerable.

The day was even warmer than the one before. A moist
wind swept up from the gulf, bringing with it the smells of
swamp muck and brine. It increased as the day advanced,
snatching new leaves from the trees by the handfuls, hurling them into the sky, and tearing petals from the flowers.
The hard gusts made it impossible to leave the doors open
due to the havoc wrought inside the rooms, and any activities conducted on the galleries had to take place on the lee
side of the house. Most of the ladies complained that it ruined their coiffures and billowed their skirts in an unseemly
manner so stayed inside.

Lisette didn't mind. The restless sweep of it matched
her mood.

She was standing on the south side of the house with her

eyes narrowed against the wind and her skirts molded to her body when she heard footsteps approaching. She looked around quickly, expecting to see Caid. It was, instead, the Englishman, Blackford. She managed a brief smile, but thought it probably did not appear particularly welcoming.

"You look like a figurehead standing there, divine and lovely protectress of those at sea," he said with a whimsical smile. "Dare I entreat your blessing for tomorrow?"

"I doubt very much that you will require help." It seemed best to ignore the implied compliment.

"Let us hope you are correct. Do I intrude? Tell me so, and I will go away again at once."

"You are a guest of Madame Herriot's, even as I am. I would not dream of it."

"Which puts me in my place quite neatly, or would if I were thin of skin," he said as he leaned a shoulder against the nearest column. "Thankfully, I am not. Are you always so plain spoken?"

"Normally, I am more so. But if you don't care for it, you have only yourself to blame. I was quite pleasant, I think, before last night."

"I see. I am properly chastened."

She gave him a sharp glance. "That I doubt."

"Observant, too, though waspish with it."

"If you expect me to be grateful that you took Francis Dorelle to task for disturbing me, then you will be disappointed. I refuse to condone a quarrel based on an excess of wine on one side and of choler on the other."

"No," he said with a smile that carved laugh lines into his face, changing it beyond belief. "Like Eve with her apple, you were only the excuse. The lack of self-control was mine."

"You admit it was badly done?"

"I could say that I am subject to megrims that make me unreasonable on occasion, but that is mere temporizing. Actually, you're quite right."

She turned to put her back to the railing. "Then you don't intend permanent damage?"

"To Dorelle? Barbarians come in all guises, but not, I hope, in my likeness."

"I am relieved. He is young and a little foolish, perhaps, but not…" She paused as she searched for the word.

"Not unreasonable, at least when sober?"

"Something of the sort."

He reached out to catch a strand of her hair that had been torn from its pins, rubbing it between his fingers. "A gentle heart, as well. Cry hosanna."

"I don't know what you mean." She snatched her hair from his grasp and tucked it behind her ear.

"Not all ladies are as concerned for the victims of the passions they instill."

"It was not my intention to instill anything."

A laugh shook him. "That should make it worse instead of better."

Was he flirting with her? Could he, by any stretch of the imagination, be attempting to ingratiate himself for the sake of her fortune? She could not tell. He might only be bored, or else in search of some small relief from what he faced in the morning.

"You aren't concerned about the skill of your opponent?"

His face turned preternaturally grave. "To the point of terror."

"I'm sure," she said tartly. "Though I believe I once heard him speak in passing of visiting Croquère's."

"The mulatto fencing master? I will certainly be on my guard."

She compressed her lips, then opened them again. "I didn't intend to offer instruction or advice."

"And least of all concern. I understand perfectly."

He smiled again with wry humor reflecting in the bright blue of his eyes. It was impossible, Lisette discovered, not to smile back, though instinct warned that his charm was too practiced and possibly too directed by intelligence to be trusted.

Just then, Blackford looked past her shoulder and cocked a brow. "O'Neill," he said in obvious greeting. "Come to frighten the hawk away from your chick?"

"Or at least dangle other bait before it," Caid replied, his tone even as he strolled to join them. His gaze clashed with that of the Englishman.

"If you make your anxiety too evident, my friend, people will assume all sorts of interesting and unlikely events."

"So I should leave you a clear field? You are an optimist."

"But one with good eyesight, especially for other birds of prey, such as nighthawks."

Caid was silent for an instant. "Meaning I am no better than you? Self-evident, I think."

"Clumsy, as well, which I like to think is not usually one of my traits. I spoke, merely, of watchers in the dark."

They were talking over Lisette's head, of matters beyond her ken. Or were they? Was Blackford suggesting that Caid had been keeping watch outside her bedchamber, even here at Maison Blanche? It was an interesting thought.

"Nighthawks have talons," Caid said softly.

"Assuredly. The question is one of intentions."

Caid flung up a hand as if to ward off a touch. "God, not you, too!"

"An impossible task requires an improbable solution."

"But not," Caid answered in grim tones, "from you."

Blackford winced. "Such directness quite spoils the game."

"As was intended."

"Then I leave you to your prize, *mon brave,* untouched and untouchable." The English sword master made them a bow tinged with irony and walked away without a backward glance.

"Did he just say what I think he did?" Lisette asked with a frown, watching him go.

"Pay no attention. Our English friend enjoys being cryptic. And his mood is contrary at the moment. Some men practice before a duel, some seek out friends and family, some drink. Then there are those who would as soon make an opponent of the whole world."

"Out of distress of mind?"

"Or rage at their own stupidity and a code that makes it as likely that a man may die for a ridiculous reason as for a worthy one—shall we talk of other things?"

His voice was brusque, though whether because he felt he had said too much or from some inner pain was difficult for Lisette to tell. "Such as?"

"Your headache of last evening is better?"

"Not noticeably."

"But you slept after the excitement."

"How could I?" How strange it seemed, such politeness between them after the intimacy they had shared. They might have been strangers.

"You shouldn't blame yourself."

She hunched a shoulder. "So Blackford said, yet he and Francis Dorelle would not have had words if not for me."

"Blackford sent your poet about his business. Do you mind?"

"Not at all. It was rather embarrassing, if you must know."

"And more so afterward. But you won't, I hope, make a hero of Blackford for the rescue."

"I'm not likely to do that," she said with precision. "Though I don't know why you should care."

"He is a penniless younger son."

"Marriages are often made with that kind of imbalance, a man of breeding and a woman of fortune. It matters little who has the money as long as the pedigrees are not too unequal."

"I hate to tamper with your illusions concerning your position in the world, but Blackford can probably trace his lineage to the Doomsday Book. It's doubtful his family in England would consider the match equal."

"But we are not in England," she answered in cool tones. "His position makes him nearly as eligible as Rio de Silva who turned out to be a Spanish count. More than that, it seems likely that he, like you, could easily fend off any action taken against me by my father-in-law."

"You are taken with him, is that it?"

"I didn't say so. But it is extremely irritating to be told who I can and cannot consider as a marriage prospect by one who has no intention of filling that position himself."

"I told you…"

"So you did," she interrupted. "But have you asked me what I wanted? Have you listened when I explained it to you? Please don't dictate to me, then. I will choose my own husband. Now you must excuse me, for it's time I rejoined the others."

She turned from him, but he put out a hand to grasp her arm. The firmness of his hold made it plain that fighting him would be useless, still she stiffened, her gaze defiant, while the wind blew her skirts against his ankles and the loosened strands of her hair flicked his chest like tiny red-gold whips.

"Lisette…" The low timbre of his voice seemed to hold an entreaty. Then he released her with an abrupt, open-handed gesture. "Never mind. Go. I can't stop you."

It was the perversity of women, no doubt, but she suddenly had no desire whatever to leave him. That she did it anyway was due to pride alone.

Civility reigned for the rest of the damp, gray day. The duel, if mentioned at all, was spoken of in whispers; certainly it was not a topic of general conversation. The principals, in particular, behaved as if dissension was the last thing to have occurred between them. They talked and laughed along with all the rest, and if their voices showed an edge of strain now and then, no one elected to notice. No loss of appetite was observed at the midday dinner, nor did anyone seem reluctant to retire for the usual restorative naps. It was as though nothing had happened or was going to happen.

It was maddening, at least to Lisette. The inevitable march of time toward the appointed dawn with nothing done to stay it seemed a sacrilege. What might be essayed to bring the whole thing to a halt was more than she could say, but it seemed that someone should at least try.

That was unfair, of course. She was sure the seconds of the pair had done their best to discover a solution that did not compromise the honor of either man. Still, more desperate measures would not come amiss in her opinion. She wished it was possible to have both Blackford and Dorelle shut away until their tempers cooled and the incident became a rather comical memory. Unfortunately, she had not that power.

She was sitting in the morning salon, reading over her lines for the play that would be enacted that evening, when Francis Dorelle came into the room. He started a little as he saw her, then came forward with a tentative smile on his face.

"How glad I am to find you alone, Madame Moisant. I have been wishing for an opportunity to apologize for the disturbance last evening."

"Think nothing of it, please." Her smile was warmer than it might have been under other circumstances. He was so very young, and would be handsome one day. Pray God. "I am just sorry that…that it turned out as it did."

"Yes." He sat down gingerly on the fauteuil next to her. "Not that I'm in the least uneasy, you know."

She might have come closer to believing that if his face had not been so pale or his eyes so shadowed. But since he had mentioned the meeting himself, she felt at liberty to at least attempt to set matters right. "Sometimes things happen that we don't intend," she said quietly. "If you could just explain to Monsieur Blackford, I'm sure—"

"Never! He would be certain to think me milk-livered, and that I could not bear. Besides, he had no right to call me down in front of you."

"He was not feeling well, you know. I'm sure he regrets his part in the business."

"So you say," he returned in bitter tones. "It's my belief he wants me out of the way."

"Surely not. What would be the profit to him?"

"A clear field with you, of course. If I am killed, there will be one less suitor for your hand."

That had not occurred to her, perhaps because she had never seriously considered Francis Dorelle in that regard. Somewhere in the back of her mind began a niggling worry that someone else might have considered it, however.

Oh, but that was impossible. Sane, ordinary people did not think in such terms. She gave a slow shake of her head.

"Yes, yes, I know it is wrong of me to say such things while you are still in mourning. But I am afraid for you. You have only a year or two advantage of me in years, nothing to signify at all. It would give me great satisfaction to be able to protect you from those who might take advantage of you. There is something about you, *madame*, so tender yet valiant, that makes men want to care for you, some men. In others, it brings thoughts that are…are quite otherwise."

To be described in such terms was uncomfortable. In an effort to distract him, she said quickly, "You wrote me a poem, but I have yet to hear all of it. I don't suppose you have it with you?"

He began to pat his pockets. "How kind. I am overcome that you wish…that you have the patience, the understanding to hear it, *chère madame*. Now where could I have… Oh, yes, here it is!"

He pulled a sheet of paper from the pocket of his tailcoat and unfolded it, smoothing it out on his thigh where it had obviously been crumpled, perhaps in some sudden anguish of mind. Clearing his throat, he began to read.

It was a sincere effort, and affecting for that reason. Lisette listened with the silent consideration any literary effort deserved. At the same time, she allowed her gaze to rest on the earnest features of this young man, studying the plane of his jaw, the way his brows grew, the deep sockets of his eyes with their thick brows. His lips were soft, almost unformed, his ears protruded a little and his Adam's apple moved jerkily in his throat when he swallowed. His shirt collar had wilted with the dampness, and the flowing Romantic's scarf that he wore instead of a cravat was on the point of coming untied. Now and then his voice came near to breaking, though more from emotion than mere youth. He had annoyed and embarrassed her in the past few days, still there was something so endearing about him in that moment that her heart ached with it.

"That was lovely," she said with the utmost gentleness when he had finished. "I can't thank you enough for letting me hear it, or for the sentiments that it conveys. I fear I don't deserve them, but I am honored that you addressed them to me."

"They are you," he said simply, his dark eyes shining as he gazed at her.

How truly brave he was to sit there smiling and reading poetry while knowing that he must rise in the morning and face an expert with a blade as the sun rose in the sky and birds sang and the spring wind blew the leaves on the trees. It did not bear thinking of, and so Lisette leaned forward and placed a kiss on his cheek.

She feared, for an instant, that he might presume too

much from that small act, might try to catch her in his arms or take other liberties. He did nothing of the kind. His face turned crimson, even to the tips of his ears and back of his neck. A smile of singular sweetness curved his lips. "Thank you, *madame,* my very dear Madame Moisant."

He reached to take her hand and press the poem into it. Then he got to his feet and sketched a bow, every inch the dignified gentlemen, before walking quickly from the room.

Lisette sat holding the paper, staring down at it until a tear fell to smudge the lines. She took out her handkerchief and wiped it away with care.

The audience for the play that evening was sparse and their enthusiasm muted. That matched the performance which was lackluster at best and distracted at worst.

Still, it was impossible to make a total muddle of Sheridan's masterpiece, and there were a few moments when the thing flowed and the laughs came in the right places in spite of everything.

The storm swept down upon the house three-quarters of the way through the evening. Thunder rumbled and crashed overhead and the lightning flickered endlessly. All the doors, windows and jalousies had been closed earlier, still cool drafts of wind eddied through the rooms, causing the lamplight to flutter and dance behind its glass globes. The rain, when it came, was a deluge that seemed to have no end. It fell through the supper hour and was still pouring down when they all straggled off to bed.

Lisette lay listening to the windswept sheets of water as they lashed the house. She was still awake when the storm grumbled away into stillness and the rain stopped. Lying there, staring into the dark, she thought of the dueling field and how wet it would be underfoot. She wondered if the duel would be postponed, if not called off, wondered if the combatants would oversleep if the sky was cloudy at dawn. She pictured them taking the path to the pecan grove where the practice bout had been held, and wondered if they would walk side by side like the best of companions to the field, or if there was some protocol for who would go first and who follow. She thought of many things in endless progression, none of them of any moment. And only when she had given up all idea of sleep did it finally come to her.

Cries, shouts and the babble of voices jerked her awake. The whole house seemed in an uproar. Before she could slide from her bed, the door flew open and Agatha entered in a rush.

"Oh, my dear, the most terrible thing. Young Monsieur Dorelle has been dreadfully injured, and Monsieur Blackford, as well. Such a to-do, you would hardly believe, and no one seems to have the least idea how to go on."

"They had doctors in attendance? They are being treated?" Lisette sprang from the bed, turning to the armoire where she snatched out the first thing that came to hand, then reached for the hem of her nightgown to yank it off over her head.

"Only one was available here in the country, and he is looking after Monsieur Dorelle. The Englishman insisted."

"Where have they put them?" She accepted Agatha's help with her corset, even as she climbed into her petticoats and hastily tied the tapes.

"They are bringing Blackford into the house just now. Madame Herriot is having his bedchamber prepared. As for Dorelle, I believe he is being installed in the summer dining room on the lower floor. He…he is too desperately injured to attempt bringing him upstairs."

A sudden feeling of déjà vu assailed Lisette as she recalled the morning Eugene had been brought to the Moisant town house after being killed on the field of honor. There had been so much blood; his body had been so slack, so still. Then she had ordered his valet to prepare the body, had chosen clothing for the burial, had gone through the house stopping the clocks, turning mirrors to the walls, doing all that was required while in a daze. During the entire time, Henri Moisant had raged and threatened, screaming that she didn't care because she was not prostrate with her grief, because she could still reason and speak and move from place to place.

Facing away from Agatha while her companion fastened the row of small buttons up the back of her day gown, Lisette was suddenly overwhelmed by this devastating outcome to another duel and the dreadful possibilities it raised.

"Oh, Aggie," she said, putting a hand to her mouth.

"Yes, love," her companion said on a deep sigh. "I know."

"He…he wrote a poem for me." Tears stung the back of Lisette's nose then, and welled into her eyes though she held her chin high as she tried not to let them fall.

"Such tragedy as has been caused by these meetings, all the young men cut down before they have lived. What a waste, what a terrible waste."

Agatha's voice held such weary acceptance that it moved Lisette to anger. "It should not happen."

"There is nothing we can do about it." Finished with the buttons, Agatha turned her and straightened her bodice with a quick twitch. Then she gave her a quick hug. "It's the part of women to do what we can for those who manage to survive."

Lisette rested her forehead an instant on Agatha's bony shoulder, then straightened. "How bad is Monsieur Blackford? Did they say?"

"Bad enough. They were shouting something about an accident. I shudder to think what that may mean."

"If he is receiving no attention from the medical man, then we must see what may be done for him," Lisette answered as she turned toward the door.

The wound was a great, jagged hole in his shoulder, just

under his collarbone, one that had bled with great profusion, soaking his shirt and staining the men who had carried him to the house upon a storeroom door quickly pried from its hinges. To staunch the flow was the first necessity. Caid had made a pad of his cravat that he held to the wound with considerable pressure. His hands were red with blood, still he persevered. As Lisette stepped to the bed where Blackford was stretched out on an oilcloth, Caid called out for her to make a heavier pad from the old sheets stacked on a bedside table, then be ready to slap it into place when he removed the soaked cravat.

Lisette had never been particularly affected by the sight of blood, nor was she now. It was the fresh smell of it that bothered her. However, she knew from experience that if she took short, shallow breaths it would be all right. She had been nominal mistress of the Moisant household, so called on to look after the slaves when there was an accident. This could be no different. She would not allow it.

"What happened?" she asked as she tore a long strip from a ragged, well-washed sheet and began to fold it.

"A damnable thing, really. Blackford had no intention of such a drastic turn of events."

"No, he said as much." She glanced at the face of the Englishman. He lay so pale and still, his eyelids closed so his lashes rested on his high cheekbones, his breathing fast yet silent. With his lack of response to pain or anything being done for him, it was difficult to say whether he was unconscious, extremely stoic or just acquiescent in the stunned manner of the recently injured.

"It happened so fast. Dorelle launched his attack an instant before the command to begin was given—not a deliberate attempt at defeating his opponent, I think, but the effect of overwrought nerves. Blackford parried with considerable force, as you can imagine. Dorelle's rapier broke from the blow, snapped right in two. He was already in a desperate lunge and could not draw back. The sword stump that was left, about a foot long, struck Blackford in the shoulder. Blackford staggered back, slipping in the wet grass. His sword point was flung up purely by reflex. Somehow, Dorelle managed to impale himself on it."

"Oh, *mon Dieu*," Lisette whispered, even as she felt something inside, some close held pain, ease a little. "I…I'm glad it was truly an accident."

Caid gave a short nod. "Others may not be so quick to accept it."

"If he dies, they will think I killed the young Caesar," Blackford whispered. His lashes fluttered a little though he lay perfectly still. "And they will be correct."

"It could not be avoided," Caid said with precision.

"Except by tolerance and less temper? Where is my hostess? I must apologize for ruining her house party."

"You must lie still before you make it a worse calamity," Lisette told him with some severity. She thought the awkward sword thrust had not severed anything vital, but could not be sure. He was alarmingly pale and beginning to shiver, though he held his arms across his body as if trying to control it. And still the blood soaked the cloth under her hand. Agatha, at her side, was busily making another, larger cloth pad to be added to the one she held.

"Where is Maurelle now?" Caid repeated Blackford's question in quiet tones.

"Sending a groom to summon Monsieur Dorelle's family," Agatha answered, since she had paused briefly to speak to their hostess on her way to the sickroom. "Also making sure that her remaining guests will have breakfast as usual and saying her farewells to those who have decided to depart immediately."

"Which will be most of them, I expect. Nothing like a scandal to break up a house party."

Even as she agreed, Lisette heard a sound at the door and turned her head to look. It was not the doctor, however.

"May we be of any help," Celina asked. Behind her could be seen Rio de Silva and Nicholas Pasquale.

"You might find a quilt or blanket," Lisette said. "And he would be more comfortable, I feel sure, if someone removed his boots."

Celina went away to execute her commission while Rio and Nicholas came forward and dealt with the footwear in a few swift moves. The two swordsmen backed up then to lean against the walls, watching the man on the table who had become their comrade. The level of restrained edginess that hovered in the room was multiplied by three.

"Where the hell is that doctor?" Caid muttered under his breath.

"I'm sure he'll be here as soon as he is able."

"Isn't there anything we can do, anything we can get him? Maybe a shot of brandy?"

"I don't think that's a good idea," Lisette said. "He would have to sit up to drink, and he probably doesn't need to be moved."

"Yes. It's just…I hate not being able to do something."

He would, of course, Lisette thought. He was a man of action. Waiting was not in his nature.

Celina returned then with an armload of utility quilts. Quickly, the others spread them over Blackford, though Nicholas brought a knife and cut away his bloody shirt, removing it, before tucking the quilt edges under his body. The efficiency and care with which it was all done was impressive, though Lisette was forced to wonder if it was all for nothing.

The bleeding was slowing, however. She discovered that much when she released a little of the pressure she was holding on her pad in order to add yet another. She thought of wiping away some of the crusted and drying blood that stained his skin, but decided it could wait.

Yet it was difficult to know what else to do, difficult to realize that a man's life could be in her hands. That was not strictly true, of course. The responsibility was shared.

Raising her gaze from the wounded man, she looked at Caid across the table from her. He met her gaze, his own unsmiling. His eyes were dark blue with concern, yet seemed to allow no chance of disaster.

It was a fallacy, that confidence. Men died every day. Any man, no matter how strong or skilled, could fall on the dueling ground. The next time Caid appeared, he could receive a fatal injury. Like that of Blackford's, it need not be life threatening at the outset. Death could come from excess bleeding, blood poisoning, gangrene or pneumonia. Caid, valiant in his strength and honor, could die.

That knowledge had always been with her, had been implicit from the beginning of their acquaintance. Knowing it was one thing, seeing the evidence of it in front of her in Blackford's inert form was another.

Caid, who had courted death on the dueling field for her sake many times over, could be killed tomorrow, the next day or the day after. He could die, and there was nothing she could do to stop it.

Just then, the door opened and the doctor came into the room. His features were set as he approached the bed, and if he realized that his coat sleeves were red-black with blood, he made nothing of it.

Blackford's face lost even more of its color. Raising his head on the pillow, he asked, "Dorelle?"

"The young gentleman has no more need of my services," the doctor answered with crisp finality. "Now, let me see what I may do for you, sir."

Francis Dorelle was dead. The knowledge came with an unrelenting flood of pain and grief. He would write no more poems, declaim no more by the light of the moon, devote himself to no more ladies, feel no more anger or joy, love nor chagrin, adoration or pain. He had fought for honor and died by it. He was gone.

Lisette, relinquishing her place to the doctor, stepped away from the bed. Turning away, she walked slowly to the door.

"Lisette?" Caid called after her.

She made no answer. Leaving the bedchamber, she closed the door quite gently behind her.

17

Caid relieved Nicholas at Blackford's bedside shortly after breakfast. Two days after the duel, the patient was progressing nicely except for a fever that the doctor assured them was no more than to be expected. This rather heartless sounding diagnosis may well have been because Blackford cursed at him with considerable inventiveness as he poked and prodded at the wound.

The fever and inactivity, not to mention the watch being kept to see that he didn't overtax his strength, had given Blackford the temper of a pit viper. He kept insisting that he could get up, and was inclined to cut to ribbons with high-flown invective anyone who disagreed with him. As a result, the swordsmen had taken the nursing duty on themselves to spare the ladies the language and, just possibly, the sight of an unashamedly naked Englishman trying to crawl out of his bed.

Blackford was lying with his gaze turned toward the window where sunlight fell in a bright square onto the floor as Caid stepped into the room. He appeared pensive and curiously bereft.

"Headache again?" Caid asked as he looked across the patient to lift a brow at Nicholas, who reclined in a slipper chair with one long leg thrust out in front of him.

"That or he's blue deviled," the Italian sword master drawled. "If you can discover which, it will be more than I've managed." Folding the news sheet he had been reading, he set it aside and rose to his feet. "The nod-cock refused to eat his breakfast so it may be merely hunger."

"If that's it, I'm sure something could be found to stave off the pangs," Caid suggested.

"So Madame Moisant suggested a half hour ago, and was grunted at for her effort." No flicker of response came from the man in the bed. Nicholas grimaced. "You see? A thankless task. I wish you joy of it."

"You're all heart," Caid said dryly.

"Indeed, and the proof of it is that I haven't murdered him yet." With that, Nicholas stalked from the bedchamber, closing the door behind him.

Caid gave a short laugh before stepping to take up the news sheet, scanning the brief sidebar of political news and disasters before sweeping his gaze over the usual notices of sales, foreclosures, arriving and departing steamboats and cargoes of goods for sale at various emporiums. One notice in particular caught his attention, and he glanced from it to Blackford.

"Nicholas been reading all the latest to you?" he asked.

"In tripping Latin accents."

"Including notice of the tournament, I suppose."

"He thought I should be interested."

"Which you were, no doubt, in your fashion."

Blackford said nothing.

"It did not occur to Nicholas, apparently, that your fashion might be negative."

Still no answer.

"That's what has you at low ebb, isn't it? The fact that you will be unable to compete in the coming tournament. Or are you still sulking because people may say you were injured by a rank amateur who should never have been able to touch you?"

The reply was profane in the extreme, which was much as Caid expected given the provocation. To goad the Englishman from his sullen mood seemed better than allowing him to lie brooding like some character in a Shakespearean tragedy.

"You should consider yourself lucky that you need not meet Thimecourt. I hear he has the devil of a temper, and is like as not to call you out later if he doesn't care for how the bout goes between you."

"Your problem," Blackford said without concern, "since you may have the honor of sparring with him after he defeats whoever takes my place."

"Or not, depending on how many more drop out between now and then."

"I didn't drop out, as you so kindly put it."

"And that will be taken into consideration the next time around. There will be other tournaments, you know. I heard before we left New Orleans that another was being considered for next month because all the entrants could not be accommodated."

"My indifference," Blackford said distinctly, "is beyond measure."

Caid frowned in impatience. "And surpassed only by your lack of manners."

"Ennui has nothing to do with conduct."

"Except that one should not outweigh the other. And those who are bored usually have their own lack of initiative to blame."

"Initiative achieves many goals but will not allow me to mend in time to skewer you in this tournament. Or outside it, more is the pity."

"I knew bloody derring-do was on your mind," Caid said, returning to affability. "It's the one thing sure to rouse a martyr."

Anger flared in the brilliant blue of Blackford's eyes. "I could, if you would hand me my sword, poke you in the neck. We could change places then, you and I, and see who best plays willing victim."

"Oh, I concede you the honor," Caid answered, his grin

unrepentant. "The reason being that you have so much more experience at it, you know."

"Which, like the poultry seller conceding number of kills to the hangman, is nothing short of amazing, all circumstances considered. Your sojourn in prison, for instance. Or do you think your self-denial on that account noble rather than merely tiresome?"

It was a lesson, if he needed one, Caid thought, in minding his own business. He should have known better than to spar with one known to be as adept with cutting words as with his sword. "A hit," he said, his smile turning wry. "Though it might be instructive to know just who gave you that tale."

"Not Madame Moisant, if that is the direction of your thought. Mademoiselle Agatha mentioned it in passing, as if I should know it—which comes, no doubt, from the two of us being born in the same general archipelago. She was mainly concerned that our principles might affect too closely the happiness of her lone chick."

"And expected you to remedy the matter if I proved stubborn?"

"What, by giving kindness and succor to the lady? I should be too pleased. But I believe I was to beat sense into you with the flat of my sword if all other persuasion failed."

Caid gave him a direct look. "You are welcome to try."

"Oh, I grant it might be difficult at the moment, but I won't be ever thus."

"No, you will be even more unpleasant, I don't doubt, when you are capable of holding a weapon."

"And you will be more of a snob," Blackford said in biting accents.

"A snob?" Caid inquired in incredulous tones. "I'd need to take lessons for a fortnight before standing in your supercilious shadow."

"Natural superiority and snobbery are two different things

entirely," Blackford returned, his eyes gleaming. "But neither can hold a candle to the righteous humility of the common herd. Good God, man, were you innocent or guilty? And what in the devil's holy hell makes you think it matters?"

"It matters to me," Caid said with a look that should have stopped the Englishman in his tracks.

"Only because you let it. No one can make you feel shame without your consent, my Irish friend. Nor can they prevent you from courting a willing lady."

"If you think so, you have no concept of what it's like in New Orleans."

"French New Orleans, you mean. But this is also the United States, thus a new country. The conventions that chain you to the past belong to another place that is an ocean, and distant world, away."

"Imagine that," Caid said softly. "And would you be explaining to me just why it's important to you?"

"Why do you think, you damned peat bog dandy? The wish to be renewed in a new land is not solely an Irish virtue."

Where further insult and innuendo might have led them was impossible to guess, for a knock came on the door at that instant. Caid called out the command to enter, and Lisette swept into the room at the head of a procession which included a manservant bearing a ewer of hot water and a razor box, a maid with fresh linen, and the butler carrying a tray on which reposed a silver coffeepot and a sumptuous array of pastries.

"A few comforts for the patient," she said, her smile beneficent. "Pray accept them Monsieur Blackford or the cook will feel her skill has been slighted."

Whether it was Caid's strictures, the gesture or the sight of a pretty form and face, Blackford actually smiled. Caid could hardly blame him. He could feel grim appreciation curving his own mouth. Lisette, though a little subdued still, was not only extremely pleasant to look at but almost impossible to resist in this mood of calm expectation. How she managed it, he could not tell. He knew very well that she had watched over the body of Francis Dorelle during the night and been present at dawn when his grieving parents, an elderly couple who had spoiled this son of their later years, had risen from their overnight stay and taken his body away with them.

"Dulcet and intoxicating as a pear in wine sauce, the lady gratifies my every wish, even those I was not aware I had," Blackford declaimed in his own florid manner. "How am I to refuse?"

"Excellent," Lisette said. "There is a cup for your tireless caretaker, as well, and extra cake besides. Enjoy, gentlemen."

She did not remain, probably because it appeared from the rather noble way that Blackford gestured toward the valet that he meant to make himself presentable at once, even before he ate. Caid knew that he should have thought of that comfort. With so many hirsute faces these days, however, he'd hardly noticed that Blackford was looking downright scruffy. Eyeing him, he wondered if Lisette saw him in the same light, or if she might not find the blue shadowed lines of the Englishman's jaw rather rakish instead.

Raised voices came just then from the connecting room, the salon, through which Lisette had departed just minutes ago. Caid's head came up. One of the voices was certainly hers, while the other, deeper in tone and more than a little importunate, belonged to a man.

Caid glanced at Blackford, who was propped up now with a hot towel wrapped around his lower face. The Englishman met his eyes above the Turkish fabric, his gaze intent. Almost imperceptibly, he nodded toward the door.

Permission to go or encouragement? Caid had no idea

which was intended, but it seemed they both sensed something odd in what was happening in the salon. Rising to his feet, he moved in that direction. He pulled open the door and stepped inside.

Gustave Bechet had Lisette by the wrist, attempting to drag her into his arms. The bulk of his body obscured most of what was taking place, but there was no doubt that Lisette was not enjoying it.

Never in his life had Caid felt such a strong wish that it was still the fashion for a man to wear a sword at his side like some eighteenth-century gallant. How satisfying it would be to slide it from its scabbard and apply it where it would do the most good. Though whether that was against Bechet's fat buttocks or between his shoulder blades was a question he was too incensed to decide on short notice.

"Let me go at once," Lisette said with distinct disfavor in her voice. "I have no interest in your proposal."

"Maman insists," Bechet whined. "I must beg you to listen. She says you will think on it, for if you keep encouraging men to fight duels over you, no one will receive you. It's the perfect time, before other men see the opportunity. I must seize it, must seize you."

"Don't be ridiculous," she cried, jerking against his hold as he tugged her toward him. "You can't do this in broad daylight and while a sick man lies in the next room."

"You had best not do it at all," Caid said with disgust in his voice.

Bechet made a squawking sound and released Lisette so quickly that she almost fell. Swinging around with clumsy haste, he gawped at Caid as if he had dropped from heaven. Then his expression turned belligerent.

"You," he said on a grunt. "You're always there, always first. I guess you think you'll be the first to bed the widow. Maman said…"

Caid stepped forward, caught a handful of the stout man's

cravat and shirt front and jerked hard enough to lift Bechet onto his toes. "Your maman is much mistaken in her ideas and her advice. I never again want to hear anything she may have said about Madame Moisant."

A screech rang out then from the doorway leading to the gallery. "What are you doing to my son? Release him at once, you murderous brute!"

Madame Bechet ran across the room with her skirts and her cap flapping and her fists raised in the air. Reaching Caid, she began to beat him about the head and shoulders.

Lisette stepped quickly to catch her arm. She dragged her away, spinning her around.

The woman turned on Lisette in her rage. "This is all your fault, *cocotte!* Flaunting yourself in front of men, leading them on. Monsieur Moisant tried to tell me, but I wouldn't listen. You are nothing but a *putain,* unfit for any decent man, much less my son. So you will not have him? Hah! He will never have you. Go and spread your legs for the killers you prefer. It's all such as you deserves!"

"I prefer any man to one who answers his mother's commands like a trained puppy, *madame!*"

The comparison was apt, since Figaro chose that moment to dash into the room where he attacked the skirts of Madame Bechet, growling as he pulled at them. Rage shook the older woman and she grasped her skirts, trying to jerk them from the dog's hold. "I refuse to remain under this roof with you and your vicious beast of a dog. My son and I will return to the city where I shall go straight to your husband's father. He shall hear how you trail his fine name in slime."

"Do so. Nothing would please me more." Lisette gave her stare for stare, defiance burning in her eyes

"You will not be so pleased when he puts an end to your fine dance!"

"We shall see." Lisette glanced down at Figaro. "Stop, *mon chou.* Let the cow go."

The small dog immediately removed his teeth from Madame Bechet's torn skirt and sat down. The woman turned with massive dignity and sailed toward the door that gave onto the gallery. Over her shoulder she ordered, "Come, Gustave!"

Her son backed away, his face sullen. Then he turned awkwardly, as if loath to put his back to them, and followed after his mother.

Neither Caid nor Lisette spoke for long seconds after the pair had vanished from sight. Lisette stood stiff and straight, with her face flaming and the bodice of her day gown shuddering with her heartbeat. She was upset and who could blame her, Caid thought in grim recognition. Such confrontations were obviously not everyday fare.

Regardless, she was fascinating as she stood there, so vibrantly alive in her anger. That she had come to his defense amazed him. He was also grateful for it, since it would have been difficult for him to defend himself against Madame Bechet's attack without resorting to ungentlemanly violence.

"I am profoundly sorry for this further unpleasantness," he said, his voice a little strained, his stance as correct as he could make it. "I never meant that your visit here should be like this."

A weary smile flitted across her face. "I should hope not."

"No. I imagine you would as soon be back in the Vieux Carré. I will escort you to town whenever you are ready."

"What of Monsieur Blackford?"

"He should be able to travel by carriage by tomorrow. In fact, it may be impossible to prevent it."

"I could take him in mine if he wouldn't mind the tight fit."

"A generous offer, but he will be able to recline in Madame Herriot's vehicle."

"Will she be ready to go then?"

"If not, the carriage can return for her," Caid answered.

Lisette gave a slow nod as she put her hand into the pocket of the decorative silk apron she wore, clenching it on something that made a small, round shape there. "Yes, I suppose so."

Her distant air, as if preoccupied with other thoughts, disturbed him. "It's all right, isn't it? You would not prefer to stay?"

"No, no," she answered with a quick movement of her head. "It's quite all right. There is still one more night."

One more night for what? He might have asked, but heard a noise from the other room just then, as if something had been dropped. Reminded that Blackford might be listening, if no one else, he simply inclined his head. "Excellent. We will make further plans this evening."

"Yes," she answered as one in a trance. "That will be…satisfactory."

It was ridiculous of him to find something portentous in those few words, Caid told himself as he watched her turn and walk away. Still, he could not leave them alone. They played themselves in his head as the day advanced, mocked him as he ate with Blackford in his bedchamber, came back to him while he played cards with Nicholas and Rio. They hovered near as he arranged the time of their departure the following morning, including how the line of carriages and horsemen would travel. They were still with him when he went along to his room for the night, leaving Rio with Blackford as the two of them smoked a final cigar, drank a last glass of cognac before bed.

What had Lisette meant? Yes, and what would she do when she returned to town? Caid turned over the questions yet again as he removed his watch and chain with its fobs and dropped them in a carved tray on the dressing table, then pulled the knot from his cravat, slipping it free of his collar before tossing it over the tray. Shrugging from his coat, he hung it over the back of an armchair, and then followed it with his waistcoat. Something teased at his mind, some worrisome detail that he could not quite capture.

The lady had not been herself all afternoon, staying much alone while she read or else stared out through the tops of the trees as they all sat on the gallery. Nicholas had tried to tease her out of her megrims. Even Blackford, up and dressed for the late supper, with his arm in a sling of black silk fashioned from one of Maurelle's discarded shawls, had tried, as well. Neither had any luck.

He had been rather smug about their failure at the time, Caid realized with a frown. Now it bothered him.

As he took the links from his cuffs and studs from the front of his shirt, he recalled the moment when Agatha had asked Lisette if she had the headache again and suggested a tisane. Lisette had snapped at her, something none of them had seen before. Then after supper, she had suddenly become bright eyed and full of chatter. She held sway as the hour grew late, easily eclipsing Maurelle, who seemed tired, and Celina, whose attention was given to Rio. She had even taken over from Solon the task of filling their glasses for a last round of cordial, and proposed a moving toast to the memory of all dead poets and their verses.

Yes, something was definitely amiss.

He pulled his shirt from the waist of his trousers and draped it over the back of the chair where the butler serving as his valet could find it. Stretching mightily with his hands above his head, he shook the tension from his neck and shoulders, and then slouched to the chair where he seated himself. As he began to pull off his boots, he frowned, wondering if he was making too much of a fit of ill humor. He had never noticed that Lisette was given to moods, however. Not that she lacked reason these days.

She was almost certainly feeling the death of young Dorelle, or perhaps blaming herself for it. That was natural enough, if misguided. Then the insulting names Madame Bechet had flung at her could have disturbed her more than she was willing to admit. Apprehension over the swirl of gossip that must arise from the events of this house party could be preying on her mind, as well. Yes, she had plenty to dampen her spirits or even set her to brooding. Nevertheless, he was doubtful. It was almost as if she had come to some fateful decision. What it might be, he was afraid to think.

She was not alone in that occupation, however. He had come to a few conclusions himself. Chief among them was recognition that he must stop pressing Lisette to choose a future husband. It was making life too difficult for her, not to mention for himself. She had too many suitors, few of whom seemed in any way suitable. Moreover, the activity, as restrained as it was, seemed to have brought out the worst in Moisant. The man was much too possessive. Caid gave his boots a frown before setting them beside his chair.

Rising to his feet, he began to unfasten his trousers. His back was to the screen of gathered silk on sections of mahogany framing which shielded the corner where the chamber pot was hidden away. In front of him was a set of windows with the jalousies closed behind them against mosquitoes. Since he preferred to risk being bitten for the sake of air circulation, he paused in his task and moved to put his hands on the frame holding the wavy glass, intending to pull it upward. For an instant, he could see his half-naked reflection as in a mirror, and also that of the room behind him.

His attention was caught by a flicker of movement, the barest shift of shadow on the screen. Someone was behind it.

A scant moment later, he continued his task, drawing the window open. Then, releasing the last trouser button, he let the front open, shucked them down his legs. Wearing only his knit unmentionables, he carried the trousers to the armoire as if he meant to put them away. He even hummed a catchy melody from a recent comedic opera as he opened the door and hung the trousers on one of the hooks provided.

Abruptly, he whirled and launched himself at the screen, ramming his shoulder into it. The flimsy cloth and wood contraption toppled, striking the wall behind it. His upper body struck something firm yet soft. A low cry sounded as the intruder fell backward, thudding into plastered wall before sliding to the floor.

The hair stood up on the back of Caid's neck. His brain refused to work, but instinct made him grab the screen and set it out of the way. Then he dropped to his knees beside the crumpled figure he had uncovered.

Lisette.

Her back was propped against the wall, and it appeared to be all that was holding her up. Her face was pale, her eyes closed. Bright skeins of shining hair spilled around her, trailing over her shoulders, pooling in her lap. The nightgown and robe she wore were hiked to her thighs and her feet were bare.

"God, *chère*, I didn't know," he exclaimed as he reached for her hand and began to chafe it. "I thought you were some sneak thief. Say something. Where does it hurt? Merde, what a fool I am."

"Don't," she whispered. "I'm all right, I think."

"What in God's holy name were you doing back there. What are you doing in my chamber, for that matter?"

A ghost of a smile came and went across her face though she didn't open her eyes. "How quickly the concern passes to questions. I might have known. What was I doing? Something I should not, of course."

"If you had need of me, you should have sent word. I'd have come to you immediately. Here, let me help you stand."

She allowed him to put his arms around her and lift her

to her feet. She came easily, but made no attempt to balance herself so he was forced to catch her against him, pressed to his near-naked body from breastbone to knees. Then she slid her hands upward that were pressed to his chest, threading through the hair that curled there, skimming the firm surface of his chest and along his shoulders until she reached his neck and clasped them behind his head. Gazing up into his face, she gave him a slow smile. "I could have sent someone, yes. But what would be the point of it when I so wanted to be here myself?"

"You wanted…"

"This, *mon brave*," she whispered and drew his head down until her mouth met her parted lips.

He was dreaming, Caid thought. He could not be living this fantasy of tender and pliant seduction. To have her flow against him, twining her fingers in his hair, was the stuff of fevered, late-night longing. It could not be real.

Yet she was warm and perfect in his arms, and wearing nothing under her nightclothes except her own warm skin. Her curves, gently rounded here, slender there, melted against him, molding to the hard heat of his body like the candle wax of midnight. She was all accommodation, inciting him to madness. He slid over that edge with disturbing ease, gathering her closer while a deep drawn breath lodged, trapped, in his chest.

Her mouth was sweet yet tart with the lingering flavor of the cordial they had sipped earlier. And it was his to take, every moist corner, fragile surface and porcelain edge. Invading, he laved the silken inner planes with his tongue, skimmed the small, glassy squares of her teeth, glided over the arch that was like silk over bone, and learned the minutely quilted texture of her smaller tongue as it mated with his in delicate play.

She was inexperienced, shy as a minnow in a pool, darting away, returning, sliding past and around his tongue while her breathing increased to a frantic pace and her grasp tightened upon him until he thought her fingers must be cramped with it. It was tantalizing and incredibly provocative without meaning to be. It was touching in a way he had never thought to know, much less feel or understand. He kneaded the soft, tapering lines of her back, slid his palm over her firm flesh while an odd reverence caught him unaware, like a piercing ache in the region of his heart.

He wanted her, wanted to taste her every mystery, drink her essence, bury himself in her heat and moisture while counting the world well lost for the chance. His brain ignited with flames that seared its edges. His body was as tempered and hard, as poised for penetration as a well-honed rapier. Still he had some miniscule grasp on sanity.

Releasing her lips, he put his forehead against hers as he asked in a hoarse whisper, "Are you sure you know what you're doing?"

"I'm sure."

The words were soft, humid as they tickled his lips and chin. Then she kissed the corner of his mouth, dipped her tongue into that small keystone-shaped well, traced the turned edges that led from it.

Yet he couldn't abandon the need to test her resolve. Smoothing a hand over her rib cage and under her arm, he palmed the fullness of a breast, using his ridged swordsman's calluses to abrade the nipple through the fabric. As that small bud tightened, nudging between his fingers, a low groan rumbled in his throat.

She pressed more fully into his grasp, silently entreating the stimulation, the liberties he was taking. And he felt driven to take more and still more, until there was nothing he didn't know. He was suddenly desperate to have her writhing under him in hot, slick supplication, to have her once, completely, if never again.

Lowering his head, he wet the thin batiste of her nightgown with his saliva until it was transparent, showing the puckered coral-pink of her nipple, then suckled her through it, tugging gently with his teeth. Closing his eyes, he rubbed the lids over the soft swell that surrounded his mouth. "Stop me now," he whispered while his moving lips brushed against her. "Do it before it's too late."

"I can't," she answered, threading her fingers through his hair so the thrill of it prickled his skin with gooseflesh.

"Then forgive me later," he answered. "If you can."

With the last word, he slipped his self-imposed restraint and fastened his hot, open mouth on her breast. She made a small sound, though whether of pain or intense pleasure, shock or gratification, he could not tell. Nor did he try overmuch. His concentration was on releasing the row of small pearl buttons that fastened the nightgown's deep neckline. One by one, they parted company from their holes, baring her pale skin, the sweetly rising mounds that he caressed, widening into a deeper V-shape that exposed the flat surface of her abdomen with its dip of navel, and the red-gold glint of a triangle of soft curls.

Prayers, invocation, praise, he whispered them all against her as he followed that opening with teeth, tongue and questing hands. He pushed the nightgown opening wider, shoved the cap sleeves from her shoulders and down her arms with more determination than finesse. It caught at her elbows and he left it, careless as he skimmed her waist, delving into her navel, burying nose and mouth into her soft femininity with its essential, erotic fragrance. He shoved inside in wet exploration, while filling his hands with the rounded curves of her bottom and pulling her more exactly against his face.

She gave a small cry, her fingers biting into his shoulders. Her legs trembled, threatening to give way. Caid caught her behind the bend of her legs with one arm and around the waist with the other, lowering her to the carpet that was centered on the floor. Mercilessly then, he stripped away the yards of white batiste and tossed nightgown and robe aside, dispensing with his underwear, as well, before turning back to her.

She lay bathed in the golden glow of candlelight, lying in a pool of her vibrant hair that shone like cool flames against the lush cabbage roses of the carpet. A ribbon held her tresses away from her face, but had come untied, trailing alongside her cheek. He reached to catch one end, pulling it from her so she was naked and free, unbound and unconfined before him. One hand lay at her waist while the fingers of the other still touched his shoulder. Her eyes darkened as she watched him, shadowed by half hidden, half denied fears. She was exposed to his gaze, the globes of her breasts as succulent as white and pink peaches, her thighs smooth and spread as he had arranged them on releasing her.

It was necessary to remember to breathe, to subdue the need to take her in mindless, anguished rut, stabbing deep and to the hilt. He was heavy and hot where his body touched her hip, throbbing with the ragged jar of his heartbeat. It would be so easy, such a fervid joy. Yet that way also lay the abrupt end of pleasure instead of the beginning.

She wasn't ready. She deserved more, and so did he.

Taking the hair ribbon in his fingers, he draped it over her breasts, circling the nipples, catching their tips that were knotted like sweet berries in the swirling loops he made with the length of satin. Where the ribbon went, his lips and tongue followed, sampling, gathering tastes and impressions to last a lifetime. He brushed her cheek, trailed across her lips, let the shining ribbon glide along her neck before returning to the place where her heartbeat moved under her breast. The small gasps she made touched some part of him he had never known existed, an area between his heart and his soul, and he smiled a little against her skin.

Slowly, making sinuous curves and arabesques, he draped and slid the ribbon down her body, letting it puddle in her navel, drift across her abdomen that rose and fell with her quick breathing, gliding it lower with every twist and turn until it tangled in the soft fleece that marked the juncture of her thighs. The blend of satin and silk, smooth and crisp of his incursion there enthralled him, but not half so much as the slither of satin down through the hidden, damp and tender crevice.

She moved restlessly, touching his hair, his shoulders, skimming quick, inquisitive fingers over his muscled hips and the hot length of him. He clenched his teeth, enduring, for he still wanted her to need him as desperately as he needed her, wanted her to feel and wonder what touched her, parted her, whether the ribbon, his gently stretching fingers or his tongue. He wanted proof of her desire.

And he had its abrupt, slick abundance. An ecstasy of gladness swelled inside him as he carefully tied the ribbon he held around her thigh like a damp garter, then made a perfect bow. Inserting a finger under it, he tugged, opening her. Then he rolled to cover her, pressed into her. He felt her clinch around him in hot, wet anointing while she grasped his arms urgently, crying his name.

He took her completely then, sliding deep in a single plunge that pushed aside the remaining barrier and took her breath. She stiffened for an endless instant, and then relaxed profoundly, flexing her knees, so that he sank into her until he could feel the throb of the blood in her internal veins, sense the first warning spasm of her release.

Then came the furor, the striving that stroked them both into jolting, astonished pleasure, joy beyond measure. Still he propelled them both, taking from the joining every last flutter of subsiding glory, not wanting it to end, needing something more than mere conclusion, something more that was just out of his reach.

It could not be gained, and so he thrust deep a final time and was still while his chest heaved and his eyes burned with unshed tears. Then he eased from her, rolling to his side where he gathered her against him, holding her while staring into the far corner of the room that was still mellow with candlelight.

After a time, he roused. Picking Lisette up bodily, he carried her to the bed. He stripped back the covers and joined her on the sheet where he made love to her again with swift efficiency and because he could not resist. And this time, when it was over, he closed his eyes and let his swordsman's hard resolve gather sleep around him.

No more than a minute later, or so it seemed, Caid felt Lisette stir, then move away. Instantly, he put out a hand to catch her upper arm, holding her at his side.

"Let me go, please." Her voice was low and not quite steady.

"What is it?"

"I can't be here." She twisted abruptly from his grasp and slid from the high bed. Crossing the room, she scooped her nightgown from the floor, fumbling with its folds as if needing to cover her nakedness.

Caid came off the bed so quickly that he caused the bed candle to flutter on its shortened wick and almost go out. "Why? What is it?"

"This is wrong…all wrong." She backed away at his approach, holding the nightgown in front of her.

"Not to me." He could hear the stubborn anger in his voice, and the intimation of pain. He reached out, clasping her arms that were cold to the touch, fighting the urge to pull her against him to warm her. Or to warm them both, for he felt an icy chill spreading in his chest.

"You don't understand," she said with a shake of her head that made her hair slide over her shoulders, fall across her half-covered breasts, tickling his wrist where he held her.

"Make me."

She came up against the window frame where she stood staring at him with desolation in her face. "It was a mistake," she whispered. "I made a terrible mistake."

18

"What are you saying?"

Caid's voice was tight. He released her and eased away, putting a little distance between them. Lisette made a brief gesture toward the bed. "This…what took place between us…"

"People call it making love, unless that particular emotion has no bearing."

"Don't." Her protest was instinctive, edged with pain as she met his eyes. "I just…I'm trying to tell you that…that whatever you felt wasn't you, wasn't real."

"It felt real all right." He watched her, his shadowed blue gaze intent, breathing through his nose so quickly that his chest rose and fell as if he'd been running flat out.

"Please, this is hard enough without…" She stopped, pushed her fingers through her hair, raking it back so it fell behind her shoulders. Closing her eyes for an instant, she opened them again, said clearly, "What I am trying to say is that I gave you a potion, a Voodoo love potion."

His face, in shadow since the candlelight was behind him, seemed to go blank for an instant. Then he gave a short laugh. "In the cordial, I suppose. And why was that?"

"To…to make you want—"

"I know what it's supposed to do. What I'm asking is why you desired the effect?"

She pressed her lips together for a second before she answered. "That must be obvious."

"Not to me."

He was going to make her say it. She should have expected nothing less. "I wanted you to make love to me."

"All you had to do was ask."

"Indeed? To the best of my recollection, I did that and was refused, or at least denied the final consummation."

"That was different."

"Oh, yes. It was to your plan and purpose and under your control."

"I'm sorry if I disappointed you, but you still haven't explained why."

She looked away from him. "I wasn't disappointed, at least…"

"I remember," he said, his voice rough. "But you accuse me of having a plan and purpose. What was yours?"

He was relentless, though it was possible that he had every right. She wished briefly that she had kept quiet. It would have been more cowardly, but far easier.

"I thought it would end the search for my new husband," she said quietly. "I thought you might become my lover. Or even marry me yourself."

"You meant to trap me."

"Only if you wished it."

Something, some remnant of passion or intent, shadowed his face, then was gone. She knew in that instant that she had been right, that he would have made a permanent place in his life for her. She put out a hand to touch his arm. "Oh, Caid…"

He moved away so her hand dropped back to her side. "That was the desired outcome, perhaps, but you haven't given the reason why it was so necessary a consummation, if you will forgive a crude pun."

The harshness was a sign of his anger, she thought. He had a right to it. He also deserved to know the full truth. Since it seemed that she had destroyed all hope of any closer relationship between them, it was pointless to keep the secret any longer.

"I told you once before that you are one of the very few

men in New Orleans with whom I might feel safe. That is truer than ever now. But there is more to it than that. I owe you a debt, and it isn't simply that you removed me from a marriage that was never a real one in any sense. There is something more that touches on your sister's death."

"Brona's? What could you possibly have to do with that?"

"It's a long story. Would you like to sit down?"

"I am not, I assure you, in need of support."

"No, I suppose not," she said wearily, "but I think I might be." Moving past him, she sought the armchair and sank down on it, perching on the edge of the seat. With a few quick moves, she straightened her nightgown and slipped it on over her head, doing up the buttons. As a shield, it was barely adequate but served to make her feel less vulnerable.

Caid waited until she was settled, his face mirroring his impatience. "What about Brona?"

"You know that she was Eugene's mistress. Did you know that the house on Rampart Street where she lived with Eugene was bought for her by his father? Yes, he bought it just as he would have if his son had chosen a quadroon at one of the balls. He thought he was providing his son with an outlet for his male needs while assuring that he did not frequent the brothels where he might become diseased."

"Eugene told you this?"

She gave a quick shake of her head. "Henri Moisant, rather."

"But you knew it before you married his son?"

She gave a low laugh; she couldn't help it. "By no means. It was explained to me later. My father-in-law thought that he was enlightening my ignorance concerning the ways of the world, you see. Which he was in a way." She paused a moment in pensive remembrance, before going on. "The question concerning Brona came up when he accused me of failing as a wife because I had not yet given him a grandchild after nearly two years of marriage. I defended myself by telling the truth, that Eugene preferred his mistress. Henri was at pains to tell me that such things made no difference. I convinced him, I think, that he was mistaken."

A frown drew Caid's brows together. "You make it sound as if your husband was in love with Brona."

"He was," she said simply.

Caid turned and walked away from her, setting his hands on his hips while he stared at the floor. The muscles across his back stood out with the tension that gripped him. "Why in the name of hell did he let her die then?"

"He didn't. Oh, Caid…"

"Tell me. Just tell me."

She gathered her thoughts, doing her best to make the thing clear in her own mind so she could relay it to him. "Henri Moisant desperately wanted an heir. Eugene was his only child to live to adulthood, his one hope of seeing that his line continued. He had arranged Eugene's marriage, accepting my mother's terms concerning my dowry, terms he had little intention of keeping, because he was eager to see this happen. More than that, Monsieur Moisant is a man who enjoys controlling those around him and he was sure that Eugene would be a dutiful son and do as he was told. He was correct, as far as it went. Eugene married me because he had no wish to embarrass his father by refusing, but he declined to change his manner of living."

"He went back to Brona."

"If things had been different, if his father had been a more tolerant or understanding man, we might have come to some accommodation in time, even some form of affection." She lifted a shoulder in a fatalistic gesture. "He was not, and so Eugene spent just as much time on Rampart Street after the wedding as before."

Caid turned to face her. "And none in your bed."

A flush moved over her in a wave, but she refused to let it matter. "It was, I think, his way of declaring his independence. Or perhaps it was only stubbornness, I don't know."

Voice abrupt, Caid asked, "How old was Eugene?"

"Two years older than I am. He would have been two-and-twenty on his next birthday."

"God, I thought he was older." Caid put a hand to his face, wiping at it as if he had walked into a spider's web.

"He seemed so because he was so serious." She shook her head. "The real trouble came when his father discovered that there was no possibility of me having a child—but that Eugene's mistress was going to have one."

"He was not happy."

"A gross understatement. Monsieur Moisant was enraged that Eugene had wasted his seed, as he styled it, and was deliberately withholding from him the legitimate heir that he craved. Eugene defied him openly for the first time in his life by telling him he wanted only Brona. His father could not endure that. And so it all began."

"What began? I thought…"

"The tragedy, at least that's the way I've come to think of it in my mind. You see, Henri Moisant, discovering that he could not move his son, went to your sister. What he said to her no one will ever know—possibly that she was ruining Eugene's chances for legitimate children, maybe that he would have her sent back to Ireland. Whatever it was must have been devastating. At the end of it, he took her to a midwife known for helping women who cannot afford to have a child, and when she returned, she was no longer in an embarrassing condition."

"Jesus, Joseph and Mary," Caid whispered. "He killed his grandchild."

"Brona took it hard, or so I understand, crying constantly, praying for what she saw as the sin she had committed. She could not seem to regain her strength and the little she had was spent while on her knees at the Cathedral. It was a terrible time. Eugene was distraught himself, and it was then that he became somewhat…violent. He blamed me for telling his father about our arrangement as man and wife, and so for everything else."

"You? Not his father?"

"He loved him, you know. And I was a useless encumbrance whose mere presence had destroyed his happiness."

Caid gave a slow nod. "I see. Go on."

"What happened next, I had from Eugene in one of his rages, but I think it must be so. When Eugene still refused to honor his wedding vows, spent even more time with Brona, his father sold the house on Rampart Street and hired men to move your sister into the street. It was done while Eugene was away in the country on an errand for his father, so he had no idea it had taken place or where she had gone for several days. When he found her, she was feverish and weak. They spent the night together and, some time during it, decided that if they could not be together in life, then they would be so forever in death. They drank laudanum then lay down on the bed in each other's arms. Eugene woke up. Brona did not."

"Mother of God."

Tears burned their way into Lisette's eyes and she lifted her head to prevent them from falling. "I expect you can guess the rest. Eugene, with no real wish to live, saw you as his deliverance. When you accused him of the death of your sister, he did everything in his power to convince you it was true. Perhaps he felt that guilt in all honesty, who can say? Then he met you at dawn on the field of honor and allowed you the vengeance of ending his life for him."

Caid took a step back from her, the blood draining from his face. "I killed an innocent man."

"I'm sorry," Lisette said through the thickness in her throat. "I'm so sorry."

Caid didn't answer. Turning from her, he moved to the

end of the bed where he braced his arms on the footboard, holding tightly to it. Lisette had no idea what images might be in his mind, and did not want to know.

When the silence had stretched to the breaking point, she cleared her throat and went on. "What I was trying to say earlier was that I thought marriage might make amends in some way for Brona's death, and Eugene's that had been forced upon you. I had seen you in passing on the street, knew your circumstances insofar as gossip allowed. It seemed you deserved an easier life. It seemed as well that we had both lost something that we valued, the only family left to us."

"So you intended to share your fortune with me. Is that it?"

"You could put it like that. I just…wanted to make up for what I had done."

"You?"

"By allowing Monsieur Moisant to know how things stood between Eugene and myself. But for that slip of the tongue, it all might have ended otherwise."

A short grunt left him. "Unlikely. What other end is there for a bog Irish lass who is with child and without a husband or way to live?"

"They might have gone away somewhere together, Eugene and Brona. Or an annulment of my marriage to him could have been arranged."

"Or he might have grown tired of her and fonder of his wife."

Lisette gave him a strained smile. "I don't think so. He loved her, they loved each other."

Caid pushed away from the bed, moving to the window where he leaned a shoulder on the frame while staring out through the glass. "It appears then," he said over his shoulder, "that your Eugene was in some sense a lucky man. Now I must ask you to allow me a little privacy to dress, I think. We leave for town an hour after breakfast."

She was dismissed, just like that. Whatever she had expected, this wasn't it. Rising to her feet, she reached a hand out to him. "You don't think we might—"

"No," he said deliberately. "I have no wish to trade my freedom for a fortune, be the bride ever so lovely."

She felt every word as if it were a flung stone. The bruises, she was sure, would be with her for the rest of her days. Blindly, she turned away, suddenly frantic to be out of the bedchamber, desperate to leave this place of humiliation and pain. She broke into a run, her bare feet thudding on the floor. Snatching at the door handle, she turned it.

"Lisette…"

"You need say no more," she told him in strangled tones, her back still to him. "I understand perfectly."

Mere seconds later, she was in her bedchamber with her back to the door. She stood there for endless minutes with her eyes closed. She couldn't seem to get enough air into her lungs though her chest rose and fell with frantic effort. Reaching up with both hands, she put her fingers to her temples and palms to her cheekbones, pressing hard.

He had withdrawn from her. Yet what had she expected? Absolution, perhaps? She had caused the death of his sister. It was unintentional, to be sure, but still a fact.

Her time with Caid was done. It was over. He would never want to see her or speak to her again. And she couldn't cry, shouldn't cry, must not under any circumstances allow tears to fall because she had to dress and go down to breakfast in a few moments. She must face all of Caid's friends and fellow sword masters and pretend that nothing had happened, nothing had changed.

Everything had changed. After today, Caid would be no more than a stranger seen from a distance. He might pass her in the street and never speak. Certainly, he would have no wish or need to call, no desire to waste his time seeing that she was safe. He would care nothing for who she married or what became of her. The visits of the other sword masters would doubtless fade away as they saw that she was at odds with Caid. She would be left alone with Agatha and the most hardened of her fortune-hunting suitors. Oh, yes, and with her fears.

How delighted her father-in-law would be to know that he had managed to separate her from her protector, after all. What a far-reaching arm past events had, that they could destroy long after they were committed.

She had hoped for so much, someone to love and who would love her, a family, a circle of friends bound by a common background, laughter, joy, and the end, finally, of useless regret.

Now there was nothing.

She felt ill. The breakfast Caid had mentioned was the last thing she wanted. She would bathe and dress, then go down to her phaeton only when everyone else had assembled. She would smile and speak to this one and that, then climb to the seat and set out as if hell's hounds were after her. And if she were very lucky, she might reach town without saying another word to anyone other than Agatha.

Tears welled up, burning the back of her nose, crowding into her throat until it ached as if it were being cut by a rusty knife. She swallowed them back, clenching her fists with the effort to prevent them from falling. She would not go down with a red nose and eyes. She wouldn't. And if the tears gathering like acid in her chest chanced to dissolve her heart, she would be glad, for then she might be free of its terrible pain.

The journey back into town, contrary to Lisette's fullest intention, proceeded with all the ponderous slowness of a funeral cortege. Blackford's injury, as he rode in Maurelle's carriage, prevented anything more rapid. It being impolite in the extreme to simply bowl away, leaving them all behind, Lisette, with Agatha and Figaro beside her, was forced to keep to the sedate march.

Slow or fast, it mattered little, after all. Once back at the town house, there was nothing to do. The days drifted past with little to mark them. The evenings were quiet, and Lisette made no attempt to change them, certainly did nothing to revive her literary salon. She and Agatha sat reading or plying their needles with Figaro at their feet, their only company, only guard. Denys Vallier and his friends Armand and Hippolyte made morning calls now and then, and Neville Duchaine put in an appearance once. Lisette sustained a proposal from the Comte de Picardy's cousin which she refused with emphasis, and she saw him no more.

Caid most certainly stayed away, though she caught a glimpse of him now and then from her balcony. A dozen times, she sat down to pen a note, asking him to come to her, to allow her to explain further. Just as many times, she tore up the missives without sending them. What more was there to say?

The street boys still kept their vigil outside her town house, still slept in the *garçonnière* storeroom when the nights were wet or blustery. One morning, she saw them playing with lengths of wood, no doubt taken from the site where the new St. Louis Hotel was about to be rebuilt to the design of the architect, De Pouilly. They chose partners, squared off, bowed and shouted *"En garde!"* before attacking each other with verve and relish, as if they had every intention of doing bodily harm.

Lisette stood the shouts and clacking of the sticks as long as she could. Fearful that someone was going to wind up with a cracked head at the very least, she descended the stairs and marched across the street.

"What in the name of heaven are you doing?" she demanded. "Don't you know someone could get hurt?"

They ceased their play and stood staring at her all agape, as if the words coming out of her mouth were in a foreign tongue. Perhaps it was to them, since they were unused to anyone showing interest in what became of them.

"Well, answer me! Do you want to kill yourselves? Have you no thought for what could happen if you stabbed each other? You could be crippled for life, or blood poisoning might set in and you could die."

"Monsieur Caid said…"

"Monsieur Caid? What has he to do with it?" She could guess, perhaps, but required proof.

"Taught us to sword fight, he did, him and Monsieur Nicholas. Said we wuz good at it. We get better and we maybe can be like them one day."

"Fighting for a living, you mean?"

"Teachin' men to fight, teachin' how to save their lives. 'Tis a good trade, *madame*."

She supposed it was, for those who had aptitude and no chance of anything better. Changing tactics slightly, she asked, "And did Monsieur Caid say that you were to practice on the banquette where you might injure anyone who passes by as well as yourselves?"

They looked down, looked away, studied their grubby hands and their makeshift swords that had been, several of them, whittled into something resembling a blade with a tapered point. After a while, Squirrel shook his head. "Told us not to."

"That's what I thought. And did he say you were to practice when he was not there to oversee the matches and point out your errors?"

Another head shake was the only answer.

"Then I trust you will refrain from annihilating yourselves unless it's under his supervision," she said tartly. She fairly itched to take the weapons from them but could not bring herself to wound their touchy pride when it was virtually all they had. "Now. Cook has made a gumbo that is far larger than Mademoiselle Agatha and I can possibly eat. I wonder would you all be so kind as to help us be rid of it?"

Squirrel looked at the one called Faro who glanced under

his brows at Weed. Some silent communication passed between them, though by what means Lisette could not tell since she had not seen a single muscle move in their faces. It was a performance she had noticed before, though it was usually Felix who invited them inside to eat.

"We can do it," Squirrel said magnanimously.

"Excellent. I believe there is an excess of berry pie, too. If you will accompany me?"

"*Madame.*" Squirrel sheathed his sword by the simple expedient of shoving it into the top of his ragged pantaloons, then sketched a bow and held out his arm.

Absurdly enough, tears rose to Lisette eyes. The gesture was so like Caid's that there was little doubt who had taught it to him. "Thank you," she murmured, then placed her hand on the thin arm of the street boy and sailed regally back into the town house.

Finally, the solemn holidays arrived, Palm Sunday, Good Friday and Easter with their attendant observances. Hardly had the palm branches blessed by the priest and placed behind the salon mirrors begun to dry before the invitation to the wedding of Celina Vallier and Damian Francisco Adriano de Vega y Riordan, Conde de Lérida, appeared. It was an instant before Lisette remembered that this noble-sounding groom was only Rio.

It came to her then that this was the first such social occasion to which she had been invited since the house party. Apparently the tactics of Monsieur Moisant had worked admirably and she was a pariah. Not that she minded. There was no one she wished to see and no place that she wanted to go.

Briefly, she considered staying away from the wedding, as well. That was mere lack of nerve, of course, and not to be borne. She would go to honor Celina and Rio and wish them every happiness. She would hold her head high and look people full in the face. And if she saw Caid, she would smile politely, distantly, as if they had never made love in the moonlight with only a curling silk ribbon between their warm bodies, never touched in joyous wonder, never even shared a kiss. She would do it if it killed her.

The wedding was a magical occasion of candlelight and incense, white lace and flowers. The usual detail of Swiss Guards met the bridal party at the cathedral doors where flambeaux guttered on either side, then led them down the aisle. Celina, beautiful in a gown ordered from Paris, of embroidered silk with a bell skirt and demitrain, followed the guards on her father's arm. Rio came directly behind her, escorting Celina's Tante Marie Rose in place of her mother who had died years before. After him came his best man, Caid, with the maid of honor on his arm, a cousin of Celina's on her mother's side of the family, while Denys Vallier trailed after them with legions of Vallier cousins and numerous family friends trooping on his heels.

There was no mass as the Church did not permit its celebration after noon, still the vows were simple and moving. The expressions on the faces of Celina and Rio as they gazed at each other in the candle glow brought a hard knot of tears to Lisette's throat. The alliance ring from the groom to the bride was of gold, a double ring made of two interlocking bands which, when opened, displayed the initials of the bride and groom and the date of the wedding. A matching ring was presented to Rio from Celina. Afterward, the couple and their relatives, some thirty-five people, signed the register, then all the guests trooped down the rue Royale to the Vallier town house for the wedding supper.

This repast was truly sumptuous, with a *pièce montée* of nougat in the shape of Cupid, God of Love, centering the table and surrounded by turkeys, roasts, hams, rich cheeses, silver and glass bowls filled with salads, gelatines, cakes in elaborately ornamented and beautifully iced pyramids, charlotte russes, thick custards and jellies, Mont Blanc of whipped cream and sherbets and ice creams in baskets carved from orange peel and decorated with candied rose petals and violets. Champagne and wine were deftly served to all, even the children, and conviviality and pleasure were the order of the evening. The bride cut her cake, and every girl present received a piece to slip beneath her pillow that night along with the names of three eligible bachelors, since it was believed that the man she dreamed of then would be her husband. After an hour or two, the bride and groom slipped away to the bridal chamber that had been prepared for them elsewhere in the house, but the party continued.

Lisette remained on the fringes of the group as much as possible, eating but little and talking less, and then only when approached by those few she knew. She seldom glanced in Caid's direction, not because she feared he might be looking her way, but because she was sure he would not.

Once the bride and groom disappeared, she did not linger. Making her excuses to her host, Monsieur Vallier, she left with Agatha. An escort was offered, but she declined, saying most mendaciously that one was already arranged. The distance to her town house was a mere four blocks straight down the most respectable and well-traveled thoroughfare in the city and there were two of them to keep each other company. What had they to fear?

Her thoughts were not on safety but on the ceremony she had just witnessed and her ambivalent feelings toward it. She was happy for Celina and Rio, but could not help contrasting their febrile excitement at joining their lives together with her own marriage and present circumstances.

"Celina made a lovely bride," Agatha said, her voice warm and a shade sentimental.

"Indeed she did."

"And Monsieur de Silva! So handsome and manly, and so devoted."

Lisette smiled her agreement.

"I do worry about this charivari, I must say. Such a barbaric custom for so civilized a people. I wonder that it continues."

"What charivari?"

"Did you not hear? It was spoken of at length where I sat among the older ladies."

She should have paid more attention to what was going on around her and less to her own misery, Lisette thought. "Such things are for widows and widowers who remarry or those with a great age difference between them, not a couple like Celina and Rio."

"Nonetheless, it seems to be planned. The whole thing appears rather sinister. I heard Monsieur Nicholas saying that The Brotherhood must be on guard."

Agatha knew as much as she did about the chastisements handed out by the sword masters who had become known by that title. "You think there might be a connection?"

"I heard a whisper or two. It would be a way for those who suspect Monsieur Rio's involvement to get back at him."

"Mob revenge? Surely not." Most charivaris were mere noisy harassment, Lisette knew, but they could turn violent on occasion.

"What other reason could there be?"

"Rio's elevation as a Spanish count, perhaps. Some might resent his rise from the ranks of the *maître d'armes*."

Agatha did not look convinced. "Whatever the cause, I expect he and Celina will simply order the usual feast for the hecklers and that will be end of it."

"Or else it will prove to have been no more than a rumor."

No sooner had the words been spoken than they heard the first shouts, the clanking of iron on iron and clanging bells that signaled the crowd gathering for the ritual chivying of bride and groom. It was coming toward them, judging by the noise, approaching from the outskirts of the Vieux Carré. Since it seemed to be at least a block away still, they might, with luck, avoid it. They picked up their skirts and walked quickly toward the town house now only a short distance away.

It was then that they heard the clatter of horse's hooves. Some of the men were on horseback, thudding along the street in advance of the others. These riders emerged onto rue Royale at the cross street directly in front of Lisette and Agatha. They wore masks or false faces with long cloaks over their clothes, and carried flambeaux that flared and smoked in the draft of their passage.

Lisette came to a halt as she was struck by the similarity of this group of men to those in the Mardi Gras parade not so long ago. Then the horsemen swept toward them, clattering past so close that she could smell warm horseflesh and the sweaty wool of the men's cloaks. Behind them surged a raucous crowd of merrymakers, perhaps forty in number, some carrying shovels and rakes, some banging on pans with ladles and hammers or blowing horns to deafening effect.

This was no jesting crowd out to make fun of an unpopular bride and groom. They appeared to be the flotsam of the docks area: boatmen, sailors and hangers-on from the saloons that lined the rue de la Levée. Some were having a good time, eager to get to the fun and free food, but many appeared the worse for drink and some few wore expressions that could only be described as vicious.

"Dear God," Agatha gasped.

Lisette wasted no time on words. Grasping her companion's arm, she stepped back into the inset doorway of a milliner's shop, pulling her companion with her.

All might have been well except for the reeling progress of a one-eyed backwoodsman in greasy leather. Stumbling against Agatha, he reared back to stare at her. A ribald grin spread across his face. He gave a whoop as he snagged an arm around the waist of Lisette's companion and dragged her into the crowd.

Lisette shouted at him as she grasped her companion's arm and set her feet. It did no good. She was pulled into the press of bodies, as well. The two of them were carried along with the rest of the charivari-bound horde.

The mob was moving faster now, and an ominous growl came from their throats. Something animalistic seemed to have them in its grasp, like a monster with a deadly aim from which it could not be deflected. Agatha's bonnet was knocked askew so it dangled in front of her face, and she was having trouble keeping her feet as the sailor towed her along. Lisette's hold on her seemed to be throwing her off balance, so she reluctantly let her go. An instant later, she saw Agatha stumble and fall to her knees. Lisette tried to stop, tried to reach her, but was pushed along from behind. She looked back over her shoulder, but could catch only a glimpse of her clothing, a flash of her pale face, before the mass of men closed in between them.

In less than a moment, they were back once more in front of the Vallier town house. The hideous din of bells and horns and drums increased, echoing like raucous thunder off the buildings on either side of the street. Wedding guests appeared on the balcony above the town house entrance and were greeted by jeers and catcalls. A group of men filed out of the *porte cochère* and took up stations at the gate where they drew swords, barring access.

Fearful admiration rose inside Lisette as she recognized Caid and Nicholas, Bastille Croquère and Gilbert Rosière, Juan Pépé Llulla and even Blackford with his sling. How daring they were in front of the undisciplined crowd, how willing to put their comfort, safety and even their lives on the line for their friend. That men of such stringent honor existed filled her with wonder.

"Feast! Feast! Feast!"

The crowd chanted, demanding their due as decreed by tradition. The horsemen clattered up and down in front of the
swordsmen, rearing their mounts, while the shouting and
noise rose ever higher in volume. Rake and shovel handles
hammered the paving stones, bells and pot lids were banged
on the metal posts that held up the gallery. The swarming host
of men milled around, pushing at each other and particularly
at the shop doors and windows on the ground floor, rattling
the wrought iron screens that covered them.

Abruptly, a lone horseman wearing a beaked vulture's
mask reared his mount and plunged forward with a hard kick
of a spurred heel. The stallion he rode was tall and heavily
built. He rammed forward through the crowd, knocking men
aside like stuffed dolls. Making straight for Caid, he knocked
him backward, jamming him against the wrought iron of the
porte cochère gate.

Lisette screamed and started forward. She could move no
more than a few feet for those who gawked in frozen stupe-
faction. Caid was down, she knew for she had seen him fall.
Nicholas was beside him, she thought, his sword flashing as
he beat men back with its flat edge.

Then from above them came a rain of silver. Handfuls of
coins bounced and rang as they hit the street and rolled into
the gutters. Lisette looked up to see Celina, dressed in a
nightgown and negligee of embroidered batiste, her golden-
brown hair shining, cascading around her as she flung more
coins in a wide arc. Rio, grim of face, naked to the waist and
barefoot, held his hat as a container for the largesse that his
new wife so freely distributed.

Within seconds, the crowd dissolved into a mass of men
on their knees, scrabbling for coins in the dirt and filth of
the street. Lisette spun back toward the spot where Caid had
fallen, seeking his long form with a desperate gaze.

He was gone, as were the swordsmen who had been with

him. The gate of the *porte cochère* clanged shut as their shadowy figures vanished back into the Vallier courtyard. The metal bar that locked it was slammed into place.

Was he hurt? Maimed? Dead? She could not say and had no right to ask. If it was the least of those things then all was well, if the worst, then she did not want to know.

She could not bear it, not when she had just realized a truth that should have been obvious to her days ago when Caid had held her inside a tent of white netting while teaching her the nature of passion and taste of love.

She loved him.

She loved him, and she had hurt him, used him, set him on a path that left him with no choice except to face death again and again. She had made him the target for a father's violent and deadly rage that should have been directed at her alone. She might have killed him, and she couldn't bear it. Not now, perhaps not ever.

Swinging around in a whirl of dirty and bedraggled skirts, she picked her way through the jostling, crawling men who scrambled for coins, thankful that they had the silver to occupy their thoughts and their hands. Then she lifted her gown and petticoats and ran at breakneck speed back toward where she had been forced to leave Agatha. She saw her sitting as if dazed, her forehead bruised, against a shop wall. In breathless haste, she reached the spot and dropped to her knees beside her.

"Oh, Agatha, are you all right? Tell me where it pains you."

"My head. I hit it as I fell." Agatha put up one hand, gently probing the front of her temple, even as she lifted the crushed millinery confection in her lap with the other. "My bonnet seems to have suffered more than I."

Lisette felt a weight leave her chest. "Thank God. If only I had not insisted on leaving without an escort."

"Don't be ridiculous. How could you know this would happen?"

Such acerbity meant that Agatha really was recovering. Lisette swallowed a hard lump in her throat. "Come, let me help you up. Then we will get home before anything else happens."

"Indeed, but Lisette…"

She made a distracted noise of inquiry as she levered her companion to a standing position and put an arm around her.

"I saw his face, the man who led them on his horse. He took off his mask as he rode back past me."

Stillness invaded Lisette's body, perhaps even her soul. "And?"

"I can't understand it. Why he should exert himself to make a mockery of the Vallier-De Silva wedding…it makes no sense."

"Who? Tell me!"

"But yes, my dear. It was Monsieur Moisant."

Moisant. Agatha could not know it, had not seen, but his presence made perfect sense, considering the attack on Caid. The charivari had been a trumped-up excuse, cover for an attempt to remove the man who was keeping him from gaining control of his dead son's wife.

He might have achieved it, certainly had managed to injure her companion. How pleased he must have been to see her and Agatha on the street. Or had that been carefully timed in hope of meeting them? Could the man who had drawn Agatha and her into the melee been instructed to do so? Had Henri Moisant intended her to witness his attempt to crush the life from Caid?

Lisette's head began to pound with the sudden rush of fury to her brain. She felt on fire with the urge to do a serious injury to another human being. She hated Henri Moisant with every fiber of her being for what he had done to his son, to Caid's sister and to her, and would until the day she died. Most of all, she despised him for his attack on Caid from behind a coward's mask.

And yet, and yet.

Too many people had become involved in the quarrel between them. She could bear no more deaths or injuries on her account. Her longed-for freedom had been no more than an elusive dream. She had thought to force it by running away and setting up her household under the protection of a man strong enough to deter her father-in-law. That had been foolish. Freedom, if it was to be achieved, had to be earned, she thought. She must stop running and turn to face the man who seemed determined to imprison her. She had to end the contest, had to find some means of appeasing her father-in-law's wrath and make peace with him.

She could see no other way.

19

The St. Philips Theater, on the rue St. Philippe between Bourbon and Royale, was a Palladian-style building of two stories with a tall pediment and arched openings which framed the entrance loggia on the ground floor and also the balcony above it. Built more than thirty years before, it had come down in the world since the construction of the *Théâtre d'Orlèans, Théâtre de la Renaissance,* American Theater and others that were newer and more elaborate. A few productions were staged there from time to time, but tended toward vaudeville skits and raucous comedies of the kind that appealed to the common crowd. Quadroon balls were held there, as well, as a way for the management to meet expenses.

An article Caid had seen in *L'Abeille* had called the theater a den of thieves and pickpockets, and that seemed close to the mark. Any grandeur it had once claimed was long faded away. Its gilt carvings were peeling, the velvet draperies threadbare and split in long slits and the girandoles on the walls held the stubs of smoked and melted candles. Dust motes spun in the sunbeams falling from the tall second-floor windows where the coverings had been pulled back to let in light. The smells of whitewash and warm broadcloth, dust and sweat rose to pollute the air, and a fine grit lay everywhere, tracked in on the boots and shoes of those who came and went. Regardless, with seating for some seven hundred and a parquet area that covered over to form a sizable flat surface, it was more than adequate for the tournament of sword masters.

Five fencing strips had been laid out with lengths of canvas cut to the correct width and length and roped off to prevent spectators from crowding too close. A number of officious gentlemen strode here and there with flapping lists in their hands, while the tournament judge and his four jury members were seated on low platforms on either side of the rectangle of fencing strips. Sword cases, in this instance holding competition foils, were stacked conveniently to hand, each marked with the name of the man to whom it belonged. The dress circle boxes were full of spectators, all male of course, who stood around talking, joking and placing bets while waiting for the action to begin, and the tiers of seats that mounted to the ceiling had a respectable number of takers. The *maîtres d'armes* who stood about, waiting to demonstrate their skill, would have an audience.

The hum of voices was like a hive of angry bees as the sound reverberated through a space designed to carry speech to every corner. Beneath it lay an undercurrent of the kind of excitement that comes from the anticipation of seeing blood. Masks and padding would be used today and the foils would have buttons firmly affixed to the ends, but accidents happened and every soul in the theater knew it.

Caid was of two minds about the exhibition. He understood quite well the economics of it, that the man who triumphed today would have his fortune made as the young bloods of the town flocked to his atelier. More than that, he was aware that the whole purpose for a swordsman was competition, to face other men and prove which of them was more agile, aggressive, skilled and, above all, favored by Lady Luck. To be proven the best swordsman in New Orleans was a tremendous prize and he felt its allure with the rest. Recognition of his prowess was all he had sought for more than a decade. The little he had managed to gain was all that he could claim for himself. From the moment he had heard of this vaunted *assaut d'armes,* he had burned to win it, to show New Orleans that he was a man of note, someone other than a pinch-penny Irishman who could be pushed around at will by those who had power and noble names.

Now the tournament seemed merely an exercise in crass showmanship, a matter of arrogance and self-aggrandizement with money as the only reward. That he was forced by the tenets of his profession to take part affected him with a free-flowing anger. Or perhaps it was everything that had happened in the past few days that fueled his fury. He resented the men who came to gawk, despised those who, like ancient Romans, gathered in hope of blood sport, and disdained the dandies who thought to choose a man worthy of teaching them the art of swordplay by judging how he hacked and sliced at his fellow masters.

Still, what could he do except compete? He was committed. And what else was there for him anyway?

"Well, my friend, what think you of your chances this morning? Or are you, like the tiger eyeing a flock of peacocks, merely considering which to have for breakfast?"

Caid turned at the quietly ironic tone of Blackford's voice. "Since you are still wearing your invalid's badge," he drawled with a nod toward the sling on the Englishman's arm, "I rate my chances better than a few days ago."

"Polite. Also accurate. But sincere?" Blackford shook his head in a sardonic negative. "We won't quibble over it, not until we are able to test blades, one against the other. Until then, I am a bearer of fair tidings."

"Fair?"

"Rather than excellent or even good, a nice distinction. Nicholas bids me tell you that he saw the lady in question safely home with her companion, and that her rest was undisturbed through the night. At least no additional incident disturbed her peace."

"She was unhurt?" It galled Caid to be forced to obtain

answers concerning Lisette at second hand, but it was as much as he allowed himself these days.

"Apparently. Bandages and ointments were called for, but applied to the scrapes and bruises sustained by Mademoiselle Agatha."

"Nothing more serious, I trust?"

"No doctor was summoned."

He must be satisfied with that, he supposed, though it was far less than he wished to hear. "Did anyone say how the pair of them came to be in that melee?"

"As we surmised, according to one of the street boys who overheard the butler telling the cook. They were caught up in the mob after leaving the wedding. It was almost avoided, and would have been except for the order of the devil on horseback who saw a chance to include them."

"Something must be done," Caid muttered.

"Assuredly. If I may be of service…"

"Thank you, but I believe I can handle it. And will when this business here is over."

Caid's grip on the foil he had been testing tightened. Dear God, but he would never forget the moment when he had caught sight of Lisette being carried along by the seething mob of wharf trash bent on mischief. How could he have missed her? She had stood out among them like a pearl in a pail of slops. The idea of her being touched, mauled, or worse, by such scum make his skin crawl and the blood pound like a drumbeat in his head. There had been a moment when he had recognized Moisant, seen his fine hand behind the charivari, that he had been inclined to murder.

He had no right to extend his protection that far, no right to guard Lisette from any form of harm. He had forfeited anything of the sort he might have claimed on a night of passion almost two weeks ago, and so was left to this second-hand news of her, information gained at one enormous remove.

"What of Squirrel and the others?" he asked abruptly.

"Keeping watch, as usual. It's their pleasure as well as their duty these days."

"Meaning?"

"They are all more than half in love with the young widow simply for the sake of her smiles. Not to mention her cook's tea cakes."

"And you?"

"Oh," Blackford said, at his most ironic, "I'm no more immune than any."

Caid snorted, no wiser than he had been before he asked.

"Jealous, old man?"

"Of a bunch of guttersnipes? I should hope not," he said with derision.

"Of any who might steal away the heart of the lady," Blackford said, his eyes brightly blue.

"Is that what you intend?" The idea of the Englishman courting Lisette, kissing her, lying with her, with or without a wedding ring, set his teeth on edge. For a brief instant, he was lost in sensual memory of her naked among cabbage roses and the silk of her own hair, with a ribbon bow adorning her thigh. The instant molten heat in his veins was something he had been living with from minute to minute since his return from Maison Blanche, but was hellishly inconvenient just now.

"Not," Blackford answered with a courtly bow, "in my present condition."

He meant while he was *hors de combat*, Caid realized after a disordered instant, so unable to protect himself against attack. Which indicated, of course, that Blackford thought him capable of it to protect his place as the lady's guardian. And he was right, damn his eyes.

Caid wondered if Blackford felt anything for Lisette in truth or if the point of the gambit had been to force him to admit his own interest. The Englishman seemed prone to such interference.

"What of yours, my friend?" Blackford went on. "Your condition, that is, not your intent?"

Caid put his hand to his left shoulder, flexing the muscles that had been bruised as Moisant's horse had driven him into the Vallier wicket gate. "Tolerable. Use should help the soreness."

"Bad luck, that it should come just before the tournament."

"As yours did, you mean?"

"Oh, mine was something beyond mere unlucky fate."

The words were light but the look in Blackford's eyes was not. He was troubled still by the accident that had resulted in Dorelle's death, and who could blame him?

"Mine, as well," Caid replied.

"Meaning the element of luck was absent," the Englishman said without noticeable surprise. "You think the aim was to see that your chance of winning today was reduced or simply to remove you permanently?"

"You doubt that it was an accident?"

"Don't try to cozen me," Blackford recommended. "We all recognized the attacker, as I suspect was intended."

Caid gave a resigned sigh, since it seemed this affaire of Moisant and Lisette must always be played out before an interested audience. "I'm not sure there was a rational aim."

"Pure malice then?"

"So I suppose."

Blackford's gaze was trenchant with consideration. "Were I you, I would still be on my guard, particularly against those who seem too interested in your health."

It was excellent advice. How to reply to it from one who should have had no concern was Caid's dilemma. He solved it by ignoring it. "I should tell you, I think, that I may not be quite so active for The Brotherhood in the future."

"You have a reason?"

Caid kept his gaze on the blade in his hand, testing its

edge with his thumb. "I'm no longer quite so comfortable avenging the sins of man."

"Because of Moisant," Blackford said with a nod, since the tale of Eugene and Brona that Lisette had given him had been imparted to the others of the cadre during the return from Maison Blanche. "To discover that you have been forced to assist in a suicide must have been damnable, but that doesn't make every accused man innocent."

"One was enough."

"So you doubt your judgment?"

"I am just a man with a sword," Caid said, harking back to something someone—was it Maurelle?—had said weeks ago. "I thought I knew right from wrong, that they could be told beyond question. Because of that certainty, a man is dead who should not have fallen. I can still see his eyes—" He stopped abruptly.

"As I see those of the man who died so needlessly on my blade," Blackford said softly.

Caid gave a sharp nod. "Forgive me. I meant no reminder."

"Yet some deserve the fate that comes to them. Make no hasty decision. You are needed in The Brotherhood."

Caid had no ready answer. None proved necessary, in any case. The Englishman walked away then, strolling toward the other side of the room where Nicholas was stretching his muscles with a series of lunges.

The first round, or *phrase d'armes,* of the tournament, would be fought without Caid. Ten men would meet in this initial set of encounters, two on each of the five strips. The winner of each bout would be the first man to achieve five touches as noted by the tournament jury members who called out these to the judge and the combatants as they occurred. Each time one man in a pair was eliminated, another pair would take their places on the free strip in a constant progression. Few bouts lasted more than ten minutes, which meant that the first elimination bouts should cover a couple of hours, at most, and narrow the field of fifty swordsmen to twenty-five. The remaining bouts, as the number of combatants was reduced to twelve, then six, then four and finally two, would take perhaps the same amount of time, allowing for a rest period here and there. The whole thing should be done in time for the usual early dinner.

To be placed in the second round was to Caid's advantage since it allowed him to watch the other contenders. He knew something of the strengths and weaknesses of many of them from the friendly competitions fought among them or just from dropping into the *salle d'armes* of other masters on the days when his own was closed. Still there were some he had never seen. These were the ones he gave his closest attention. To discover their relative speed, stamina, variety of technique, method of defense, and from what distance they preferred to strike could be invaluable later.

He watched Eduoard Sarne for a few extra moments, since the betting on him was high. Aggression, as Caid had learned in their abortive duel, was the major component of Sarne's play. His eyes burned with it, and he relied heavily on savage attack as a means of intimidating his opponent. Nothing in his style was new then. Caid soon moved on.

The competitor who troubled him most was Nicholas Pasquale. The Italian was left-handed, a detail that made him automatically formidable. Most men were nervous of such a fighter because it forced them to defend against a counterclockwise attack coming from an unexpected angle.

That was not Pasquale's only advantage, however. Intelligent beyond most in his strategy, he was stronger, as well. His will was relentless, his mechanics perfection. He scorned flashy moves, did not attempt to overwhelm with fancy technique. Called La Roche because he did not skip up and down the strip in the style of many, the reason for his immobility was the variety of the moves at his command.

He had no need to move away from an attack that could be countered by other means. Yet he could be lightning quick when required, so fast that it was impossible to follow the tip of his sword. Above all else, he possessed the one quality which marked him as the most likely man to survive the rounds ahead, and that was intuition. He seemed to know with great accuracy what stratagem his opponent would attempt next.

Caid could find no fault in the Italian's play. That was disturbing since he might be forced to meet him in the final round for the title of Best Swordsman in New Orleans.

Turning away, Caid began to make ready. He removed his coat, waistcoat and cravat, but left his shirt buttoned under the padding that he donned, and retained his gloves, with cuffs which covered his wrists, in the manner of the teaching bouts in his salon. He tested the mask allotted him, checked the buttons on his foils a final time. Then he attempted to wipe all considerations from his mind, concentrating solely on the match that lay ahead of him.

A bit of excitement broke out during the second round. Another Italian sword master and expert with the broadsword, Poulaga, had been matched against the former French cavalry officer Thimecourt whom Blackford had originally been scheduled to meet. During their bout, Poulaga accused Thimecourt of stealing one of his touches, that is, failing to acknowledge a touch that the judges did not call. Thimecourt, incensed at a charge he held to be a lie, instantly responded with the offer of a cartel.

Caid didn't catch the action, being involved at the time with a match of his own, but he heard about it the instant he was done. From the heightened tension that he could feel in the air, he suspected it would not be the last such exchange. Tempers were strained, and it was plain that the judges, for all their hard work and impartially, were unequal to the task of following the swift blade tips of the masters or of keeping watch over so many matches in succession.

Nor was he wrong. A half dozen other challenges had been extended by noon. That he was not among the future combatants was due to luck and his training that allowed him to remain calm under provocation. His opponents, so far, had been either overconfident or strung out with nerves so they grumbled and cursed at the calls or lack of them. Noting the distraction of the jury members and judge, Caid had deliberately scored as many touches as possible and as clearly as he was able, so that even if a few went uncalled, he might still win the bout. The tactic had worked to this point. At least he was still in contention.

Even so, he could not help thinking that the result might have been different if Rio de Silva and Gavin Blackford had been competing. He really would have liked matching blades and wits with those two in something other than a mere exhibition between friends. That feeling was the result of the hot blood of competition that pumped in his veins, he knew, still it was no less true for it.

An hour's break was declared before the final two bouts. Caid spent it virtually alone to maintain his focus and work his shoulder so it wouldn't stiffen up on him. It had been loose enough to this point, though he knew he would pay later for this intense exercise.

He could have had company in plenty, as he received several offers to buy him drinks or coffee. He refused them all. His preference was wine rather than hard liquor, but he eschewed even that on the days he was to fight or even only to teach. It dulled the senses, and no swordsman could afford that, least of all in a tournament.

He noticed Nicholas standing alone, as well, and almost decided to join him for the last few minutes of the hour. Even as he moved in that direction, however, he saw someone approach the Italian. The man spoke with a grin, jerking a thumb toward the entrance doors. Nicholas glanced in that direction, then frowned.

Caid followed his friend's line of sight, but could see nothing for the press of men. Then he was called as the next round of bouts began, and concentration wiped the incident from his mind. It did not recur until he had defeated his fifth opponent and looked around to see if it was indeed La Roche that he would face in the final *phrase d'armes*.

Nicholas Pasquale was nowhere to be seen.

Eduaord Sarne stood at his ease nearby, foil in hand with its strap around his wrist and the blade point-down against the floor as a support. Lifting his voice above the hum of the crowd, Caid called out to him. "Have you seen Pasquale? How did he fare in this round?"

"Gone, alas." Fàlse sympathy coated the words.

"Defeated?" Caid paused in the act of wiping the sweat from his face with a damp towel.

"He was called away, that's all I can tell you," Sarne said with an elaborate shrug. "Since he has not returned, he has been declared in default."

"In your favor."

"As it happens."

"Unbelievable." For Pasquale to come so far and then be denied a chance to win on the turn of a rule was hard indeed.

Sarne stiffened. "You are saying I could not have advanced to this final round otherwise?"

That was exactly what Caid thought, though it was both impolite and impolitic to make his opinion clear. "Certainly not, *monsieur.* It's only that I can't conceive of anything that might take him away, unless…"

"Monsieur?"

The street boys, Nicholas's protégés. He might have gone if something had happened to one of them, Caid thought. It was he who had set them to watch Lisette, though it had seemed more an excuse to make them feel useful while earning a small wage. What if someone had deliberately injured one of them? What if the whole thing was a trick, a means of getting Nicholas out of the way, thus clearing the field for Sarne's meeting with him and final try at the prize. Such a low ruse was by no means unlikely.

It was also possible that the messenger had been one of the boys with a report concerning Lisette. With a scowl between his brows, Caid asked, "Pasquale left no word with the judges, none for me?"

"Not that I am aware.

He eyed Sarne, his cocky stance, his self-satisfied smile. It was possible that he should have dealt with this swordsman earlier, while he had the chance. "So we meet in the final bout?"

"Odd, is it not, how these things arrange themselves?"

The words were innocuous enough, but Sarne's tone hinted at something more. Did he actually know what had taken Nicholas away or was he merely referring to their duel that had been stopped by the arrival of the gendarmes? Was he suggesting that outside influences had been at work there, just as they were here? Or was he only attempting to play on Caid's imagination, creating a distraction that would give him an advantage? If the latter, it was a mistake. The mere idea fanned Caid's low-burning anger to white heat.

The sooner he was done with this popinjay, the sooner he would be able to find out where Nicholas had gone and why. Stalking to his end of the fencing strip, he indicated the opposite side. "Shall we begin?"

The jury member for their strip came forward. Caid and Sarne swept up their blades in salute then crossed the buttoned tips in firm contact. The call rang out, *"En garde!"*

It was only then that Caid looked directly into the eyes of the man across from him. He had found in the past that it was best to reveal no expression, no promise or threat prior to the match that might permit his opponent to guess the intensity of his will to win. Now he deliberately allowed it to be seen. He wanted Sarne to know. Much of what happened in a competition between two masters was in the mind rather than the muscles. He wanted Sarne to understand that he was confident of his ability to defeat him. If the other sword master believed it, the battle would be half won.

Fencing, the French sword master who had been his teacher once said, was like polite warfare between two men armed with identical weapons. As in the midst of military conflict, the swordsman who could maintain the initiative was usually the winner. Since his adversary was always attempting the same thing, victory was only possible by outmaneuvering, and outthinking, his opponent. Caid, standing ready, relaxed and allowed his fighting instinct to take over.

Sarne lunged into a jumping attack the instant the order to begin was given. The maneuver was strong, direct and no doubt had achieved instant victory for him in many bouts, many duels. It was also flawed in that it was his signature. Caid was expecting it and parried just as strongly, just as simply, before swirling into an attack of his own with split-second timing and speed.

The battle was joined.

In less than a moment, Caid recognized, as he had not had time before, that Sarne was a highly mechanical fighter. His timing was excellent, his movements precise and strongly executed, but both were so rigidly practiced that they allowed little deviation. He brought scant variation to the fight and less mental ability.

He had a whipcord strength of the kind that came from endless practice, however. He was also free of injury. Therein, Caid thought, lay his own greatest danger. He could win the phrase, he was almost sure, but only if he made no mistakes.

He settled into a rhythm to the musical ringing of the

blades. Back and forth he moved while sweat stung his eyes, dampened his shirt and even his leather glove. He touched Sarne twice in succession in the first five minutes, and knew that he could do it again as long as Sarne continued as he had begun.

The strip they were on was not one he had used that morning. Its surface seemed rougher, as if it covered uneven floorboards. In his concern for Nicholas and, yes, Lisette, he had failed to take note of where the worst unevenness lay before stepping onto it.

Hardly had the thought occurred when he realized that Sarne was driving him back. In his tight concentration on the other man's play, there was no time to check what was behind him.

A torn place in the canvas, one that surmounted a ridge. Caid felt it, but it was too late. He stumbled, caught himself with wrenching effort while defending with an attempted counterattack.

One touch to Sarne.

Caid's shoulder burned as if touched by hot iron. He refused to acknowledge it. His play became a thing of instinct and well-honed reflexes, the result of endless hours of attack and parry, foray and riposte. Yet the pulling ache of the cramp threw off his timing by that split second that mattered. Sarne saw, and grew more confident. His movements became faster, more aggressive. They seemed directed at the injury, as if he knew, with diabolical cunning, just where it lay. It was all Caid could do to hold his ground while waiting for the pain to ease. He and his opponent traded touches back and forth until they each had three.

Then Sarne seized the initiative, swirling into an attack. It was the moment Caid had been watching for, waiting for as the panther waits for an unwary buck. He answered it with verve and speed, taking advantage of the bad execution caused by overconfidence.

Fourth touch to him. Only one more to go and the title would be his.

The unexpected ease of Caid's last touch seemed to enrage the man across from him. He bared his teeth, breathing heavily, while the glare of his eyes was unblinking. His attack grew more uncontrolled, relying on strength and automatic efficiency rather than finesse.

Dimly, Caid was aware of the spectators, of their cheers at each touch, their cries of encouragement or derision. They made a background noise that he accepted and ignored as a commonplace of all fencing salons. It never bothered him unless it changed.

Abruptly, the sound stopped. At the same time, something flashed at it spun upward from between his blade and that of his adversary in the midst of a parry in sixte. A second later, it fell to the floor with a metallic clatter.

It was the button from a foil.

That it was not his, Caid knew well. The weight of the button was always noticeable. To remove it left the weapon much lighter and more balanced in the hand. The same thing had to be instantly obvious to his opponent.

Caid expected Sarne to withdraw at once. Even so, he did not lower his guard as a matter of form, a precaution drilled into him from his first lesson with a blade.

It was as well. Sarne lunged into an attack of such desperate power that Caid was forced back from it. The sharp, unprotected tip of his foil gleamed like a blue star, a glittering, dancing beacon of death that could easily penetrate the padding Caid wore. Sarne knew the button was gone from his weapon, might have known all along that it was loose. He intended to kill if he was able.

If.

Caid had been angry before, but it was nothing to the rage that swept through him now. That fury brought power surging into his arm and shoulder. He ceased to feel the bruised soreness, the strain of the endless bouts of the day or even the fear of what had prevented Nicholas from meeting this man with his unprotected foil. He attacked with every ounce of point control, every vestige of hand control he possessed and every variation he had ever learned. He sent Sarne stumbling back, parrying in mindless answer to his movements, until, abruptly, he found the place for the perfectly timed thrust.

Caid took it, and felt his sword tip thud against Sarne's padding.

It was the final touch. The judge shouted out for them to halt. With a snarl in his eyes, Sarne dropped his guard.

This time, it was Caid who pretended not to hear. Disengaging, he reached with his gloved hand to rip the button from his own foil. Then in a lightning move, he stepped forward and pressed the point to Sarne's chest directly above his heart. The limber foil bent in an arc, cut into padding, reached flesh.

"Mon Dieu!" Sarne gasped, his skin turning a sickly yellow. "Will you kill me here?"

"If necessary." He would, indeed. The nerve for it coiled inside him in spite of his past mistakes on the dueling field. It waited only on a purpose.

"O'Neill, for the love of God."

"I want the message that called Pasquale away." Caid did not raise his voice. "I want it now."

"I can't tell you."

"I think you can." Caid leaned on his blade the fraction of an inch.

"All right, all right. It was one of Pasquale's brats come to say their leader had followed Madame Moisant to the town house of Henri Moisant. The idiot boy sneaked inside and had not been seen since."

"And Madame Moisant?"

"I don't know, I swear it!"

It was all he was going to get. Caid lowered his arm, stepped back. Immediately, a half dozen other masters rushed in from the sidelines with swords in hands to take Sarne's foil and prevent further contact.

Then a great cheer began, echoing under the gilded dome of the old theater, swaying the chandelier with its chains festooned by soot-blackened spiderwebs. Caid executed his bow of acknowledgment. He also bowed to the judge and jury members. But he did not stay to be awarded the trophy, did not remain for the speeches or the rehashing of the many thrusts and parries of the day.

Placing his foil under his arm, he tore off his mask, ripped the padding from his upper body. Then he flung the gear to the floor. Scant moments later, he was in the street, striding at speed toward the Moisant town house.

20

Lisette went alone to visit Henri Moisant. Agatha was still not feeling well after the distress of the night before, for one thing, but she preferred not to have a companion. There were things she needed to tell Eugene's father, after all this time, things better said without an audience.

She was oddly calm, almost fatalistic. She had made her arrangements, true enough, but still expected to feel the old awe caused by his age, so much greater than her own, and the fear once inspired in his household by his anger. He was going to be angry indeed, but that hardly seemed to matter. She had abandoned fear for the moment, though it might return at any time.

At the Moisant town house, she was ushered inside as if she was a stranger, though it had been only a matter of weeks since she had left the place. That she was inside its walls again, the same enclosing walls she had wished so fervently to escape, seemed not quite real. To follow the housekeeper upstairs to the salon took tremendous effort. Still she did it with a regal tilt to her head and no outward sign of trepidation. She owed herself that much.

She was asked to wait while the master of the house was told of her arrival. She wandered around the room, noticing with new awareness the threadbare carpets, stained upholstery and sagging curtains with their soot stains from the coal fires of many winters. Against such shabbiness, her new black silk walking gown with its lace collar and cuffs seemed too pristine, too flagrantly affluent. She had not noticed such things before. Had she grown just as shabby before Eugene died, refraining from buying for herself because of unspoken condemnation?

How many hours had she sat here doing needlework or reading while waiting for her husband and her father-in-law to return from their manly pursuits? She had been lonely beyond belief without realizing the true extent of it. Odd, how such things came on so slowly that they soon felt natural. She had lived here as if under a spell until released by Eugene's death.

At a sound behind her, she turned. Henri Moisant stood just inside the room. She wondered if he had really been busy elsewhere or simply determined to let her know how little he valued her presence. She wished she knew, not because the question disturbed her but as a gauge of his humor. He did not move, obviously expecting her to come to him. Lisette did not, but merely waited for his acknowledgment.

"An unexpected pleasure," he said, the words clipped as he advanced into the room. "I would not have thought that you dared come here."

"You suggested it, as I remember."

"Perhaps. Be seated."

It was an order rather than an offer, as he waved her toward a settee with short cabriole legs designed to accommodate the full skirts of ladies. It was necessarily low and wide, which would put her practically at his feet. Her voice even, she said, "I would as soon stand. What I have to say will not take long."

"You intrigue me."

He was anticipating victory. There was no point in delaying the inevitable. Moistening her lips, she said, "I have come to the conclusion that you are owed some consideration."

"I thought you might after the other evening."

"No doubt, since you have been at pains to see that any other course has dire consequences for those who are important to me. Since I cannot bear more bloodshed, I am now willing to return to this roof."

"Excellent," he said, rubbing his palms together with a dry, rasping sound. "I am pleased we finally understand each other."

His lips were moist and red and the light in his eyes almost feral. This evidence of his excitement and perhaps his illness was abhorrent to Lisette, but she hid it as well as she was able. "I trust that you are satisfied."

"Indeed, and so will you be. This I swear. We will forget any ugliness that has gone before and become as we were when Eugene was with us. It will be quite like old times, with my family around me."

Lisette gazed at him, her features impassive. "I was never your family."

"I considered you so," he said firmly. "You were as a daughter to me. Like a stern father who secretly adores his child, I was reluctant to let you go from me for that very reason. Now we shall be cozy together again."

His eagerness was almost pathetic. Did he really think that she could put all that he had done from her mind? If so, he had never really known her. "You have not heard my stipulations."

"Don't be foolish, *ma petite*. How shall there be stipulations between us? No, it is I who will allow you to know how we shall go on. Time is with us, you know. If we make haste, no one shall be the wiser."

"Make haste?"

"With your return, I mean to say, and the alteration in the relationship between us. We will leave for Europe immediately, and remain away for a year, perhaps two—I suspect credibility may be stretched that far, wouldn't you say? As long as my heir is born within eighteen months or so of Eugene's death, he can always be passed off as his posthumous offspring."

His posthumous offspring…

A rippling of goose bumps swept over her skin. She had hoped his ranting about this before had been from mere thwarted anger. It had seemed too unbelievable to be anything else. Her voice hardly more than a whisper, she said, "You really do expect to sire your own heir."

"It is my due. That is why I accepted you as my son's wife. He cheated me in deliberate and malicious defiance because he knew it was my heart's most fervent wish. Family is everything to me, family and my name. It must go forward in this way, my blood must go on."

"That's obscene!"

"It's necessary!"

"It was my dowry and the fortune left me by my mother that you wanted before. Surely that's enough."

"I am due that, as well, of course, and will have it signed over immediately. But it isn't of paramount importance now. My son is dead. My line will die with him without this subterfuge. You could not attract Eugene, could not wean him from his Irish whore, but you attract me and will serve me in this manner. I demand it. You will not defy me as did my son."

He was lost to all reason, all decency. She knew what had caused it for Eugene had told her. He had a disease contracted in the brothels of the town, a disease that was eating away at his mind. He had brought it home to his wife, so she was unable to have another child after Eugene was born, and had died, finally, as much from shame as from illness. It had taken Moisant's wife, the love of his son and his sanity, but it would not take her.

"No," Lisette said simply.

Moisant took a step forward. "That is not a word I care to hear from your lips. You will retract it please."

"I don't believe so. You have told me how you envision our future. Now I will explain how it will actually be arranged."

"How dare you?"

She dared because she had learned that she could control her life, if she chose. She had always known that in an objective fashion, but now she felt it inside where it mattered.

Caid had given her that, she thought. He had extended his protection and under its shelter she had bloomed like a flower under a glass cloche. More than that, she had seen how he had risen from the depths of a prison hulk to create a respectable life for himself using nothing other than his own mind and hands. If he could do that, surely she who had manifold advantages could manage a similar transformation.

She would not be free in the same way she had imagined, no. Still, she would have peace, security and respect. She would have it, or she would have nothing at all.

"I dare because I am Lisette Helene Saine Moisant, my mother's daughter who is not a fool," she said, her voice steady. "I would not sign over my fortune to you when I was a young bride who thought all adults were honorable and all-powerful. Why would you think I might do it now? Nevertheless, I have discovered the uses of money. Shall I tell you of them?"

"I have no interest in your prattling."

"I fear you must bear it for a short while." She had not planned what she would say, but now the words came welling up from inside her in chill, hard streams. "I called on my mother's former lawyer, Judge Reinhardt this morning. He proved most knowledgeable concerning certain matters. With his aid, I now hold the mortgage on this house in my name as well as the mortgage for the Moisant plantation up-river. The contents and household slaves attached to both properties are also mine by virtue of buying your notes which list them. In addition to these arrangements, I have directed that a sum be paid to you each month, one which will allow you the small necessities of life, such as an evening or two a week with friends at a café or restaurant, but with no excess for games of chance or other dissipations. And I have made it clear to your numerous creditors that I will not be responsible for any further debts you may incur. You are, in effect, my pensioner and will remain so for the rest of your life."

"Impossible." His voice was hoarse, his eyes so wide it seemed he might be seeing demons.

"Not at all," she contradicted him, continuing with hardly time for a breath. "Before you receive even a picayune from me, however, you will sign a sworn statement admitting to posting the scurrilous broadsides concerning Monsieur O'Neill and myself, to spreading false rumors concerning my lifestyle and guilt in the death of my husband and to attempting to have both Agatha and Monsieur O'Neill killed in order to force me to your vile purpose. I have the papers here."

Taking the document from her reticule, she stepped forward to place it on the table beside him. Then she stood back, waiting for some comment. When he only stared at her with hatred in his eyes and spittle flecking his lips, she went on again.

"We will live quite separately here in this house, you and I. To insure that this is so, that you keep well away from me, I intend to hire a pair of strong men to act as guards. Should you attempt to circumvent our agreement, should you become violent or subject me to any unpleasantness, should illness make you incapable of normal behavior, these guards will be instructed to confine you to a secure place in the attic. There you will stay until you see reason or are carried from it to the cemetery."

The echoes of her words died away between them. In the quiet, she could hear the labored sound of his breathing. He opened his mouth once, twice, but no words emerged. Finally he said on a croak, "Bitch."

"Only because you force me to act the part."

"You can't do this."

She clasped her gloved hands loosely at her waist. "I would not depend on that."

"I am a man of standing, a Creole of the *crème de la crème!* No one will allow you to use me so!"

"How will they know? They may hear eventually that you have become ill, perhaps a fit of apoplexy or the effects of absinthe poisoning. Few, I think, will be surprised. Your conduct has not been particularly rational these past weeks."

"So you will take over my house."

"*My* house," she amended. "Unless you are able to redeem the notes?"

"You know I am not."

"Well, then."

"You think you have every answer, don't you?" he asked, glaring at her. "You think you can do as you please, queen it in my house, order my servants. No doubt you expect to have your fancy swordsmen friends here as your guests, to have this Monsieur O'Neill stand behind you to enforce your orders, or even to invite him into the bed you shared with my son."

She gave him an icy smile, in spite of the pain in her heart. "What I do is my affair."

"You may find it difficult," he said with a smile of grim satisfaction, "to conduct such a liaison with a dead man."

"I suppose you mean something by that?" She couldn't think, could hardly breathe for the pain squeezing her heart.

"O'Neill will never pollute the sheets where my son once lay, never wallow there between your white thighs, daughter-in-law. At this moment, your swordsman is dying, choking on a blade thrust through his gullet."

She put a hand to her own throat where sharp pain seemed to lodge. "He fights in a tournament, not on a dueling field. Such a thing cannot be."

"No?" Moisant laughed, a cackling sound that slipped in

and out of his control. "Accidents happen, even at tournaments. And you are not the only one who can make arrangements, *ma chère.*"

"How…Who?"

"You have no need to know. It should be over by now, the tournament done. Such a tragedy. Such an annoyance for you, too, since you will have to find someone else to back you up while you play the lady of the house—*my house.*"

He seemed so sure. If Caid were really dead—but no, she refused to believe, would not until she had seen it with her own eyes. Still, whether he lived or died, she would have to stand alone. She could not depend on his protection or authority to remain safe in the life she must make for herself.

"If you are right, then it will be a great grief," she said at last. "I will miss the support of Monsieur O'Neill as the morning dew misses the sun. Still, I have no need of a man to help impose my will here. It shall be done by my own thoughts and actions, and nothing will stay me from it. You are a danger to other people, a danger to yourself. You must not be allowed to injure anyone else."

"You dare to say that to me, you who caused the death of my son!"

"It was not I who did that," she said, her voice perfectly clear. "You killed your son with your expectations and demands and lack of understanding. You killed him by forcing him to marry me, demanding that he provide the heir you wanted. You killed him by destroying the small home where he had found solace from the death of his mother and your madness. You killed him by taking away the life of the woman he loved. Oh, yes, and you killed his child, your grandson and the last of your line, when you commanded its mother to be rid of it. The child, I am told, was a boy."

Henri Moisant stared at her while his face turned purple and a white line formed around his mouth. Then he spun away and stamped to the writing desk which stood in one corner. Jerking open the drawer, he snatched something from it and turned to face her.

The silver-black bore of a pistol was fixed upon her. It shook with the rage that gripped him, but wavered little from its target.

"Nothing can stop you?" he asked in a harsh croak. "You think there is nothing? What is one death more to me?"

Fire and smoke exploded from the end of the pistol barrel. In that same instant, Lisette brought her hands up in front of her as if to ward off a blow even as she whirled away from the blast. Something snatched her hand, flung it against her chest. Her fingers went numb, her arm dropped, dangled.

Then a skinny figure flew past her like an angry wasp, a boy whose bare feet thudded on the thin carpet. "No!" he yelled at high pitch. "Not Madame, not my Madame!"

It was Squirrel, hurling himself at Moisant. The older man warded him off but the boy clung to his coat, stumbling. Grabbing on to one leg, he sank his teeth into his thigh. Moisant staggered back, cursing. He brought up the empty pistol he held and swung it down toward the unprotected head of the boy. Horror surged up inside Lisette. She screamed, a shrill sound of despair as she swayed on her feet.

The blow did not fall. Figaro was suddenly there, following after Squirrel. With a leap worthy of his wolf ancestors, he snared Moisant's arm in flight, then hung from it, growling every breath. Then Caid plunged into the room, sprang to grasp Moisant's arm. He forced it down and back behind him even as he ripped the pistol free. Squirrel beat with his tight, hard fists at Moisant, tears streaming down his dirty cheeks as he moaned again and again.

"You killed my Madame…you killed my Madame."

Caid swung to send a stabbing look over his shoulder. His gaze, bleak and desolate beyond description, scanned over Lisette, centered on the blood that splattered her bodice.

Then he shoved Moisant from him. Her father-in-law crashed into a table and went down in a shower of palmetto fans in their vase of sand, then scuttled away on hands and knees toward the open door into the next room.

Moving to where she stood with lithe swordsman's grace and set face, Caid captured Lisette's bloody hands that she held one in the other, holding them as if afraid to touch her. Then he put his free hand on the wet, bright red blotch above her heart.

"It's my hand, only my hand," she whispered, unbearably touched by the dark pain she saw in the clear blue-green of his eyes.

"God," he whispered, then bent his head to kiss her stained fingers before taking her into his arms. "I thought I had lost you."

Suddenly the room was full of *maîtres d'armes,* all talking at once, picking up Squirrel from the floor, brushing him down while searching for injuries that weren't there, ruffling his hair, congratulating him on his bravery as if he had faced a raging lion. Lisette watched them as though from far away, watched them in wonder and gladness and an odd inexorable certainty, as if there had never been any doubt they would come to her. She felt a little light-headed but endlessly comforted by the strength of the arms around her, by Caid's scent, the firmness of his jaw that was so near she could skim her fingers over the faint stubble on his cheek if she only had use of her hands. He wore no coat, which was strange when he was always so courteous, even when making love. Her blood was wetting the white linen of his sleeve, she noticed, though he didn't seem to care. It troubled her, because there was so much of it, and it smelled so very raw.

"Watch it, Caid," Nicholas said with urgency in his voice as he stepped toward them. "You're losing her now of a certainty."

Abruptly, she was swept up, held against Caid's chest

until he set her down on the ladies' settee. Above her head, she heard him snap, "Somebody go for the doctor. Now."

It was then that the shot rang out, a flat report that shuddered through the town house. A species of uproar ensued. Distantly, she heard it, heard the clatter of feet as they searched for the source, knew the moment when Rio plunged back into the room. "It's Moisant. He shot himself."

"Dead?" Caid, kneeling beside her, rapidly binding her injured hand with his cravat torn from his neck, spoke over his shoulder.

"Extremely. It was a head wound."

"Excellent," Caid said.

Lisette sighed and closed her eyes. She felt safe, so very safe, at least for this brief and painful moment.

It did not last, of course. She was attended by Doctor Labatut, and then bundled into a hastily summoned hack and carried to her town house. Agatha received her there with cries of distress and self-blame. A short time later, bathed, bandaged and dosed with a tisane containing a tincture of laudanum, she was put to bed. She protested through it all, but to no avail. She had endured a shock, the doctor said. She required rest and a respite from the pain of her hand. A bone had been clipped by the ball, nerves severed. Though she would most likely regain use of her hand, it would be stiff for some time and there would be a scar. It would naturally be covered by her glove when she went out, but any lady must perceive it as a trying experience.

Somewhere in the midst of these proceedings, Caid and others departed. Lisette heard them go, but saw no way to stop them. When she was alone, she lay staring at the tester above her for some time. It was only the laudanum and relief from strain destroying her defenses, she knew that, but tears seeped steadily from the corners of her eyes to make damp trails in her hair.

* * *

On a warm and bright day a week later, a day when the scents of bath pinks and sweet olive drifted from over court-yard walls and along the streets, Lisette left the town house and walked briskly along the rue Royale to the turning that would lead her to the street of the sword masters, the Place de la Bourse. Agatha trotted along, protesting, beside her as they dodged the wagons and drays hauling lumber to the site where the St. Louis Hotel was being rebuilt.

Lisette paid little heed. She had waited, reclining in art-less dishabille on the fainting chaise in her salon, for her friends to visit the invalid. Few had come. Celina and Rio, the Conde and Condessa de Lérida, had paused a few mo-ments on their way to take ship for Spain. Denys Vallier, sup-ported by his friends Hippolyte and Armand, had paid her an awkward call during which he had presented a poem en-titled "The Brave Lady" that had reduced her to tears for so many reasons. Maurelle had sent hothouse violets, candied rose petals, a selection of books from Fremaux's bookshop just down the street and a box of chocolates, then followed them for a hour's visit during which she had related all the gossip currently circulating in the town.

And that was all.

Maurelle had, however, listed the twenty or more duels that had been fought as a result of the tournament, includ-ing who had won or lost, who had been injured and who buried under a marker engraved, *Victime d'honneur.* One particularly bloody contest had been that between the two sword masters, Poulaga and Thimecourt. The French cav-alry officer, it was said, had refused to declare himself sat-isfied until he had hacked Poulaga to pieces, and there was much antipathy toward him for the vengefulness of his con-duct.

Maurelle had related a final piece of scandal that was par-ticularly sensational and close to home. It was this which had prompted Lisette to cease waiting for visits that never came and embark on one of her own.

She had been hurt, at first, that the *maîtres d'armes* had deserted her. She had attempted to excuse them by reflecting that they were probably busy after the tournament—the many duelists would have required lessons prior to their encounters and the competition had stirred up a storm of interest among young men for the manly art of fencing. She thought, too, that they might have felt it was for her own good, that she would be better off without contact with their kind. Maurelle's call upon her had given a different angle to the situation. Now she was more annoyed than wounded by their defection.

But that was not all by any means. She had sent a note to Caid, asking that he call on her. He had ignored it.

Lisette had had enough.

It was Caid's day to receive clients at his atelier. The windows of the second-floor where the fencing strips were located stood open to the balmy air. The rumble of men's voices, interspersed by called instructions, rolled along the arcaded pedestrian throughway, blending with the same sounds from a dozen similar establishments. Men stood on the balconies outside the salons, sipping wine and allowing the smoke of their cigars to mount to the pellucid blue of the sky above. Uniformly, they fell silent as they caught sight of Lisette and Agatha.

"We are being stared at," Agatha said in a strained undertone. "What did I tell you?"

"It won't hurt us." Lisette marched along with her eyes straight ahead. "If it bothers you so much, you can always go back."

"As if I would! But I am sure half the men on these balconies think we are abandoned women."

"It can hardly matter since they think that of me already."

"And you will give them no time to forget it. Please, Lisette, write to Monsieur O'Neill again. Surely he will come this time."

"I cannot depend on it. And I won't."

"We will be insulted, or else embarrass ourselves by glimpsing gentlemen in their shirtsleeves."

"As if there is anything the least objectionable about a man's chest."

"Lisette, really!"

"Besides, you adore sword masters, so don't tell me you aren't staring around, hoping as hard as you may that you will see them without their coats."

This was accompanied by a roguish side glance that Agatha pretended not to see, though she pressed her lips together to keep from smiling. At least she was effectively silenced.

No such incident occurred, however, nor was there any unpleasantness. In its place was a wave of disapproval coupled with something very like embarrassment that moved ahead of them like a swell in the ocean. To brave it required considerable fortitude, and Lisette was heartily glad when she could step from view under the arcade that shaded the entrance to Caid's atelier.

A servant waited for her there, apparently alerted to her approach. He remonstrated with her when asked to show her upstairs, but finally acquiesced as he saw her temper rising. Then she and Agatha were led to an anteroom, hastily cleared of coats and canes, where they were requested to wait. Swift steps padded on the floor of heart cypress, and then the door was flung open.

"Have you no discretion whatever?"

Caid followed those words into the room. Closing the door behind him, he tossed the mask and sword he carried onto a chair, then followed it with the padding he dragged from his chest. He was coatless and wore no cravat, doubtless in token of the warm day. Virility personified, his shoulders appeared as wide as the door he had entered, his skin gleamed with perspiration, his arms where his sleeves were rolled to the elbow were strongly muscled, and sprinkled with dark hair. He looked around, apparently for his coat, but wasted no more time on the exercise when he failed to find it. When he turned back, glancing over her form in an appraisal every bit as thorough as her own, she suddenly lost her tongue.

"Precisely what I said to her," Agatha told him, stepping into the breach. "She would not listen to me. Perhaps you will have better luck."

Lisette lifted her chin as she sustained Caid's gaze. "Of what use is discretion? I wished to see you and you would not come to me. If you are discomfited by my presence, it's no one's fault but your own."

"Discomfited, no, but certainly irked. I stayed away for your benefit."

"I am aware. You might have considered whether it was truly beneficial."

"How could it not be? You no longer require a protector and my acquaintance can only harm you."

"You are in error on both accounts. And you might ask if my hand pains me should you wish to be polite."

"Politeness, like your discretion, has scant appeal at the moment." He paused an instant. "How does it fare?"

"Excellently well. While we are being so formal, permit me to express my felicitations on your victory in the tournament. Why I must hear of it at secondhand I fail to see, but I wish you joy of it anyway."

"It's of little consequence." The words were stiff.

"I doubt that, judging by the gathering of men here today."

"Which will only mean more tittle-tattle about seeing you on these premises. Lisette—"

"The very thing I have come to speak to you about. You

do know that our names are connected once more and in a truly horrific round of gossip?"

"I know."

"What is to be done? And please don't tell me you intend to challenge the offenders. We have more than enough scars, you and I. Besides, a too-violent response may convince all and sundry that we conspired to murder my father-in-law as well as my husband, just as everyone is saying."

He made an abrupt gesture with one hand. "Only fools and the malicious will repeat that tripe."

"With which, the town is well supplied," she snapped.

A soft sound left him which might have been derision or agreement. Turning away from her, he paced to the other end of the room then back again. "What do you suggest then?"

"That you make every effort not to lose me," she said quietly, then waited. It was a gamble, to repeat the words that had meant so much, but nothing else was left to her.

"Meaning?" A dark flush stained his face, but his eyes gave nothing away, seemed to deny that he had ever spoken of loss.

Lisette moistened her lips, suddenly unsure of what she was doing. What if he spurned her? What if he laughed or suggested a less honorable alternative for what she had in mind? Oh, but what did it matter when there was no one to hear except Agatha, who had moved to stand with her back to them, gazing out the window.

"You could marry me," she said finally.

A white line appeared around his mouth. "We addressed this before. I still say it's going a little far, just to acquire a permanent protector."

"Hardly. You have no idea how far I've gone already."

"The potion, you mean?"

She shook her head, though heat flared into her face. "More than that."

"I didn't drink it, you know."

She blinked in surprise. "You…but you must have, because afterward you…we…"

"Afterward," he said, his voice quietly mocking, "had nothing to do with potions or protection or even intelligent reason. I wanted you. That was all."

"You wanted me."

"I did. I do, and always will. I longed for you, Lisette Moisant, as a starving man longs for meat, a saint for his martyrdom or a knight for his grail. I took you because I could not bear to let you go unloved, and because I thought, was almost sure, that you wanted me."

She gave a dazed shake of her head. "And the cordial with the potion?"

"Vile beyond words, *chérie*. I tipped it into a cuspidor when no one was looking."

Darling, he had called her, and made his confession without evasion or doubt. He deserved no less, if she could find only a little more courage. "I chose you weeks ago," she began.

"Chose?"

She tilted her head, not quite meeting his eyes. "I did, yes, from gratitude at being released from a marriage that had become a sham and a danger, from appreciation for who and what you were, and because…oh, because I saw you on the street and my heart swelled inside until I thought it might burst and I longed to be near you."

"To share your wealth, as I remember."

"Will you forget the money! It doesn't matter, never did, except as an excuse."

"An excuse." His voice was blank.

"To save face, to keep from having to tell you that I…that I waylaid you."

"I think," he said carefully, "that you're going to have to explain that."

Her pulse throbbed so loudly in her ears that she could

barely hear herself think. She was far too aware of the tousled disorder of his hair, the width of his shoulders under his shirt, the way his pantaloons, fastened so tightly under his half boots, clung to the shape of his lower body and how well she could see it without his long coat to mask it. Yet somehow, she had to find the words to convince him.

"It was quite shameless, I assure you," she said in compressed tones. "I dressed in my finest nightgown with a cloak over it, drank a small amount of laudanum to scent my breath, and then crept out of the house to make my way to the cemetery. I waited there for you for what seemed an eternity. When I heard you coming, I threw off my cloak and hid it behind a headstone. Then I lay down on Eugene's tomb and waited for you to find me."

At the window, Agatha gasped, a small rush of sound in the silence, then she turned and quietly left the room. Caid stood perfectly still, all expression wiped from his face. Lisette wanted to rush into explanations, excuses, reasons, but could find not another word, just then, to add to the secret she had so boldly revealed. Caid stirred, passed a hand over his face. "Moisant was not persecuting you with the aim of gaining your money? He had not shut you away or abused you?"

"He did those things, yes. He even dosed me with laudanum on one occasion, when he feared guests might hear my shouts to be released. The only thing of which you must absolve him is leaving me to die of exposure. He would never have done that since it would not only have called attention to his mistreatment but closed off the little access he had to my funds."

"It was no twist of fate that I came upon you on that marble slab."

"That you often came that way through the cemetery, past the Moisant tomb, from your friend's lodgings had been remarked upon by many. They made sure I knew of it since it concerned my husband. I paid a servant to watch your movements until I knew when you would be there. I was cold but nowhere near dying when you found me."

"And when I kissed you…"

Heat flared in her face. "I was so startled that I nearly ruined everything by waking."

"Dear God, the chance you took." He thrust a hand through his hair. "What if someone else had come upon you, someone with fewer scruples? What if I had been a different kind of man?"

"I knew you would be there, and I knew the kind of man you were. There was little danger."

"You really did that," he whispered, almost to himself. "You waited for me."

"I did. And I would do it again."

His head came up and his eyes narrowed on her as he set his hands on his hips. "You do need a husband, one with a strong hand."

She lifted a brow at his tone. "Not just any husband. No popinjay from the French court, no town beau or mere gentleman will do."

"That isn't what I had in mind," he said with emphasis as he began to move toward her.

"Respectability isn't a necessity," she went on, even as she took a step backward. "In fact, I prefer a man who has little reason to care what fine Creole society thinks and who will not blanch when I do outrageous things."

"A former convict should suit you very well, then, especially since I was assured not long ago that this is a land where a man's past is his own business and his future what he can make it."

Her heart threatened to choke her, making it hard to speak. "Indeed."

"It doesn't seem such a bad business in any case, as you appear bent on making yourself just such an outcast."

"I…I also require a man who knows something of farming methods since I am now heiress to the Moisant holdings as well as holder of their mortgage. There is a plantation which requires considerable expertise and labor to be made profitable."

"Labor, yes. I see."

"I prefer one handy with a sword, as well," she said with a lift of her chin, "a celebrated fencing master who can overawe the gossips and convince them that speaking of my situation behind my back is unwise."

His smile was feral. "I am the best in the city at this moment. Men tremble at my frown and stumble over their feet to avoid giving cause to meet me."

She pursed her lips as her back came up against the wall and she leaned against it. "Modesty would be optional."

"Duly noted." Taking her injured hand quite gently, he lowered his head and touched his lips to her bandaging as she had once kissed the marks on his wrist. "And I quite agree that we have scars enough between us. If you are sure mine don't matter?"

"They are a part of you, of the boy you were and the man you have become. They stand for the things you believe in, those you cherish and risk death to protect. I honor you for them."

"Honor," he said, taking her other wrist and raising both it and her injured hand above her head while fitting the firm length of his body against her from breast to knees. "And what else?"

She met his gaze, her own pleading, or so she feared. And in his eyes she saw the vulnerability he concealed beneath his strength, at least from everyone except her. "Love," she whispered. "I need to be loved."

"And I do love you, have these many weeks since mistaking you for a cold angel, always will love you for as long as I shall live, to the last, feeble breath of my body," he said, his voice not quite even. "You are the prize I have fought for, the only one I value, greater than the crown of champion, more golden than wealth, sweeter than the most complete victory. I will be yours for as long as you want me, anyway you want me, friend, lover, husband…"

"Maître," she whispered, and lifted her mouth for his kiss. "Mine own master at arms."

* * * * *

Turn the page for a preview of
ROGUE'S SALUTE
by
Jennifer Blake,
the next book in the alluring and
passionate Masters at Arms series.
Available January 2007
from MIRA Books.

New Orleans, Louisiana
January 1842

"Send a husband for me, I pray, most Holy Mother. Intercede in this matter, if it be thy will, for I have desperate need."

Juliette Armant gripped her fingers tightly together as she stared up at the benign carved face of the stature of Our Lady before her. The prayer bench's hand rail, polished by countless hands over endless years, felt cold under her wrists and the chill of the knee rest penetrated her thick skirts of gray *cord du roi*. The emptiness of the cathedral echoed around her while the scents of ancient dust, incense and smoke from the burning prayer candles wafted about her face. The fluttering of the flames on their wicks was loud in the stillness. She had knelt here a thousand times before, yet everything seemed strange this morning.

"I don't ask this boon for myself," she went on with a brief but decided shake of her head. "You know well that I never expected to marry. To be dedicated to the church at birth was my fate and I accepted it in all humility, truly I did. But now all is changed. I lack the beauty or skill at flirtation to attract a husband and there is no one to arrange a match for me. My mother has not the will—but you know her trials. I must wed without delay or all will be lost."

Was she doing the right thing? Juliette wondered. She had tried diligently to find another way out of her peculiar dilemma but nothing that sprang to mind seemed likely to be of use. How had it come down to this when everything should have been so different?

"Oh, Holy Mother, make this husband you will send kind, if it pleases you, yet not too gentle of spirit. He must have strength and a will of steel for he will surely need it. Intelligence would be useful, and diplomacy as well. I don't ask that he be attractive, still it would not upset me if he were pleasant to look upon for the sake of our future children." She closed her eyes with a small moan and went on hurriedly, "No, no, forget I said that. You who know all things must surely understand what is required. Only send a man to me soon, I beg, as quickly as may be possible."

Juliette crossed herself, touched her fist to her lips and heart in quick succession, then pushed to her feet. She could not linger here in the sacred quiet. They would miss her at home, and she had no desire to explain where she had been or why she had left the house without even a maid as a chaperone. She might perhaps fob off her mother and twin sister with some tale, but prevarication was not something which came easily after all her years with the nuns.

To leave the cathedral, she had to pass the bank of prayer candles glimmering on their wrought iron stand near the heavy front doors. The draft of her passage seemed to make them flare up, for she caught a sudden light from the corner of her eye. As she turned her head in that direction, her gaze caught the bright flame from the taper she had set burning just before she knelt to pray. It sprang tall and strong on its wick, many times more brilliant than the rest. Dazzling in its intensity, it bloomed and danced before her like a stalwart golden star.

Juliette came to a halt with her breath trapped in her throat. She was not so superstitious as her mother who had a thousand beliefs, prohibitions and proverbs which ruled her life, still, she could not prevent the *frisson* that moved over her from the top of her head to the tips of her toes.

Was this an omen? Could it mean her prayer would be answered?

She closed her eyes tightly, crossing herself again. Then she moved on. As she quitted the church her steps were lighter and hope burned as bright in her heart as the candle set aflame for her prayer.

Pausing on the stone paving outside, Juliette took out the gloves from where she had tucked them away inside her sleeve before searching out a coin for her candle. She had almost forgotten them. How aghast her mother and Paulette would be if she were to be seen on the street with bare hands. Such things had not mattered only two weeks ago. At the convent it had been more important to have willing hands rather than perfectly kept ones. A wry smile curved Juliette's lips before she sighed and began to tug on the gloves of lavender kid borrowed from her sister.

The day promised to be fine. Already, the rays of the rising sun poked shining fingers through the river fog beyond the levee and the air was soft—almost warm. The steam whistle from a departing river packet moaned, setting off the screaming of monkeys and squawking of parrots from the shop of the bird man down the street. A light breeze brought the odors of mud flats, fish, fermenting molasses and overripe bananas from the dock area, along with the stench of refuse in the gutter which centered the alley between the church and the house of the priest beside it. It also wafted the scent of roasting coffee from the market where vendors were opening their stalls, making ready for the morning shoppers who would soon amble forth with baskets on their arms in search of fresh bread, brioche and croissants. Juliette's stomach rumbled slightly at the thought, and she wished she dared purchase a few of the goods she could smell from the nearby bakery. That would not do, of course, since it would give away her early morning outing.

Just then, a high-pitched shriek ripped through the morning air. Shrill, desperate, it came from no parrot or monkey but from a living child somewhere behind her.

Juliette swung in a swirl of heavy skirts. She was just in time to see a young boy fling around the corner of the cathedral, running flat out. Hardly more than three years of age, he was slight of body, with a mop of black curls and black eyes blared wide with terror. His short legs churned, his arms pumped and his mouth was wide open as he wailed.

Booted feet thudded on the ballast stone pavement behind the child. A man burst into view then, racing after him. Of superior height and width of shoulder, his long legs covered the ground with great strides. His face was grim with determination as he gained on his quarry, stretching out a hand to snatch at the back of the boy's ragged, flapping shirt.

The child swerved, evading capture by a hairbreadth. His new path took him straight toward Juliette. Dodging to one side, he caught a handful of her full skirts as he sped past, spinning her halfway around before taking refuge behind their crinoline-supported width.

The gentleman skidded to a halt then lunged to the left around Juliette as she struggled to face him. The boy jumped back the other way, jerking her nearly off her feet as she spun. His pursuer feinted to the opposite side. The boy dodged back again.

"Stop it! Cease this at once," Juliette cried, grasping her skirts to keep from being hauled around yet again. "Stop it, do you hear?"

It was the voice she used to quell young female pupils at the convent school. The effect was gratifying. The child stood still, his narrow chest heaving. The gentleman paused, then straightened to his full height. For an instant, the three of them were silent, sizing up each other with wary regard.

The boy's pursuer recovered first. Sweeping off his beaver hat, he executed a bow of consummate grace. "Your pardon, *mademoiselle*. I only require to lay hands on that imp of Satan behind you."

His voice, deep, rich and almost musical in its cadences, affected Juliette in the oddest way. She could almost feel it wrapping around her, invading her senses, vibrating deep inside her chest. A slow and disturbing heat bloomed in her midsection and spread throughout her body. It was a most peculiar sensation, one she had never before encountered. She stood quite still for a bemused instant, her gaze on the gentleman before her.

That he was masculine beauty personified was without question. Lustrous black hair, rakishly disheveled from his pursuit of the runaway, covered his head in dense waves that dipped forward onto his brow in an errant curl. His eyes were richly black and edged with thick lashes which curled at the tips. Dark brows with satanic arches, straight Roman nose, mouth almost sinful in its full and perfect contours formed such a perfect collection of features that Juliette was strongly reminded of engravings she had seen of fallen angels done by Italian masters.

She should know him, she thought in distraction, though she was sure they had never been introduced in a formal way. She went about so little on her rare visits home from the convent, mainly to the entertainments given by the family or their friends, that her circle of acquaintance was small. Still some dim memory teased her.

The gentleman returned her gaze, his own darkly appraising as he allowed it to drift over her face, then flick downward over the curves of her shoulders and breasts under their dull covering. It was done so quickly that she might not have been aware of it if she had not been so intent upon him.

Still, she felt it like a tingling caress, felt the peaks of her breasts tighten as if with chill, though she was sure the effect was merely the unusual nature of that regard. Most men of her acquaintance would have been well aware of how inappropriate such a thing was where she was concerned. Or that it had been until recent events, she reminded herself.

Noting, perhaps, the fresh wave of hot color across her cheekbones, the gentleman turned his attention back to the boy who still clung to her once more, taking a step toward him.

"Non, mais non," the little one cried out, dragging her from her reverie with his lisping protest. "I not go wit' you!"

"You will if you know what's good for you," the gentleman said grimly as he resettled his hat on his head.

"Non, non, non!"

"I'll give you a bon-bon—"

"You gi' a baf'. I no want baf'!" The boy's voice rose to a hysterical edge.

The gentleman feinted to one side of Juliette, then plunged to the other with a lithe twist of his body. He grabbed for the boy's thin arm, would surely have had him if he had not shrieked and plunged backward, falling on his small bottom.

"Monsieur," Juliette said with force as she stepped in front of the child, "it will be very much better if you try the effects of reason instead of frightening your son."

"What will be better is if you step aside." The gentleman barely glanced at her as he bent down, snatching at the boy's legs as he scooted backward.

"Don't let 'im get me, don't, don't, don't…" The small boy moaned, scraping his skinny backside over the rough stones that fronted the cathedral, scuttling out of reach.

"Monsieur!' Juliette darted forward as the boy's cries and pitiful smallness wrung her heartstrings.

Features grim, the father ignored her, bending over, reaching for the struggling child. Juliette thrust out a hand to stop him. Her grasp closed forcefully on the rolled velvet collar of his tobacco-brown frock coat. There came a dull, ripping sound.

The gentleman froze in position for long seconds. Then he came upright with slow precision until he towered over her. A frown drew the slashes of his arched brows together, giving him a look of demonic anger.

"Mademoiselle," he began in ominous tones.

Juliette released her grip while heat burned its way to her hairline. Her gaze on the torn fabric where the collar had been pulled away from the lapel, she spoke in stiff tones. "I am sorry for the mishap, but it is your own fault entirely. I cannot permit you to manhandle the boy. It's cruel and…"

"Cruel?" the man who faced her demanded in taut indignation. "You mistake the matter, I promise you. The brat is making a to-do over nothing and less than nothing. If you had any idea what he is capable of…"

There was more, but Juliette was no longer listening. Suddenly, the identity of this gentleman was distressingly clear. If she had been more worldly, had spent less time behind convent walls, she might have recognized him at once. News of his exploits had penetrated even those barriers, however, whispered by young girls who should know nothing of such things. He had been pointed out to her on the street by Paulette on one of her family visits during the winter season of the year before. Now her heart thudded against her ribs so hard she could barely draw breath into her lungs.

La Roche.

The man before her was the notorious sword master Nicholas Pasquale, called The Rock, *La Roche,* for his immovable fighting stance on the fencing mat and the stonelike tone of his body. He had never been touched on the dueling field, so it was said, seldom allowed a touch during the fencing lessons he imparted, was certainly never touched by the more tender emotions. The best swordsman in the city according to those who should know, he fought in the position sinister, or left-handed, which made him a formidable and rather bizarre foe. Young men aped his manners and sartorial perfection. Older men blanched at his name and tried to ingratiate themselves with him. It was whispered that he had killed a half dozen men in affaires of honor, one the husband of a woman discovered half dressed in the private rooms of his atelier. More than that, he had Lucifer's own luck, for he had just turned in the winning ticket for the state lottery, gaining a fortune worth the unheard of sum of over two million dollars.

He was the most dangerous, the most feared man in all of New Orleans, one known for his dedication to and taste in matters of dress. And she, Juliette Armant, had not only laid hands on him, but torn his coat.

The small boy, perhaps sensing an ally, scuttled behind Juliette once more. La Roche bent down again as if to seize him. Quick as a kitchen mouse, the child snatched up a handful of Juliette's ash gray *cord du roi* skirts and their petticoats and dived underneath. The heavy layers of fabric settled over him, covering him so completely that he vanished beneath their copious folds.

For an instant, Juliette stood in paralyzed chagrin. She could not breathe, could not speak. Dismay and admiration for the boy's daring, fear and wariness jarred each other inside her while she stared into the coffee-black eyes of Nicholas Pasquale.

The sword master whispered an imprecation, then flung away a few steps to stand with his back to her. He raked a hand through his hair, then clasped the back of his neck while his chest swelled with the deep breaths he drew in and out of his lungs. It was clear that he was attempting to control his temper. Juliette thought it best not to interfere with the process.

Even as she stared at the sword master's broad shoulders that tapered to the waist of his frockcoat, however, she was aware of the child squirming closer against her legs. She could feel the warmth of his small body with its lightweight, bony angles as he leaned against her ankles and shins. Her heart melted, flooding her with an odd yet fierce urge to protect him at all costs. Yes, and against all enemies, no matter how dangerous.

Pressing her lips together, she drew a fortifying breath through her nose. "Monsieur," she began in as firm a tone as she could manage. "I suggest…"

"You suggest what, *mademoiselle?*" Nicholas Pasquale demanded, cutting across her words as he turned on her. "You had no right to interfere. Now look where it has landed us. The only saving grace I see is that we haven't collected an audience. At least, not yet."

It was true enough, Juliette saw as she glanced around the cathedral entranceway and the Place d'armes which lay before it. The few people out and about paid them no heed. Such circumstances could not last, and she frowned a little as she considered it.

Seeing her hesitation, the sword master pressed his advantage. "If you are to be rid of…of your intruder without embarrassment, then it should be at once, don't you think?"

She gave him a cool look. "I don't know that I wish to be rid of him."

"Come, *mademoiselle,* be reasonable. I mean no harm to the boy beyond ridding him of his dirt and assorted vermin. All you need do is turn your back and bring him out. I'll take it from there."

"I'm sure you think—"

She stopped abruptly in midsentence. Her lips parted as she drew a sharp breath of surprise.

"Mademoiselle?"

The boy under Juliette's skirts had put a hand on the back of her knee. That would have mattered little, except that he seemed to be testing the silk of her stocking, sliding his hand downward over her calf to her ankle in slow, tactile exploration.

Juliette closed her mouth with snap. Patting her skirt, locating the boy's head beneath them, she gave him a quick tap. "Unhand me, *mon petit*," she commanded. "Stop that at once."

Nicholas Pasquale's black gaze narrowed a little as he took in her predicament. Then a slow smile of devastating attraction curved his lips. In deep tones that were rich with suggestion, he said, "You have a problem, *mademoiselle?*"

She refused to answer. The young miscreant had cupped a hand on either side of her lower leg and was brushing up and down as if fascinated by the silken glide of the fabric.

"His name, in case of need, is Gabriel." Pasquale crossed his arms over his chest as he surveyed her.

"Thank you," she said stiffly. "I somehow doubt that I can extract him, as you said, without a struggle. Perhaps you…"

"Oh, I don't know. It might be cruel to interrupt his play. Poor, mistreated mite that he is, he has scant opportunity for pleasure. I'm sure you can find nothing to fault in whatever he may be doing under there."

Juliette's face burned and she turned her head so the side of her bonnet would conceal it from him. "He is only a child, so naturally curious. I attach no importance to it, I assure you. Still you must see that it's awkward to have him…"

"To have him exploring under your skirts where no male has dared venture, or so I would guess. I could almost envy him." The sword master's smile had a molten edge.

"His invasion is entirely innocent!"

"As mine most certainly would not be, or so you mean to imply, and yet you invited me to venture there."

"I did nothing of the kind!"

"You were about to suggest I reach under and remove our Gabriel, I think. Tell me that wasn't in your mind before you thought better of the idea."

"I can do no such thing—what I mean to say is…" She shifted a step, her skirts swaying as she attempted to discourage the boy's assiduous attention. He only moved with her, shuffling on his knees so his head bobbed along under her skirts in a most embarrassing manner.

"I know exactly what you mean," Pasquale said with spurious sympathy, making a clicking sound with his tongue before he went on. "*Mon Dieu.* Such a Casanova the imp is turning out to be, and at his age too."

"I'm sure he came by the skill quite naturally," she snapped.

Laughter flared in the sword master's eyes. "Skill? Ah, yes. Like father, like son, you mean to say. I should be gratified by the compliment, though I should tell you that his touch cannot be…quite…like that of his model."

The heated promise behind the amusement in his black, black eyes took Juliette's breath. Suddenly, her whalebone stays felt too constricting around her ribs and the prim neckline of her day gown much too close around her neck. Her gaze was drawn to his hands with their long fingers, so supple and strong. It seemed she could almost feel them, strong and sure, playing around her garters as young Gabriel was doing now. Fiery heaviness invaded her lower body and she swayed a little where she stood.

"What a pity," the swordsman added softly, "that we can never know for sure."

He was engaging in flirtation with her, this sword master, the most notorious in New Orleans, Juliette thought in dazed wonder. She had watched as her twin countered extravagant praise and delicately suggestive innuendo from her suitors at soirées or the opera, but never practiced the art herself, particularly with such an opponent. How very heady it was. Yes, and how disturbing, for she was aware the gentleman's comments should not be quite so personal. She was also fairly certain that he meant not a single word of them.

In a supreme effort to gain control of her senses, she forced herself to look away. "Enough, *monsieur*. I feel sure that Gabriel will obey you if you speak to him firmly and without threat."

"Do you indeed?"

"Why should he not? He must be used to it."

"By no means. He is the devil's own spawn, if you must know. He bites and scratches like a feral cat and bends to no will other than his own."

"Good heavens, has he no mother to teach him trust and obedience?"

"She has not been seen for at least a month, and maybe longer."

His voice carried minimal concern and less responsibility. A love child then. She could not be surprised since she had heard no mention of a permanent female, much less a wife, in the life of La Roche. Poor little Gabriel.

"It's good of you to take charge of the boy, I suppose, but you obviously have not been bringing him up properly."

Nicholas Pasquale gave her an arrogant look. "And what concern might it be of yours?"

"None except normal compassion."

"Yet you would interfere."

"It's the duty of anyone who sees a child being mistreated," she said with a lift of her chin.

"I am not," he said with hard emphasis, "mistreating the little bugger."

"From what I can see, you aren't endearing yourself to him, either."

"But you would?"

"Any woman might," she answered in exasperation. "It's clear to me that what your son needs is a mother."

"A mother."

"Precisely."

He stared at her a long instant, then a grim smile tilted the corners of his mouth. "Marry me, then, and become his loving *maman*."

"Marry you! Why of all the…"

Juliette stopped short in the midst of her wrathful spate. She could not have spoken another word in that instant if her soul's salvation had depended on it.

Marry him.

He was standing there, staring at her with his hands on his hips as if waiting for an answer. But he could not mean it.

Could he?

A Dr. Morgan Snow novel

M. J. ROSE

The Scarlet Society is a secret club of twelve powerful and sexually adventurous women. But when a photograph of the body of one of the men they've recruited to dominate—strapped to a gurney, the number 1 inked on the sole of his foot—is sent to the *New York Times*, they are shocked and frightened. Unable to cope with the tragedy, the women turn to Dr. Morgan Snow. But what starts out as grief counseling quickly becomes a murder investigation, with any one of the twelve women a potential suspect.

THE DELILAH COMPLEX

"A creepily elegant and sophisticated novel, with keen psychological insights. M. J. Rose is a bold, unflinching writer and her resolute honesty puts her in a class by herself."
—Laura Lippman

Available the first week of January 2006 wherever paperbacks are sold!

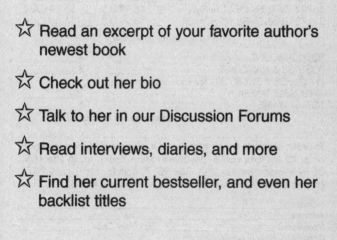

JENNIFER BLAKE

66630 ROAN	___ $6.50 U.S.	___ $7.99 CAN.
66490 LUKE	___ $5.99 U.S.	___ $6.99 CAN.
66724 GARDEN OF SCANDAL	___ $5.99 U.S.	___ $6.99 CAN.
32170 CHALLENGE TO HONOR	___ $6.99 U.S.	___ $8.50 CAN.

(limited quantities available)

TOTAL AMOUNT	$ _____
POSTAGE & HANDLING	$ _____
($1.00 FOR 1 BOOK, 50¢ for each additional)	
APPLICABLE TAXES*	$ _____
TOTAL PAYABLE	$ _____

(check or money order—please do not send cash)

To order, complete this form and send it, along with a check or money order for the total above, payable to MIRA Books, to: **In the U.S.:** 3010 Walden Avenue, P.O. Box 9077, Buffalo, NY 14269-9077; **In Canada:** P.O. Box 636, Fort Erie, Ontario, L2A 5X3.

Name: _____
Address: _____ City: _____
State/Prov.: _____ Zip/Postal Code: _____
Account Number (if applicable): _____

075 CSAS

*New York residents remit applicable sales taxes.
*Canadian residents remit applicable GST and provincial taxes.

MIRA®

www.MIRABooks.com

MJB0106BL